Death of LOVE

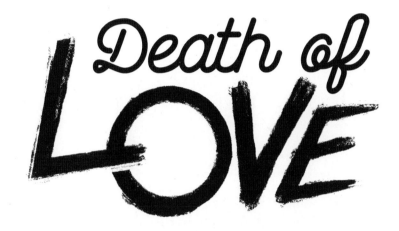

Death of Love

STORY
JUSTIN JORDAN

ART
DONAL DELAY

COLORS
OMAR ESTÉVEZ

ADDITIONAL COLORS
FELIPE SOBREIRO

LETTERS
RACHEL DEERING

LOGO
FELIPE SOBREIRO

BOOK DESIGN
ERIKA SCHNATZ

IMAGE COMICS, INC.

Robert Kirkman: Chief Operating Officer · **Erik Larsen**: Chief Financial Officer · **Todd McFarlane**: President · **Marc Silvestri**: Chief Executive Officer · **Jim Valentino**: Vice President · **Eric Stephenson**: Publisher / Chief Creative Officer · **Corey Hart**: Director of Sales · **Jeff Boison**: Director of Publishing Planning & Book Trade Sales · **Chris Ross**: Director of Digital Sales · **Jeff Stang**: Director of Specialty Sales · **Kat Salazar**: Director of PR & Marketing · **Drew Gill**: Art Director · **Heather Doornink**: Production Director · **Nicole Lapalme**: Controller

IMAGECOMICS.COM

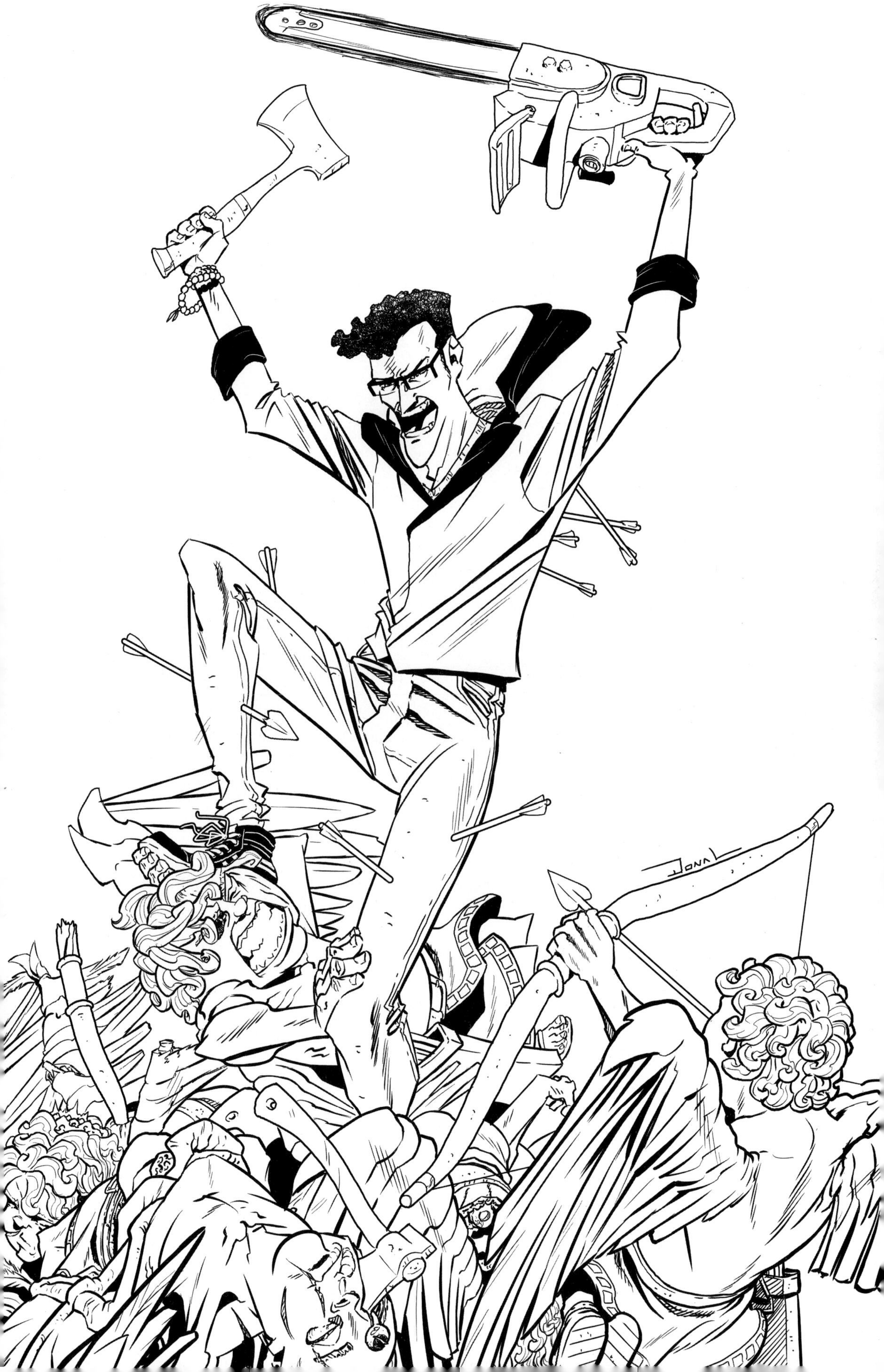

One

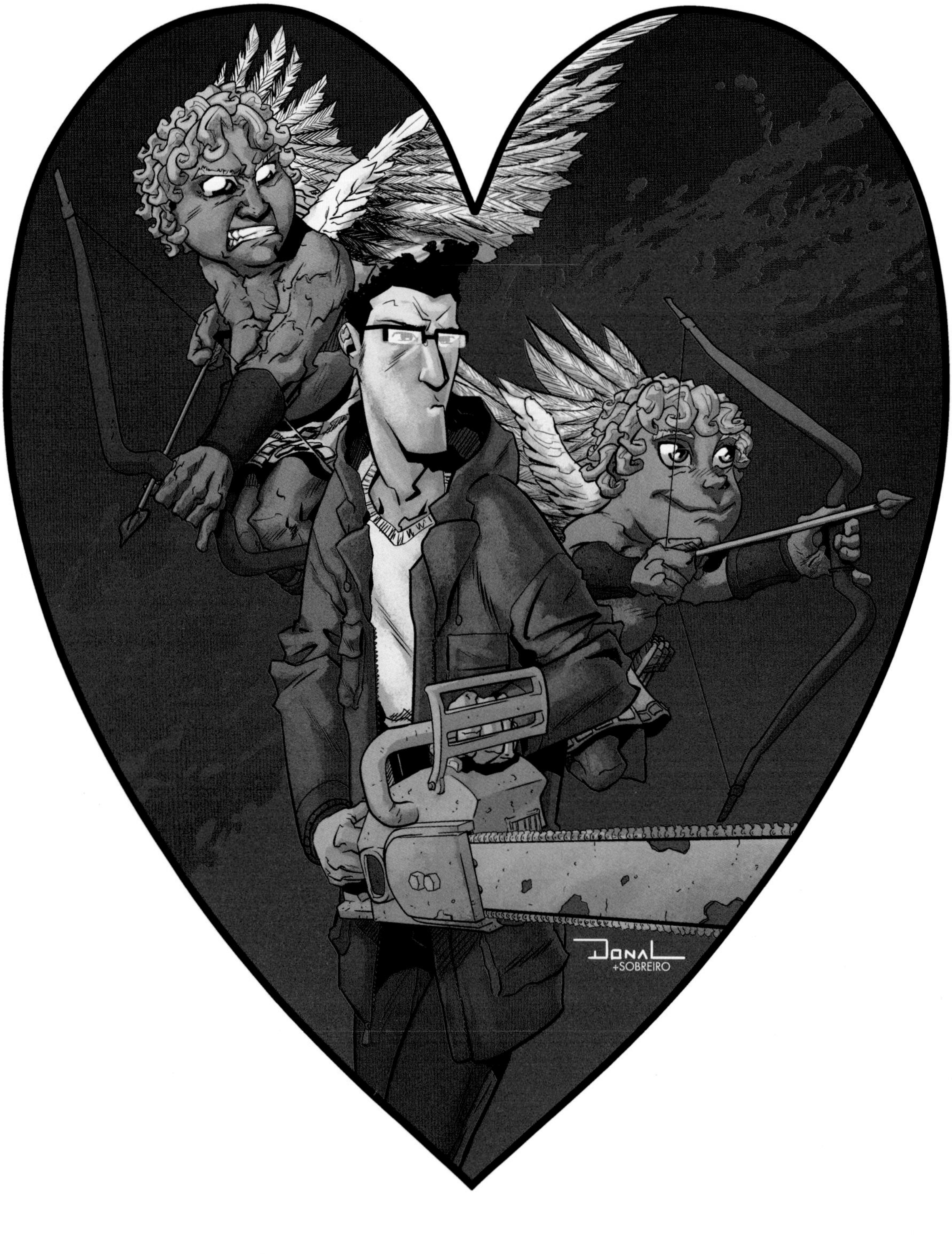
DONAL
+SOBREIRO

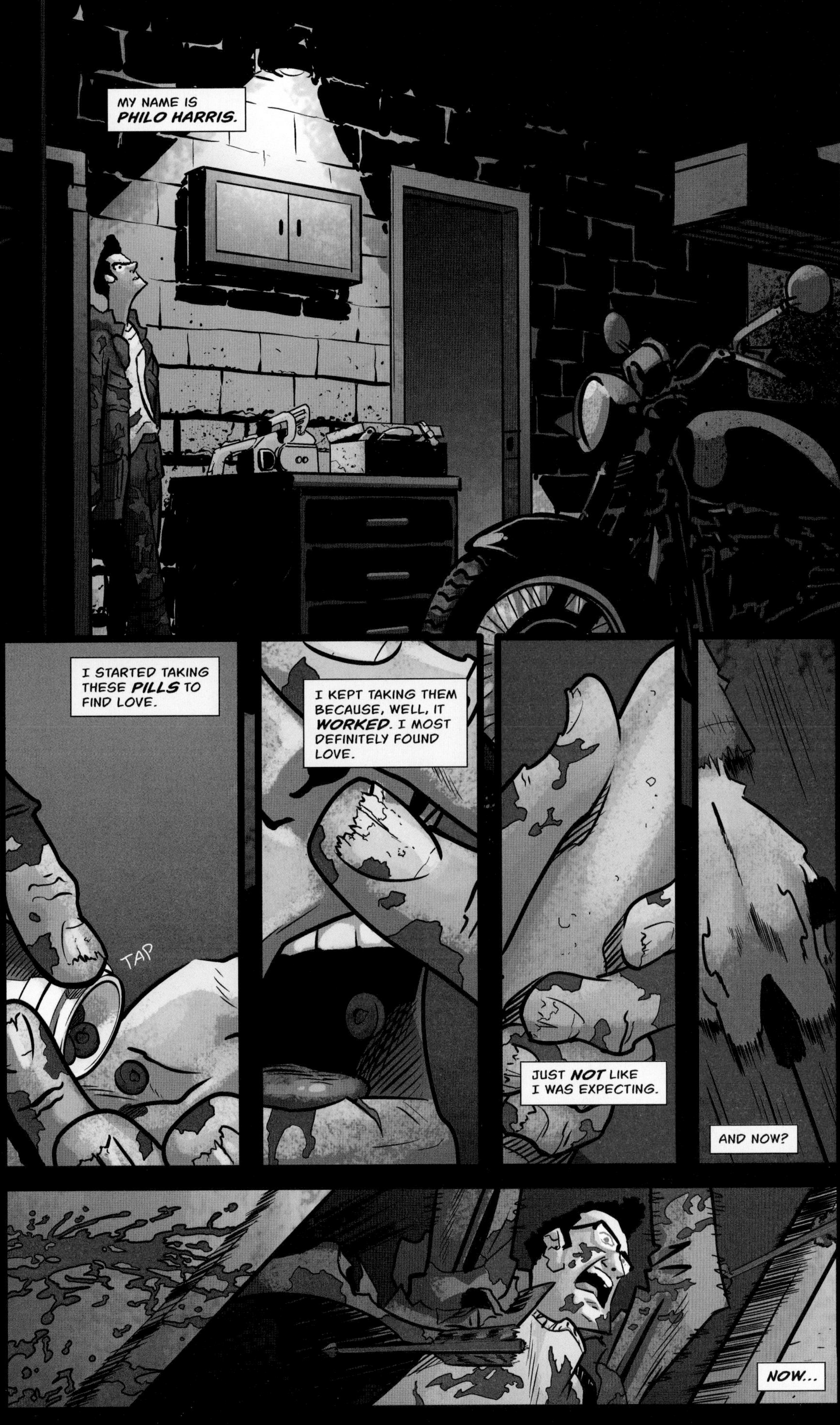

MY NAME IS PHILO HARRIS.
I STARTED TAKING THESE PILLS TO FIND LOVE.
TAP
I KEPT TAKING THEM BECAUSE, WELL, IT WORKED. I MOST DEFINITELY FOUND LOVE.
JUST NOT LIKE I WAS EXPECTING.
AND NOW?
NOW...

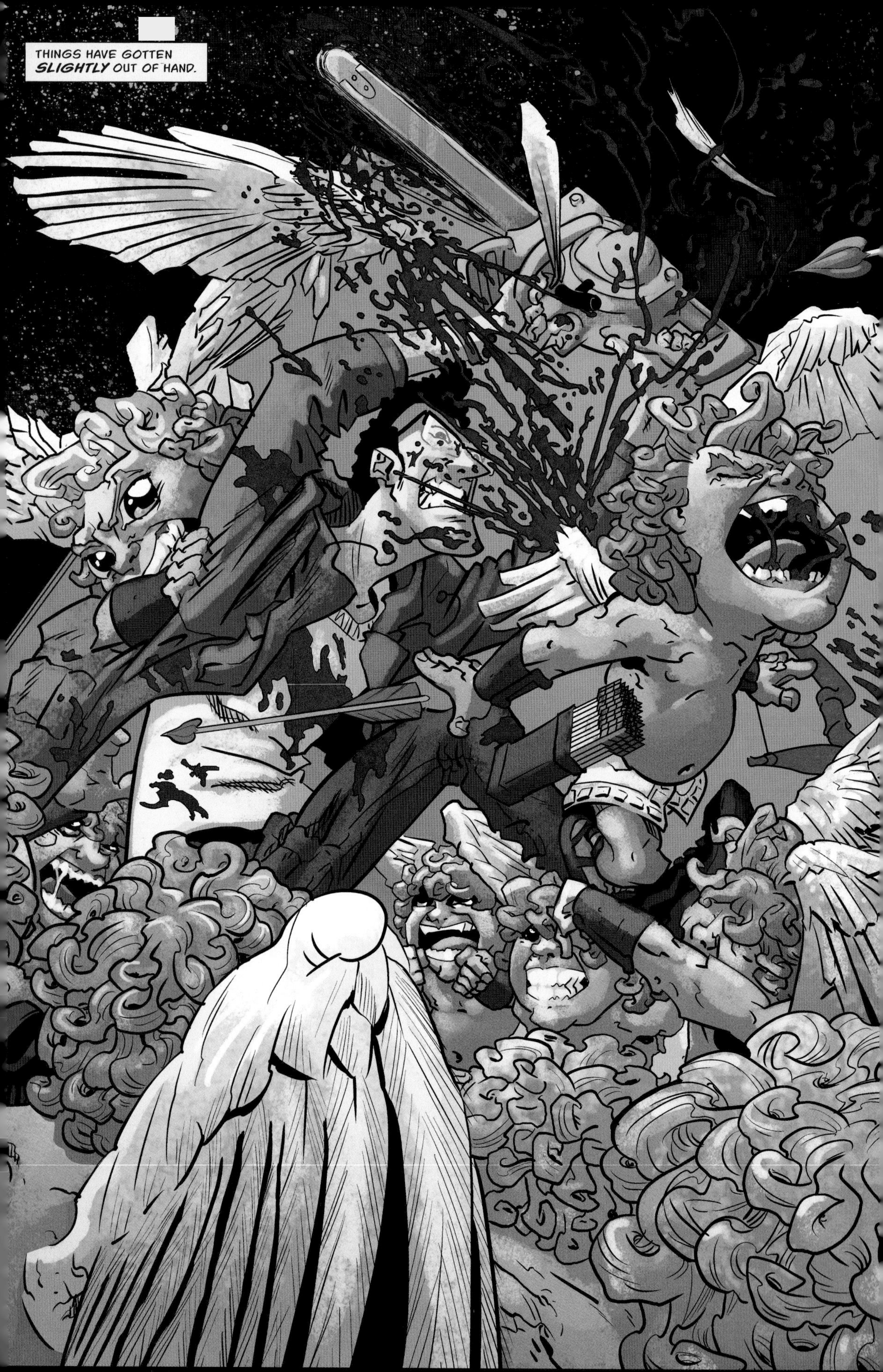
THINGS HAVE GOTTEN SLIGHTLY OUT OF HAND.

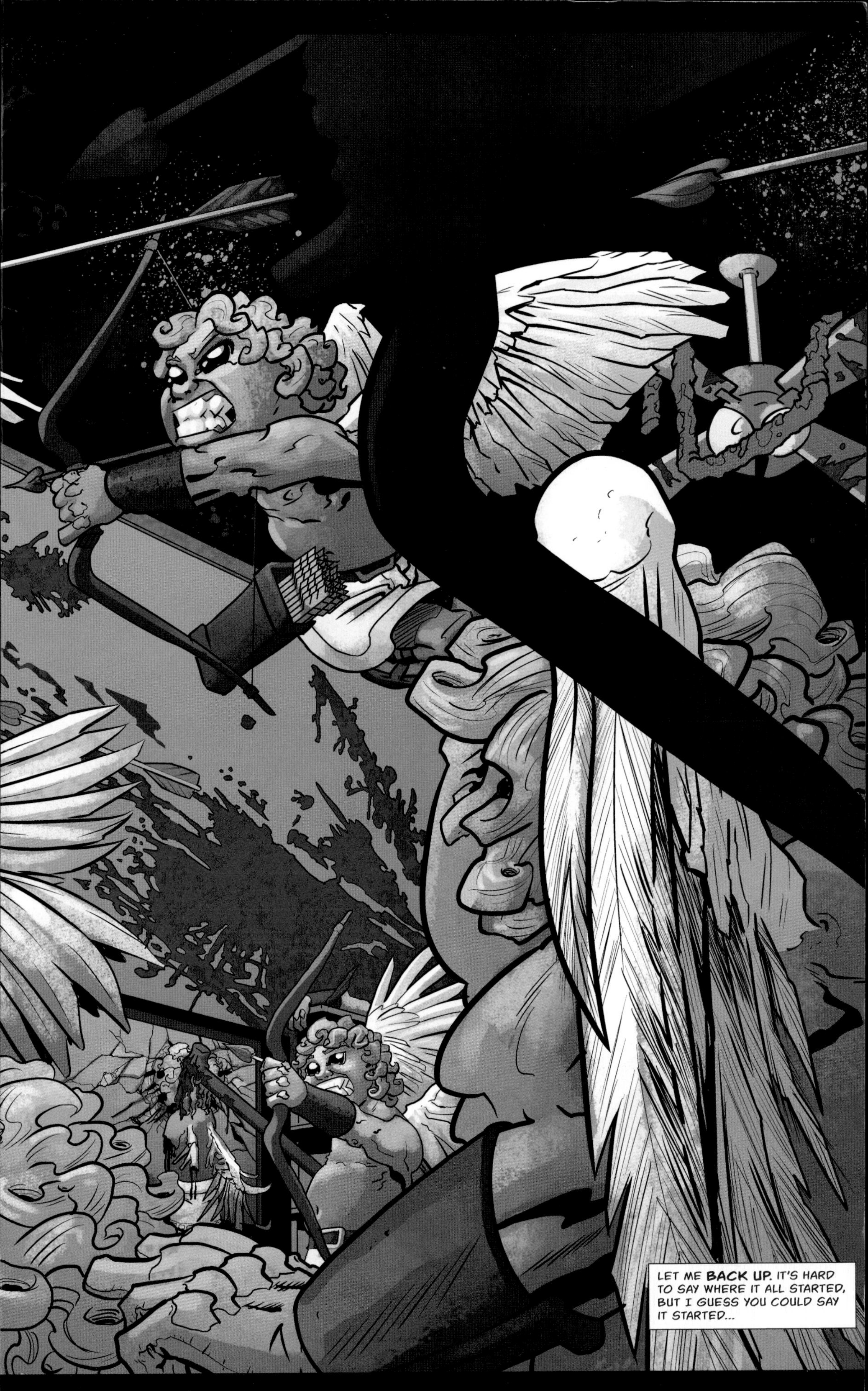
LET ME **BACK UP**. IT'S HARD TO SAY WHERE IT ALL STARTED, BUT I GUESS YOU COULD SAY IT STARTED...

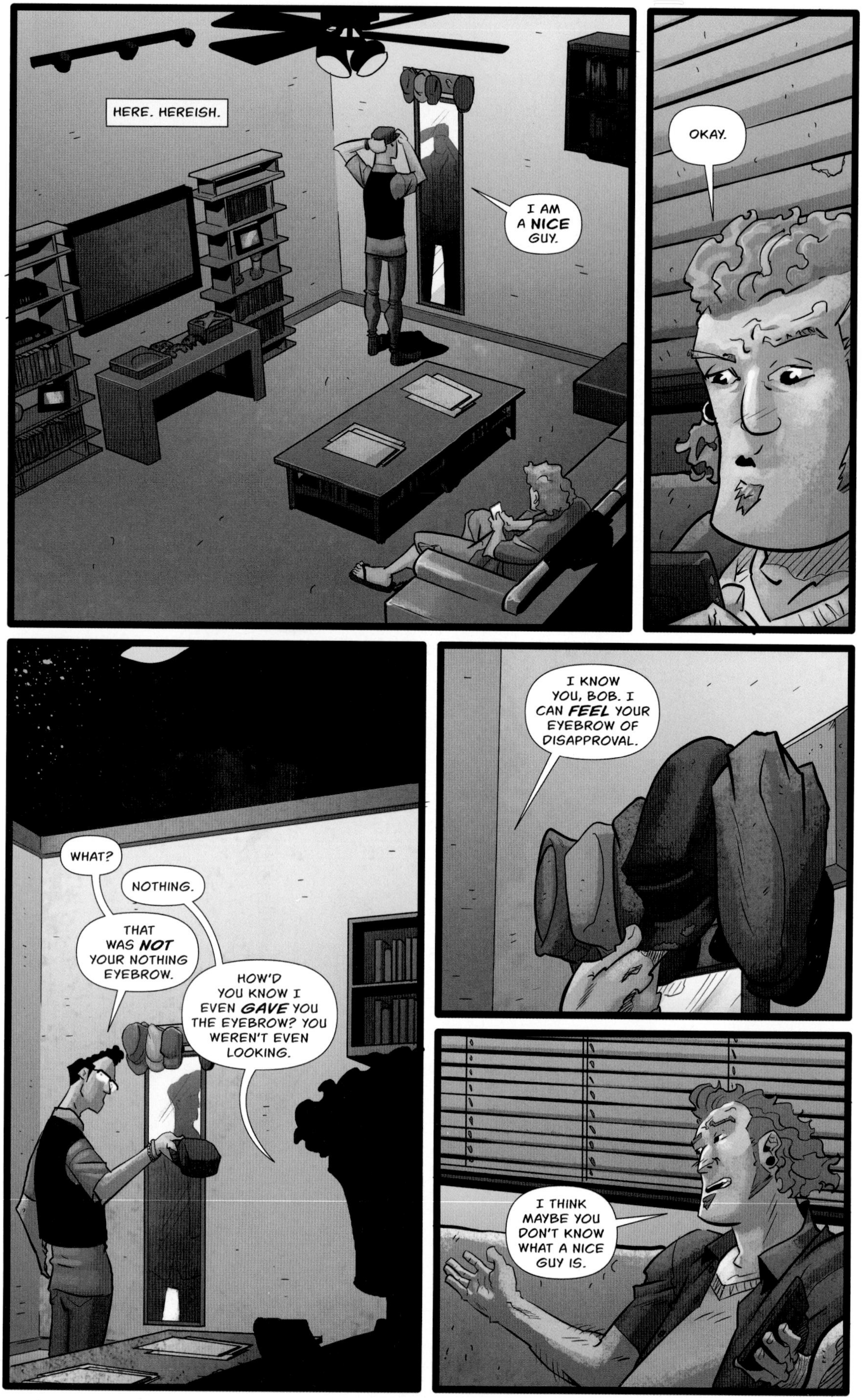
HERE. HEREISH.
I AM A NICE GUY.
OKAY.
I KNOW YOU, BOB. I CAN FEEL YOUR EYEBROW OF DISAPPROVAL.
WHAT?
NOTHING.
THAT WAS NOT YOUR NOTHING EYEBROW.
HOW'D YOU KNOW I EVEN GAVE YOU THE EYEBROW? YOU WEREN'T EVEN LOOKING.
I THINK MAYBE YOU DON'T KNOW WHAT A NICE GUY IS.

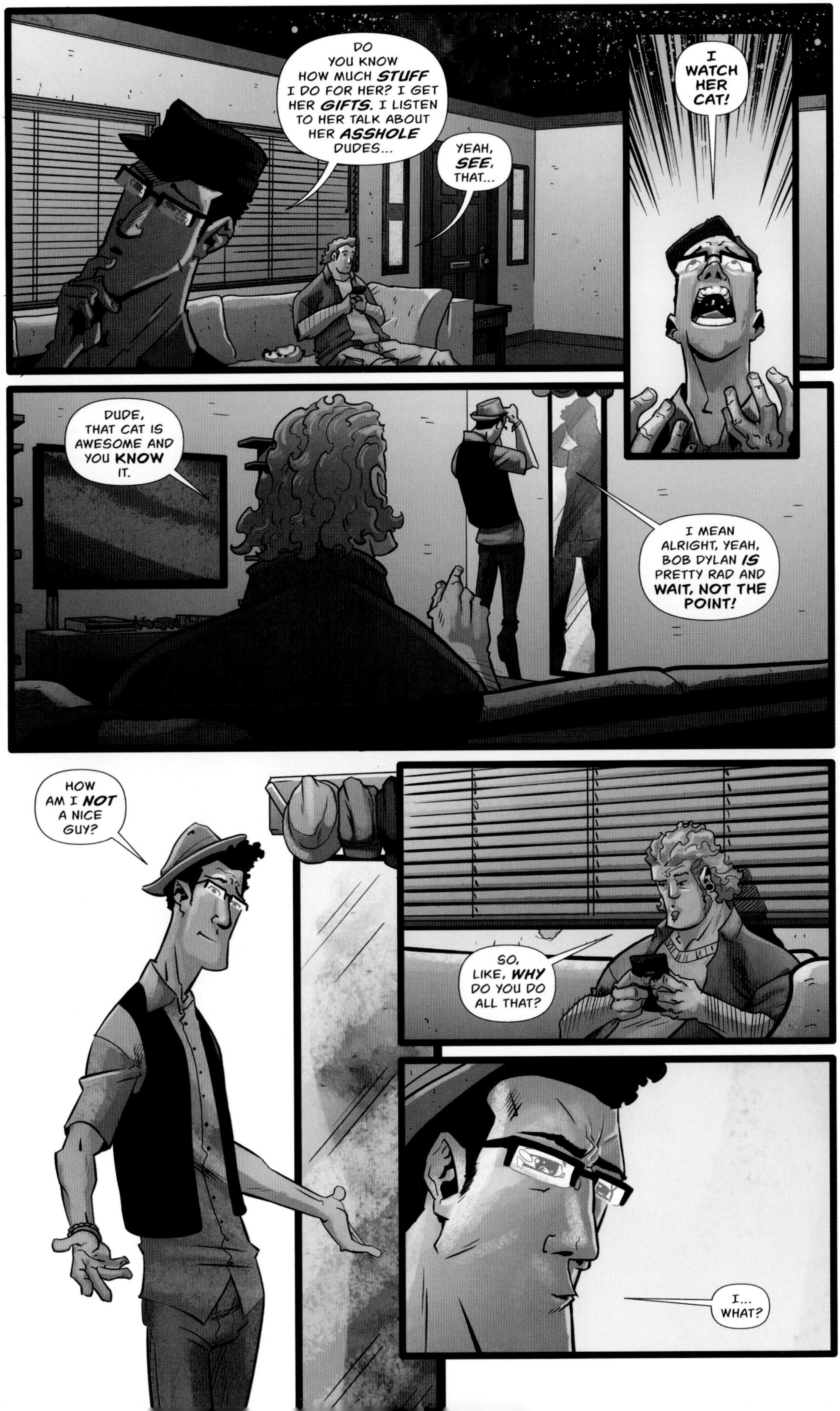
DO YOU KNOW HOW MUCH STUFF I DO FOR HER? I GET HER GIFTS. I LISTEN TO HER TALK ABOUT HER ASSHOLE DUDES...
YEAH, SEE, THAT...
I WATCH HER CAT!
DUDE, THAT CAT IS AWESOME AND YOU KNOW IT.
I MEAN ALRIGHT, YEAH, BOB DYLAN IS PRETTY RAD AND WAIT, NOT THE POINT!
HOW AM I NOT A NICE GUY?
SO, LIKE, WHY DO YOU DO ALL THAT?
I... WHAT?

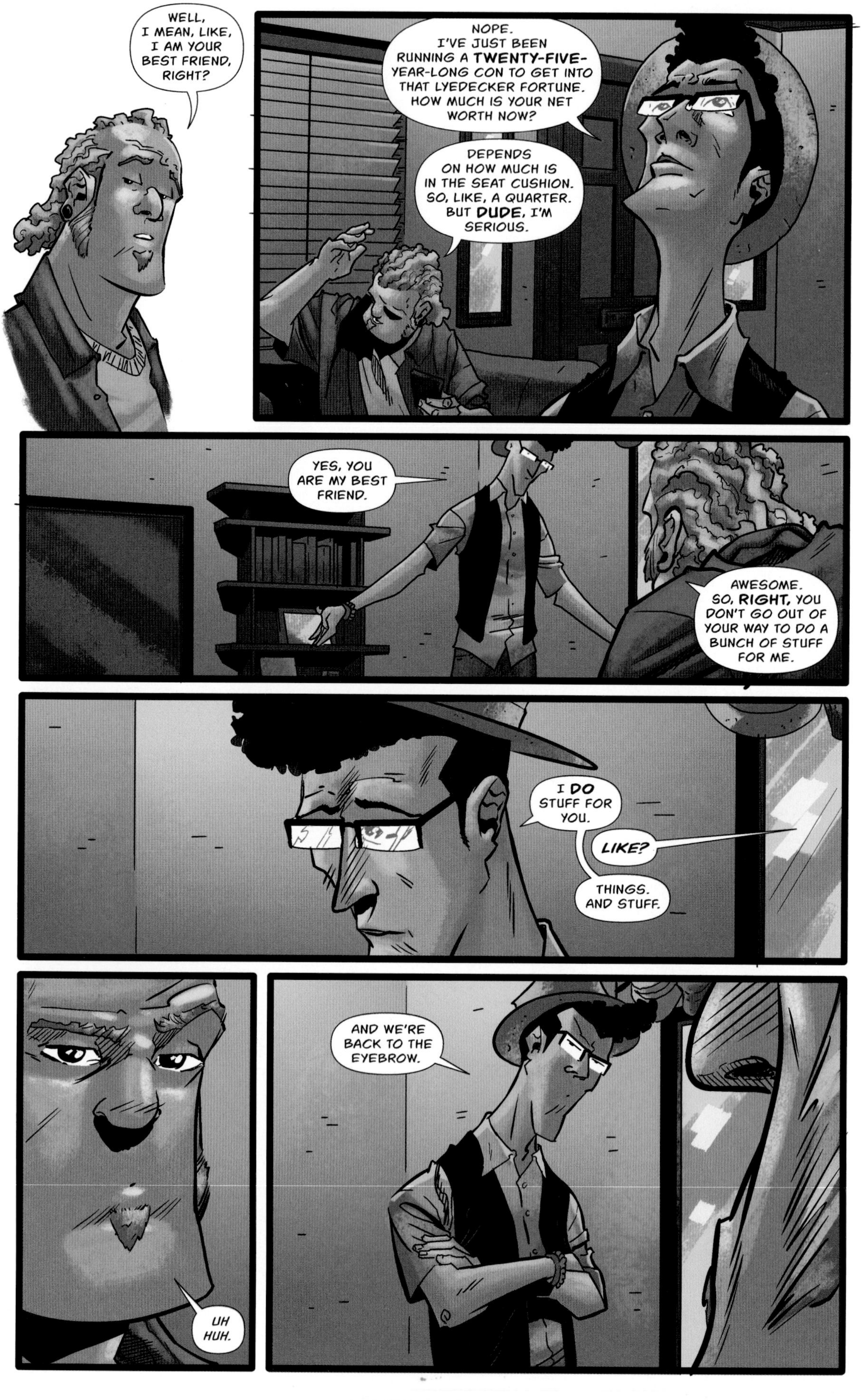
WELL, I MEAN, LIKE, I AM YOUR BEST FRIEND, RIGHT?
NOPE. I'VE JUST BEEN RUNNING A **TWENTY-FIVE-**YEAR-LONG CON TO GET INTO THAT LYEDECKER FORTUNE. HOW MUCH IS YOUR NET WORTH NOW?
DEPENDS ON HOW MUCH IS IN THE SEAT CUSHION. SO, LIKE, A QUARTER. BUT **DUDE**, I'M SERIOUS.
YES, YOU ARE MY BEST FRIEND.
AWESOME. SO, **RIGHT**, YOU DON'T GO OUT OF YOUR WAY TO DO A BUNCH OF STUFF FOR ME.
I **DO** STUFF FOR YOU.
LIKE?
THINGS. AND STUFF.
UH HUH.
AND WE'RE BACK TO THE EYEBROW.

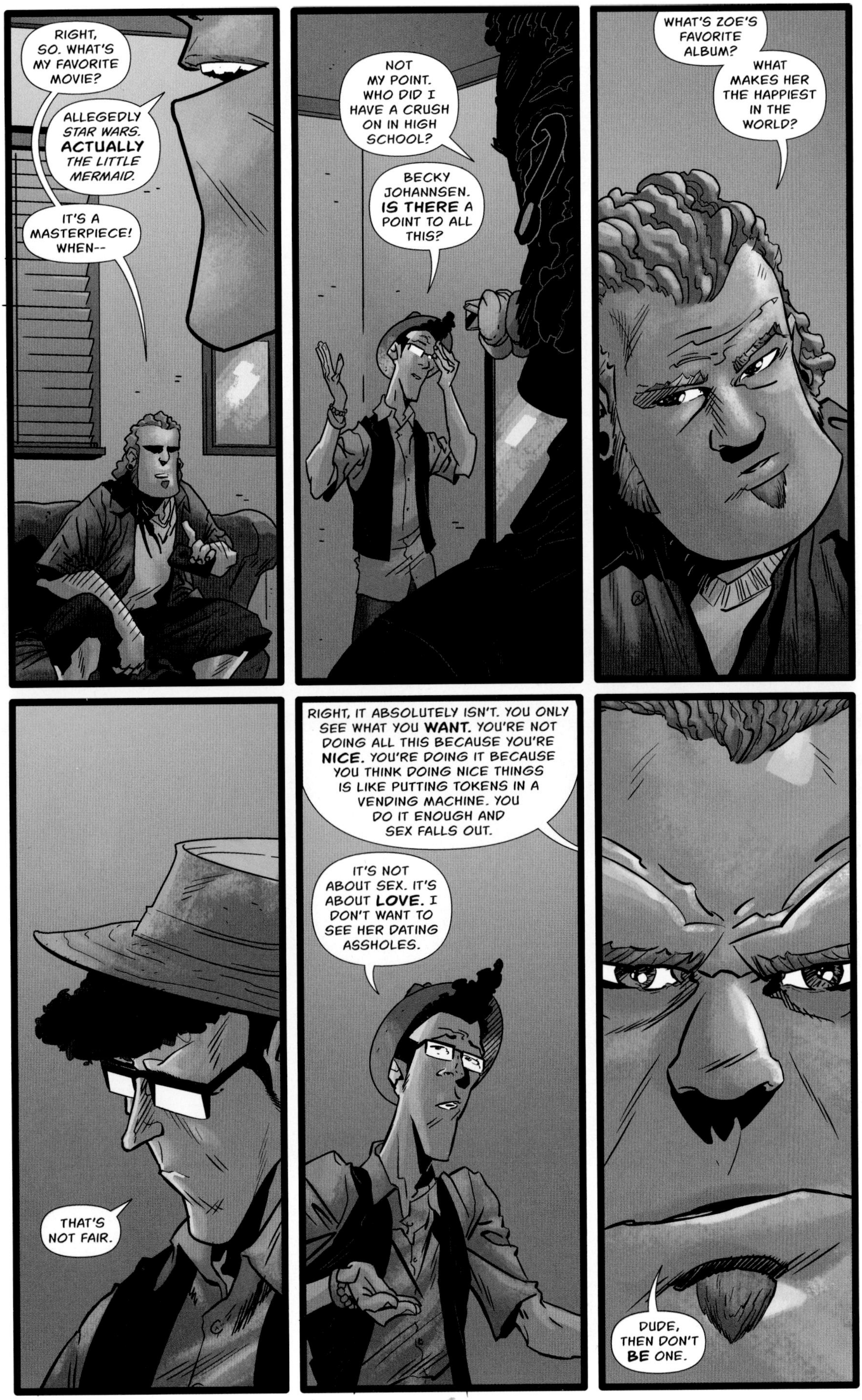
RIGHT, SO. WHAT'S MY FAVORITE MOVIE?
ALLEGEDLY STAR WARS. ACTUALLY THE LITTLE MERMAID.
IT'S A MASTERPIECE! WHEN--
NOT MY POINT. WHO DID I HAVE A CRUSH ON IN HIGH SCHOOL?
BECKY JOHANNSEN. IS THERE A POINT TO ALL THIS?
WHAT'S ZOE'S FAVORITE ALBUM?
WHAT MAKES HER THE HAPPIEST IN THE WORLD?
THAT'S NOT FAIR.
RIGHT, IT ABSOLUTELY ISN'T. YOU ONLY SEE WHAT YOU WANT. YOU'RE NOT DOING ALL THIS BECAUSE YOU'RE NICE. YOU'RE DOING IT BECAUSE YOU THINK DOING NICE THINGS IS LIKE PUTTING TOKENS IN A VENDING MACHINE. YOU DO IT ENOUGH AND SEX FALLS OUT.
IT'S NOT ABOUT SEX. IT'S ABOUT LOVE. I DON'T WANT TO SEE HER DATING ASSHOLES.
DUDE, THEN DON'T BE ONE.

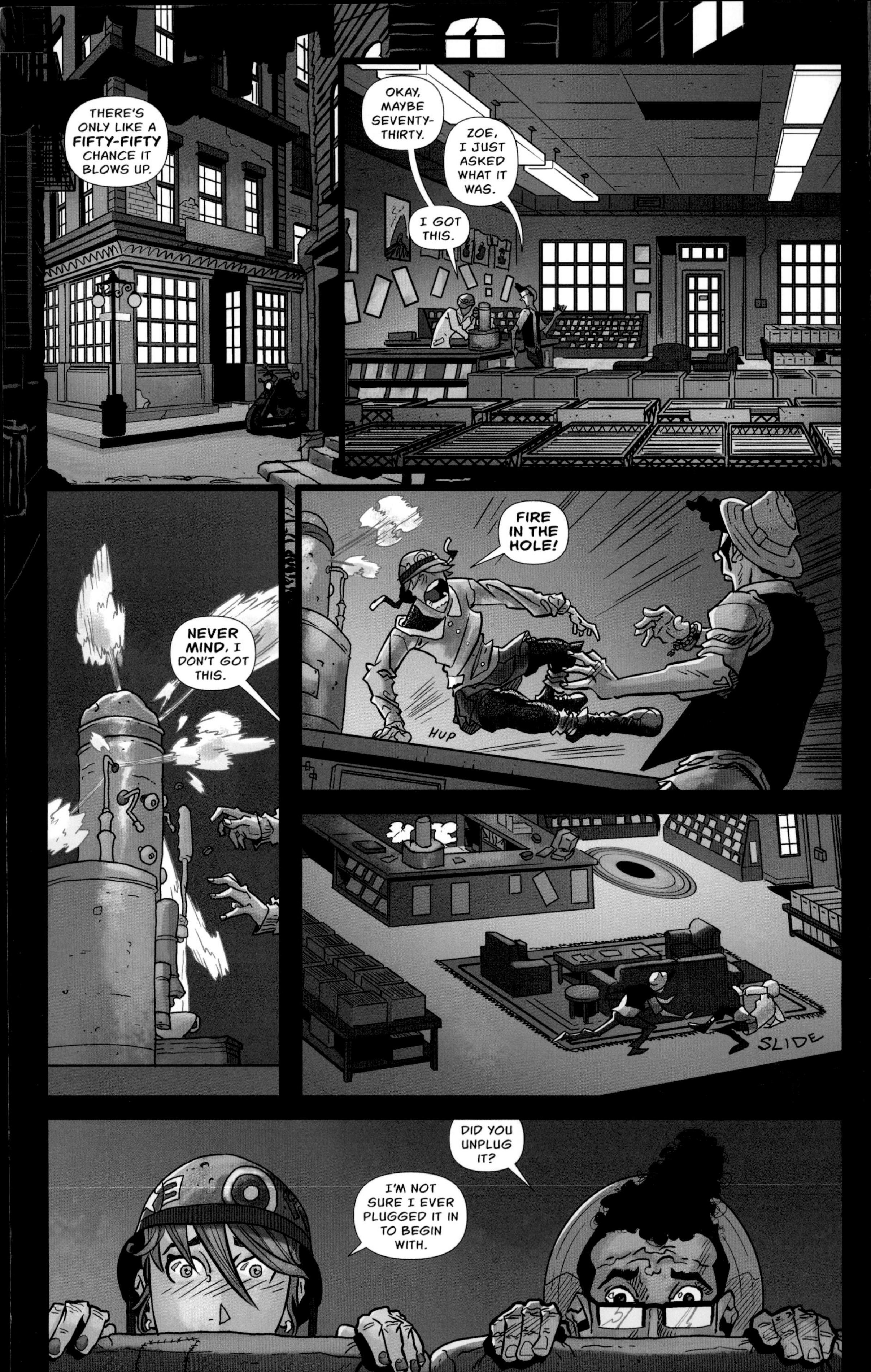

THERE'S ONLY LIKE A **FIFTY-FIFTY** CHANCE IT BLOWS UP.
OKAY, MAYBE SEVENTY-THIRTY.
ZOE, I JUST ASKED WHAT IT WAS.
I GOT THIS.
NEVER MIND, I DON'T GOT THIS.
FIRE IN THE HOLE!
HUP
SLIDE
DID YOU UNPLUG IT?
I'M NOT SURE I EVER PLUGGED IT IN TO BEGIN WITH.

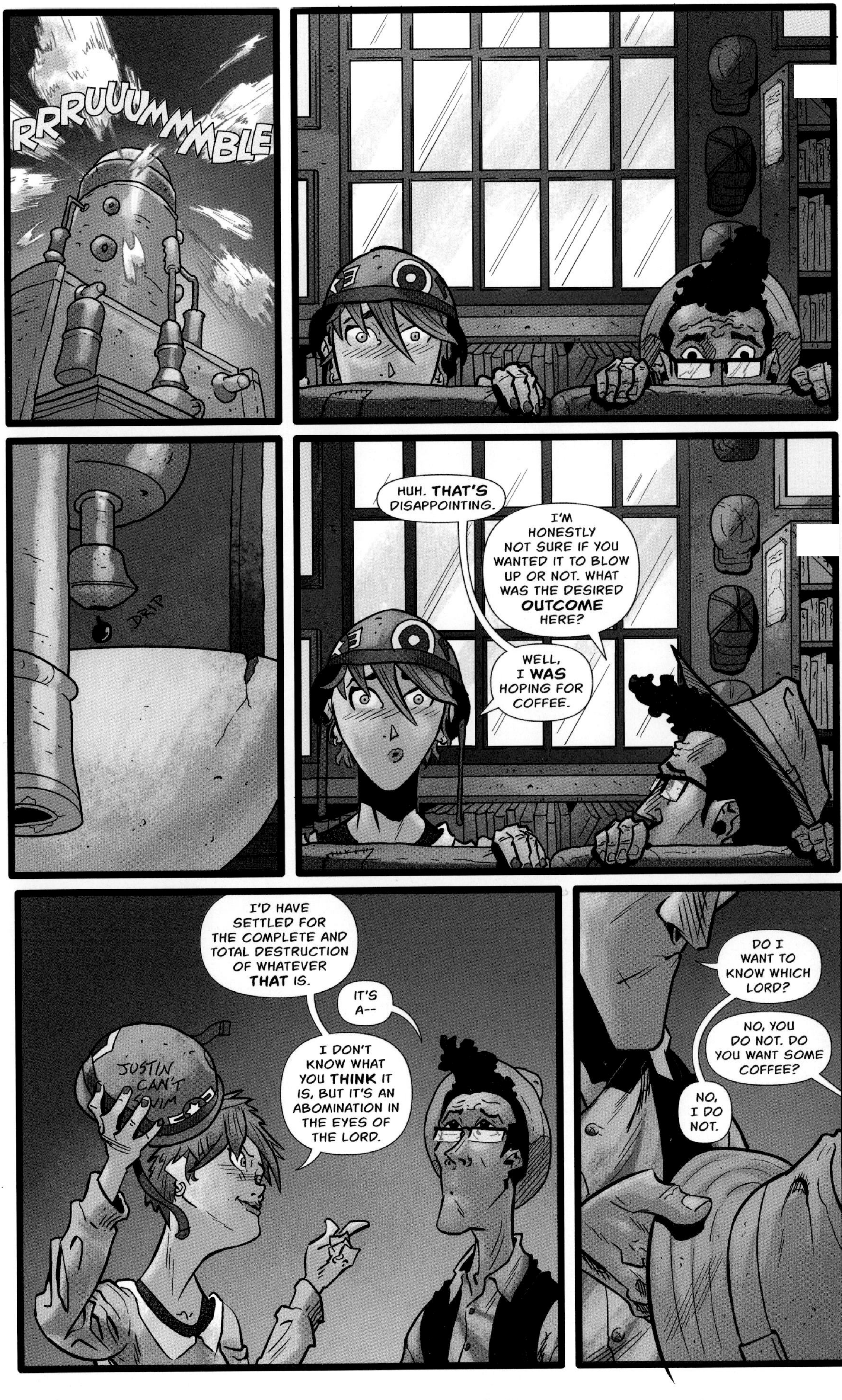
RRRUUUMMMBLE
DRIP
HUH. THAT'S DISAPPOINTING.
I'M HONESTLY NOT SURE IF YOU WANTED IT TO BLOW UP OR NOT. WHAT WAS THE DESIRED OUTCOME HERE?
WELL, I WAS HOPING FOR COFFEE.
I'D HAVE SETTLED FOR THE COMPLETE AND TOTAL DESTRUCTION OF WHATEVER THAT IS.
IT'S A--
I DON'T KNOW WHAT YOU THINK IT IS, BUT IT'S AN ABOMINATION IN THE EYES OF THE LORD.
JUSTIN CAN'T SWIM
DO I WANT TO KNOW WHICH LORD?
NO, YOU DO NOT. DO YOU WANT SOME COFFEE?
NO, I DO NOT.

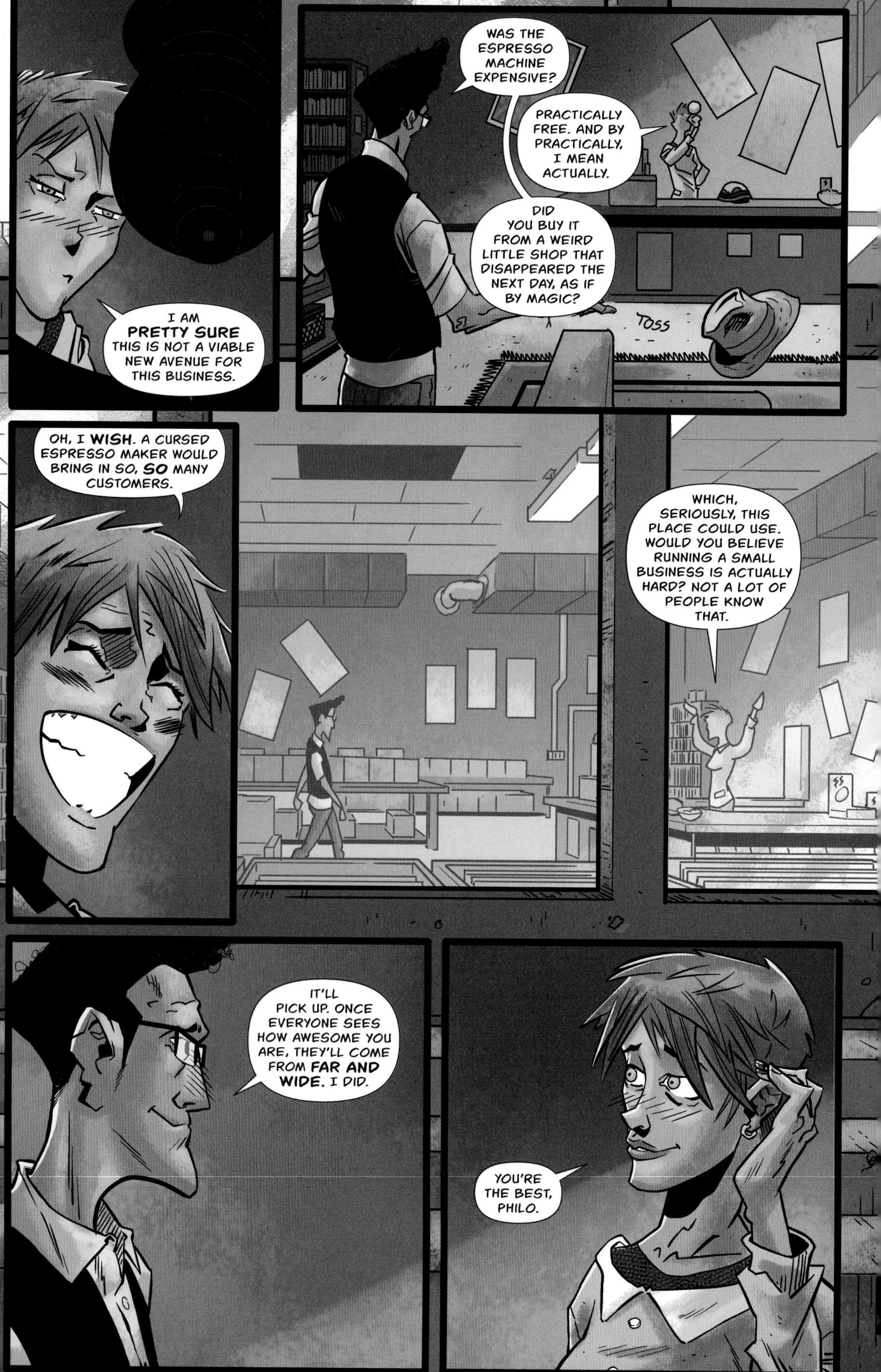
I AM **PRETTY SURE** THIS IS NOT A VIABLE NEW AVENUE FOR THIS BUSINESS.
WAS THE ESPRESSO MACHINE EXPENSIVE?
PRACTICALLY FREE. AND BY PRACTICALLY, I MEAN ACTUALLY.
DID YOU BUY IT FROM A WEIRD LITTLE SHOP THAT DISAPPEARED THE NEXT DAY, AS IF BY MAGIC?
TOSS
OH, I **WISH**. A CURSED ESPRESSO MAKER WOULD BRING IN SO, **SO** MANY CUSTOMERS.
WHICH, SERIOUSLY, THIS PLACE COULD USE. WOULD YOU BELIEVE RUNNING A SMALL BUSINESS IS ACTUALLY HARD? NOT A LOT OF PEOPLE KNOW THAT.
IT'LL PICK UP. ONCE EVERYONE SEES HOW AWESOME YOU ARE, THEY'LL COME FROM **FAR AND WIDE.** I DID.
YOU'RE THE BEST, PHILO.

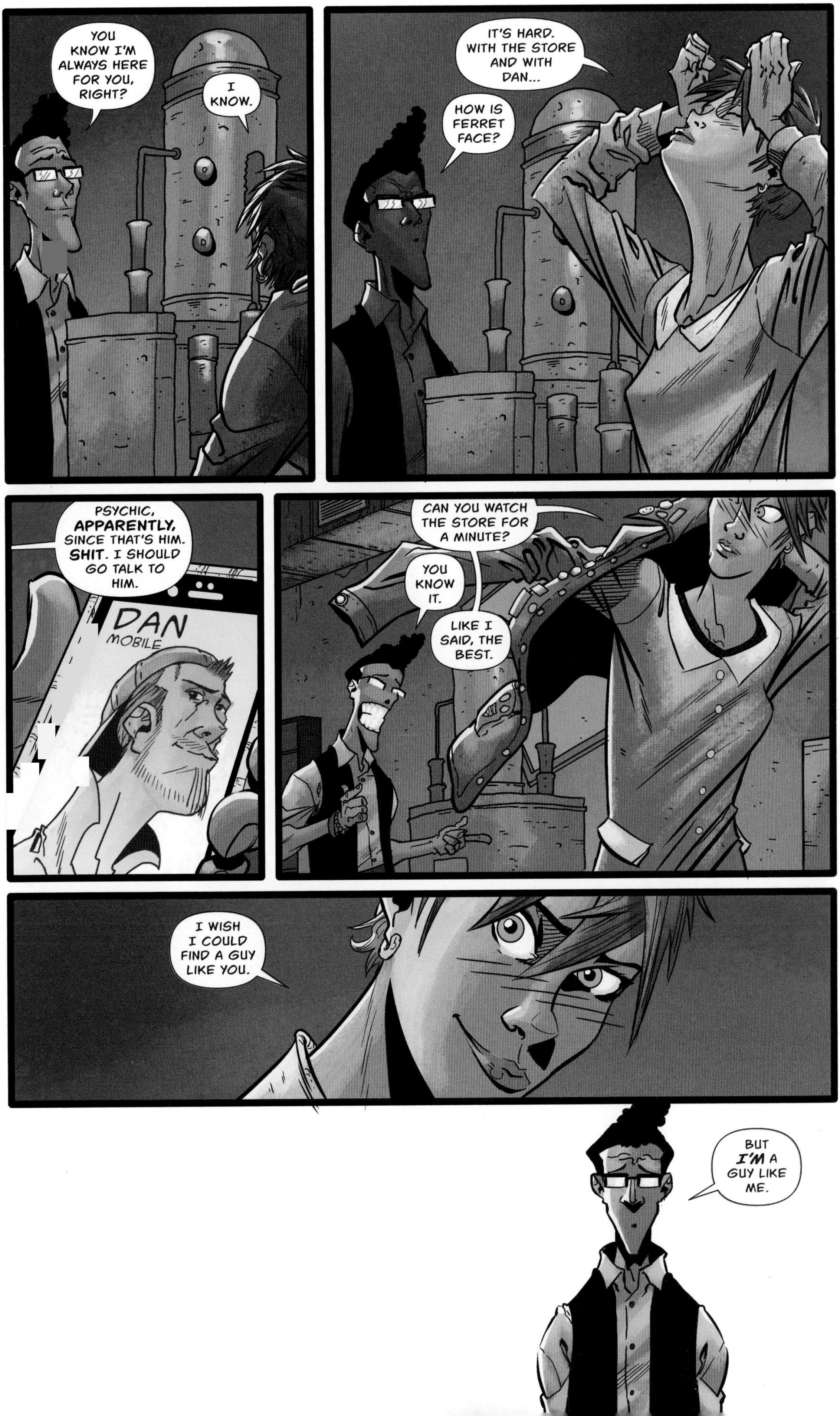
YOU KNOW I'M ALWAYS HERE FOR YOU, RIGHT?
I KNOW.
IT'S HARD. WITH THE STORE AND WITH DAN...
HOW IS FERRET FACE?
PSYCHIC, **APPARENTLY**, SINCE THAT'S HIM. **SHIT**. I SHOULD GO TALK TO HIM.
DAN
MOBILE
CAN YOU WATCH THE STORE FOR A MINUTE?
YOU KNOW IT.
LIKE I SAID, THE BEST.
I WISH I COULD FIND A GUY LIKE YOU.
BUT *I'M* A GUY LIKE ME.

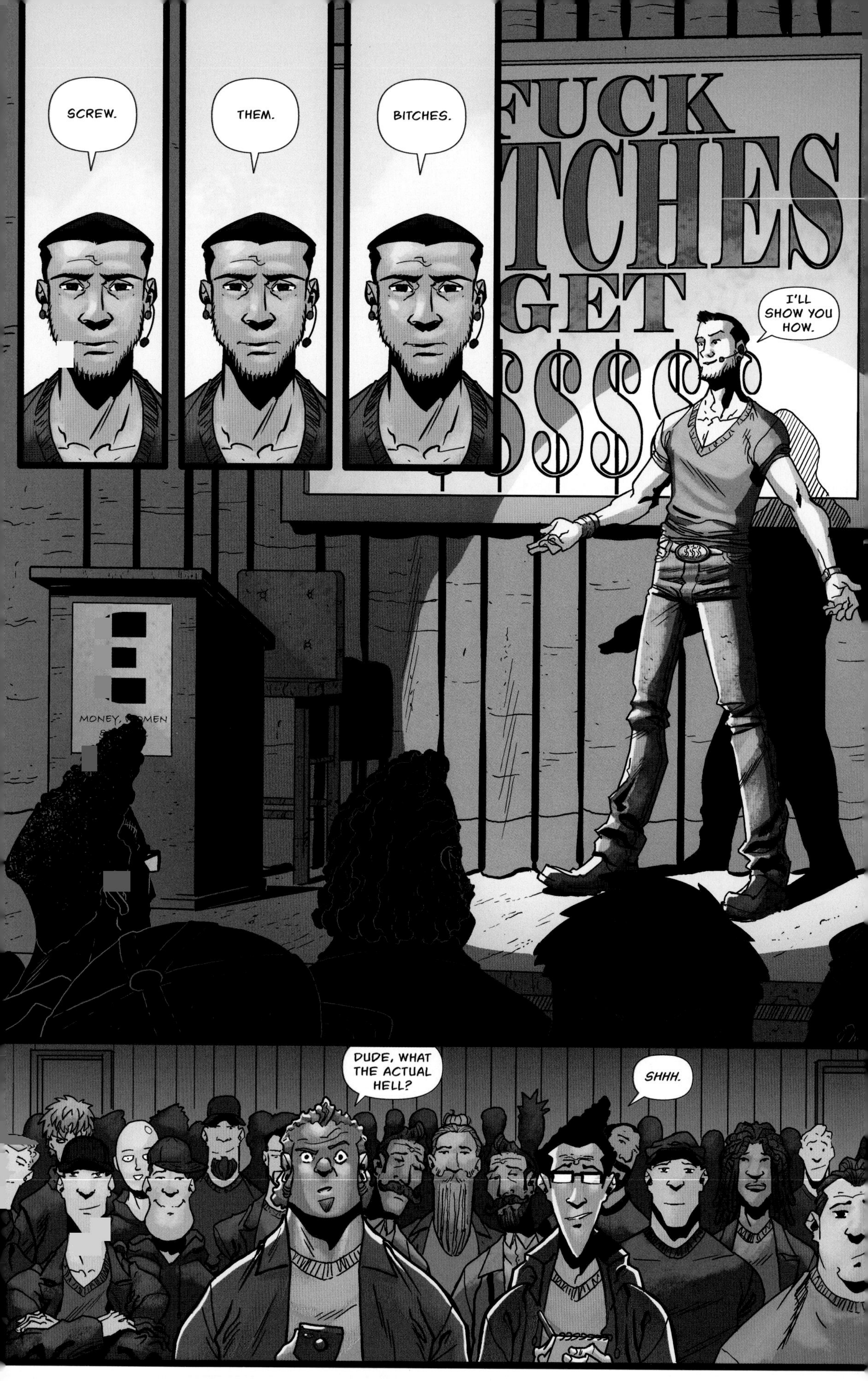
SCREW.
THEM.
BITCHES.
FUCK
I'LL SHOW YOU HOW.
DUDE, WHAT THE ACTUAL HELL?
SHHH.

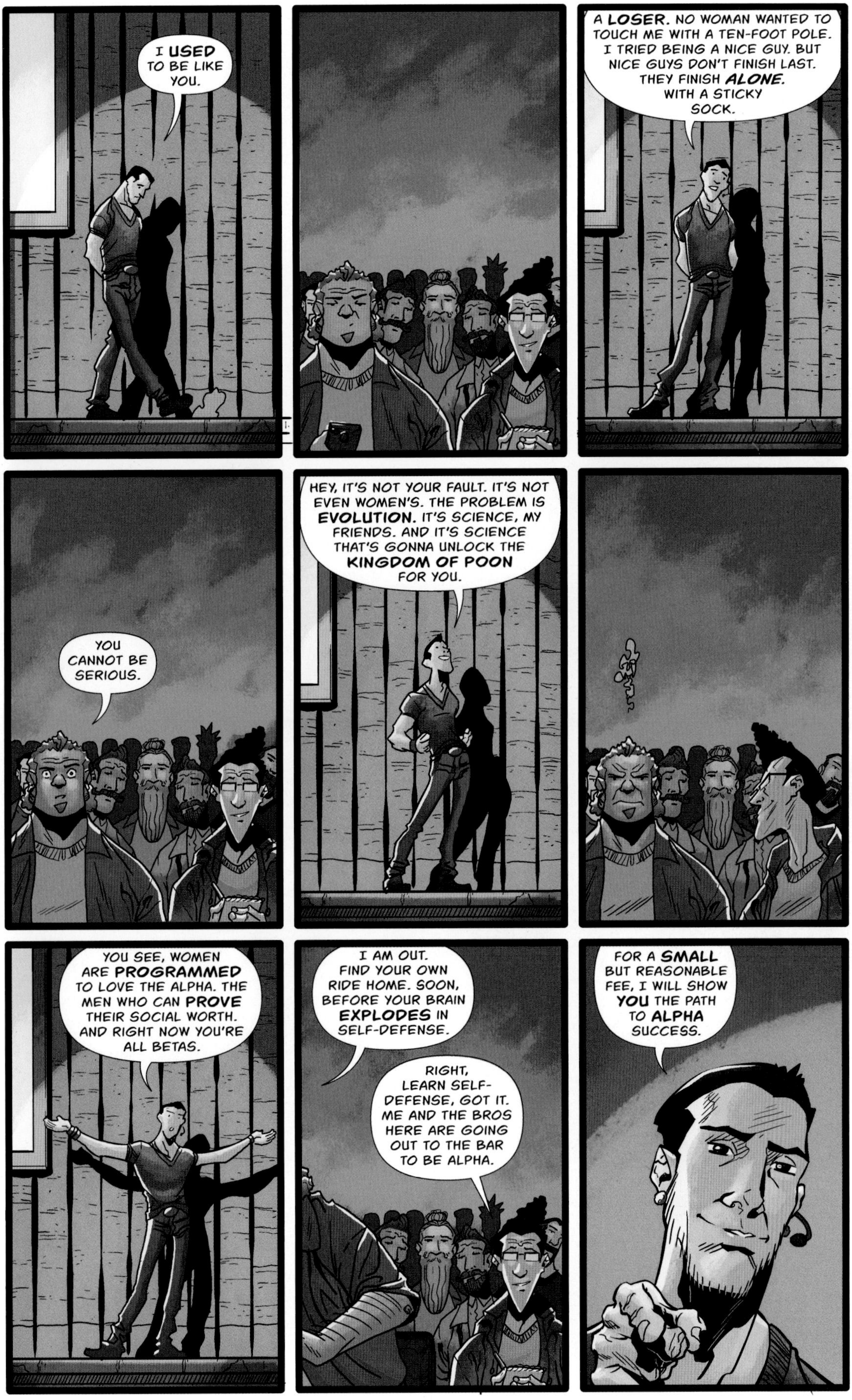
I **USED** TO BE LIKE YOU.
A **LOSER.** NO WOMAN WANTED TO TOUCH ME WITH A TEN-FOOT POLE. I TRIED BEING A NICE GUY. BUT NICE GUYS DON'T FINISH LAST. THEY FINISH ***ALONE.*** WITH A STICKY SOCK.
YOU CANNOT BE SERIOUS.
HEY, IT'S NOT YOUR FAULT. IT'S NOT EVEN WOMEN'S. THE PROBLEM IS **EVOLUTION.** IT'S SCIENCE, MY FRIENDS. AND IT'S SCIENCE THAT'S GONNA UNLOCK THE **KINGDOM OF POON** FOR YOU.
YOU SEE, WOMEN ARE **PROGRAMMED** TO LOVE THE ALPHA. THE MEN WHO CAN **PROVE** THEIR SOCIAL WORTH. AND RIGHT NOW YOU'RE ALL BETAS.
I AM OUT. FIND YOUR OWN RIDE HOME. SOON, BEFORE YOUR BRAIN **EXPLODES** IN SELF-DEFENSE.
RIGHT, LEARN SELF-DEFENSE, GOT IT. ME AND THE BROS HERE ARE GOING OUT TO THE BAR TO BE ALPHA.
FOR A **SMALL** BUT REASONABLE FEE, I WILL SHOW **YOU** THE PATH TO **ALPHA** SUCCESS.

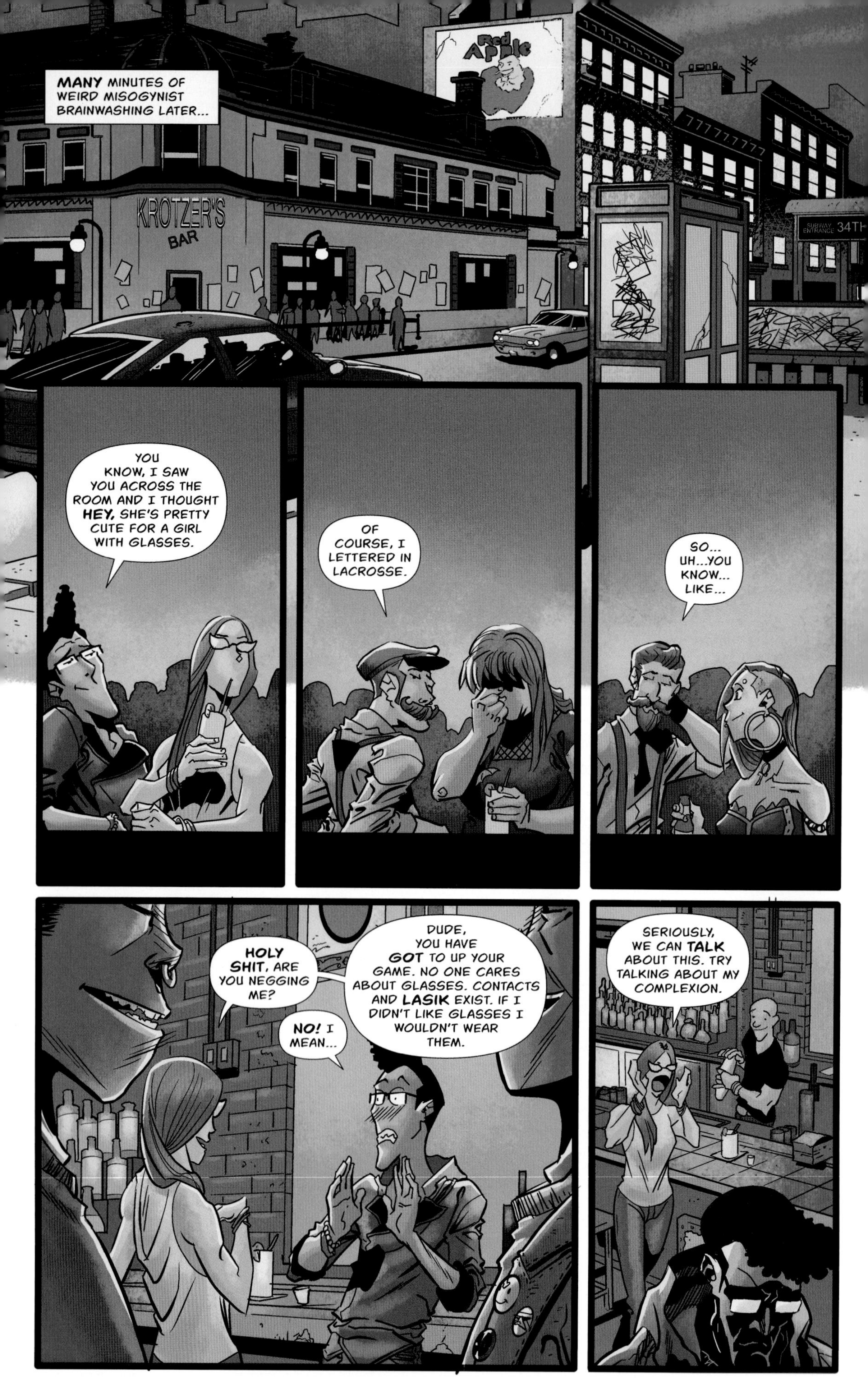
MANY MINUTES OF WEIRD MISOGYNIST BRAINWASHING LATER...
Red Apple
KROTZER'S BAR
SUBWAY ENTRANCE 34TH
YOU KNOW, I SAW YOU ACROSS THE ROOM AND I THOUGHT HEY, SHE'S PRETTY CUTE FOR A GIRL WITH GLASSES.
OF COURSE, I LETTERED IN LACROSSE.
SO... UH...YOU KNOW... LIKE...
HOLY SHIT, ARE YOU NEGGING ME?
NO! I MEAN...
DUDE, YOU HAVE GOT TO UP YOUR GAME. NO ONE CARES ABOUT GLASSES. CONTACTS AND LASIK EXIST. IF I DIDN'T LIKE GLASSES I WOULDN'T WEAR THEM.
SERIOUSLY, WE CAN TALK ABOUT THIS. TRY TALKING ABOUT MY COMPLEXION.

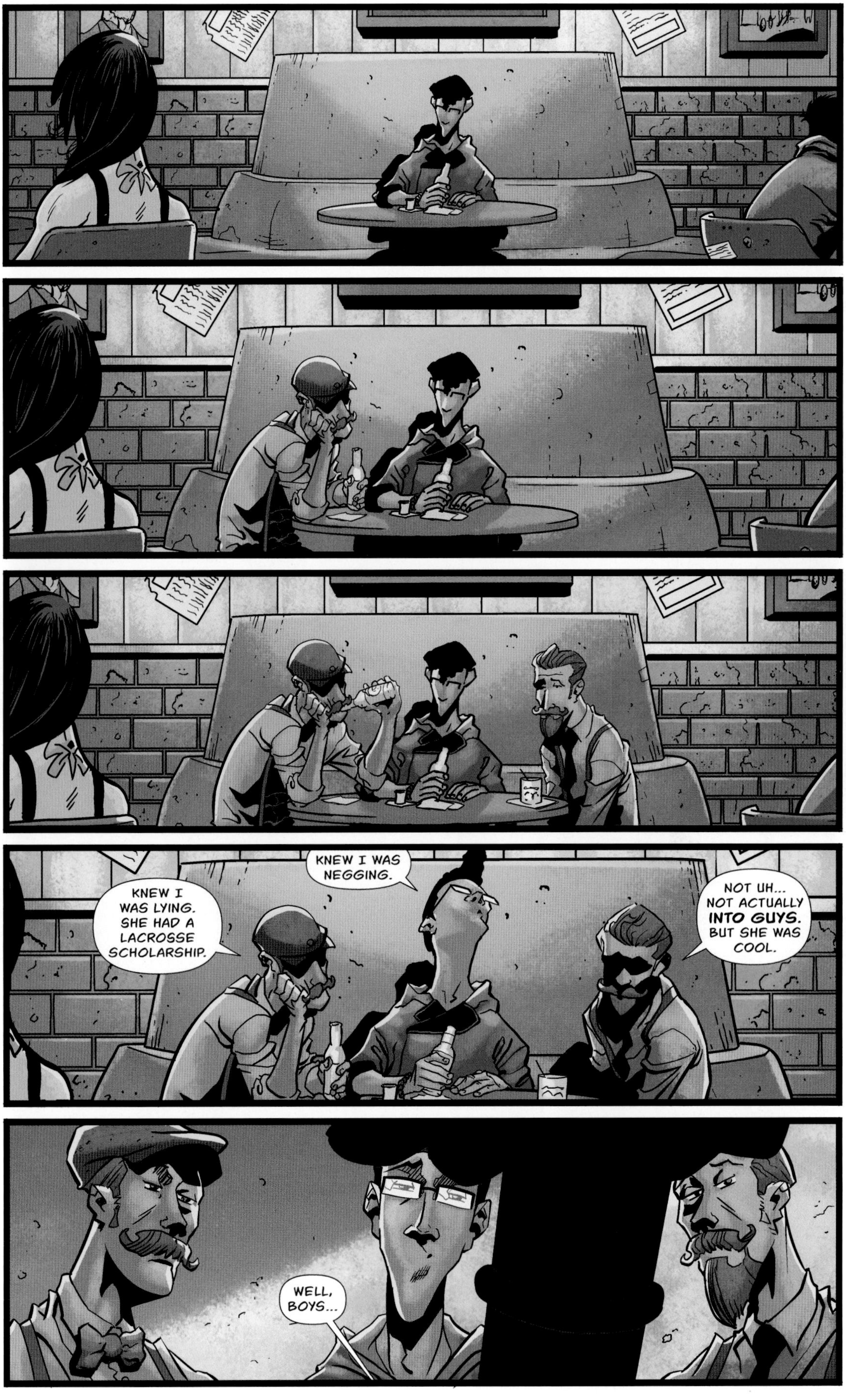
KNEW I WAS LYING. SHE HAD A LACROSSE SCHOLARSHIP.
KNEW I WAS NEGGING.
NOT UH... NOT ACTUALLY **INTO GUYS.** BUT SHE WAS COOL.
WELL, BOYS...

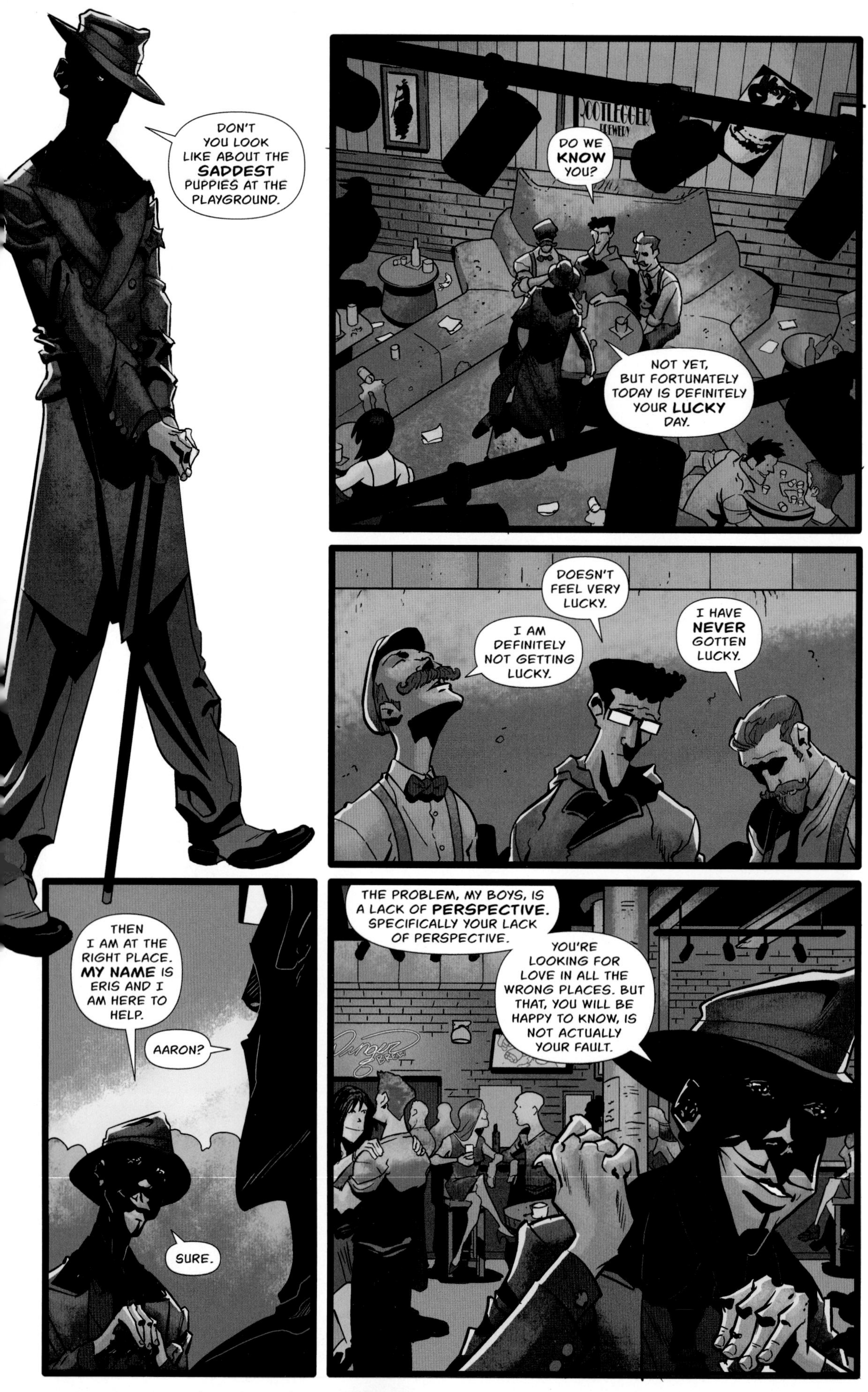
DON'T YOU LOOK LIKE ABOUT THE SADDEST PUPPIES AT THE PLAYGROUND.
BOOTLEGGER BREWERY
DO WE KNOW YOU?
NOT YET, BUT FORTUNATELY TODAY IS DEFINITELY YOUR LUCKY DAY.
DOESN'T FEEL VERY LUCKY.
I AM DEFINITELY NOT GETTING LUCKY.
I HAVE NEVER GOTTEN LUCKY.
THEN I AM AT THE RIGHT PLACE. MY NAME IS ERIS AND I AM HERE TO HELP.
AARON?
SURE.
THE PROBLEM, MY BOYS, IS A LACK OF PERSPECTIVE. SPECIFICALLY YOUR LACK OF PERSPECTIVE.
YOU'RE LOOKING FOR LOVE IN ALL THE WRONG PLACES. BUT THAT, YOU WILL BE HAPPY TO KNOW, IS NOT ACTUALLY YOUR FAULT.

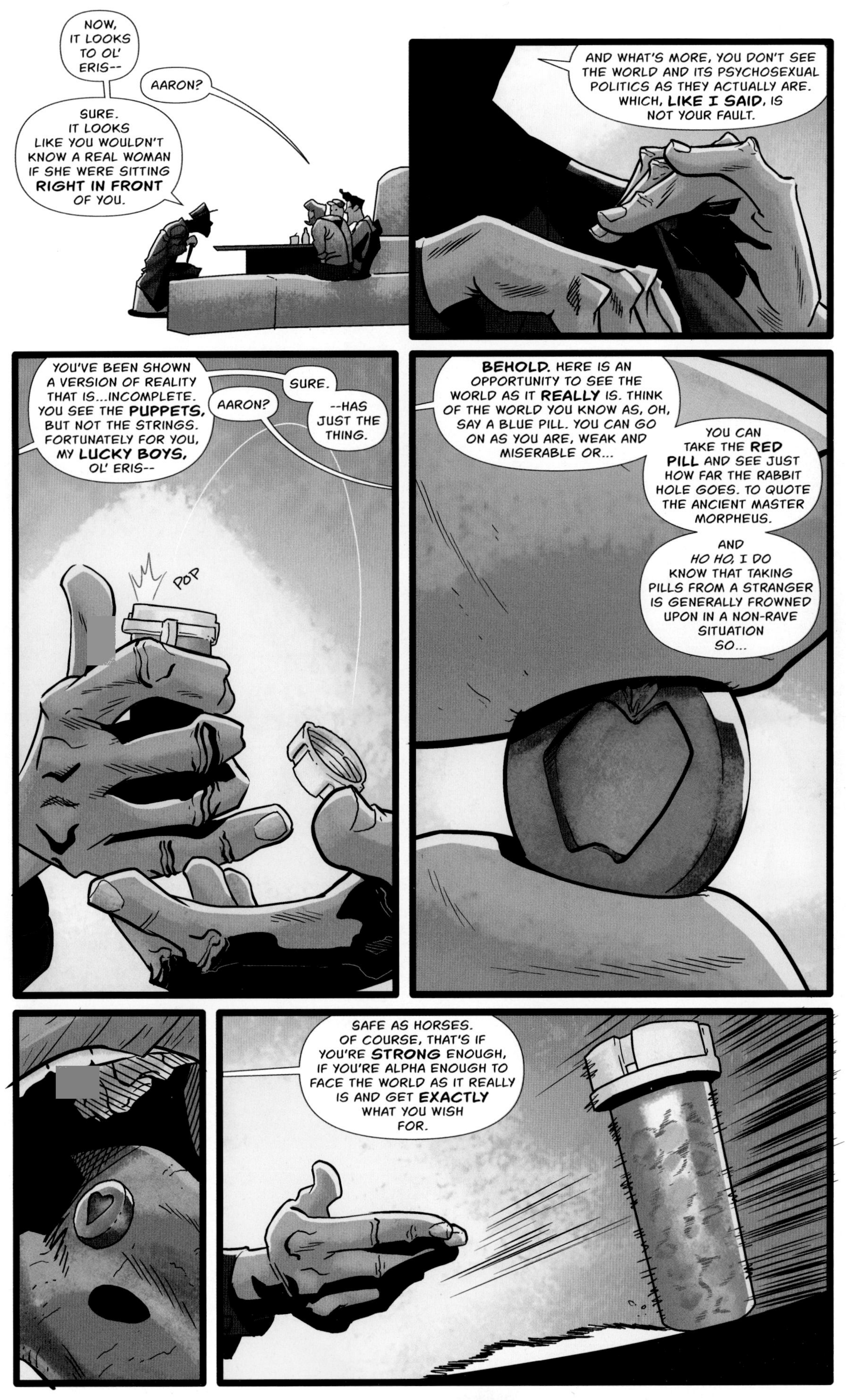
NOW, IT LOOKS TO OL' ERIS--
AARON?
SURE. IT LOOKS LIKE YOU WOULDN'T KNOW A REAL WOMAN IF SHE WERE SITTING **RIGHT IN FRONT** OF YOU.
AND WHAT'S MORE, YOU DON'T SEE THE WORLD AND ITS PSYCHOSEXUAL POLITICS AS THEY ACTUALLY ARE. WHICH, **LIKE I SAID**, IS NOT YOUR FAULT.
YOU'VE BEEN SHOWN A VERSION OF REALITY THAT IS...INCOMPLETE. YOU SEE THE **PUPPETS**, BUT NOT THE STRINGS. FORTUNATELY FOR YOU, MY **LUCKY BOYS**, OL' ERIS--
SURE.
AARON?
--HAS JUST THE THING.
POP
BEHOLD. HERE IS AN OPPORTUNITY TO SEE THE WORLD AS IT **REALLY** IS. THINK OF THE WORLD YOU KNOW AS, OH, SAY A BLUE PILL. YOU CAN GO ON AS YOU ARE, WEAK AND MISERABLE OR...
YOU CAN TAKE THE **RED PILL** AND SEE JUST HOW FAR THE RABBIT HOLE GOES. TO QUOTE THE ANCIENT MASTER MORPHEUS.
AND *HO HO*, I DO KNOW THAT TAKING PILLS FROM A STRANGER IS GENERALLY FROWNED UPON IN A NON-RAVE SITUATION SO...
SAFE AS HORSES. OF COURSE, THAT'S IF YOU'RE **STRONG** ENOUGH, IF YOU'RE ALPHA ENOUGH TO FACE THE WORLD AS IT REALLY IS AND GET **EXACTLY** WHAT YOU WISH FOR.

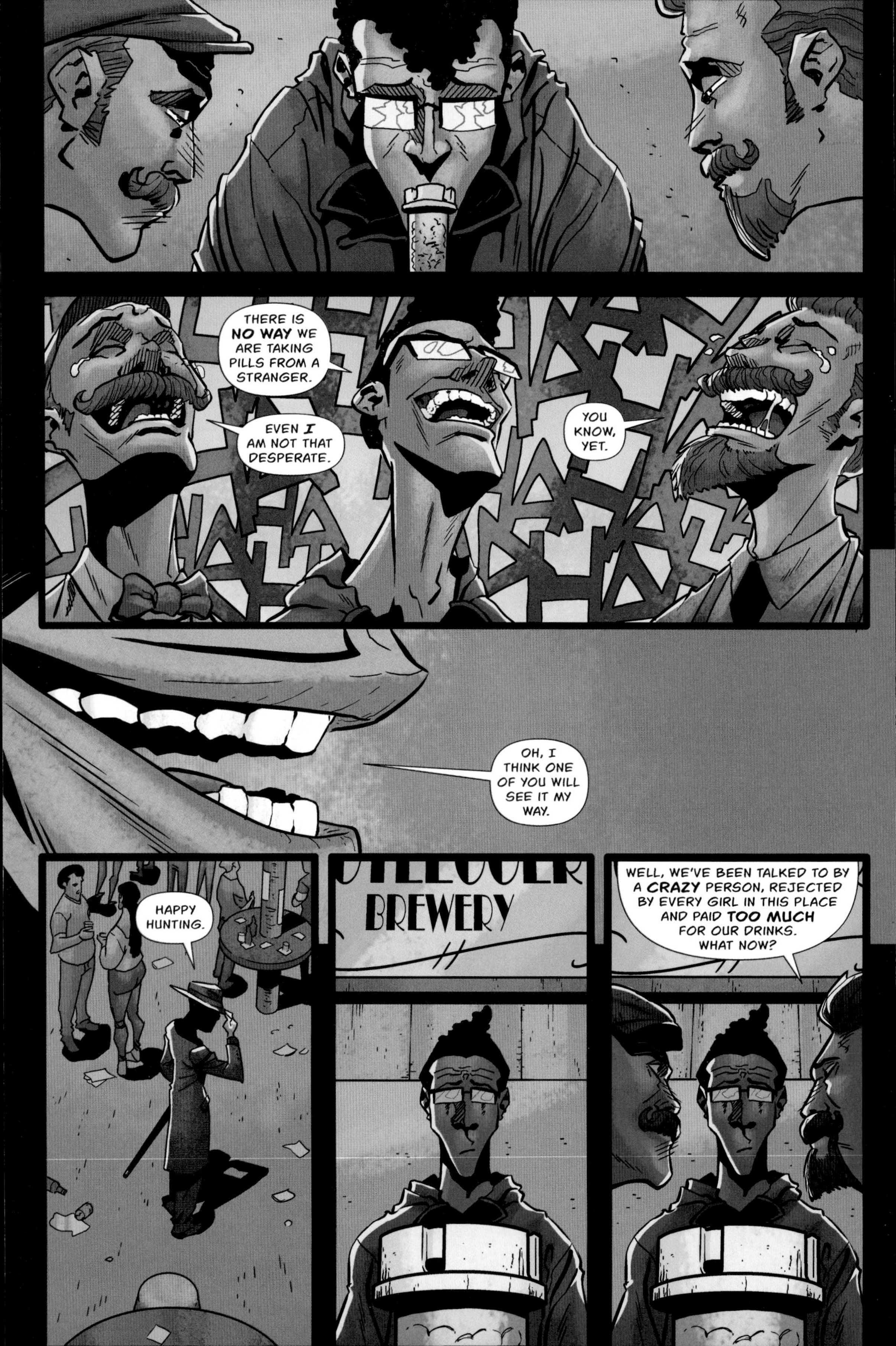
THERE IS NO WAY WE ARE TAKING PILLS FROM A STRANGER.
EVEN I AM NOT THAT DESPERATE.
YOU KNOW, YET.
OH, I THINK ONE OF YOU WILL SEE IT MY WAY.
HAPPY HUNTING.
BREWERY
WELL, WE'VE BEEN TALKED TO BY A CRAZY PERSON, REJECTED BY EVERY GIRL IN THIS PLACE AND PAID TOO MUCH FOR OUR DRINKS. WHAT NOW?

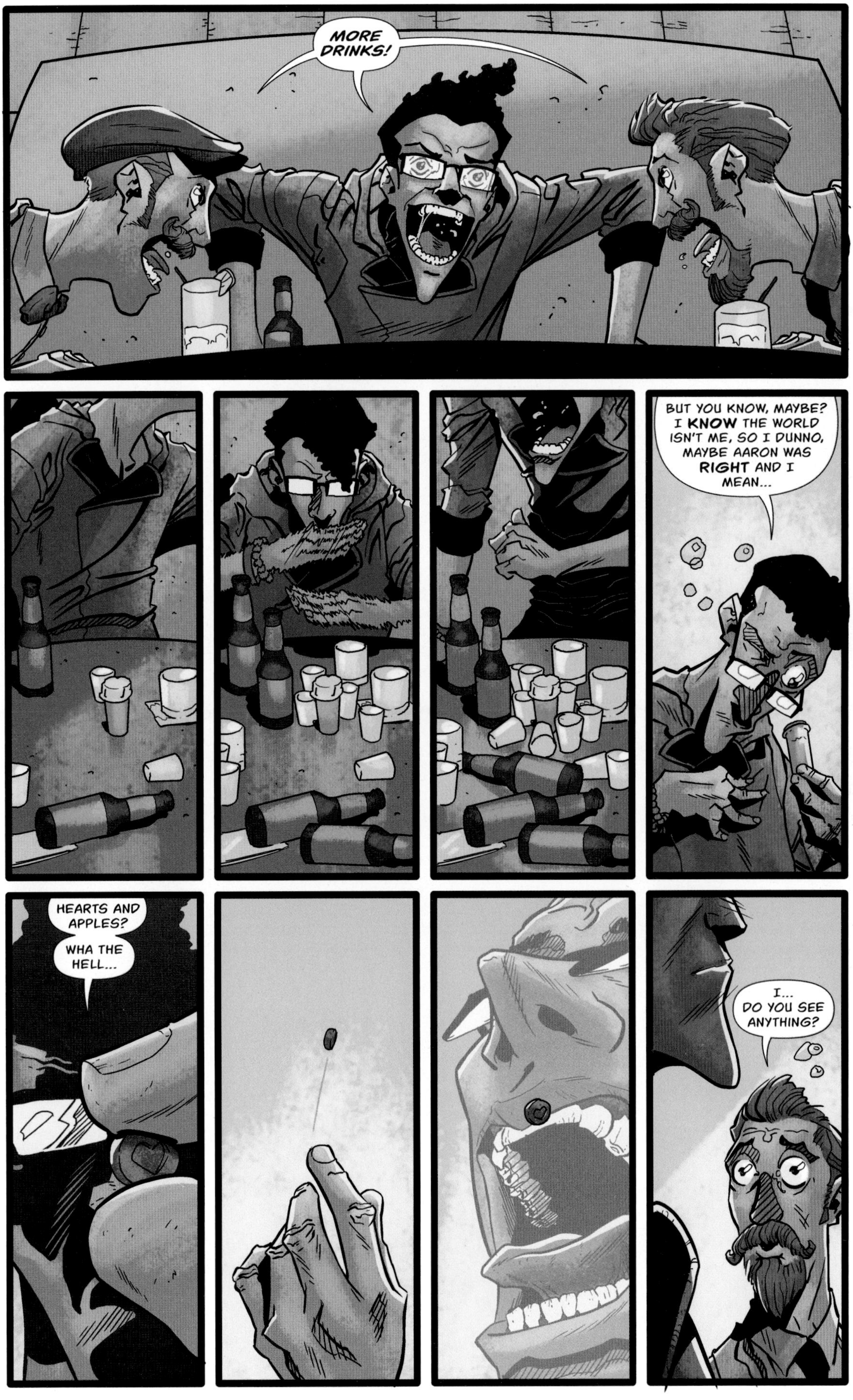

MORE DRINKS!
BUT YOU KNOW, MAYBE? I KNOW THE WORLD ISN'T ME, SO I DUNNO, MAYBE AARON WAS RIGHT AND I MEAN...
HEARTS AND APPLES?
WHA THE HELL...
I... DO YOU SEE ANYTHING?

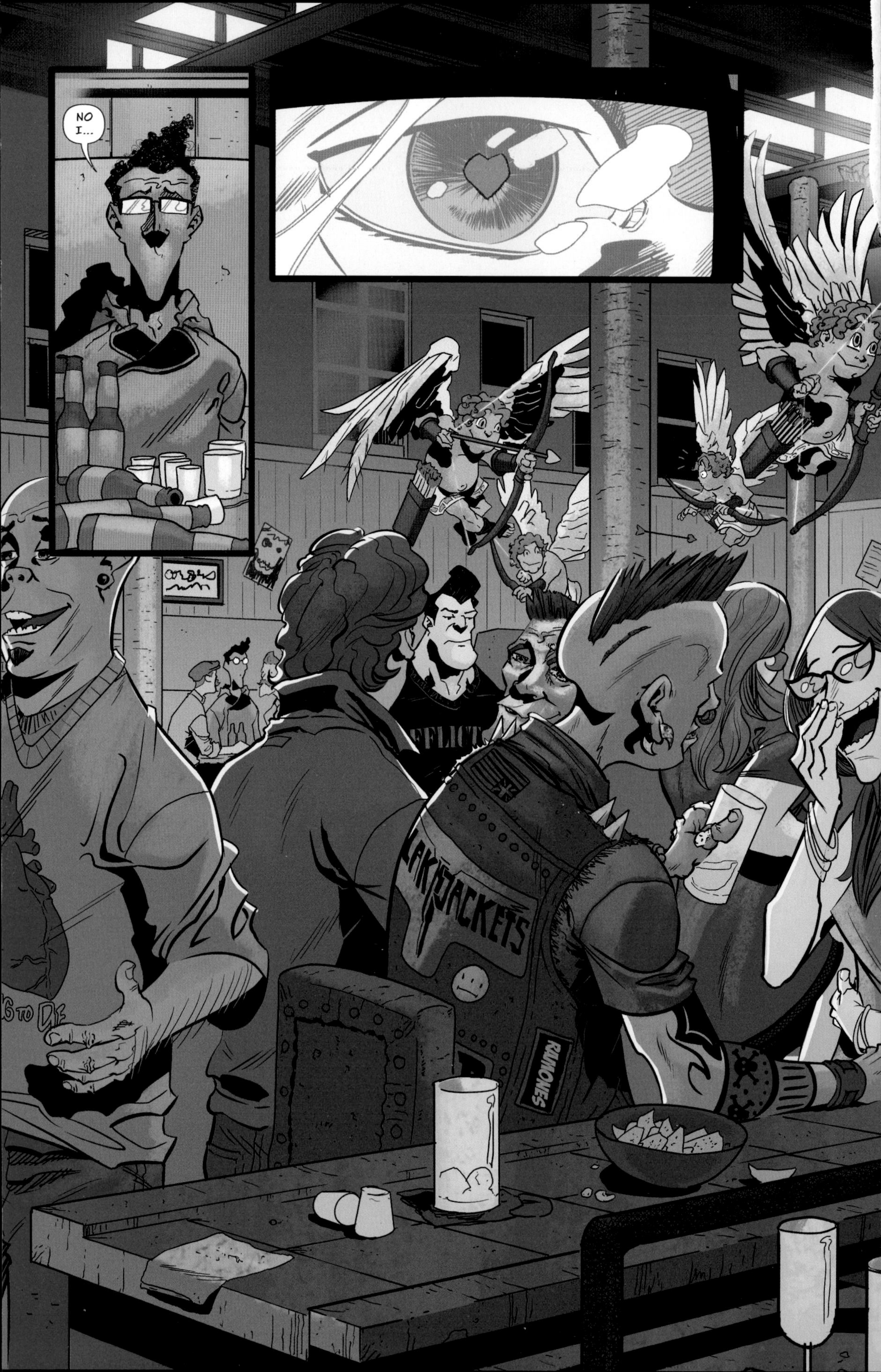
NO I...
RAMONES

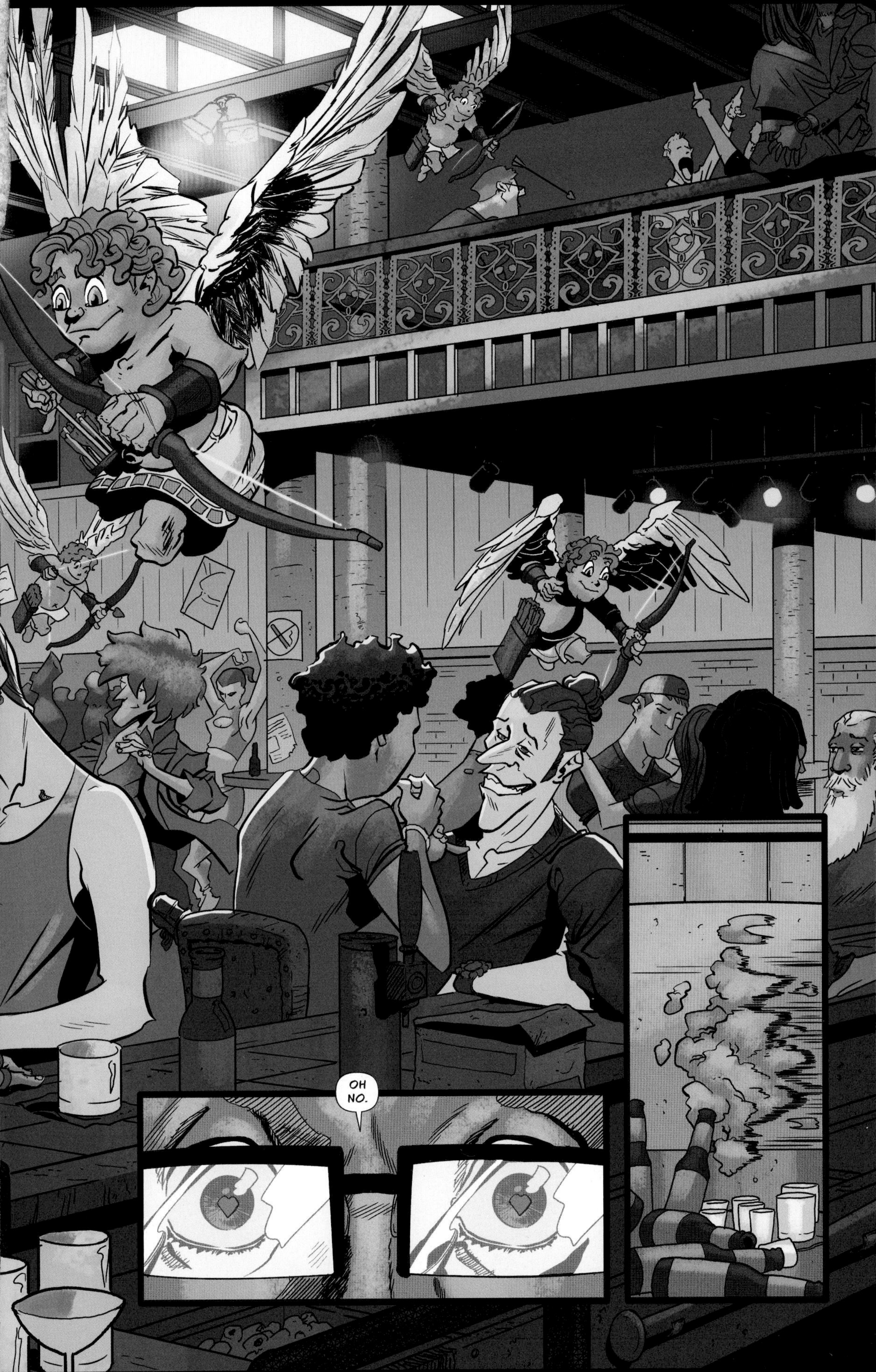
OH NO.

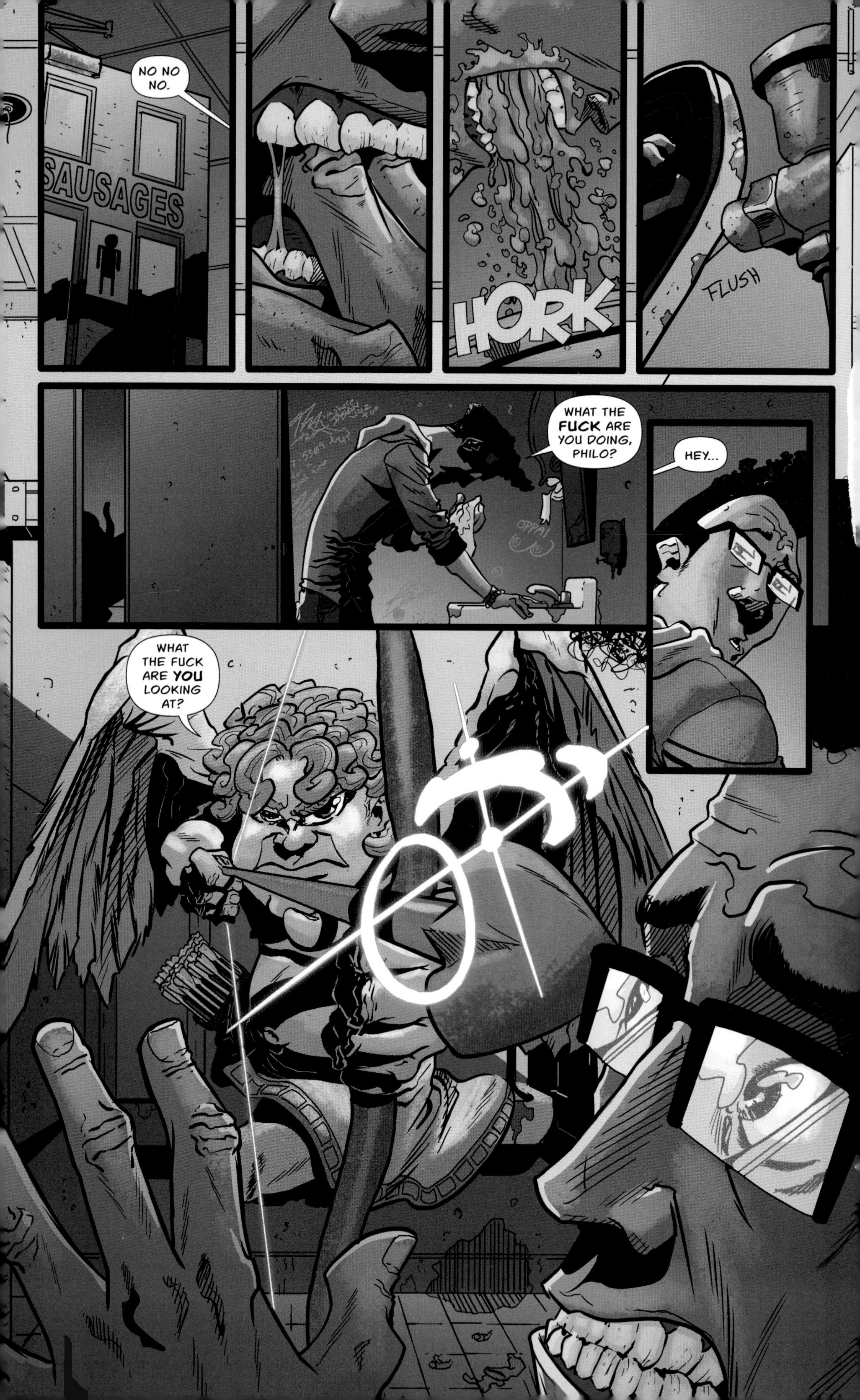
NO NO NO.
SAUSAGES
HORK
FLUSH
WHAT THE **FUCK** ARE YOU DOING, PHILO?
OPPAI
HEY...
WHAT THE FUCK ARE **YOU** LOOKING AT?

Two

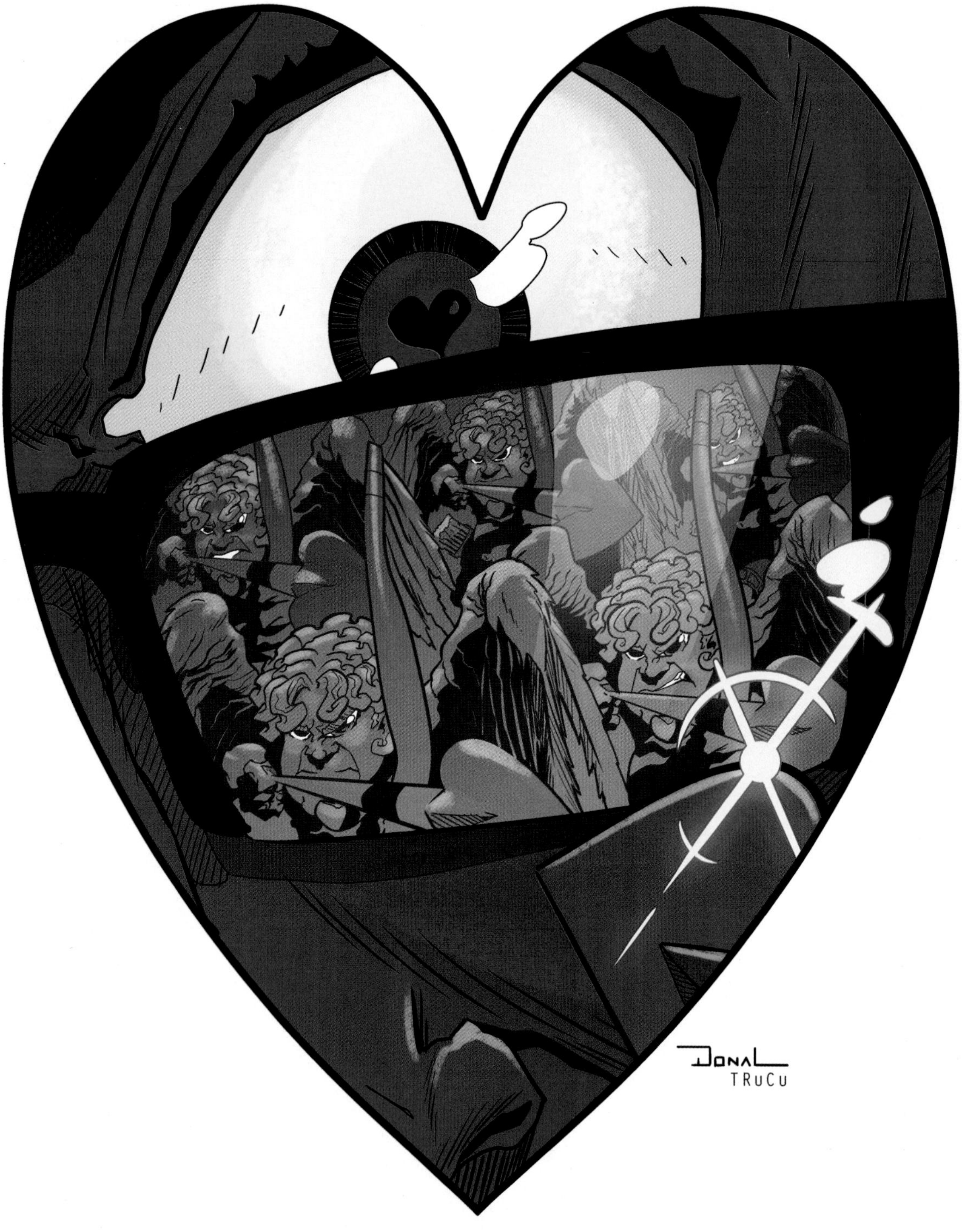
DONAL
TRUCU

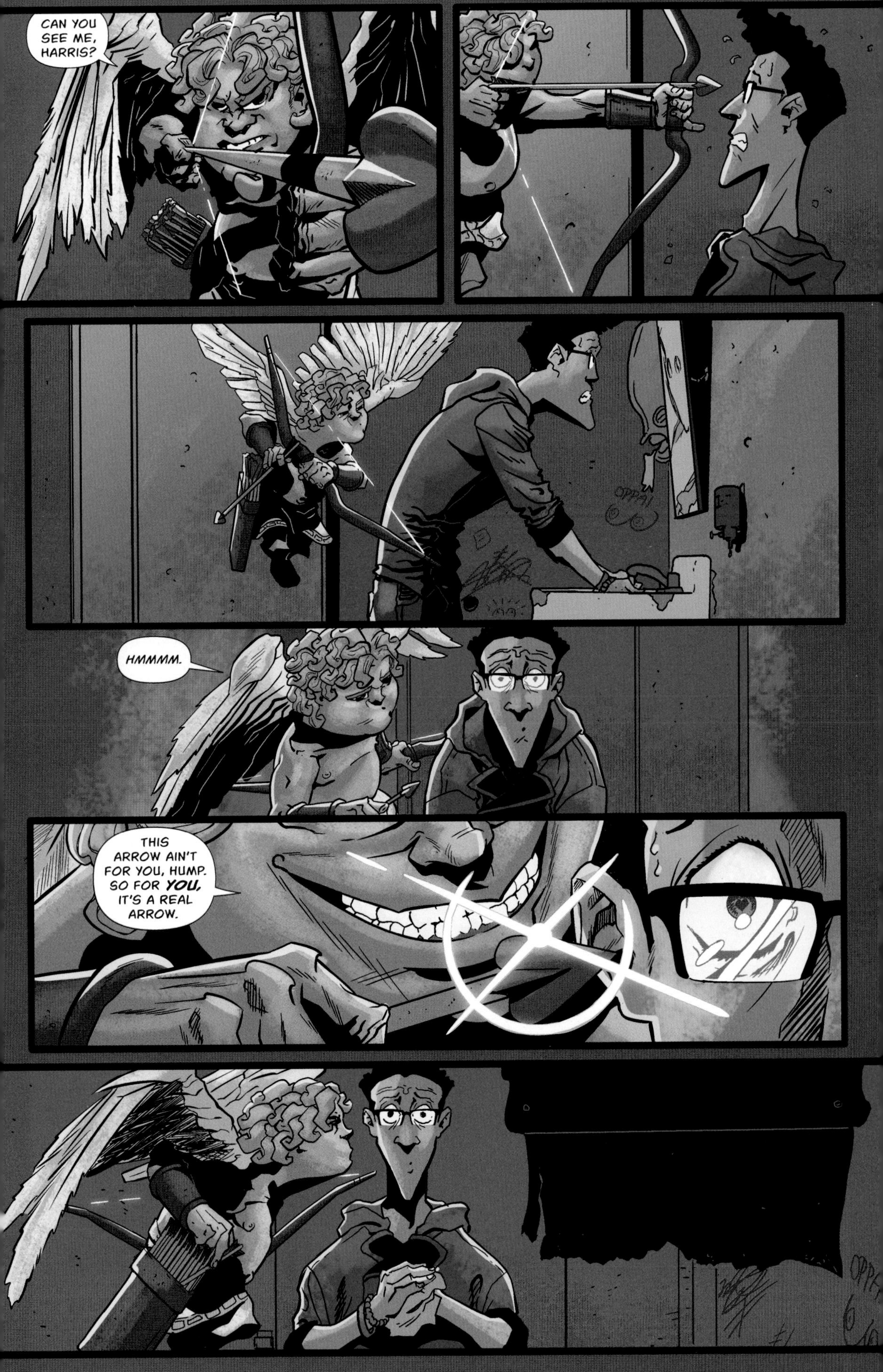
CAN YOU SEE ME, HARRIS?
HMMMM.
THIS ARROW AIN'T FOR YOU, HUMP. SO FOR *YOU,* IT'S A REAL ARROW.

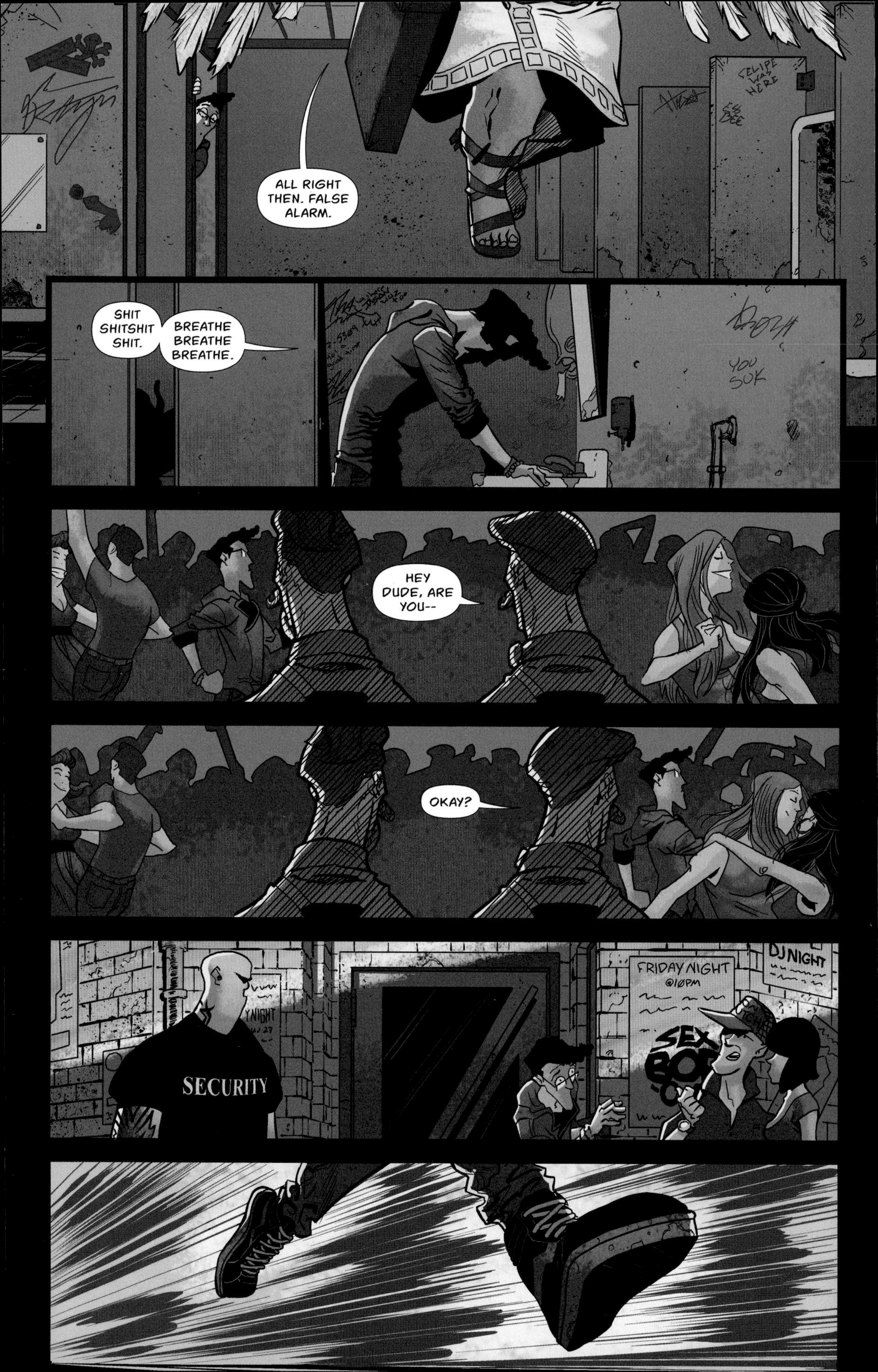
ALL RIGHT THEN. FALSE ALARM.
SHIT SHITSHIT SHIT.
BREATHE BREATHE BREATHE.
YOU SUK
HEY DUDE, ARE YOU--
OKAY?
SECURITY
FRIDAY NIGHT @1ØPM
DJ NIGHT

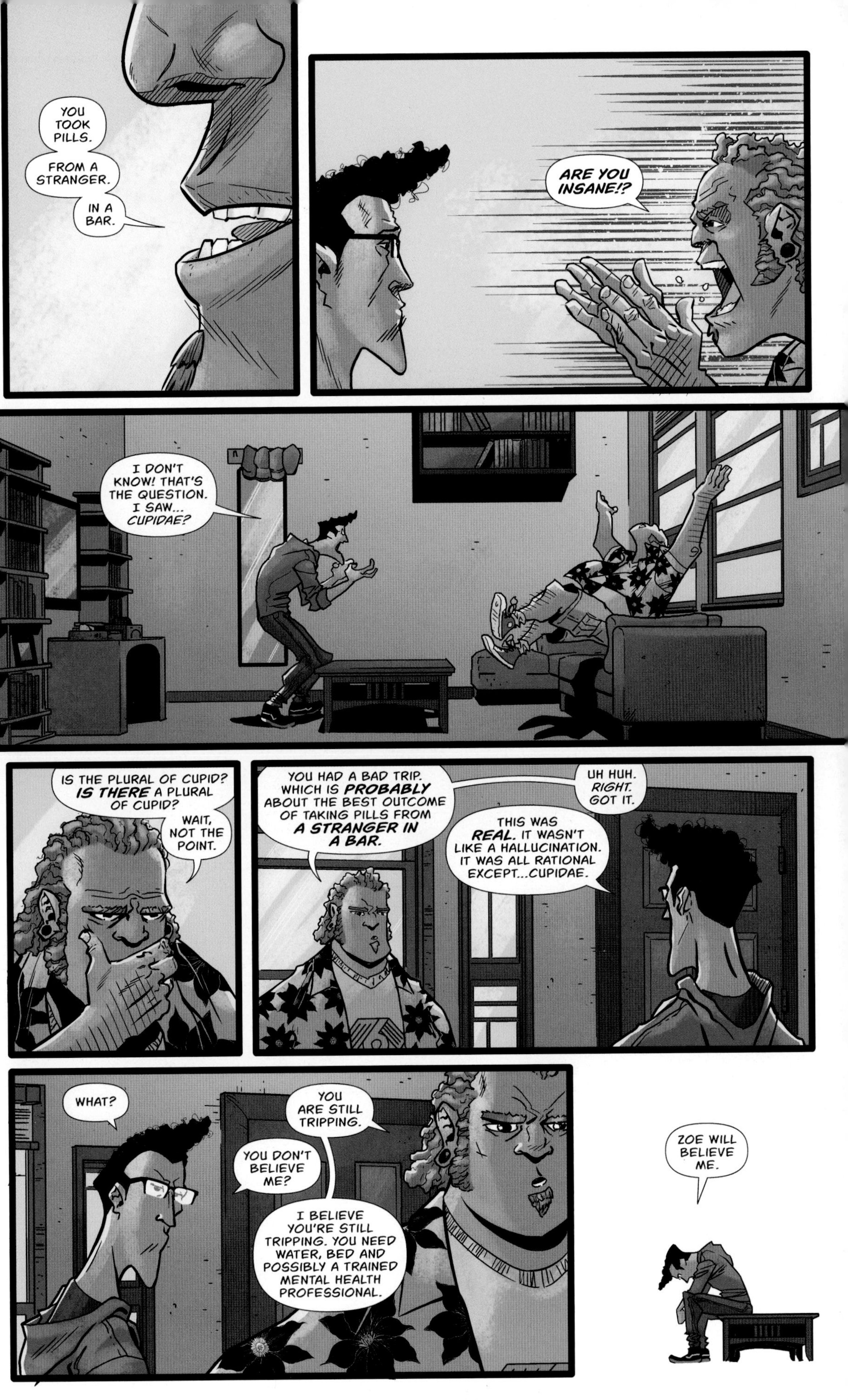
YOU TOOK PILLS.
FROM A STRANGER.
IN A BAR.
ARE YOU INSANE!?
I DON'T KNOW! THAT'S THE QUESTION. I SAW... CUPIDAE?
IS THE PLURAL OF CUPID? IS THERE A PLURAL OF CUPID?
WAIT, NOT THE POINT.
YOU HAD A BAD TRIP. WHICH IS PROBABLY ABOUT THE BEST OUTCOME OF TAKING PILLS FROM A STRANGER IN A BAR.
UH HUH. RIGHT. GOT IT.
THIS WAS REAL. IT WASN'T LIKE A HALLUCINATION. IT WAS ALL RATIONAL EXCEPT...CUPIDAE.
WHAT?
YOU ARE STILL TRIPPING.
YOU DON'T BELIEVE ME?
I BELIEVE YOU'RE STILL TRIPPING. YOU NEED WATER, BED AND POSSIBLY A TRAINED MENTAL HEALTH PROFESSIONAL.
ZOE WILL BELIEVE ME.

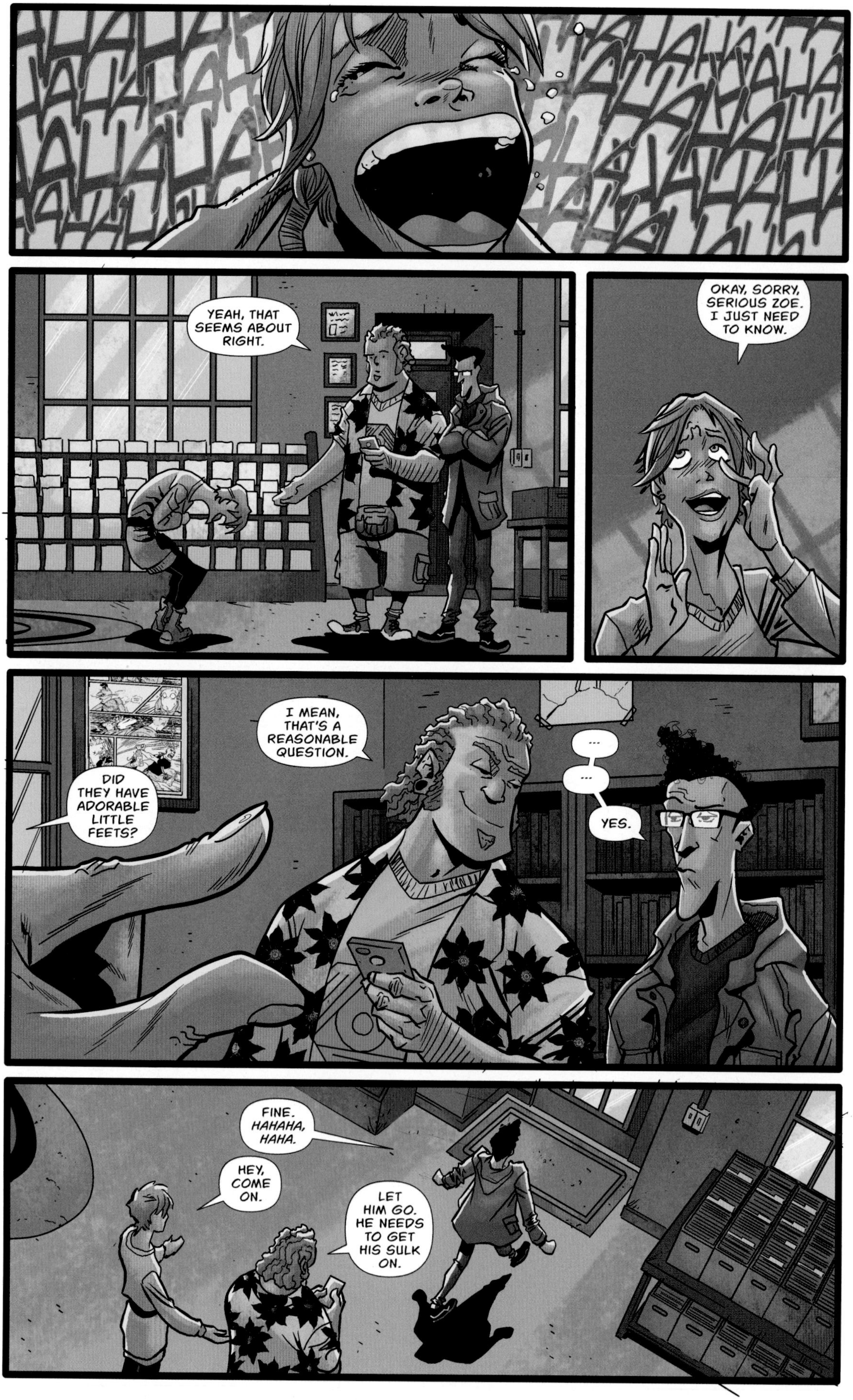
HAHAHAHAHA
YEAH, THAT SEEMS ABOUT RIGHT.
OKAY, SORRY, SERIOUS ZOE. I JUST NEED TO KNOW.
DID THEY HAVE ADORABLE LITTLE FEETS?
I MEAN, THAT'S A REASONABLE QUESTION.
...
...
YES.
FINE. HAHAHA, HAHA.
HEY, COME ON.
LET HIM GO. HE NEEDS TO GET HIS SULK ON.

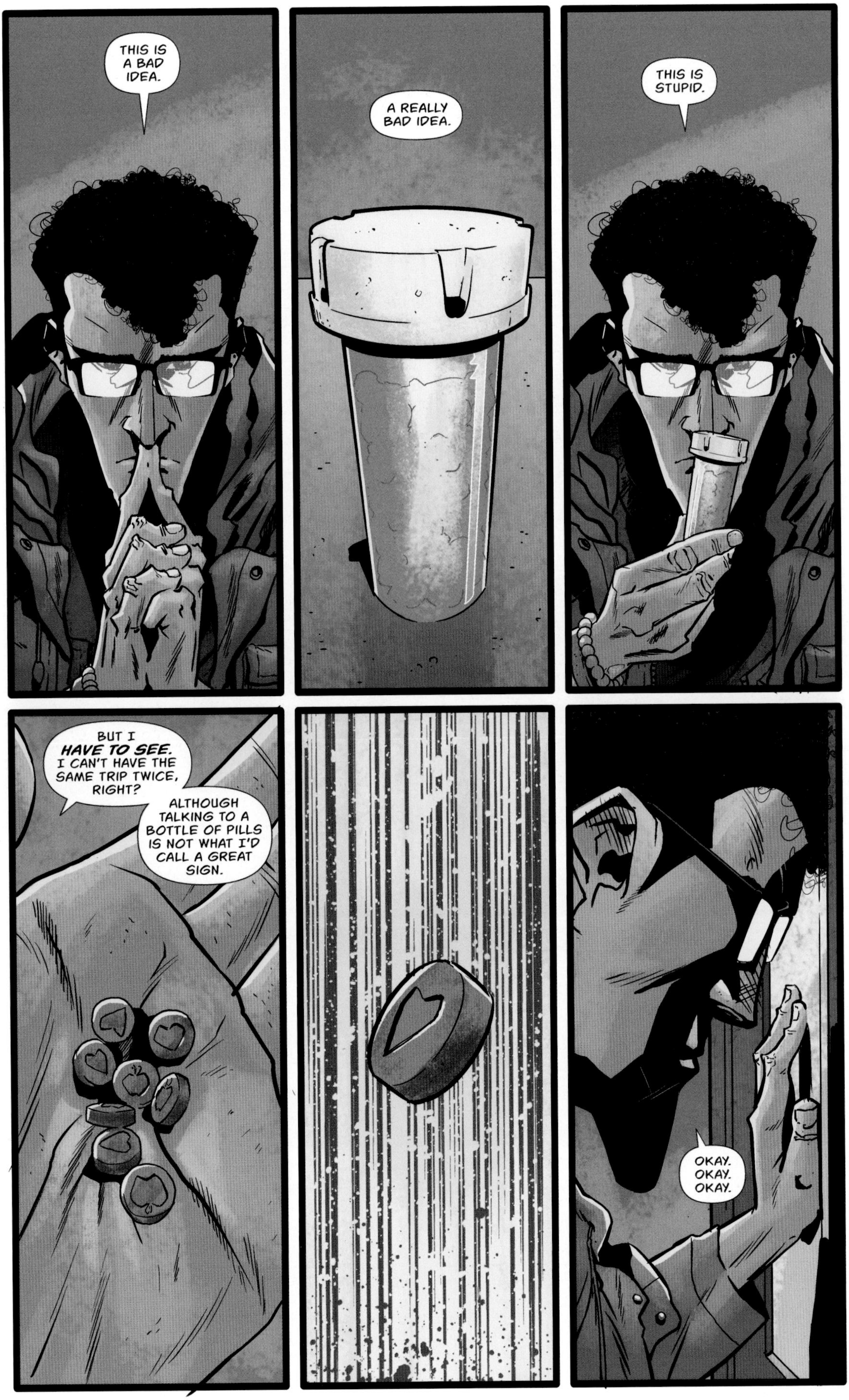
THIS IS A BAD IDEA.
A REALLY BAD IDEA.
THIS IS STUPID.
BUT I HAVE TO SEE. I CAN'T HAVE THE SAME TRIP TWICE, RIGHT?
ALTHOUGH TALKING TO A BOTTLE OF PILLS IS NOT WHAT I'D CALL A GREAT SIGN.
OKAY. OKAY. OKAY.

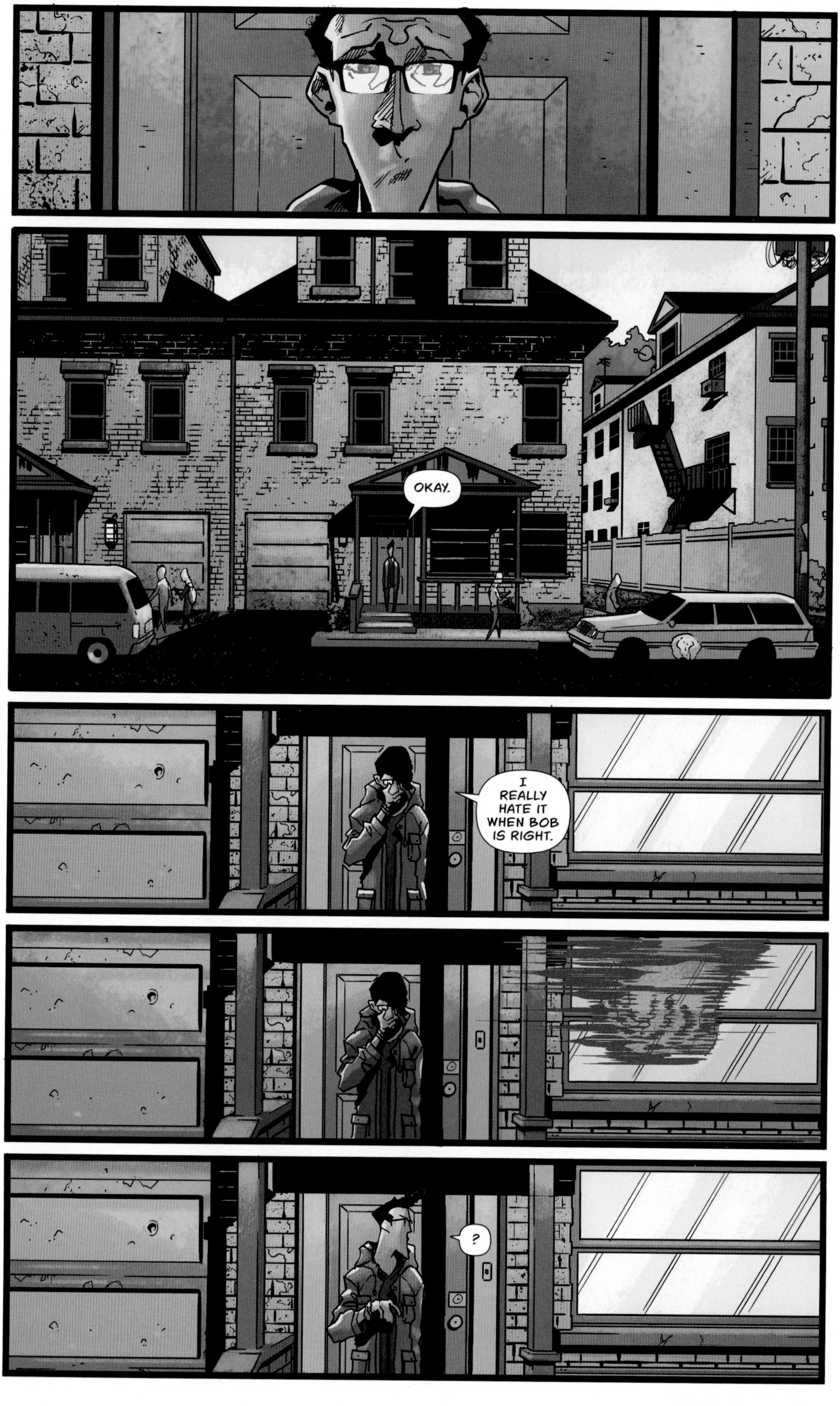
OKAY.
I REALLY HATE IT WHEN BOB IS RIGHT.
?

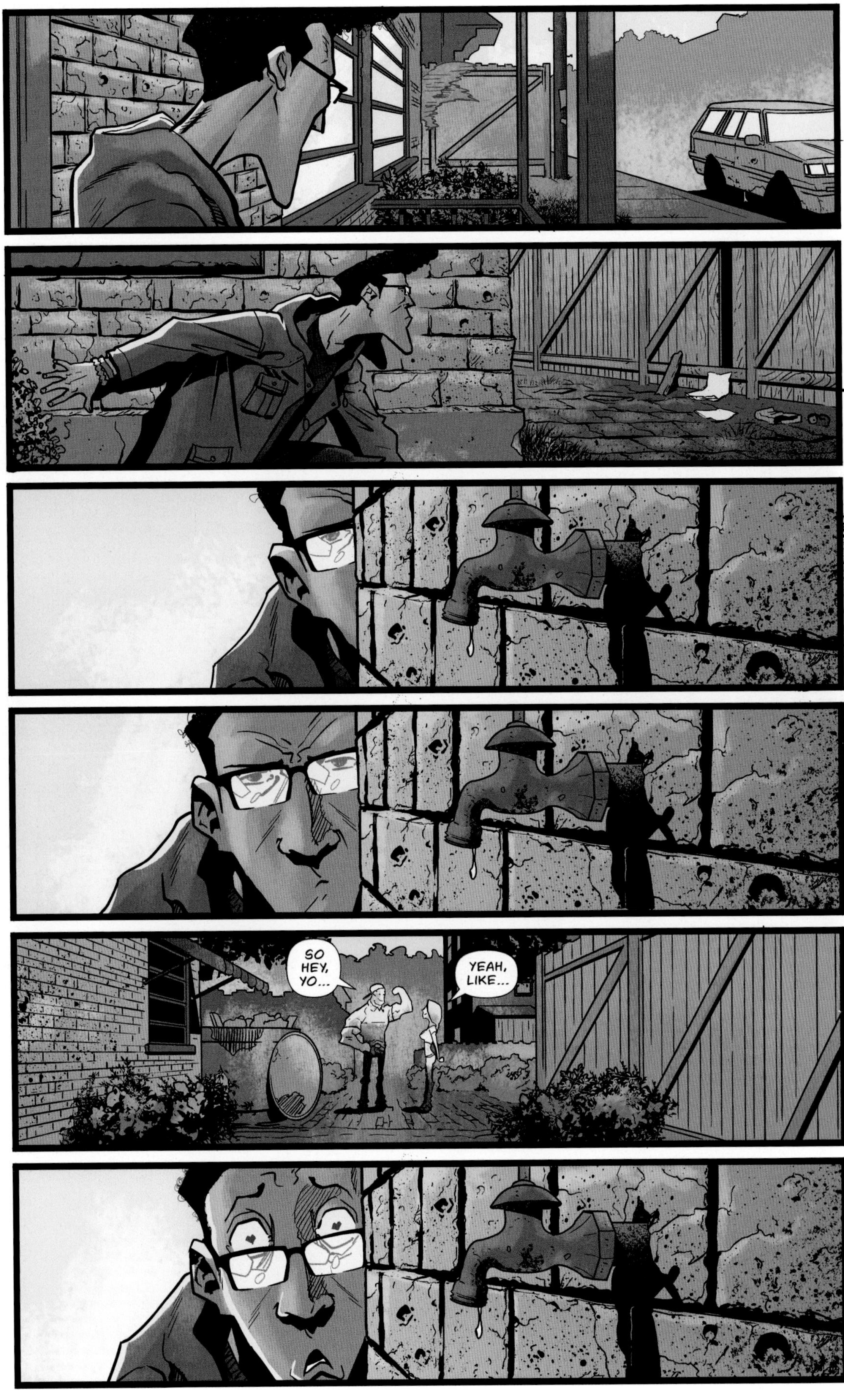
SO HEY, YO...
YEAH, LIKE...

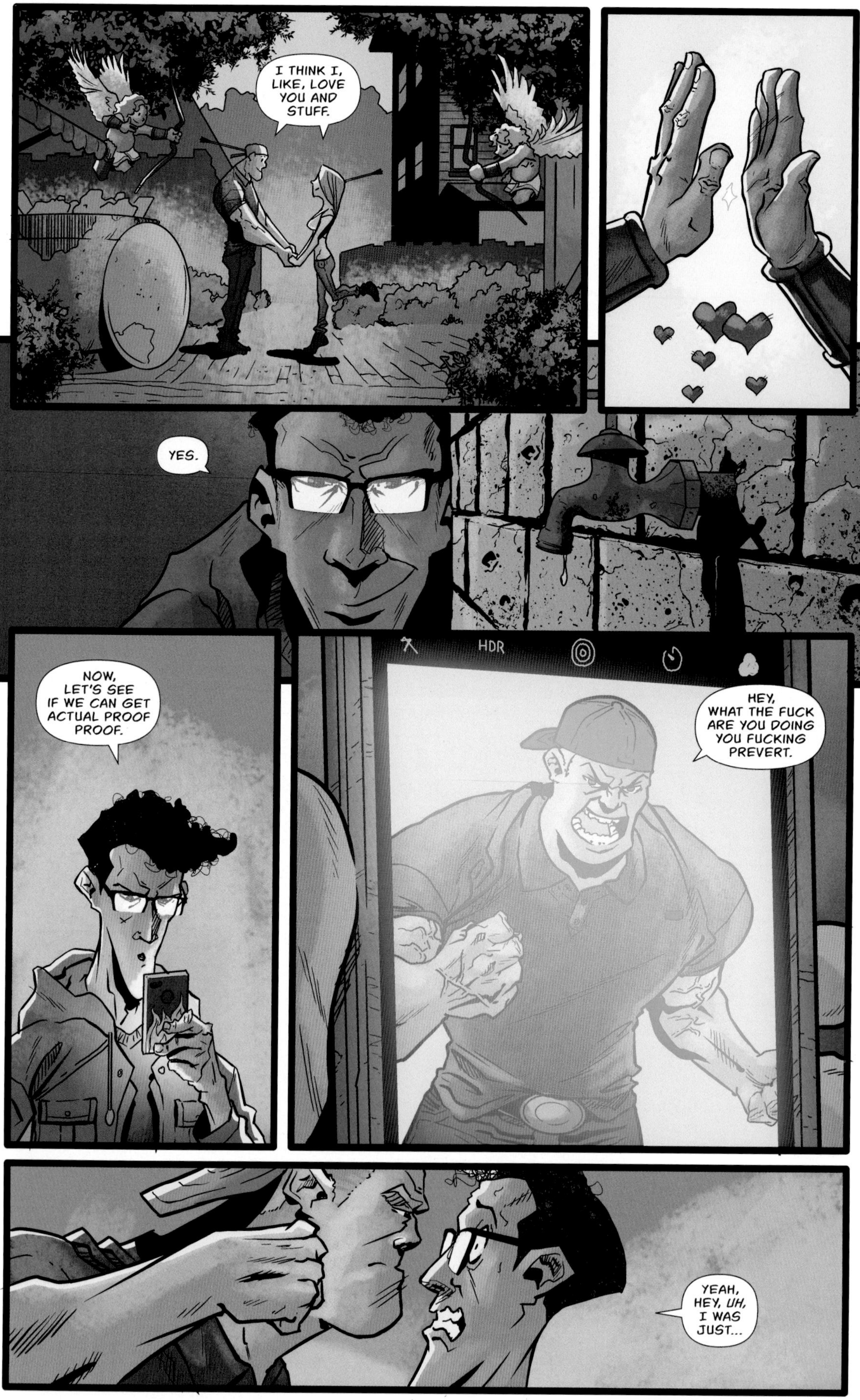
I THINK I, LIKE, LOVE YOU AND STUFF.
YES.
NOW, LET'S SEE IF WE CAN GET ACTUAL PROOF PROOF.
HDR
HEY, WHAT THE FUCK ARE YOU DOING YOU FUCKING PREVERT.
YEAH, HEY, *UH*, I WAS JUST...

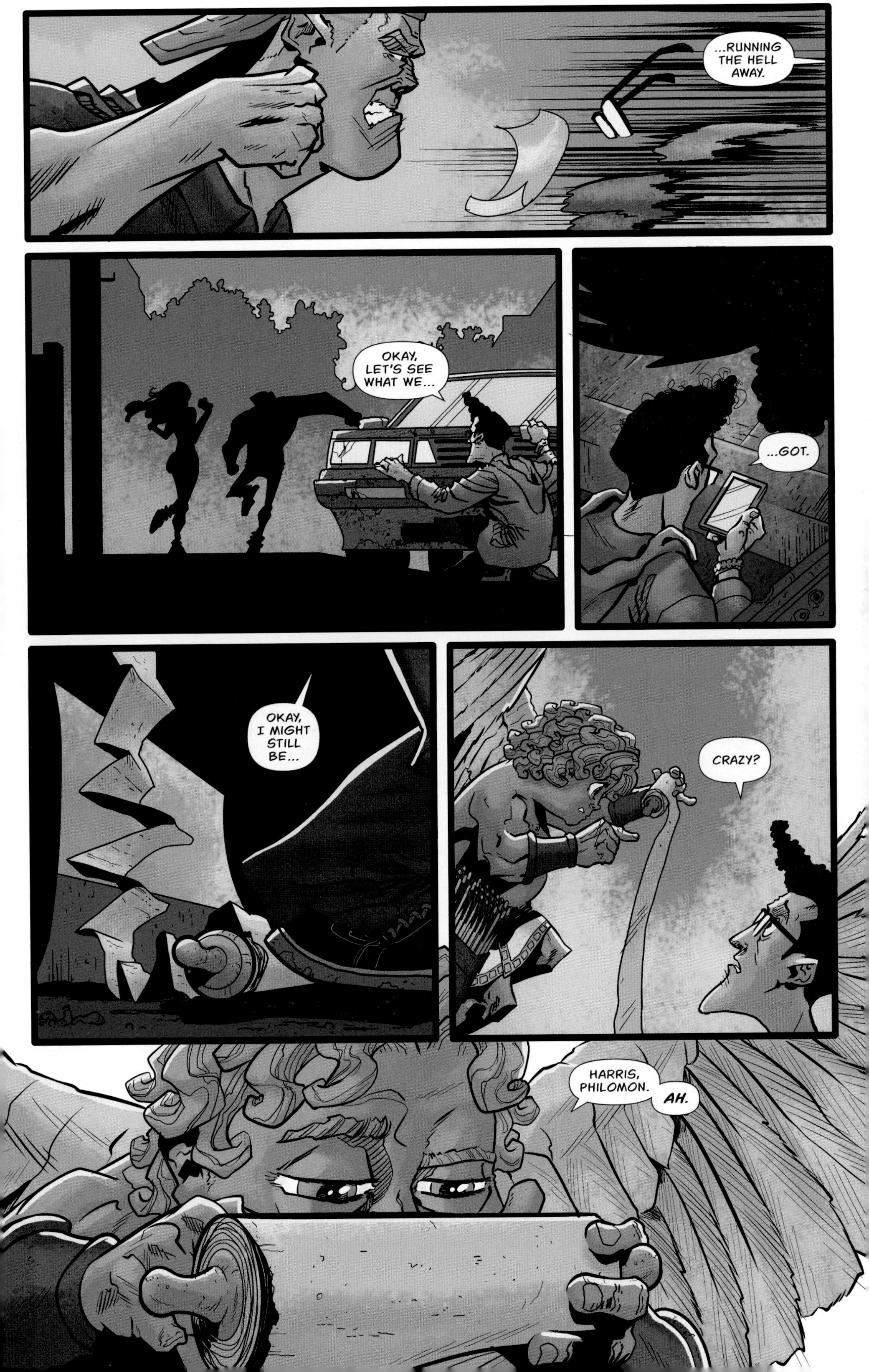
...RUNNING THE HELL AWAY.
OKAY, LET'S SEE WHAT WE...
...GOT.
OKAY, I MIGHT STILL BE...
CRAZY?
HARRIS, PHILOMON.
AH.

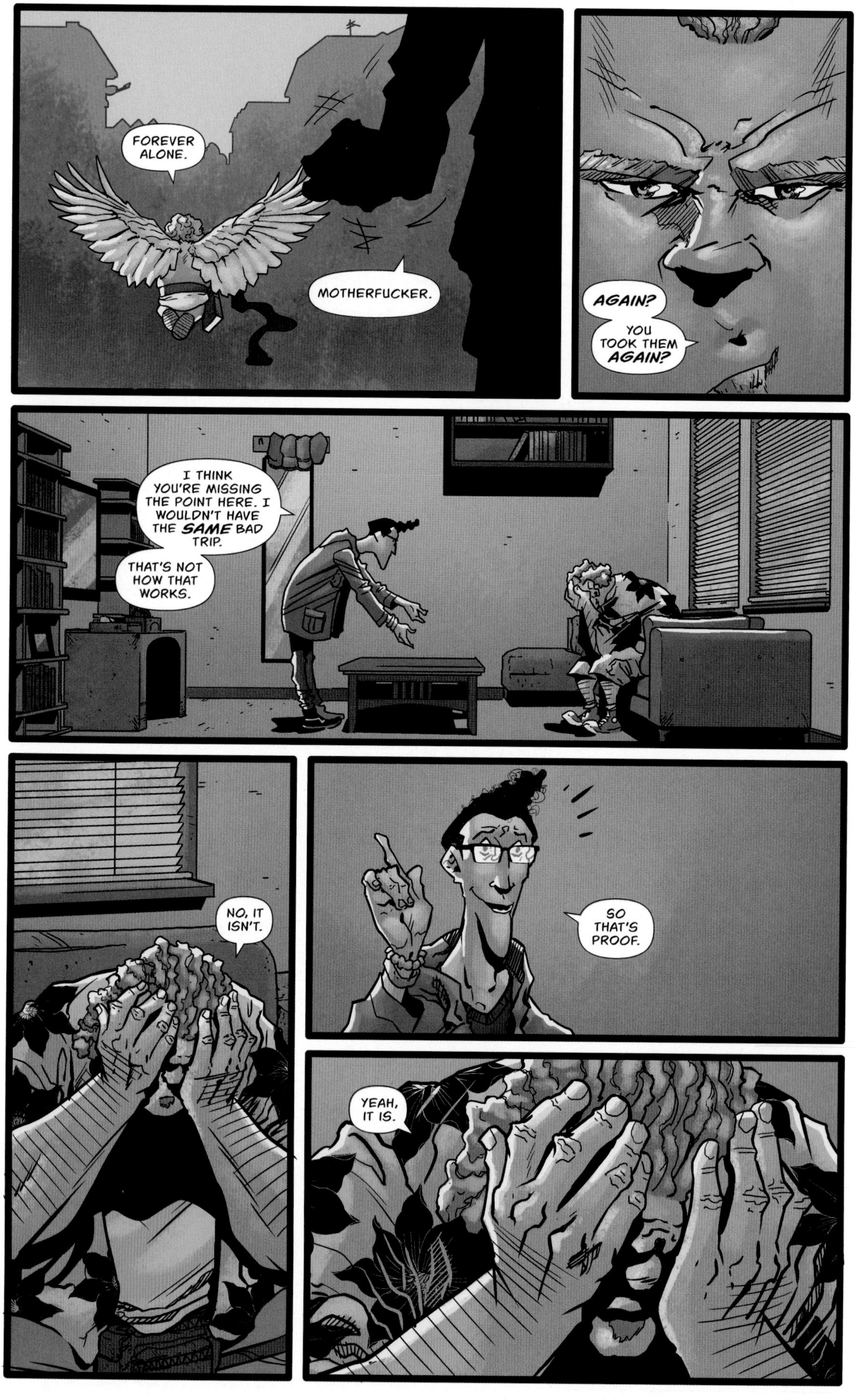
FOREVER ALONE.
MOTHERFUCKER.
AGAIN?
YOU TOOK THEM AGAIN?
I THINK YOU'RE MISSING THE POINT HERE. I WOULDN'T HAVE THE SAME BAD TRIP.
THAT'S NOT HOW THAT WORKS.
NO, IT ISN'T.
SO THAT'S PROOF.
YEAH, IT IS.

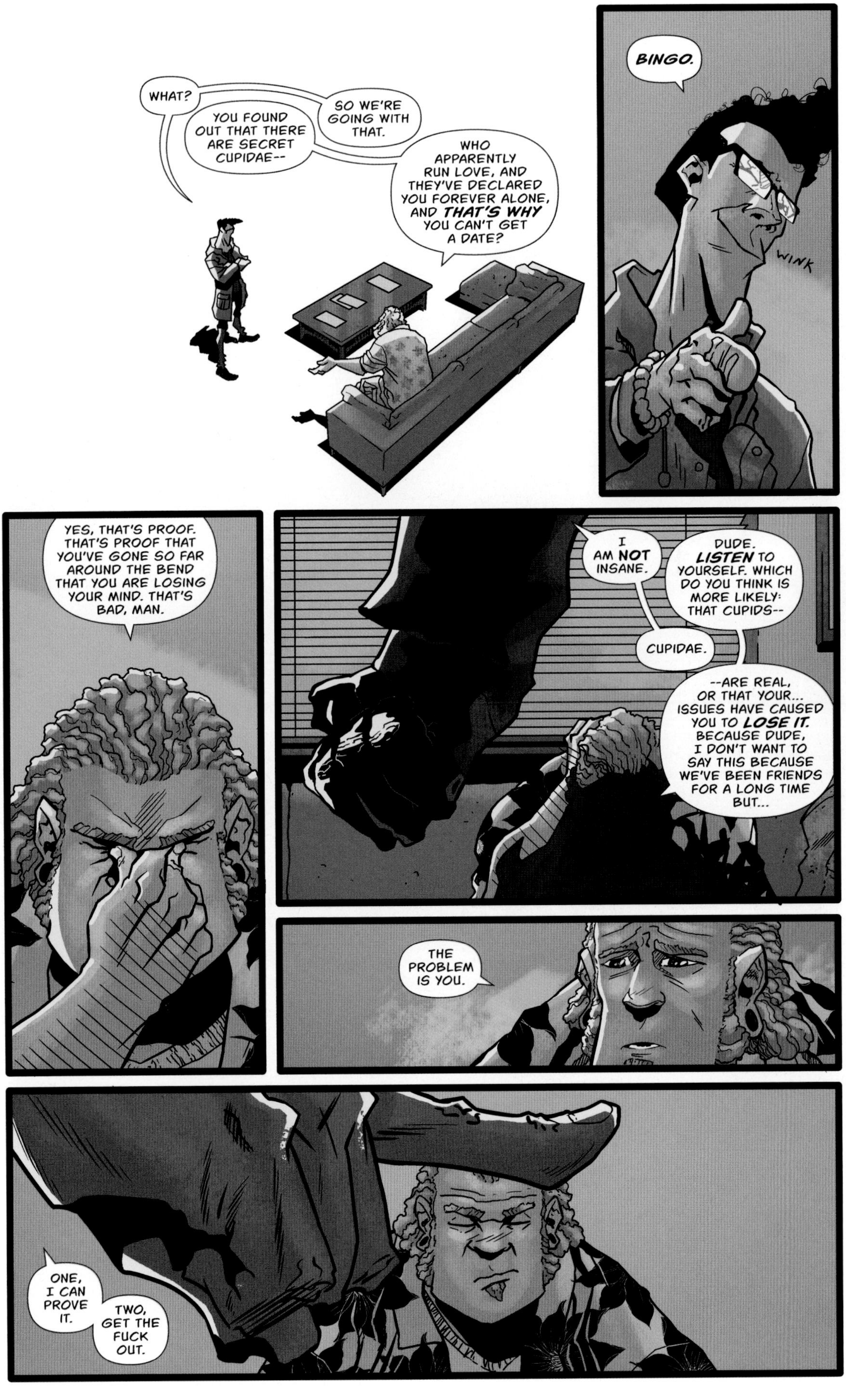
WHAT?
SO WE'RE GOING WITH THAT.
YOU FOUND OUT THAT THERE ARE SECRET CUPIDAE--
WHO APPARENTLY RUN LOVE, AND THEY'VE DECLARED YOU FOREVER ALONE, AND **THAT'S WHY** YOU CAN'T GET A DATE?
BINGO.
WINK
YES, THAT'S PROOF. THAT'S PROOF THAT YOU'VE GONE SO FAR AROUND THE BEND THAT YOU ARE LOSING YOUR MIND. THAT'S BAD, MAN.
I AM **NOT** INSANE.
DUDE. **LISTEN** TO YOURSELF. WHICH DO YOU THINK IS MORE LIKELY: THAT CUPIDS--
CUPIDAE.
--ARE REAL, OR THAT YOUR... ISSUES HAVE CAUSED YOU TO **LOSE IT.** BECAUSE DUDE, I DON'T WANT TO SAY THIS BECAUSE WE'VE BEEN FRIENDS FOR A LONG TIME BUT...
THE PROBLEM IS YOU.
ONE, I CAN PROVE IT.
TWO, GET THE FUCK OUT.

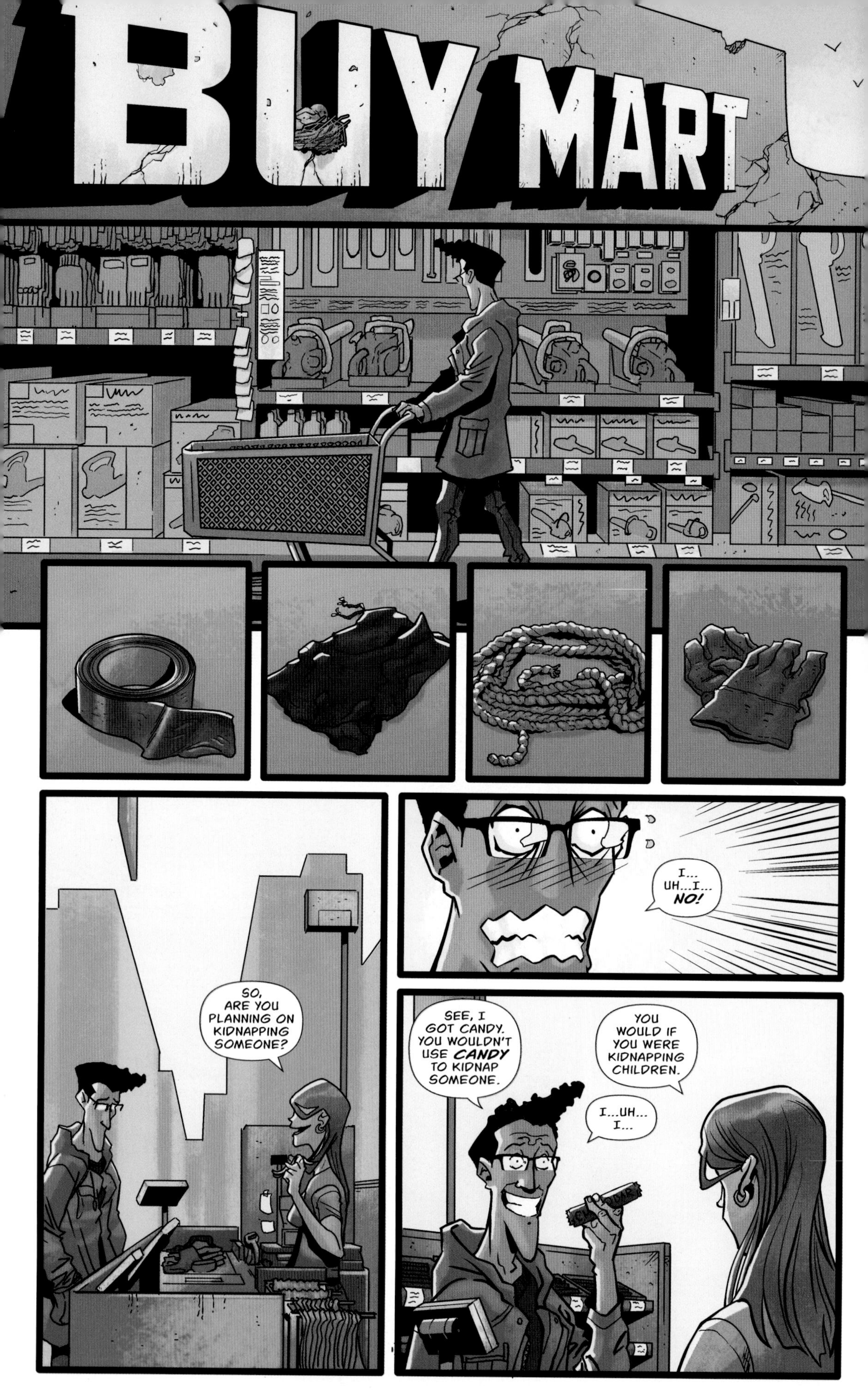
BUY MART
SO, ARE YOU PLANNING ON KIDNAPPING SOMEONE?
I... UH...I... NO!
SEE, I GOT CANDY. YOU WOULDN'T USE CANDY TO KIDNAP SOMEONE.
YOU WOULD IF YOU WERE KIDNAPPING CHILDREN.
I...UH... I...

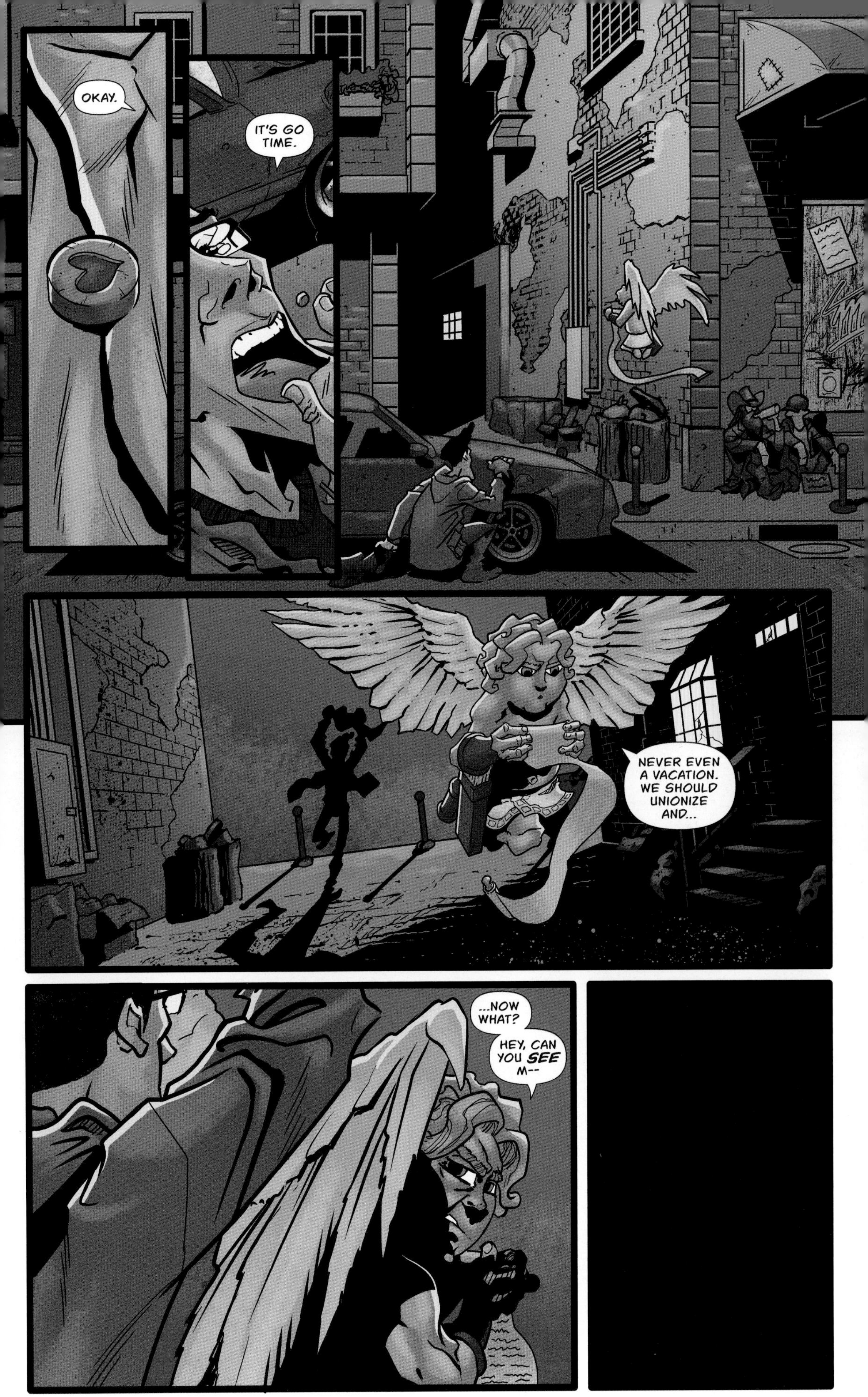
OKAY.
IT'S GO TIME.
NEVER EVEN A VACATION. WE SHOULD UNIONIZE AND...
...NOW WHAT?
HEY, CAN YOU SEE M--

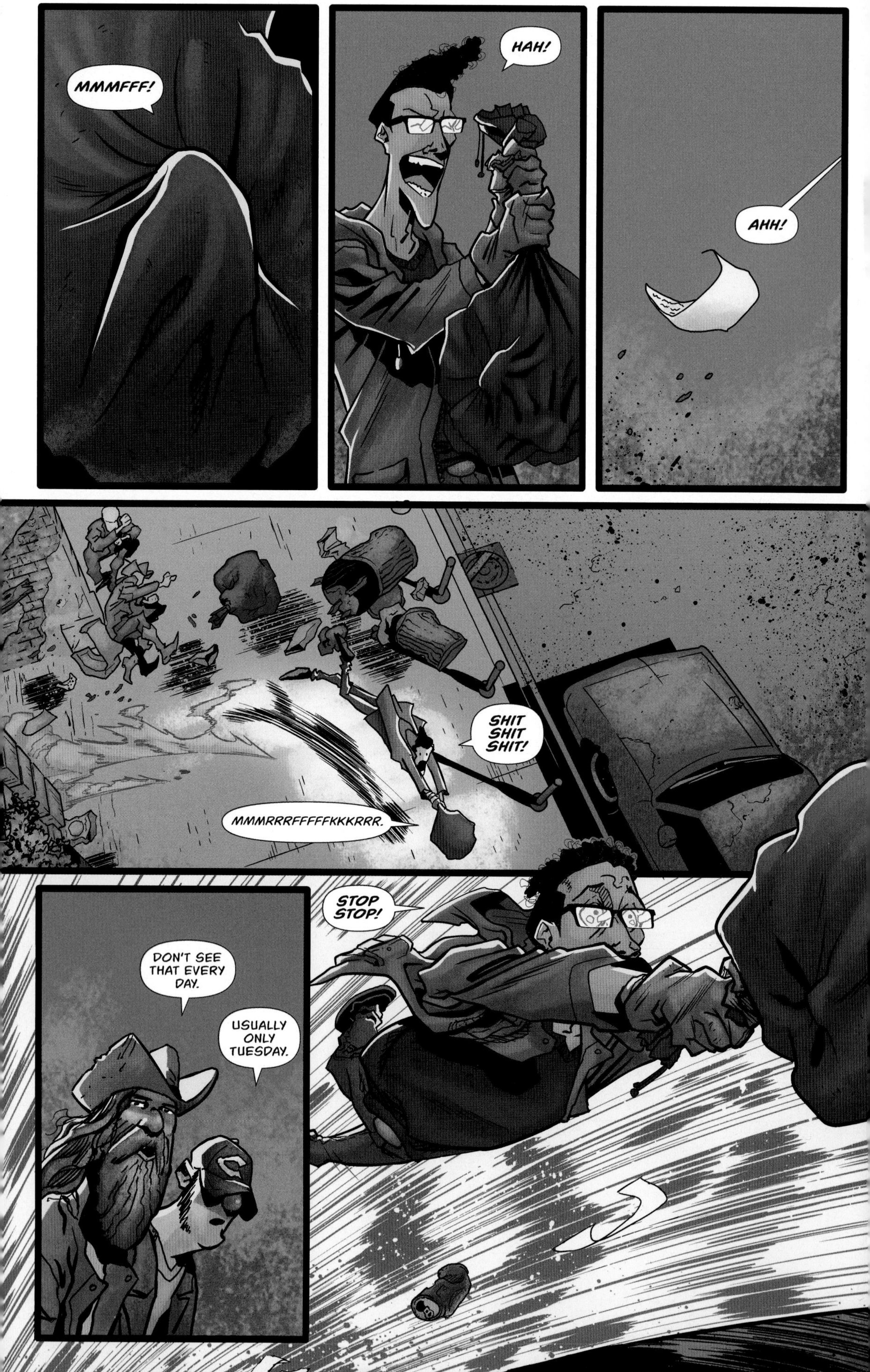
MMMFFF!
HAH!
AHH!
SHIT SHIT SHIT!
MMMRRRFFFFFKKKRRR.
STOP STOP!
DON'T SEE THAT EVERY DAY.
USUALLY ONLY TUESDAY.

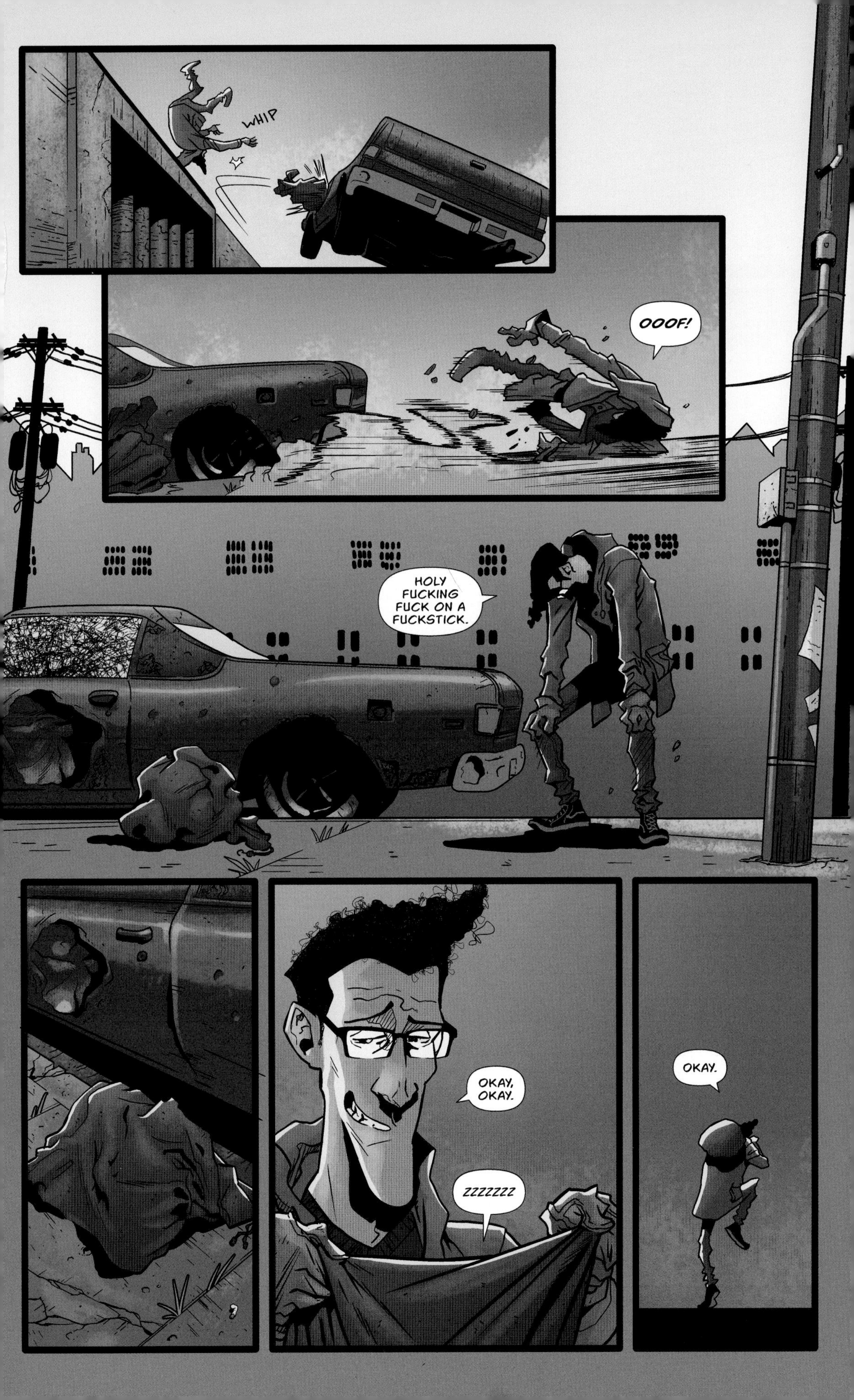
WHIP
OOOF!
HOLY FUCKING FUCK ON A FUCKSTICK.
OKAY, OKAY.
ZZZZZZZ
OKAY.

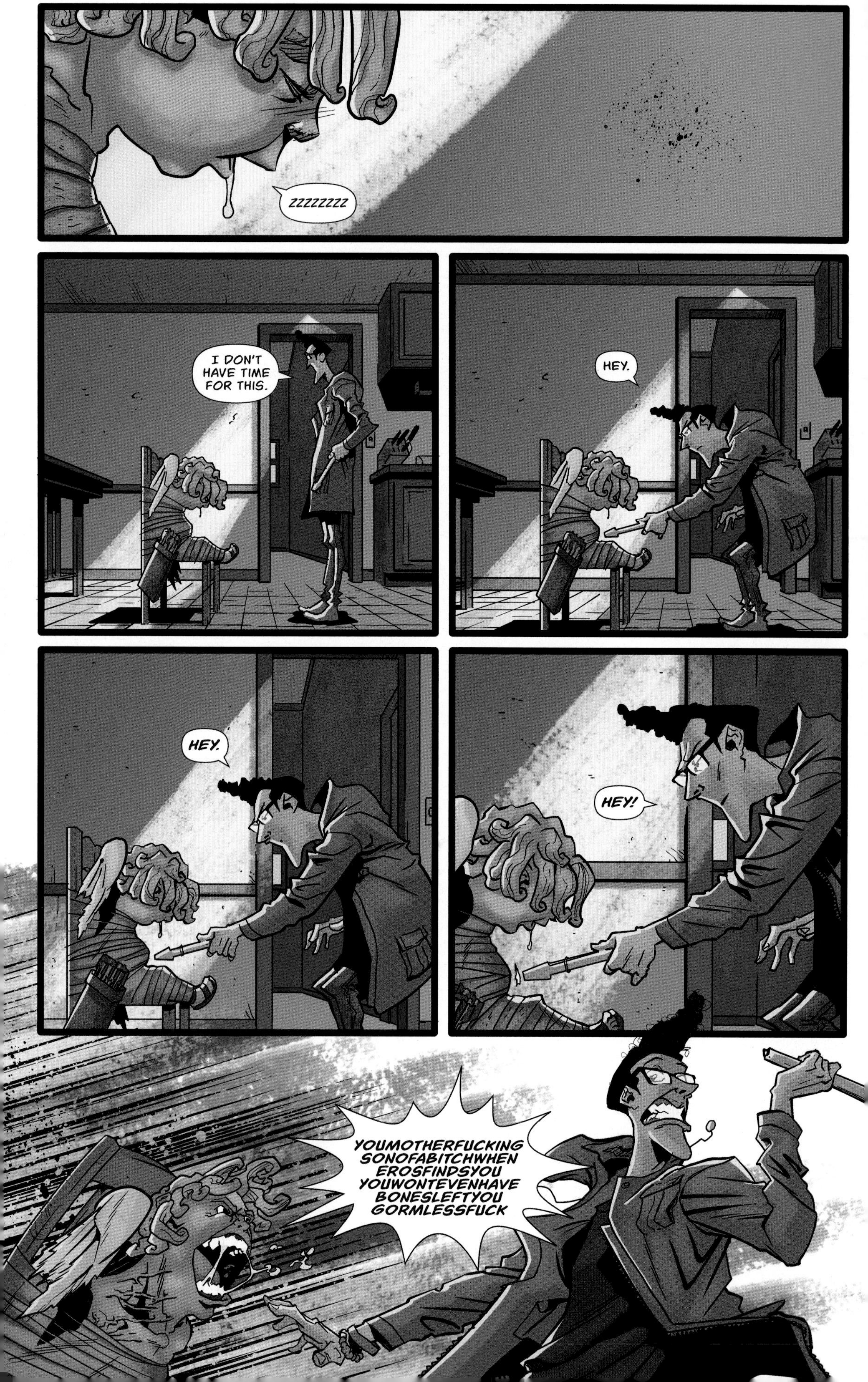
ZZZZZZZZ
I DON'T HAVE TIME FOR THIS.
HEY.
HEY.
HEY!
YOUMOTHERFUCKING SONOFABITCHWHEN EROSFINDSYOU YOUWONTEVENHAVE BONESLEFTYOU GORMLESSFUCK

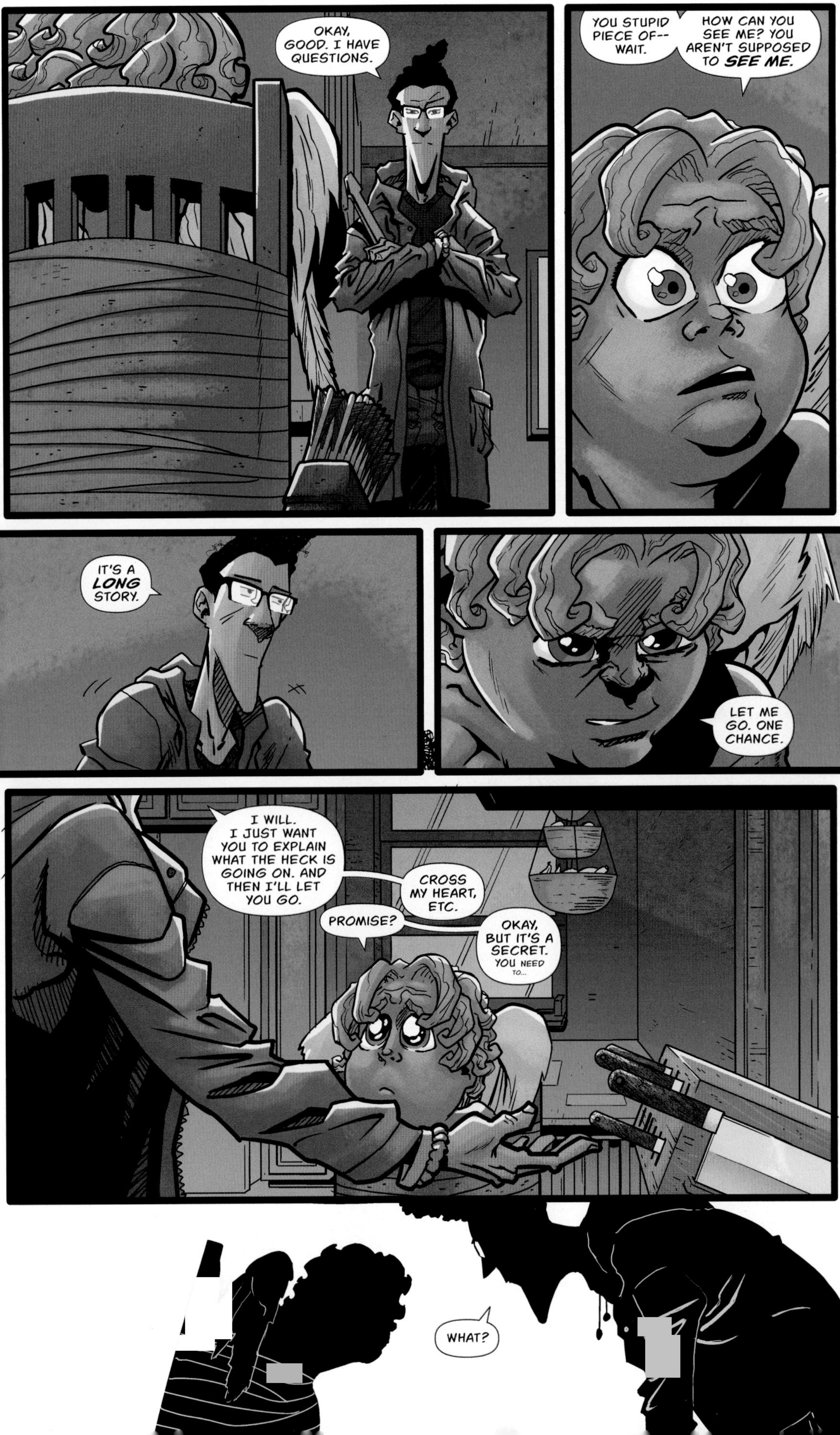
OKAY, GOOD. I HAVE QUESTIONS.
YOU STUPID PIECE OF-- WAIT.
HOW CAN YOU SEE ME? YOU AREN'T SUPPOSED TO **SEE ME.**
IT'S A **LONG** STORY.
LET ME GO. ONE CHANCE.
I WILL. I JUST WANT YOU TO EXPLAIN WHAT THE HECK IS GOING ON. AND THEN I'LL LET YOU GO.
PROMISE?
CROSS MY HEART, ETC.
OKAY, BUT IT'S A SECRET. YOU NEED TO...
WHAT?

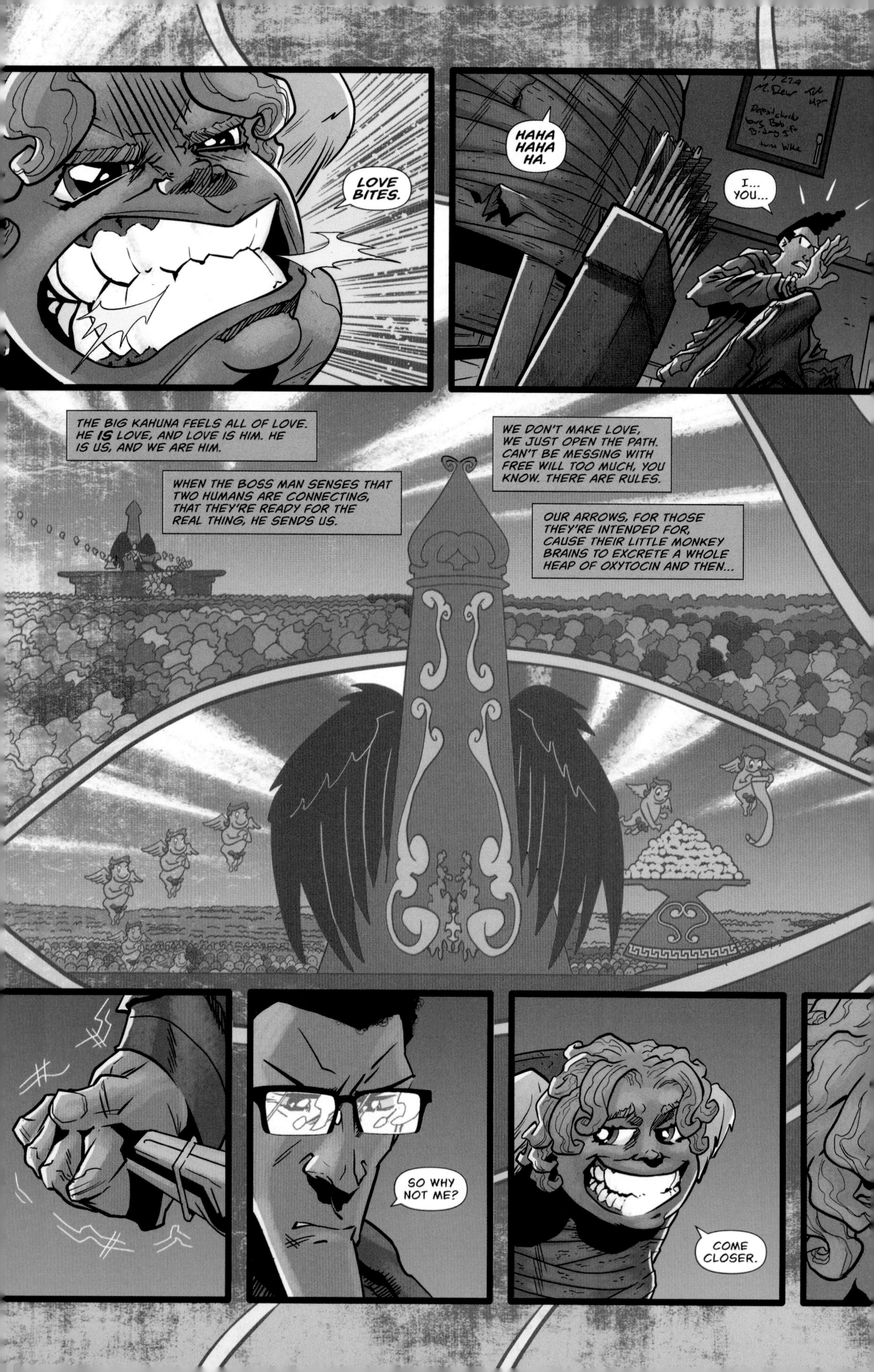
LOVE BITES.
HAHA HAHA HA.
I... YOU...
THE BIG KAHUNA FEELS ALL OF LOVE. HE IS LOVE, AND LOVE IS HIM. HE IS US, AND WE ARE HIM.
WHEN THE BOSS MAN SENSES THAT TWO HUMANS ARE CONNECTING, THAT THEY'RE READY FOR THE REAL THING, HE SENDS US.
WE DON'T MAKE LOVE, WE JUST OPEN THE PATH. CAN'T BE MESSING WITH FREE WILL TOO MUCH, YOU KNOW. THERE ARE RULES.
OUR ARROWS, FOR THOSE THEY'RE INTENDED FOR, CAUSE THEIR LITTLE MONKEY BRAINS TO EXCRETE A WHOLE HEAP OF OXYTOCIN AND THEN...
SO WHY NOT ME?
COME CLOSER.

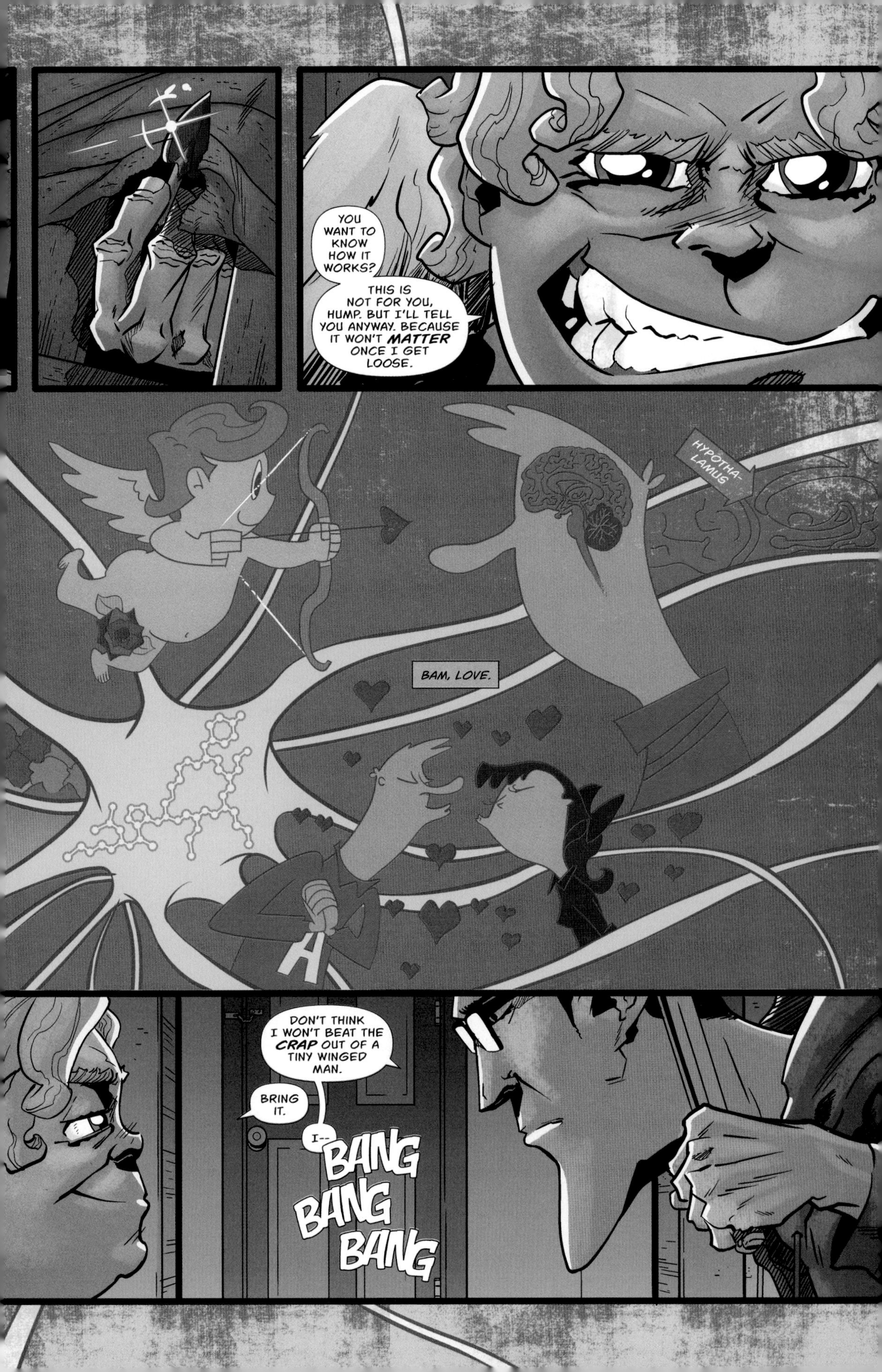
YOU WANT TO KNOW HOW IT WORKS?
THIS IS NOT FOR YOU, HUMP. BUT I'LL TELL YOU ANYWAY. BECAUSE IT WON'T MATTER ONCE I GET LOOSE.
HYPOTHA-LAMUS
BAM, LOVE.
DON'T THINK I WON'T BEAT THE CRAP OUT OF A TINY WINGED MAN.
BRING IT.
I--
BANG BANG BANG

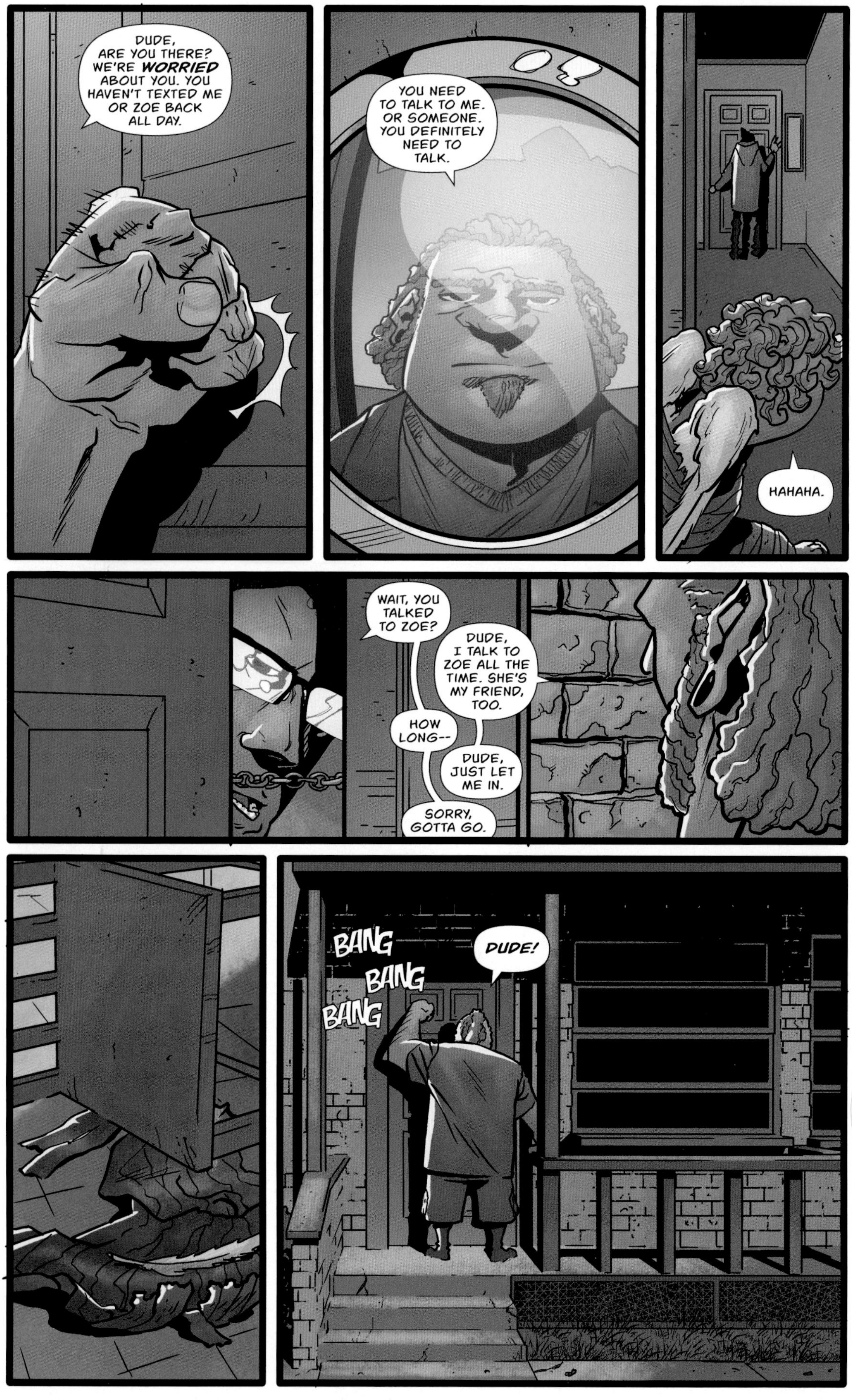
DUDE, ARE YOU THERE? WE'RE **WORRIED** ABOUT YOU. YOU HAVEN'T TEXTED ME OR ZOE BACK ALL DAY.
YOU NEED TO TALK TO ME. OR SOMEONE. YOU DEFINITELY NEED TO TALK.
HAHAHA.
WAIT, YOU TALKED TO ZOE?
DUDE, I TALK TO ZOE ALL THE TIME. SHE'S MY FRIEND, TOO.
HOW LONG--
DUDE, JUST LET ME IN.
SORRY, GOTTA GO.
BANG
BANG
BANG
DUDE!

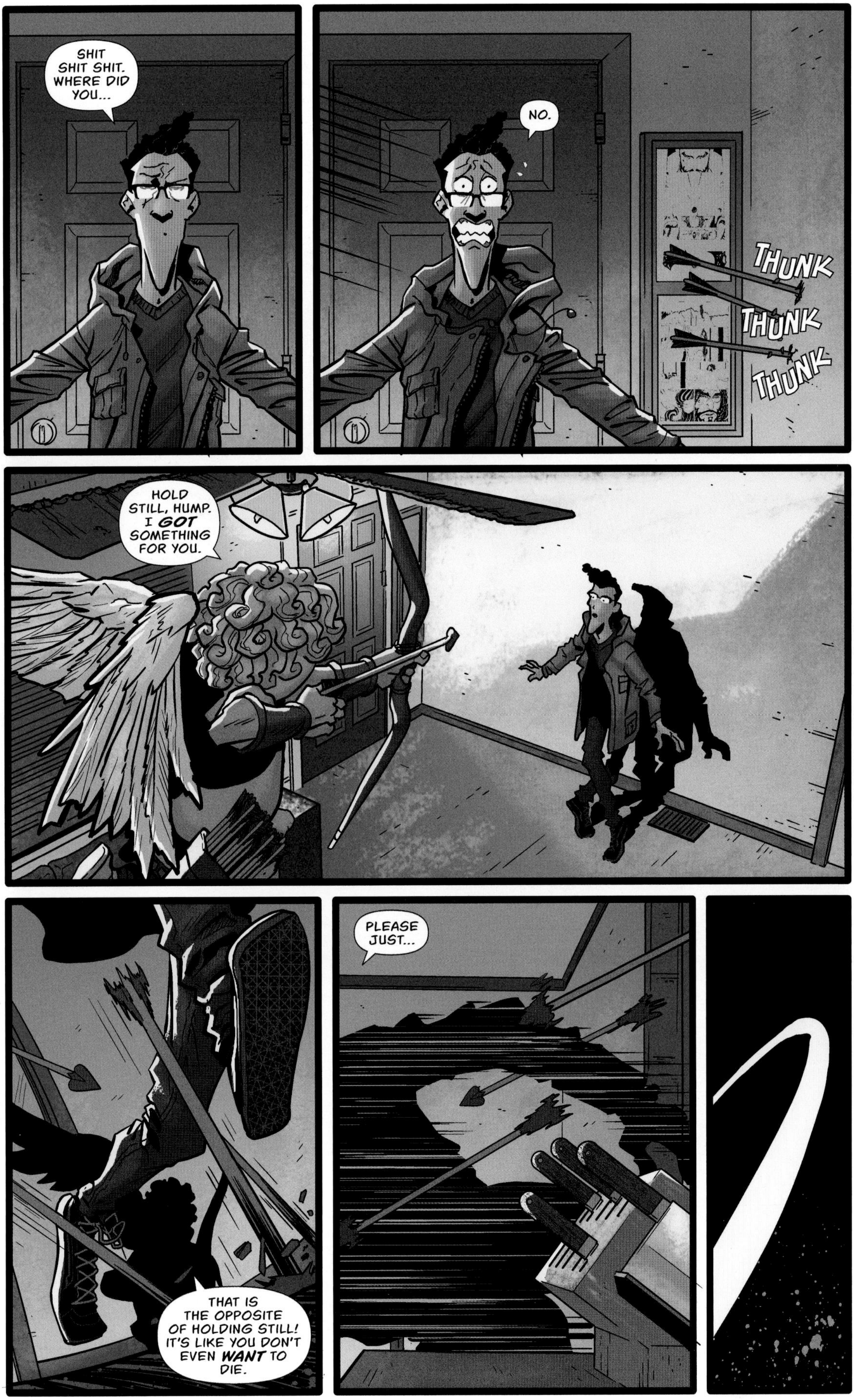
SHIT SHIT SHIT. WHERE DID YOU...
NO.
THUNK
THUNK
THUNK
HOLD STILL, HUMP. I GOT SOMETHING FOR YOU.
THAT IS THE OPPOSITE OF HOLDING STILL! IT'S LIKE YOU DON'T EVEN WANT TO DIE.
PLEASE JUST...

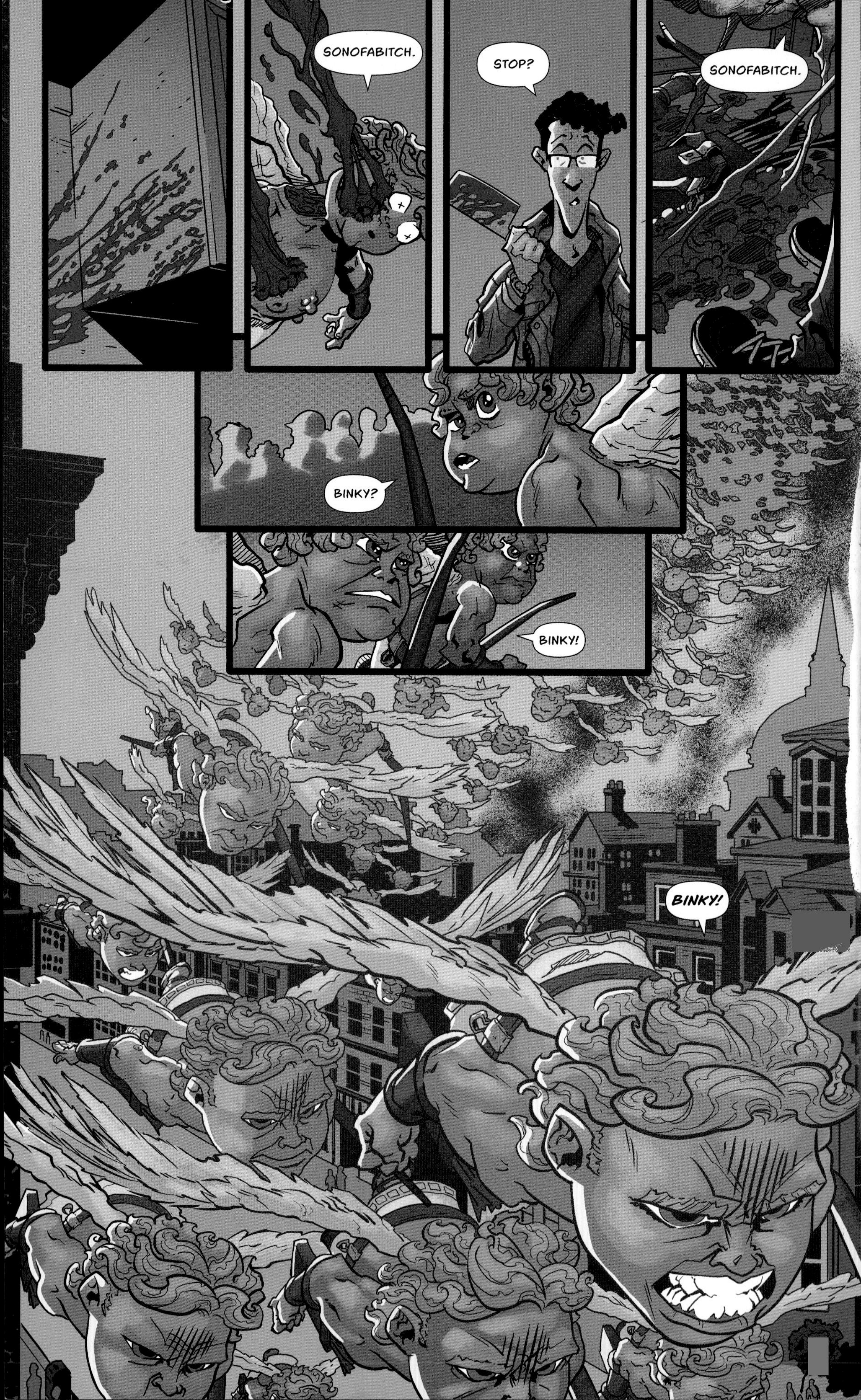
SONOFABITCH.
STOP?
SONOFABITCH.
BINKY?
BINKY!
BINKY!

Three

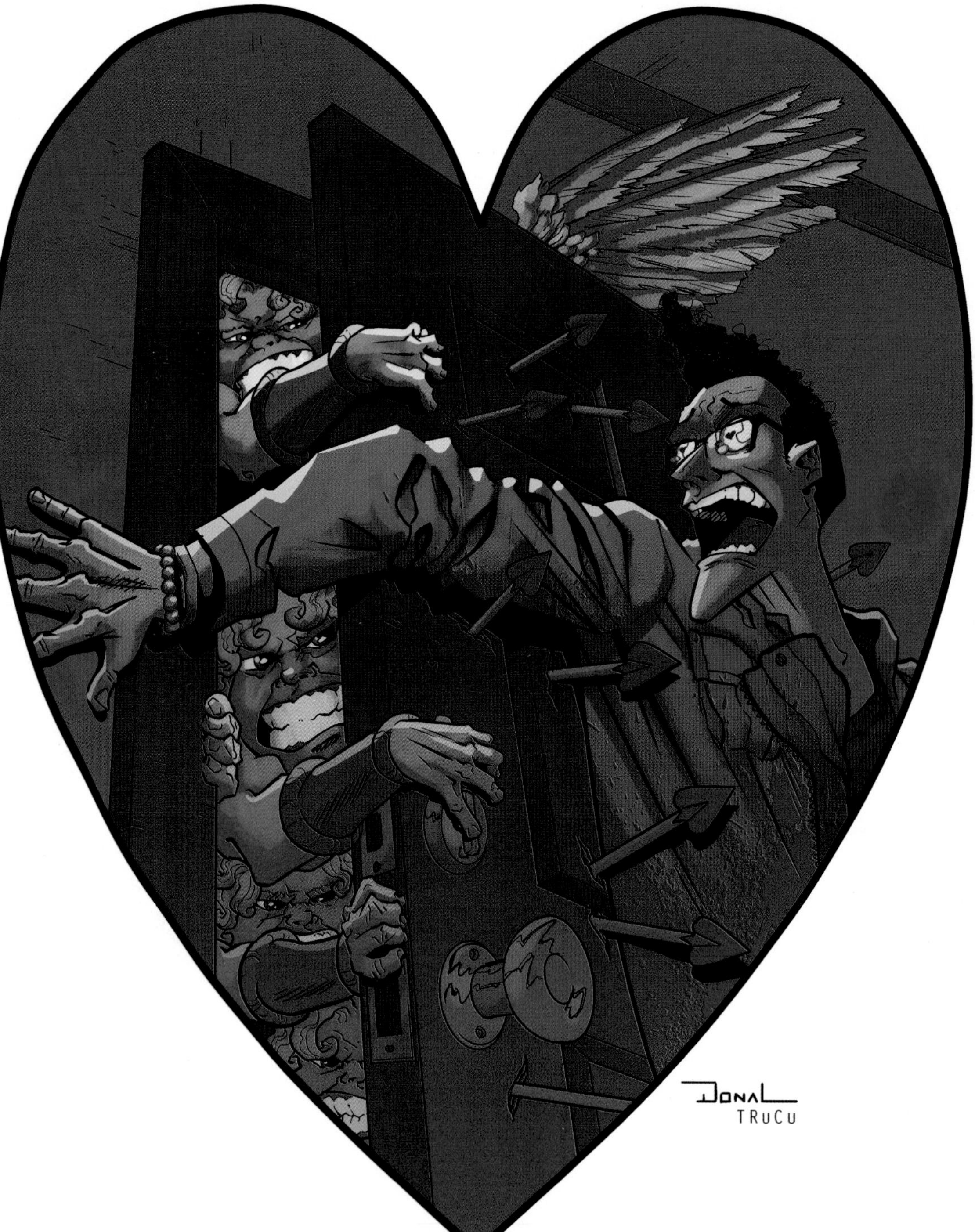
DONAL
TRUCU

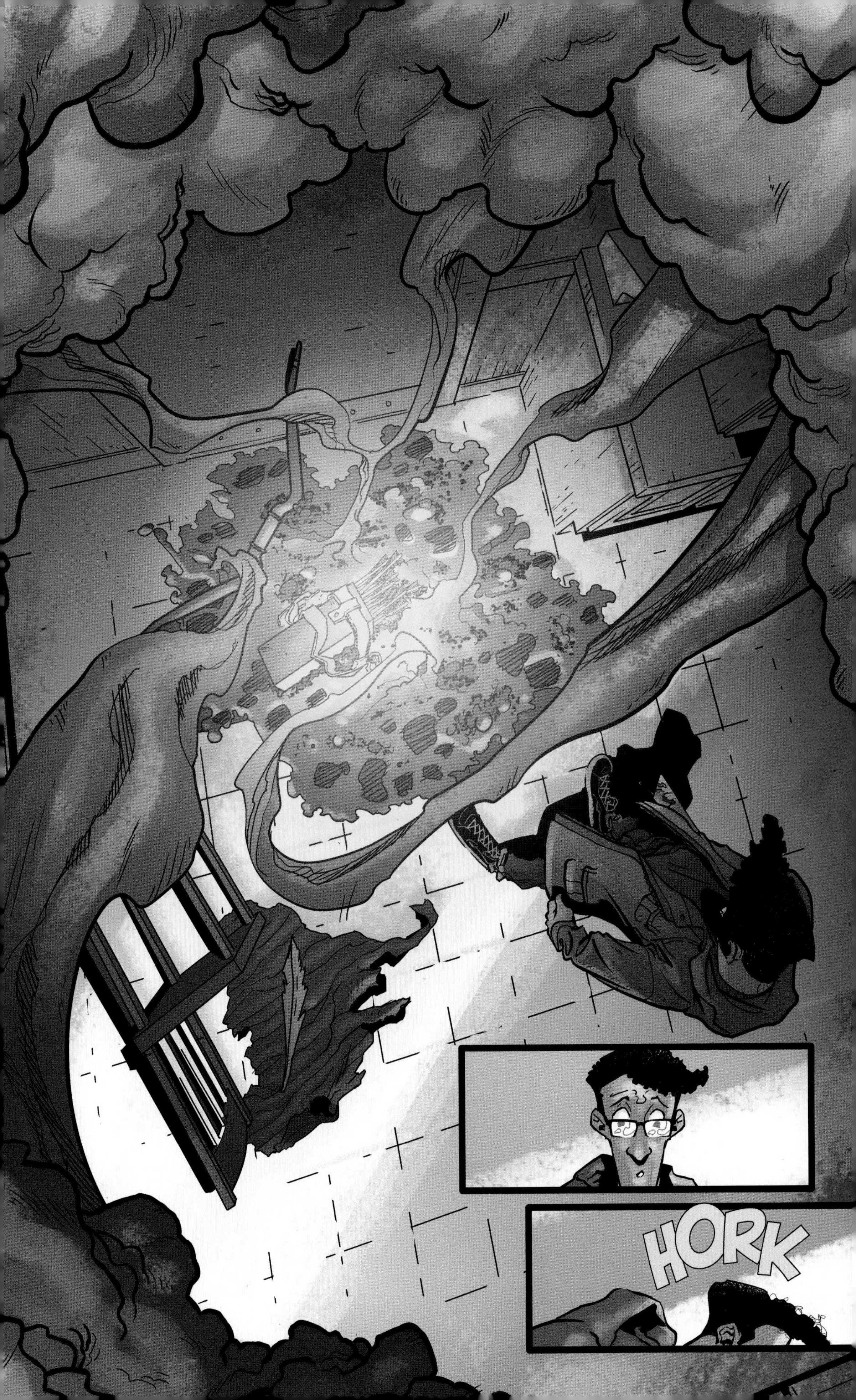
HORK

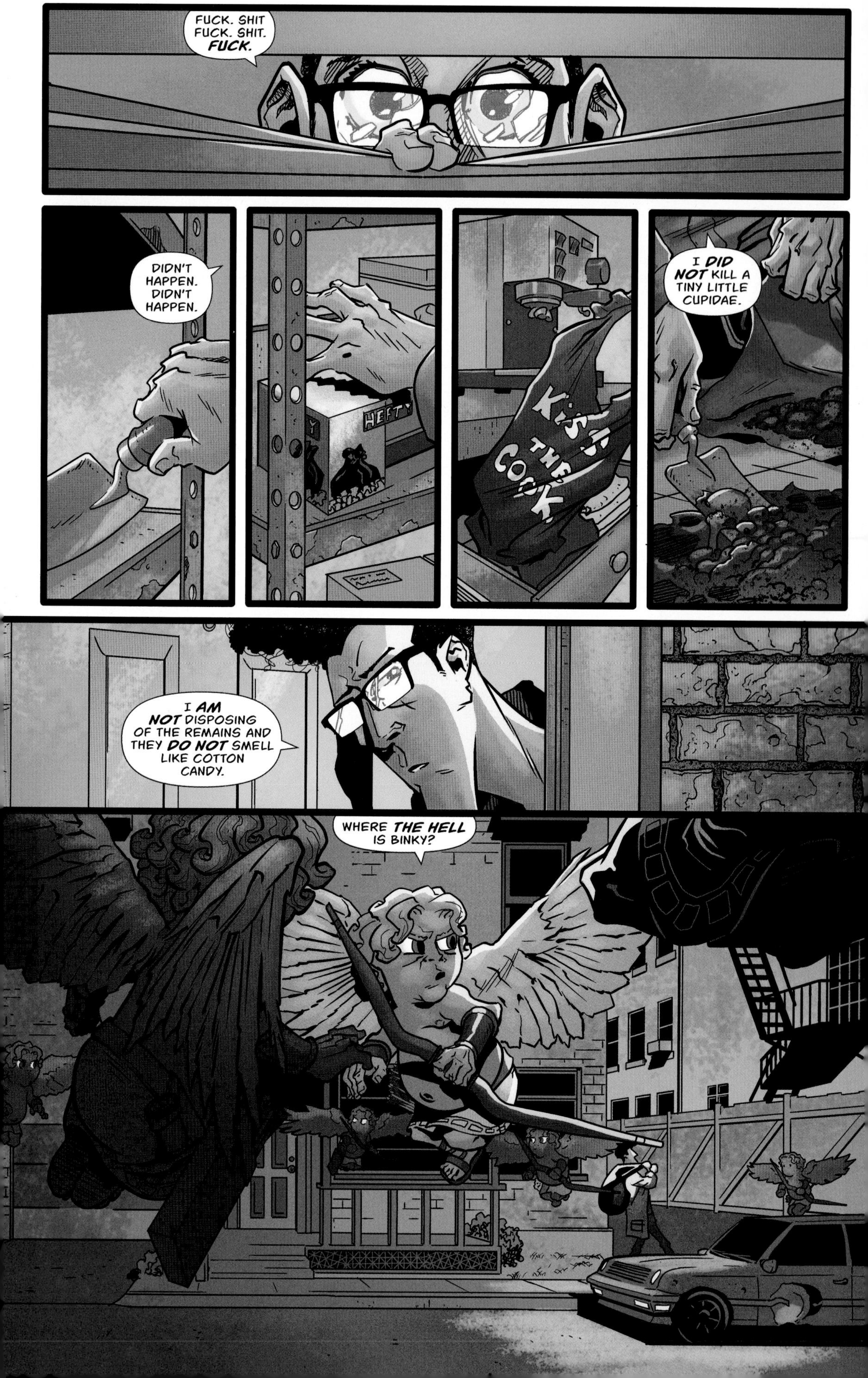
FUCK. SHIT
FUCK. SHIT.
FUCK.
DIDN'T HAPPEN. DIDN'T HAPPEN.
HEFTY
KISS THE COOK
I DID NOT KILL A TINY LITTLE CUPIDAE.
I AM NOT DISPOSING OF THE REMAINS AND THEY DO NOT SMELL LIKE COTTON CANDY.
WHERE THE HELL IS BINKY?

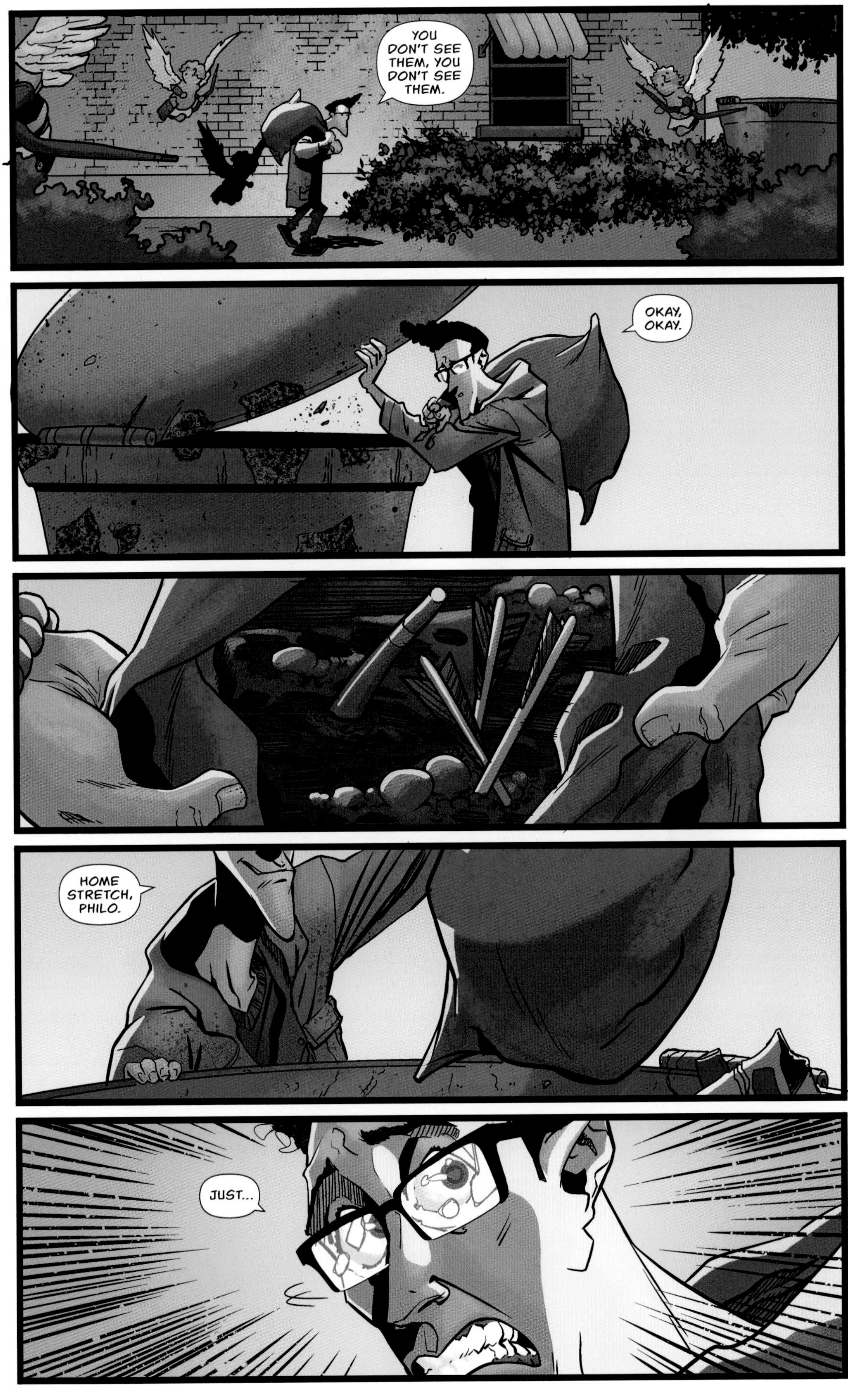
YOU DON'T SEE THEM, YOU DON'T SEE THEM.
OKAY, OKAY.
HOME STRETCH, PHILO.
JUST...

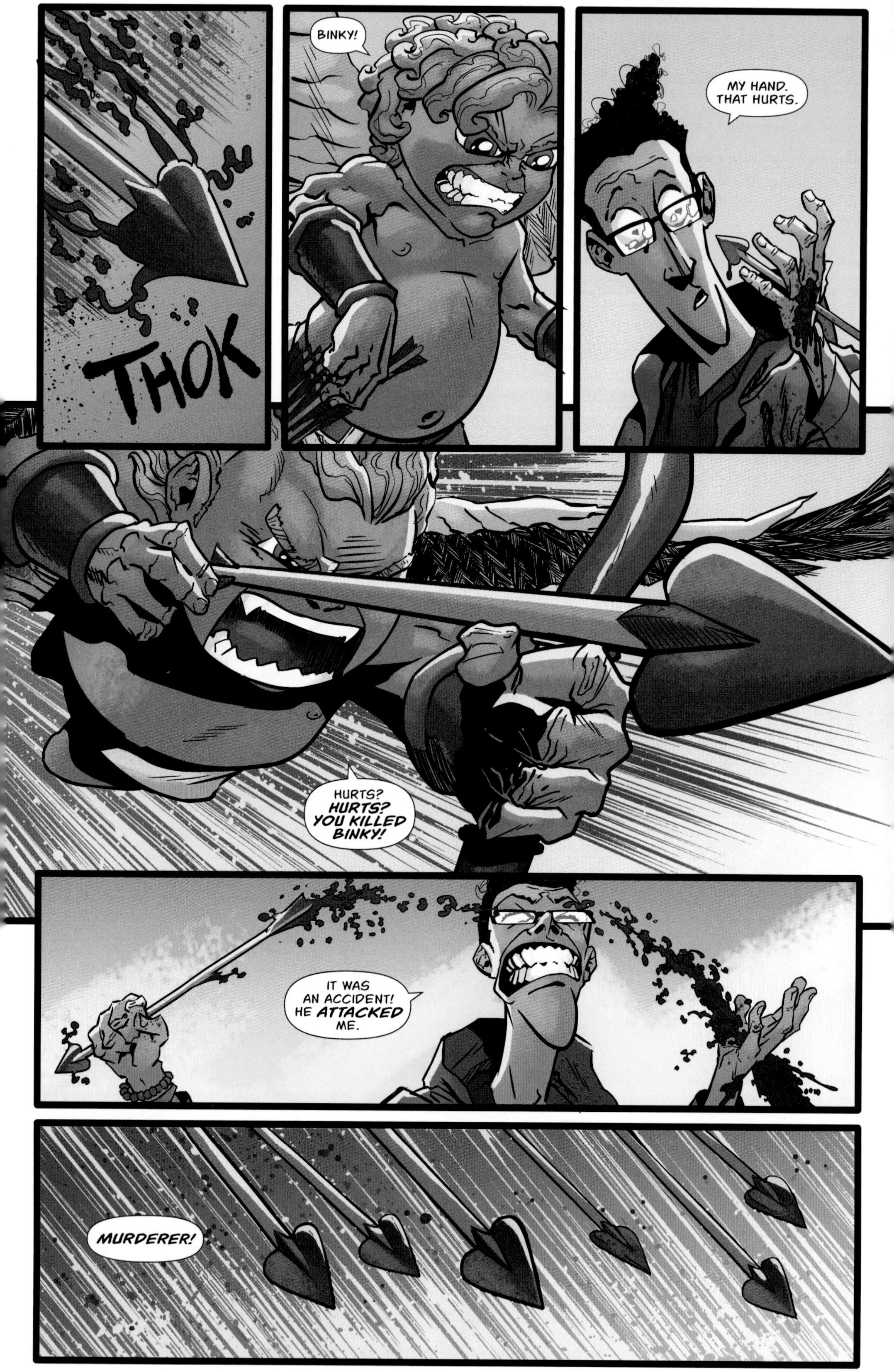
THOK
BINKY!
MY HAND. THAT HURTS.
HURTS? HURTS? YOU KILLED BINKY!
IT WAS AN ACCIDENT! HE ATTACKED ME.
MURDERER!

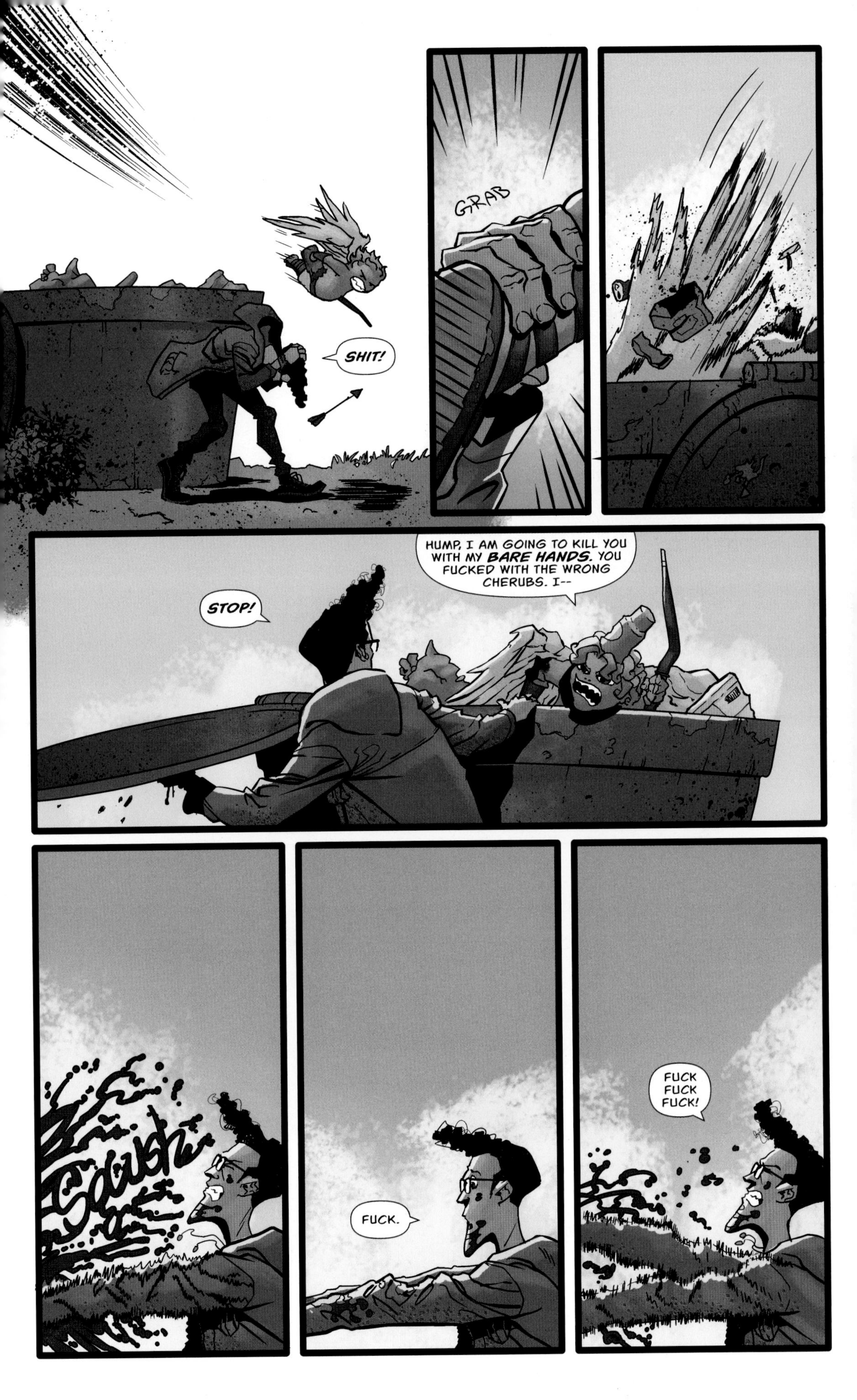
SHIT!
GRAB
STOP!
HUMP, I AM GOING TO KILL YOU WITH MY BARE HANDS. YOU FUCKED WITH THE WRONG CHERUBS. I--
FUCK.
FUCK FUCK FUCK!

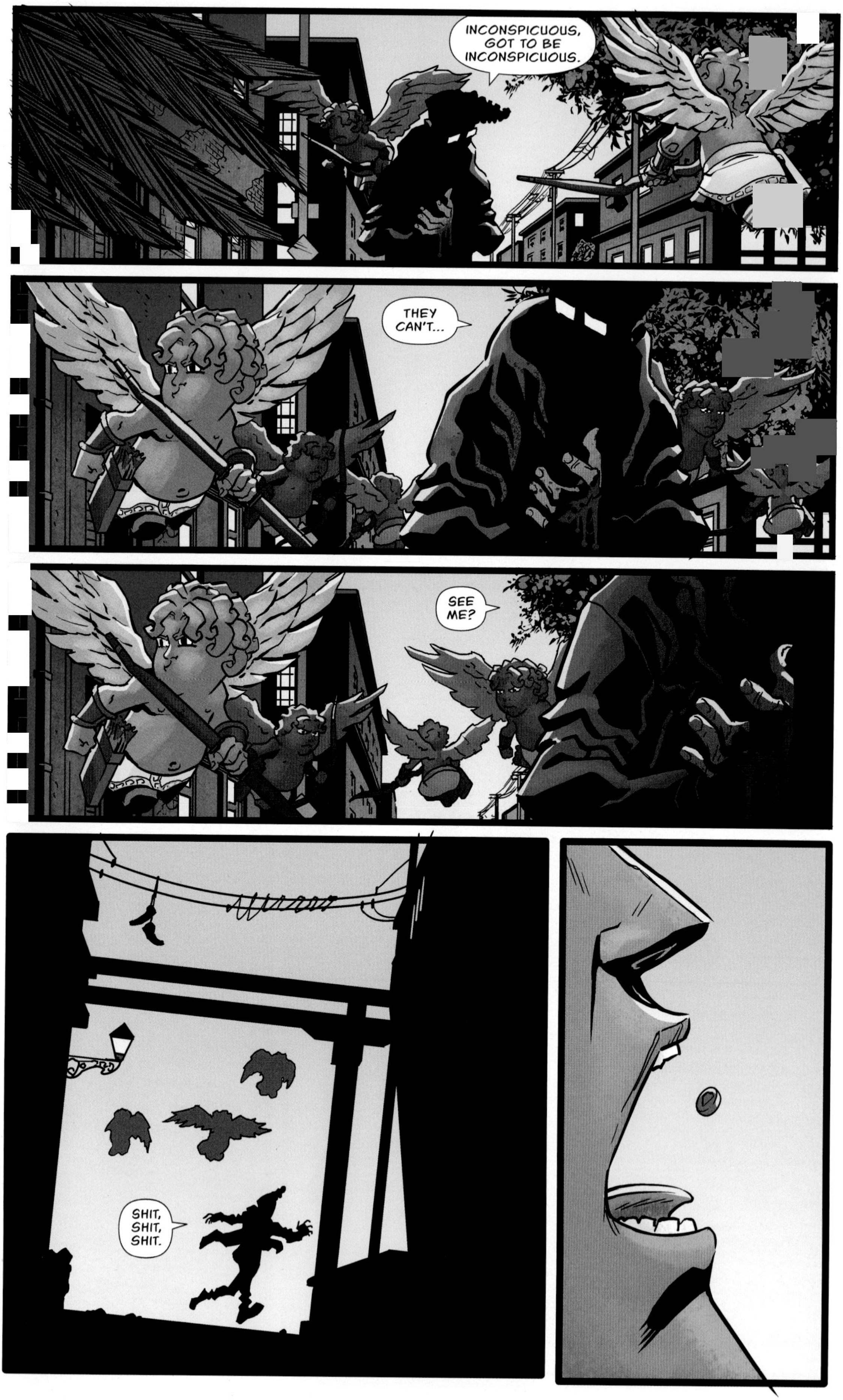
INCONSPICUOUS, GOT TO BE INCONSPICUOUS.
THEY CAN'T...
SEE ME?
SHIT, SHIT, SHIT.

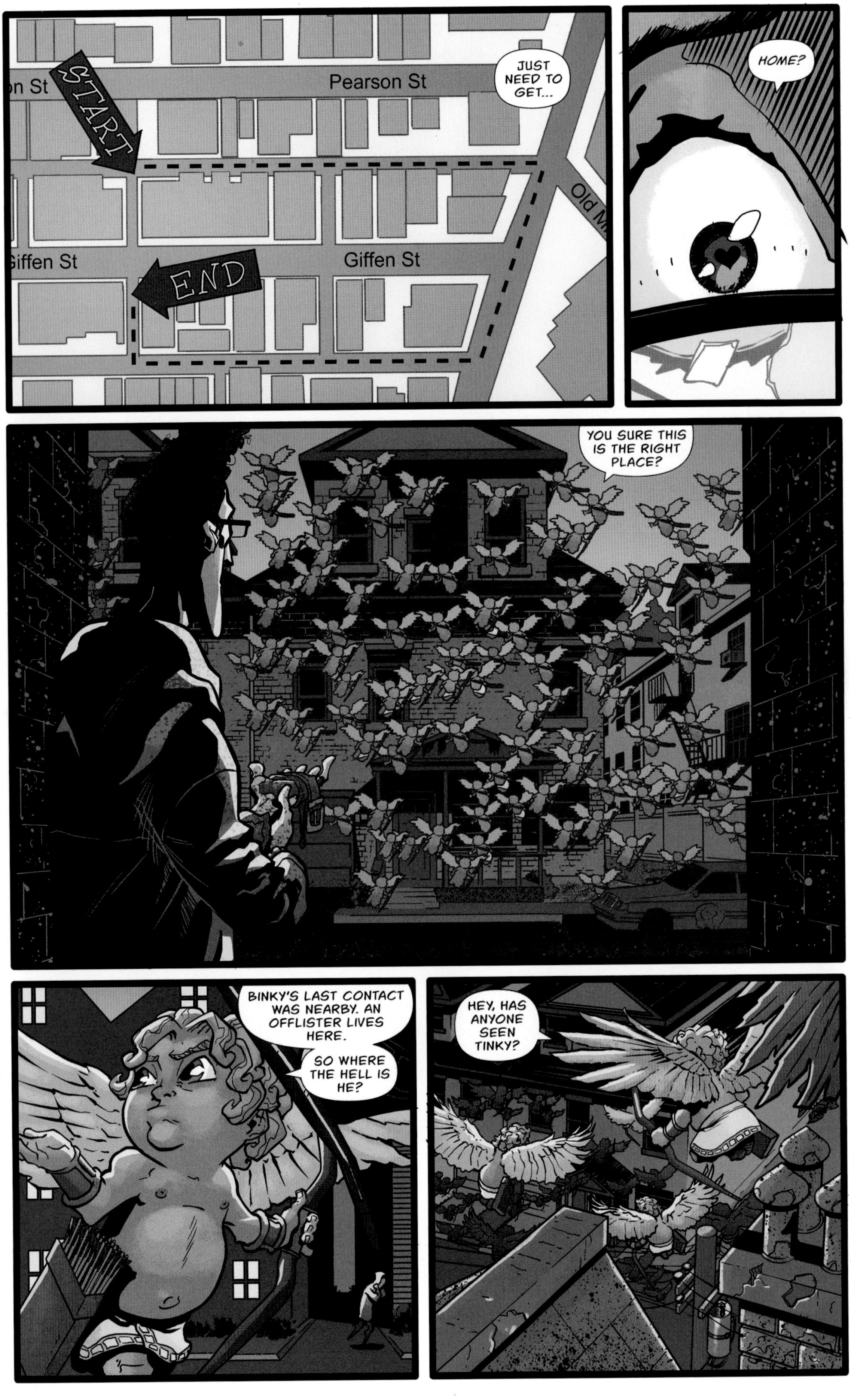
on St
Pearson St
START
Old M
Giffen St
Giffen St
END
JUST NEED TO GET...
HOME?
YOU SURE THIS IS THE RIGHT PLACE?
BINKY'S LAST CONTACT WAS NEARBY. AN OFFLISTER LIVES HERE.
SO WHERE THE HELL IS HE?
HEY, HAS ANYONE SEEN TINKY?

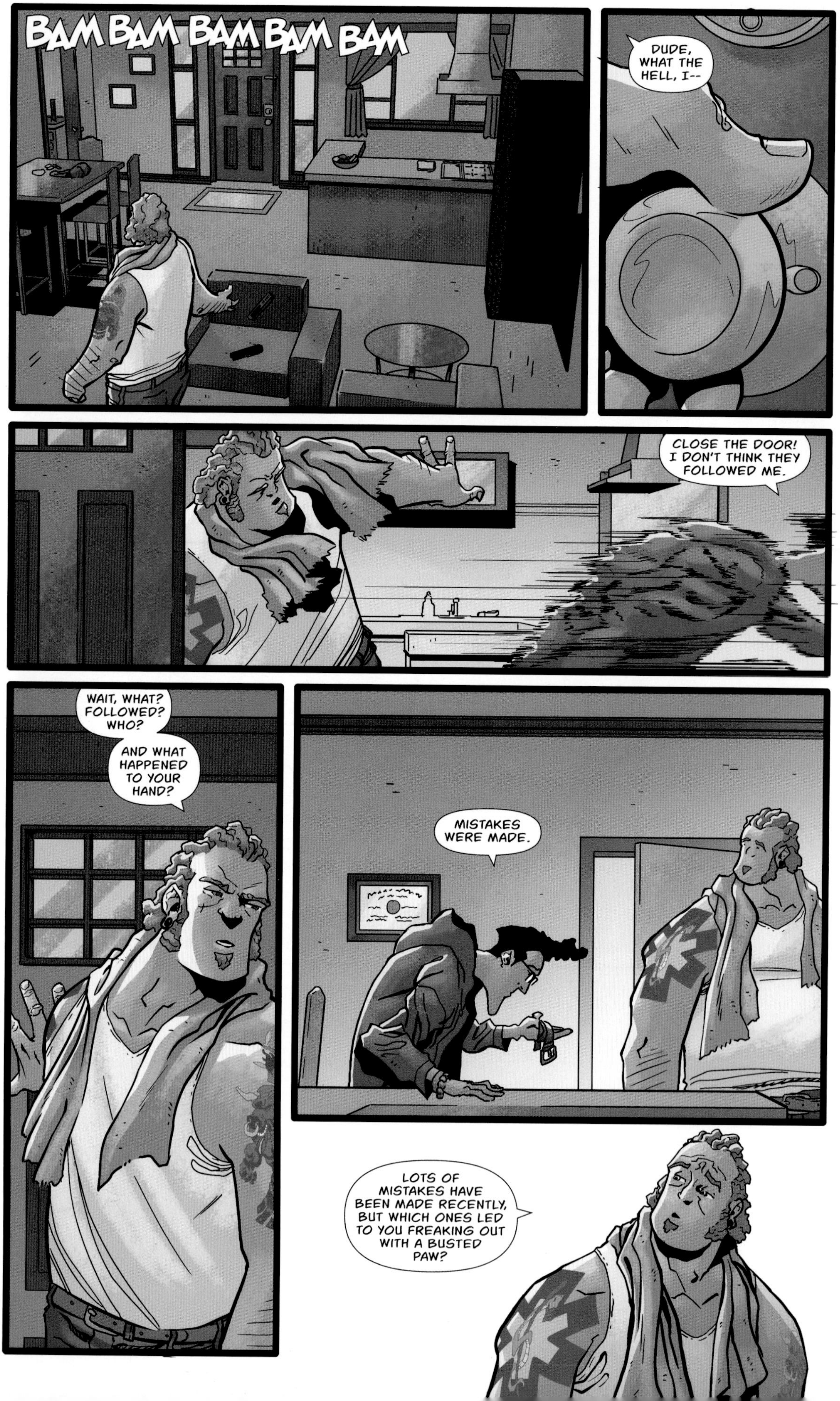
BAM BAM BAM BAM BAM
DUDE, WHAT THE HELL, I--
CLOSE THE DOOR! I DON'T THINK THEY FOLLOWED ME.
WAIT, WHAT? FOLLOWED? WHO?
AND WHAT HAPPENED TO YOUR HAND?
MISTAKES WERE MADE.
LOTS OF MISTAKES HAVE BEEN MADE RECENTLY, BUT WHICH ONES LED TO YOU FREAKING OUT WITH A BUSTED PAW?

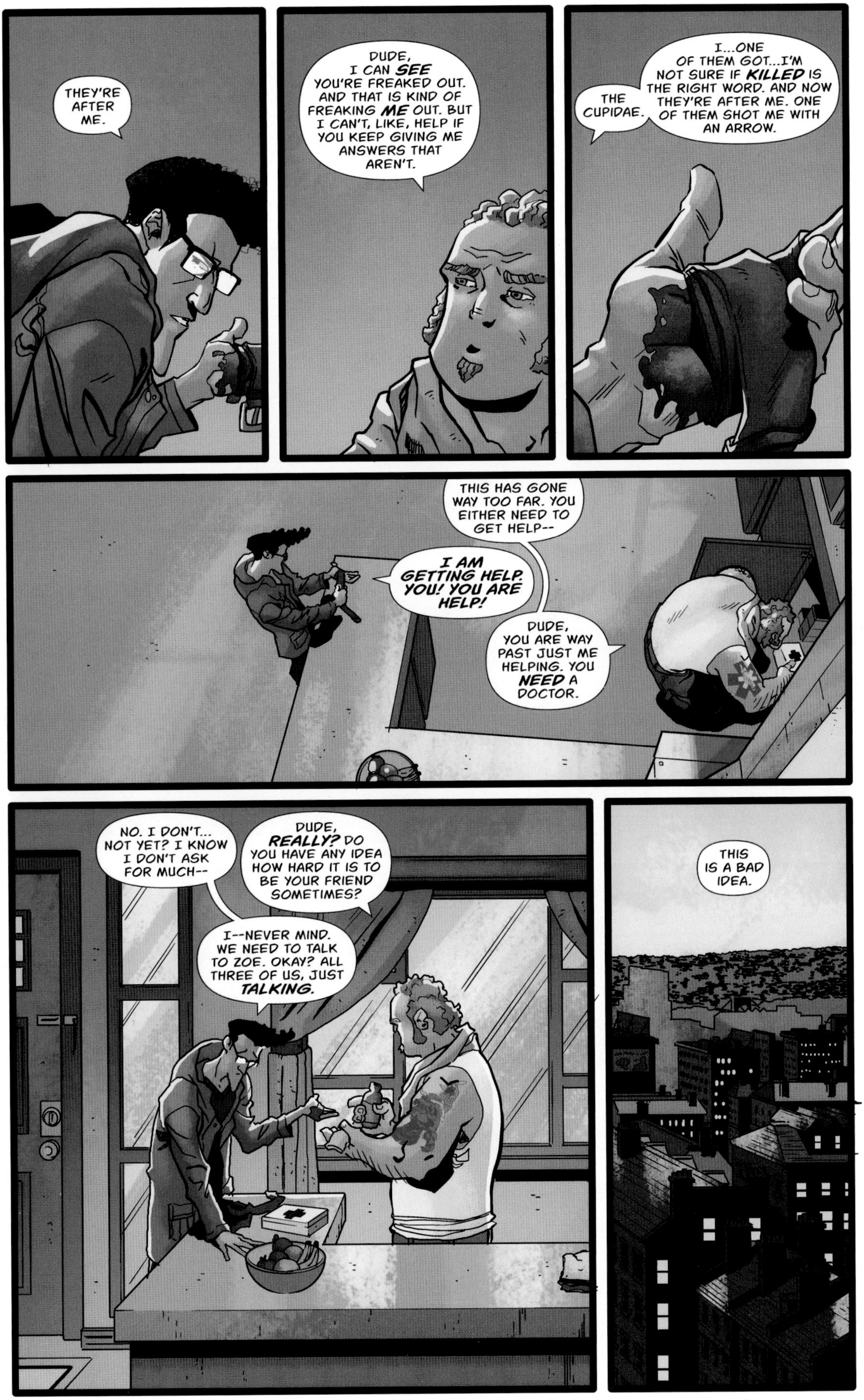
THEY'RE AFTER ME.
DUDE, I CAN SEE YOU'RE FREAKED OUT. AND THAT IS KIND OF FREAKING ME OUT. BUT I CAN'T, LIKE, HELP IF YOU KEEP GIVING ME ANSWERS THAT AREN'T.
THE CUPIDAE.
I...ONE OF THEM GOT...I'M NOT SURE IF KILLED IS THE RIGHT WORD. AND NOW THEY'RE AFTER ME. ONE OF THEM SHOT ME WITH AN ARROW.
THIS HAS GONE WAY TOO FAR. YOU EITHER NEED TO GET HELP--
I AM GETTING HELP. YOU! YOU ARE HELP!
DUDE, YOU ARE WAY PAST JUST ME HELPING. YOU NEED A DOCTOR.
NO. I DON'T... NOT YET? I KNOW I DON'T ASK FOR MUCH--
DUDE, REALLY? DO YOU HAVE ANY IDEA HOW HARD IT IS TO BE YOUR FRIEND SOMETIMES?
I--NEVER MIND. WE NEED TO TALK TO ZOE. OKAY? ALL THREE OF US, JUST TALKING.
THIS IS A BAD IDEA.

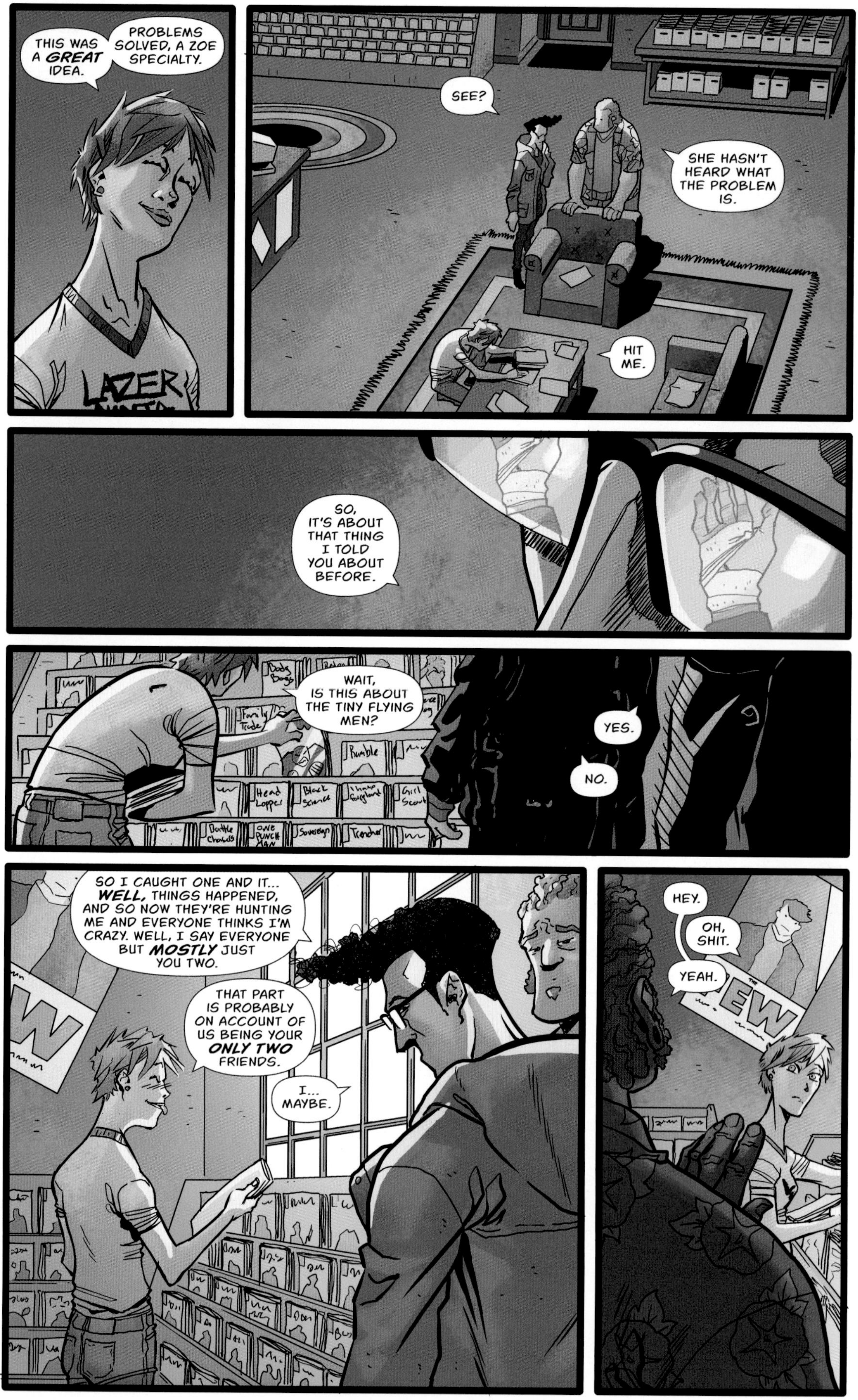

THIS WAS A *GREAT* IDEA.
PROBLEMS SOLVED, A ZOE SPECIALTY.
SEE?
SHE HASN'T HEARD WHAT THE PROBLEM IS.
HIT ME.
SO, IT'S ABOUT THAT THING I TOLD YOU ABOUT BEFORE.
WAIT, IS THIS ABOUT THE TINY FLYING MEN?
YES.
NO.
SO I CAUGHT ONE AND IT... *WELL,* THINGS HAPPENED, AND SO NOW THEY'RE HUNTING ME AND EVERYONE THINKS I'M CRAZY. WELL, I SAY EVERYONE BUT *MOSTLY* JUST YOU TWO.
THAT PART IS PROBABLY ON ACCOUNT OF US BEING YOUR *ONLY TWO* FRIENDS.
I... MAYBE.
HEY.
OH, SHIT.
YEAH.

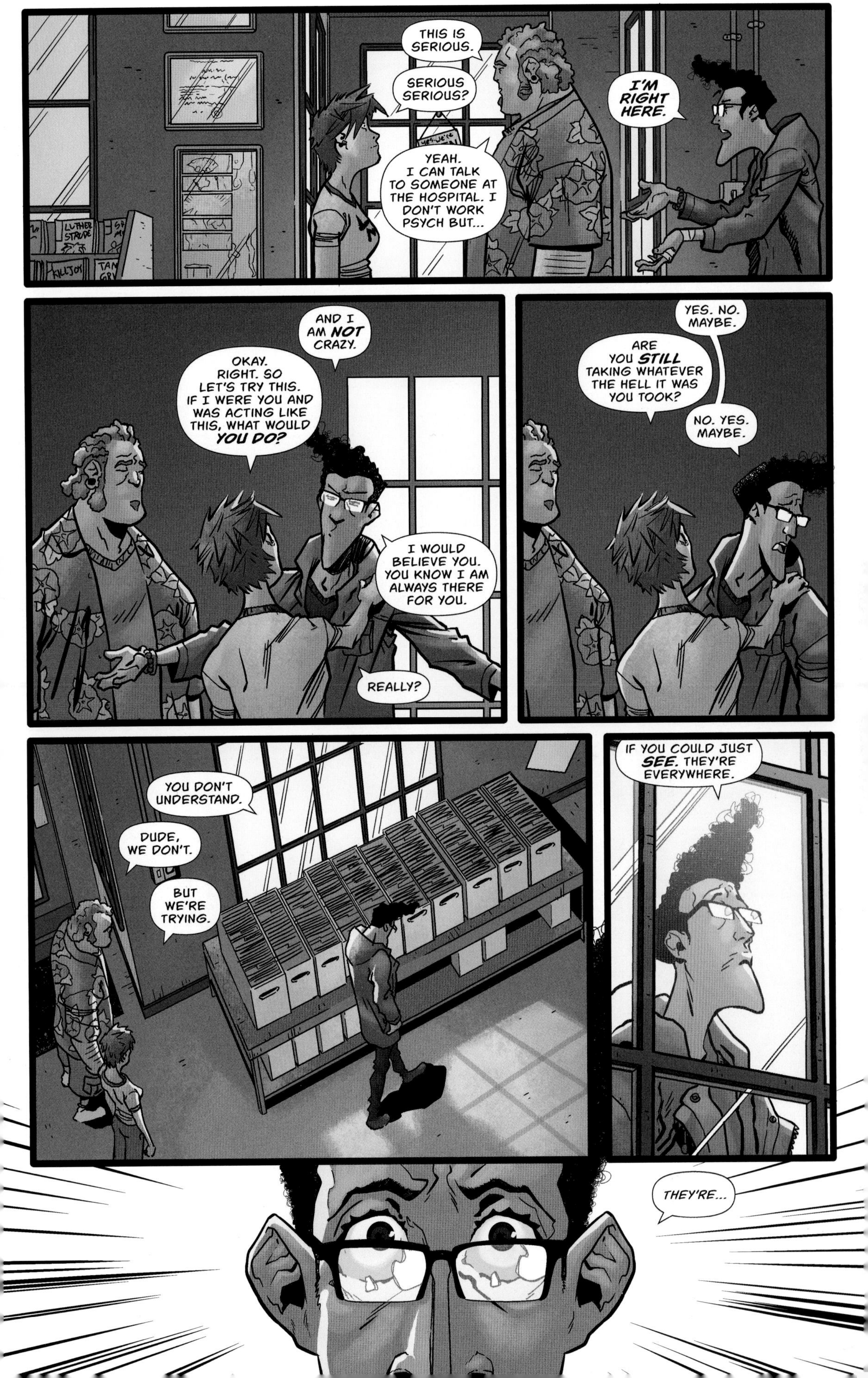
THIS IS SERIOUS.
SERIOUS SERIOUS?
YEAH. I CAN TALK TO SOMEONE AT THE HOSPITAL. I DON'T WORK PSYCH BUT...
I'M RIGHT HERE.
LUTHER STRODE
KILLJOY
AND I AM NOT CRAZY.
OKAY. RIGHT. SO LET'S TRY THIS. IF I WERE YOU AND WAS ACTING LIKE THIS, WHAT WOULD YOU DO?
I WOULD BELIEVE YOU. YOU KNOW I AM ALWAYS THERE FOR YOU.
REALLY?
YES. NO. MAYBE.
ARE YOU STILL TAKING WHATEVER THE HELL IT WAS YOU TOOK?
NO. YES. MAYBE.
YOU DON'T UNDERSTAND.
DUDE, WE DON'T.
BUT WE'RE TRYING.
IF YOU COULD JUST SEE. THEY'RE EVERYWHERE.
THEY'RE...

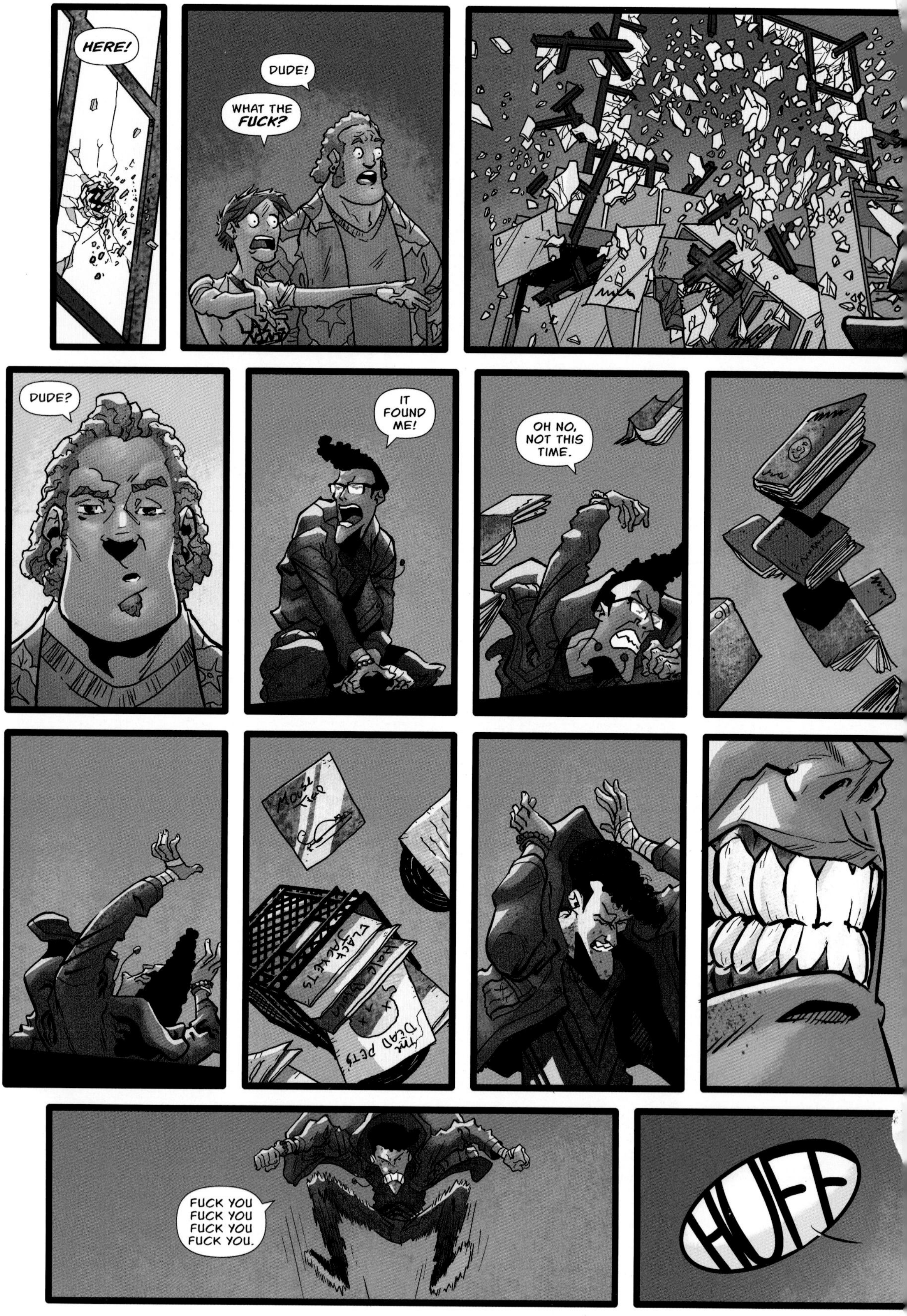
HERE!
DUDE!
WHAT THE FUCK?
DUDE?
IT FOUND ME!
OH NO, NOT THIS TIME.
FUCK YOU FUCK YOU FUCK YOU FUCK YOU.
HUFF

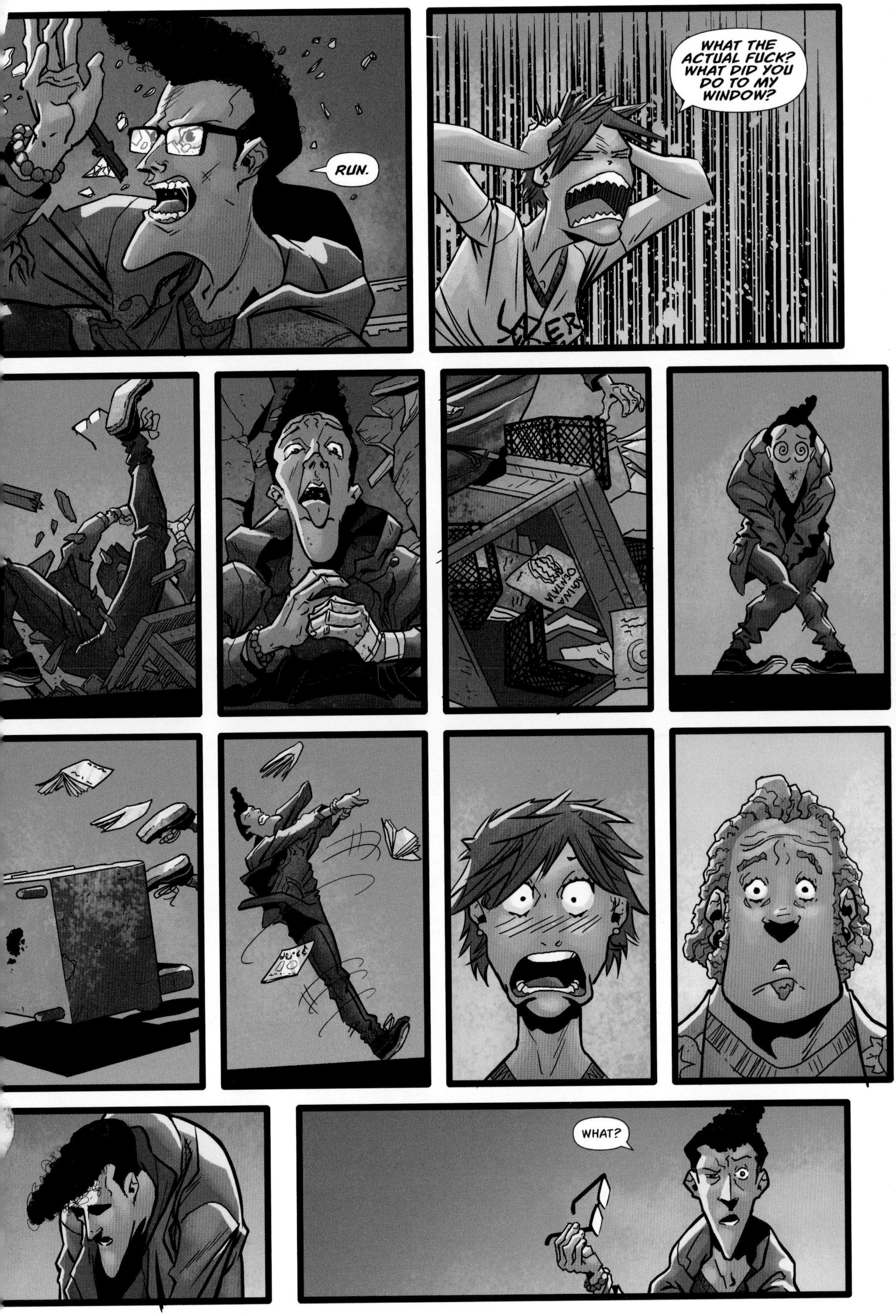
RUN.
WHAT THE ACTUAL FUCK? WHAT DID YOU DO TO MY WINDOW?
WHAT?

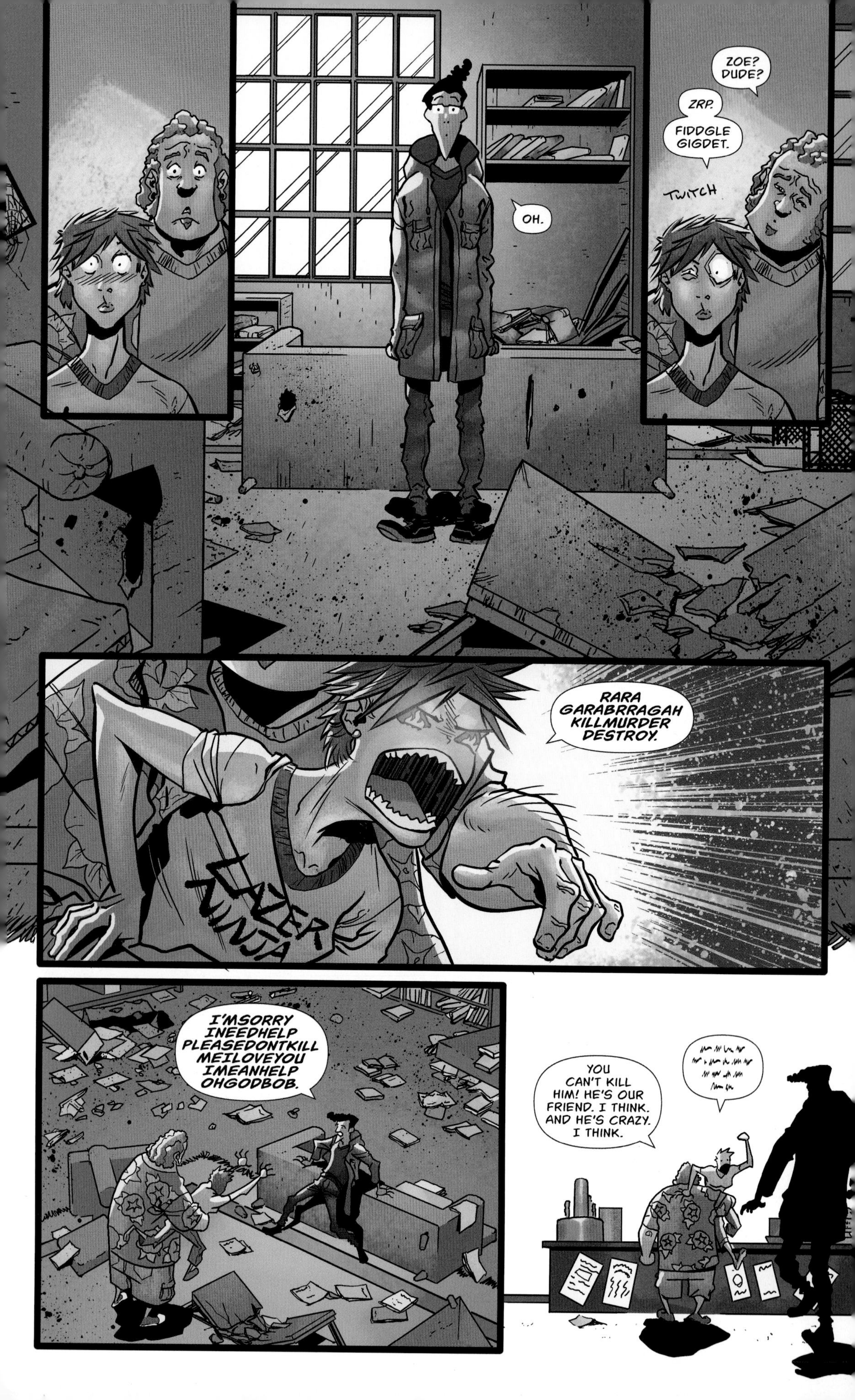
OH.
ZOE? DUDE?
ZRP.
FIDDGLE GIGDET.
TWITCH
RARA GARABRRAGAH KILLMURDER DESTROY.
LAZER NINJA
I'MSORRY INEEDHELP PLEASEDONTKILL MEILOVEYOU IMEANHELP OHGODBOB.
YOU CAN'T KILL HIM! HE'S OUR FRIEND. I THINK. AND HE'S CRAZY. I THINK.

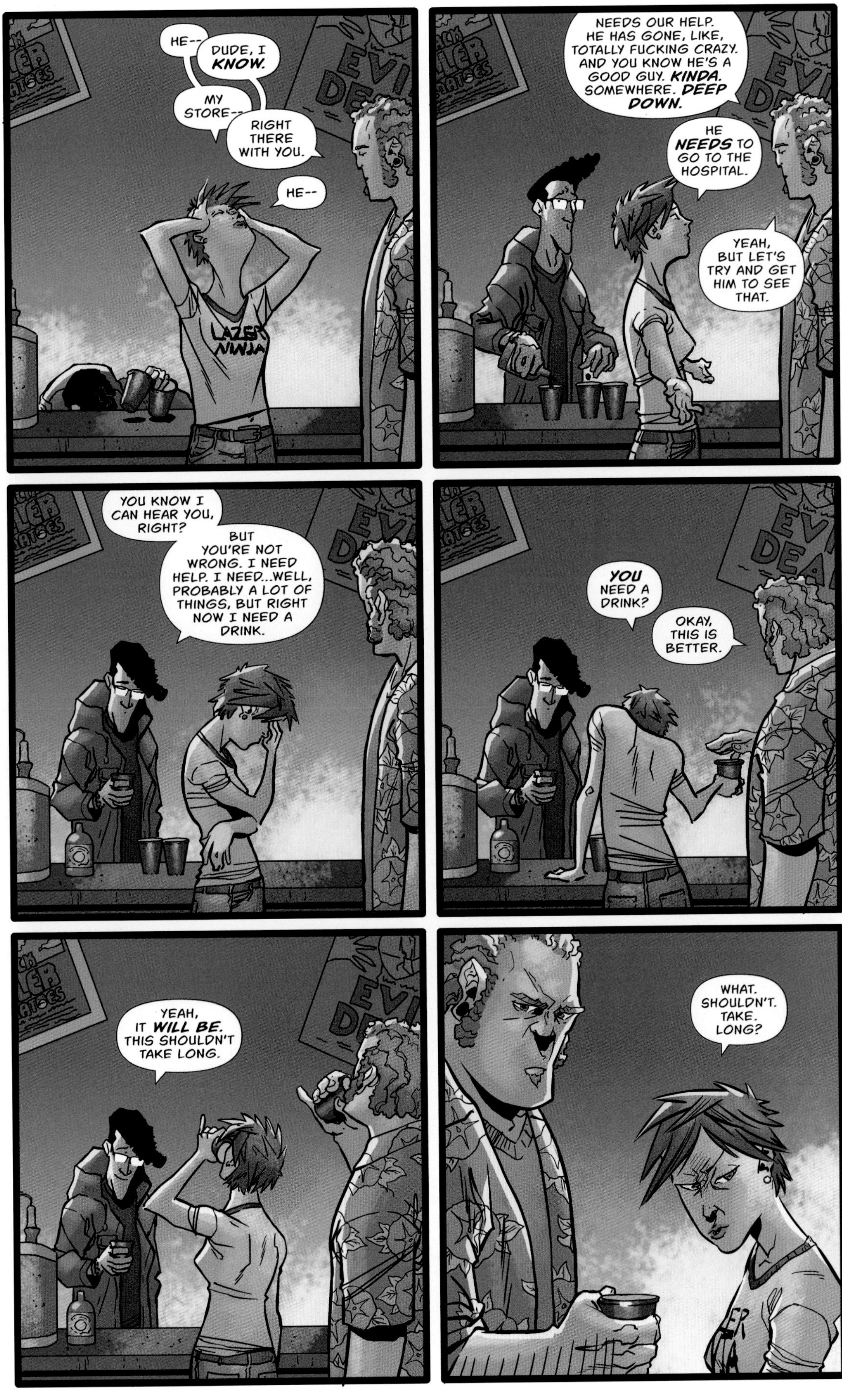
HE--
DUDE, I KNOW.
MY STORE--
RIGHT THERE WITH YOU.
HE--
NEEDS OUR HELP. HE HAS GONE, LIKE, TOTALLY FUCKING CRAZY. AND YOU KNOW HE'S A GOOD GUY. KINDA. SOMEWHERE. DEEP DOWN.
HE NEEDS TO GO TO THE HOSPITAL.
YEAH, BUT LET'S TRY AND GET HIM TO SEE THAT.
LAZER NINJA
YOU KNOW I CAN HEAR YOU, RIGHT?
BUT YOU'RE NOT WRONG. I NEED HELP. I NEED...WELL, PROBABLY A LOT OF THINGS, BUT RIGHT NOW I NEED A DRINK.
YOU NEED A DRINK?
OKAY, THIS IS BETTER.
YEAH, IT WILL BE. THIS SHOULDN'T TAKE LONG.
WHAT. SHOULDN'T. TAKE. LONG?

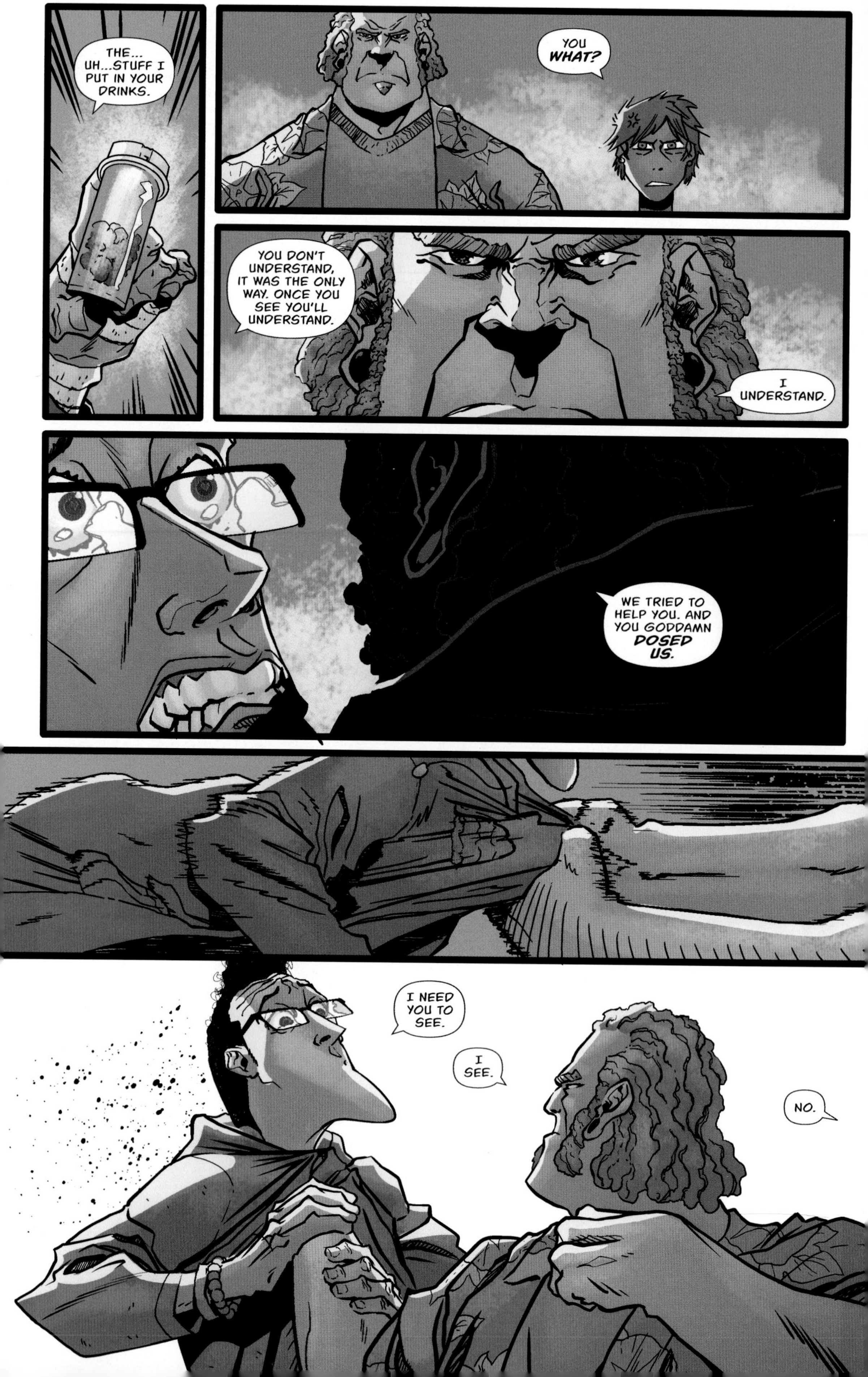
THE... UH...STUFF I PUT IN YOUR DRINKS.
YOU WHAT?
YOU DON'T UNDERSTAND, IT WAS THE ONLY WAY. ONCE YOU SEE YOU'LL UNDERSTAND.
I UNDERSTAND.
WE TRIED TO HELP YOU. AND YOU GODDAMN DOSED US.
I NEED YOU TO SEE.
I SEE.
NO.

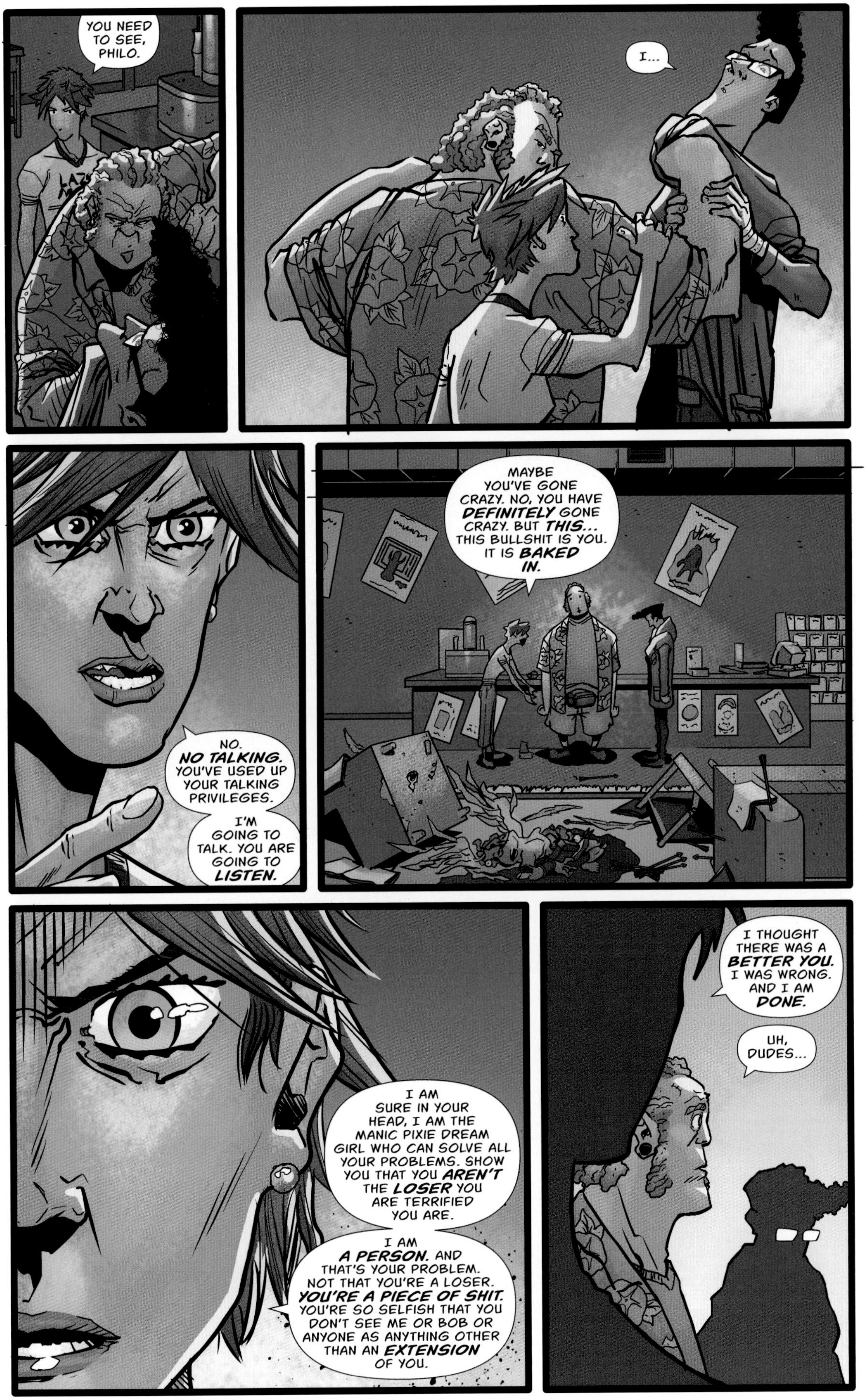
YOU NEED TO SEE, PHILO.
I...
NO. NO TALKING. YOU'VE USED UP YOUR TALKING PRIVILEGES.
I'M GOING TO TALK. YOU ARE GOING TO LISTEN.
MAYBE YOU'VE GONE CRAZY. NO, YOU HAVE DEFINITELY GONE CRAZY. BUT THIS... THIS BULLSHIT IS YOU. IT IS BAKED IN.
I AM SURE IN YOUR HEAD, I AM THE MANIC PIXIE DREAM GIRL WHO CAN SOLVE ALL YOUR PROBLEMS. SHOW YOU THAT YOU AREN'T THE LOSER YOU ARE TERRIFIED YOU ARE.
I AM A PERSON. AND THAT'S YOUR PROBLEM. NOT THAT YOU'RE A LOSER. YOU'RE A PIECE OF SHIT. YOU'RE SO SELFISH THAT YOU DON'T SEE ME OR BOB OR ANYONE AS ANYTHING OTHER THAN AN EXTENSION OF YOU.
I THOUGHT THERE WAS A BETTER YOU. I WAS WRONG. AND I AM DONE.
UH, DUDES...

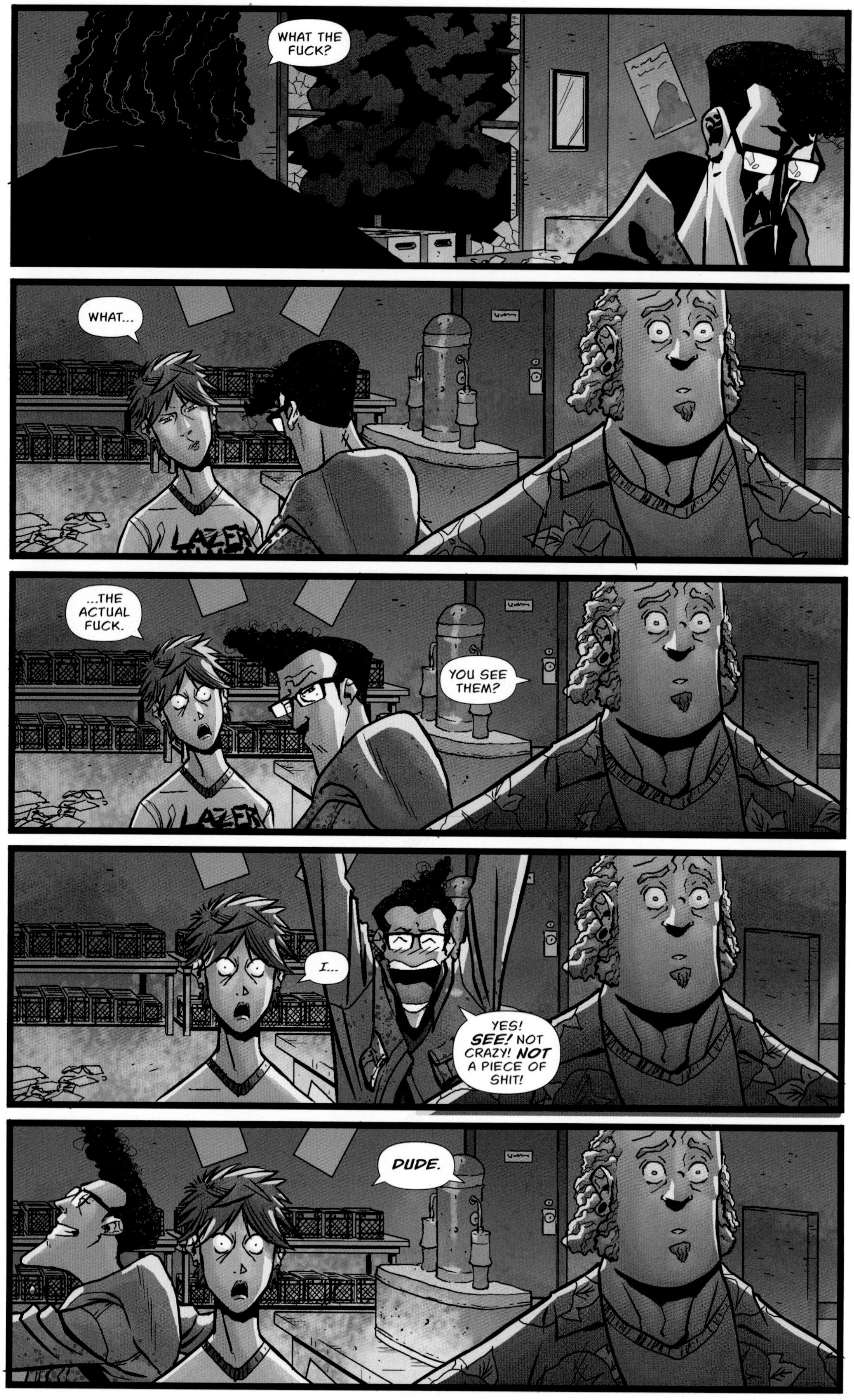
WHAT THE FUCK?
WHAT...
...THE ACTUAL FUCK.
YOU SEE THEM?
I...
YES! SEE! NOT CRAZY! NOT A PIECE OF SHIT!
DUDE.

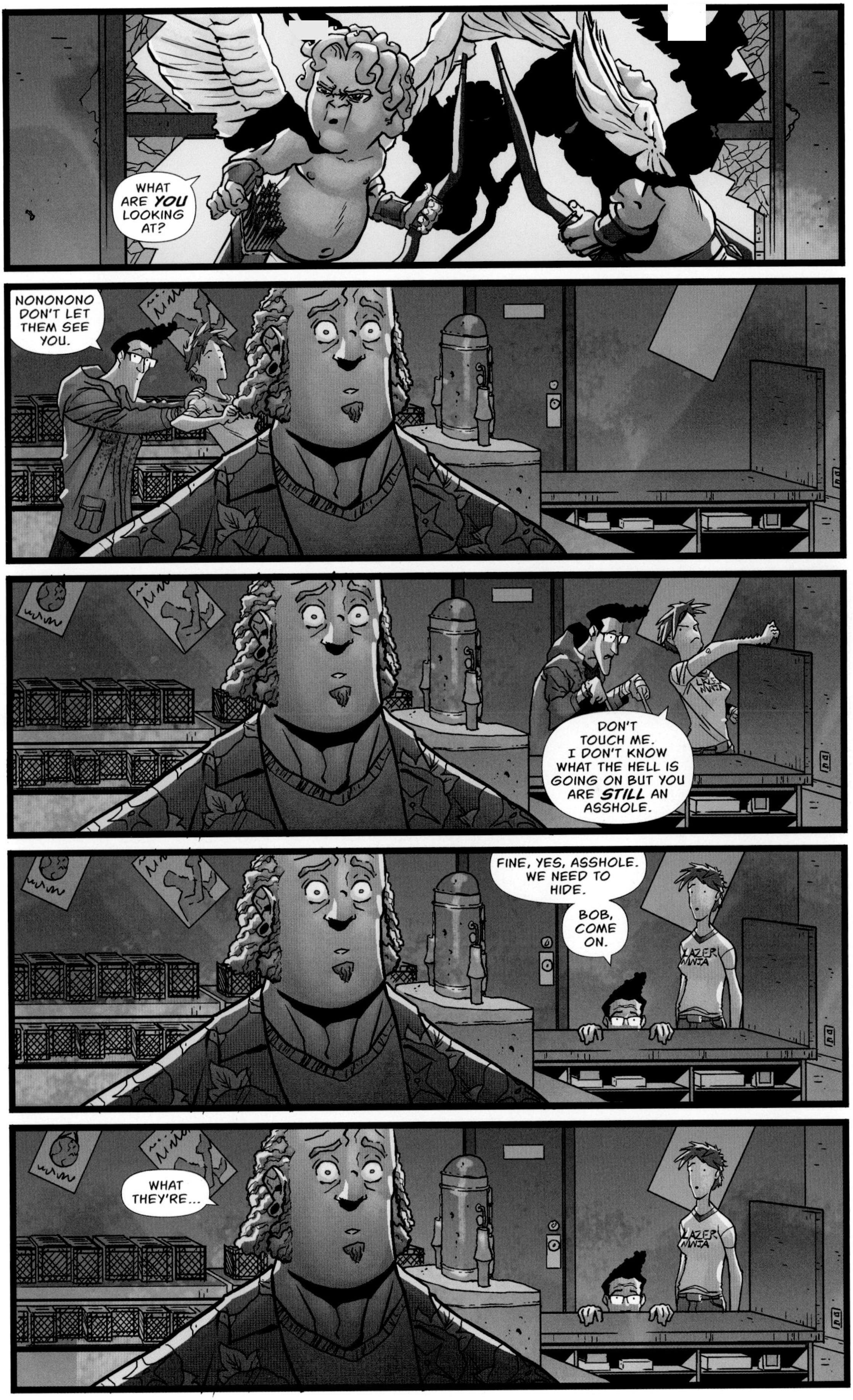
WHAT ARE *YOU* LOOKING AT?
NONONONO DON'T LET THEM SEE YOU.
DON'T TOUCH ME. I DON'T KNOW WHAT THE HELL IS GOING ON BUT YOU ARE *STILL* AN ASSHOLE.
FINE, YES, ASSHOLE. WE NEED TO HIDE.
BOB, COME ON.
LAZER NINJA
WHAT THEY'RE...
LAZER NINJA

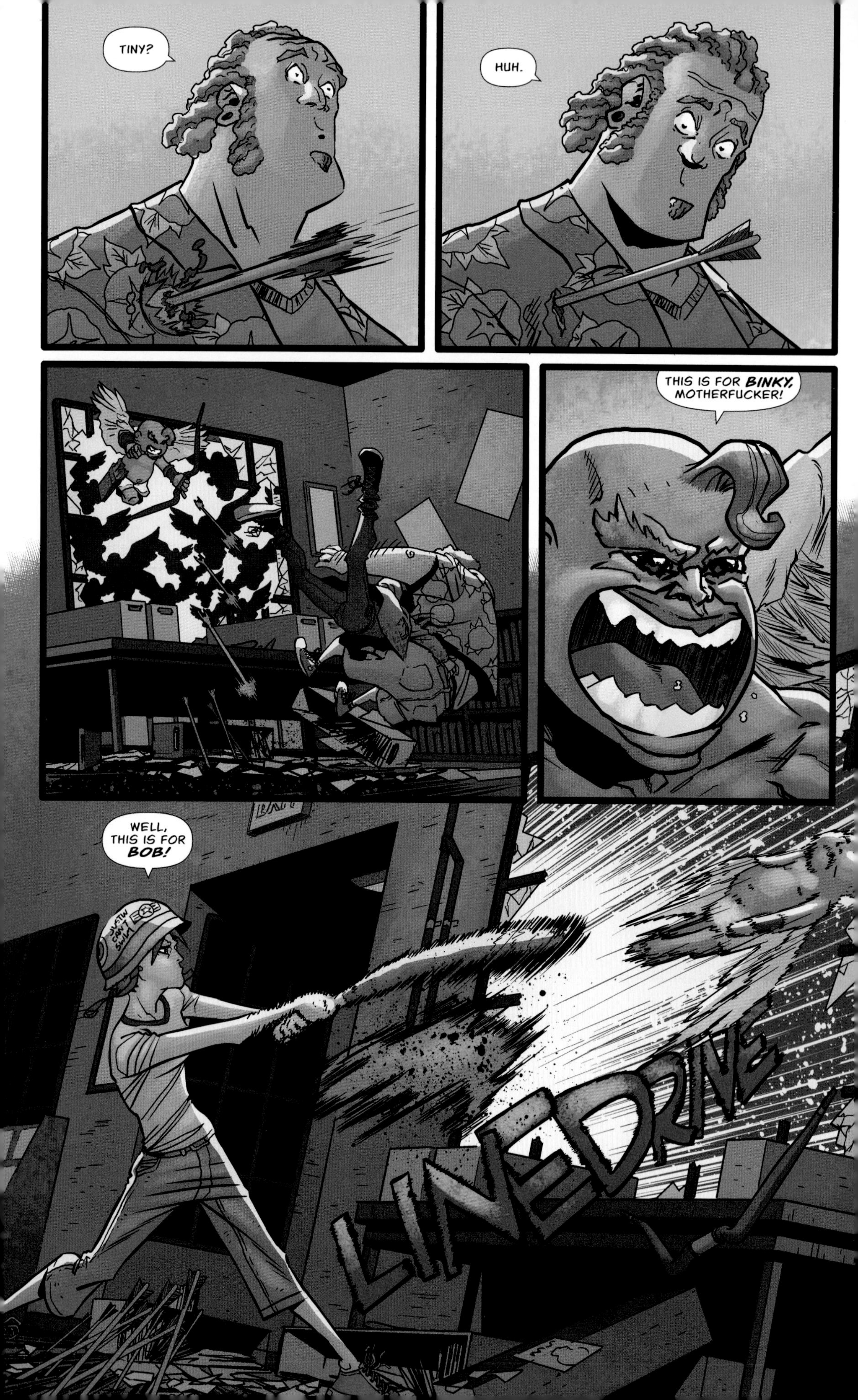

TINY?
HUH.
THIS IS FOR BINKY, MOTHERFUCKER!
WELL, THIS IS FOR BOB!
JUSTIN CAN'T SWIM
LINEDRIVE

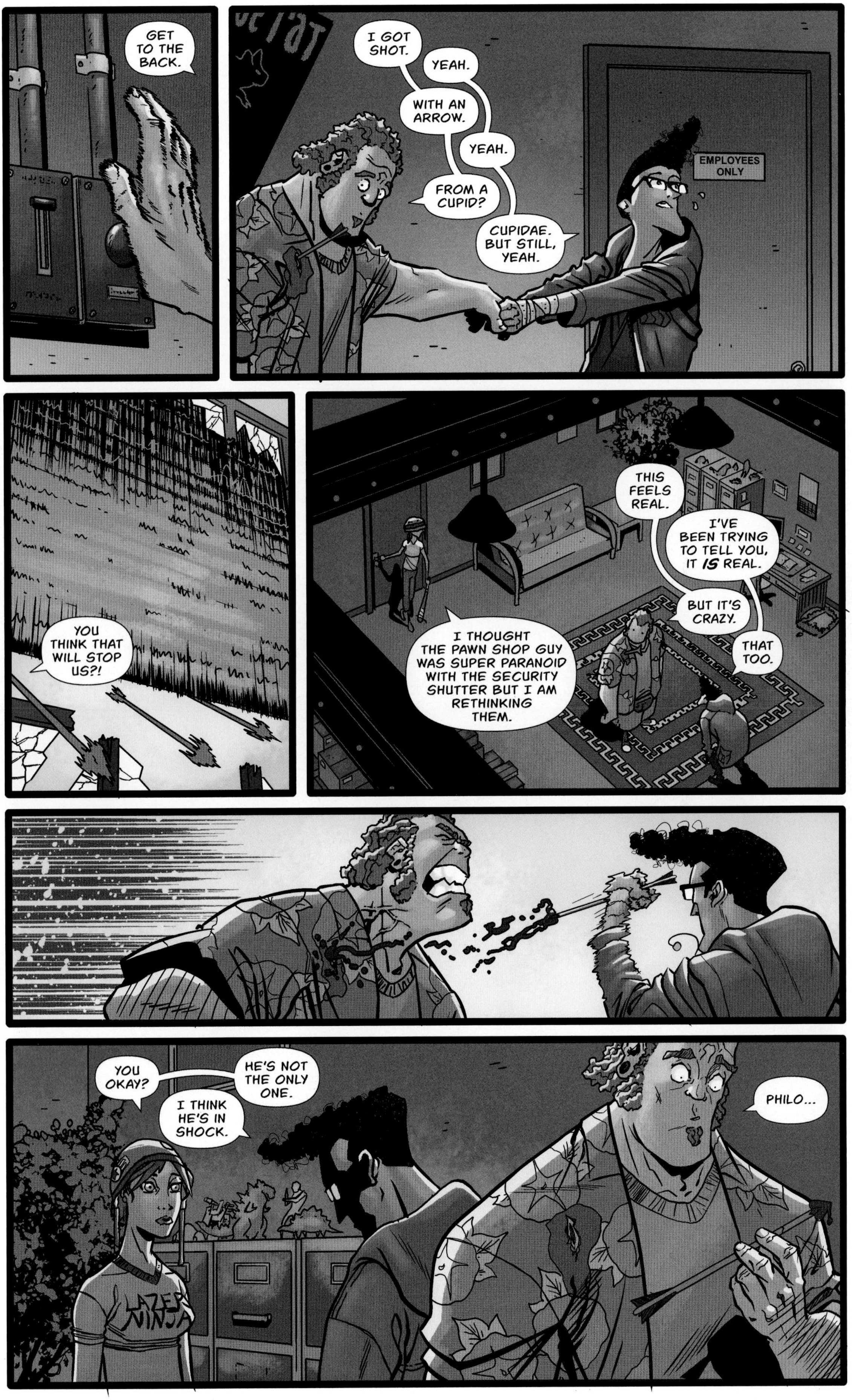
GET TO THE BACK.
I GOT SHOT.
YEAH.
WITH AN ARROW.
YEAH.
FROM A CUPID?
CUPIDAE. BUT STILL, YEAH.
EMPLOYEES ONLY
YOU THINK THAT WILL STOP US?!
THIS FEELS REAL.
I'VE BEEN TRYING TO TELL YOU, IT *IS* REAL.
BUT IT'S CRAZY.
THAT TOO.
I THOUGHT THE PAWN SHOP GUY WAS SUPER PARANOID WITH THE SECURITY SHUTTER BUT I AM RETHINKING THEM.
YOU OKAY?
HE'S NOT THE ONLY ONE.
I THINK HE'S IN SHOCK.
PHILO...
LAZER NINJA

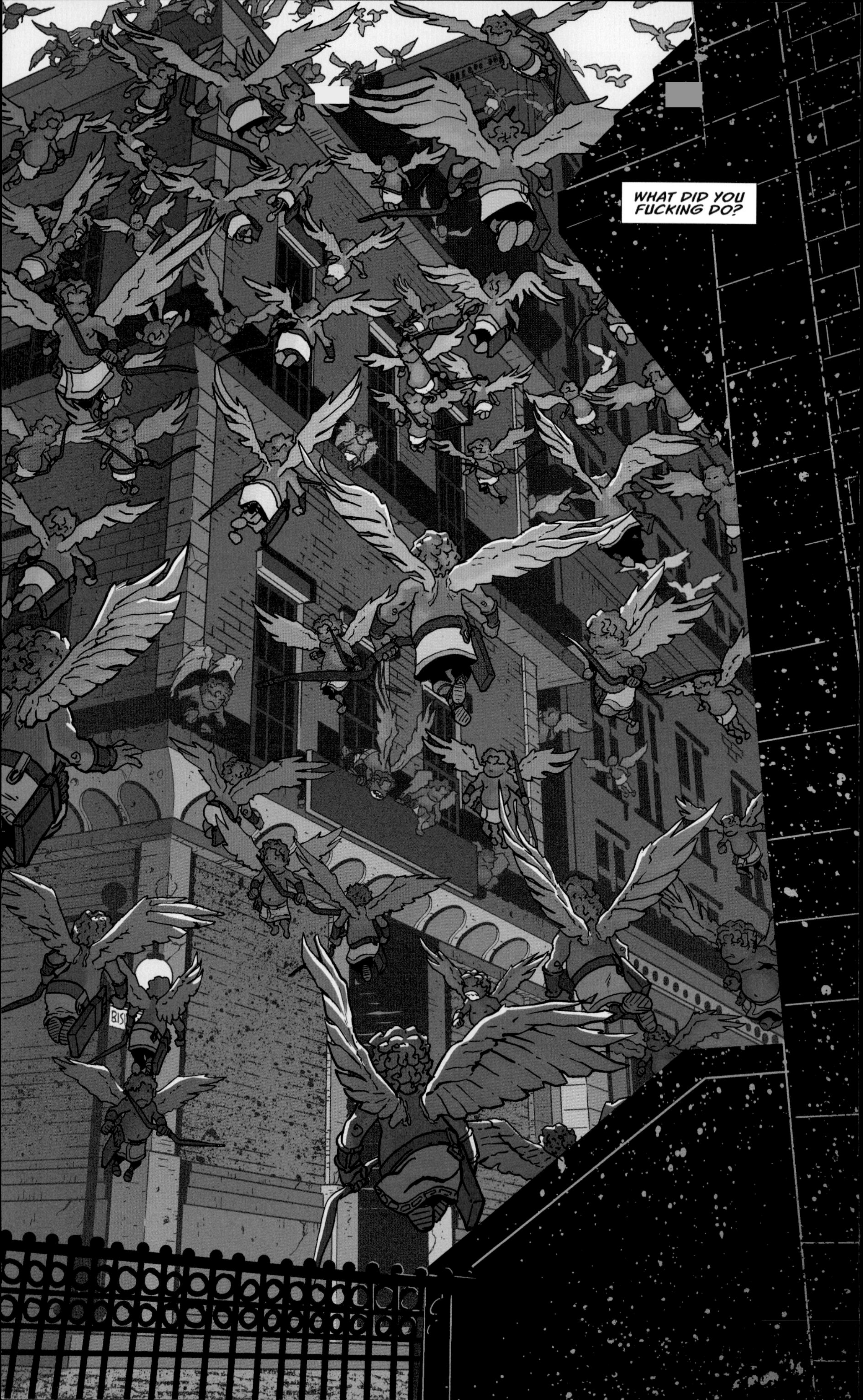
WHAT DID YOU FUCKING DO?

Four

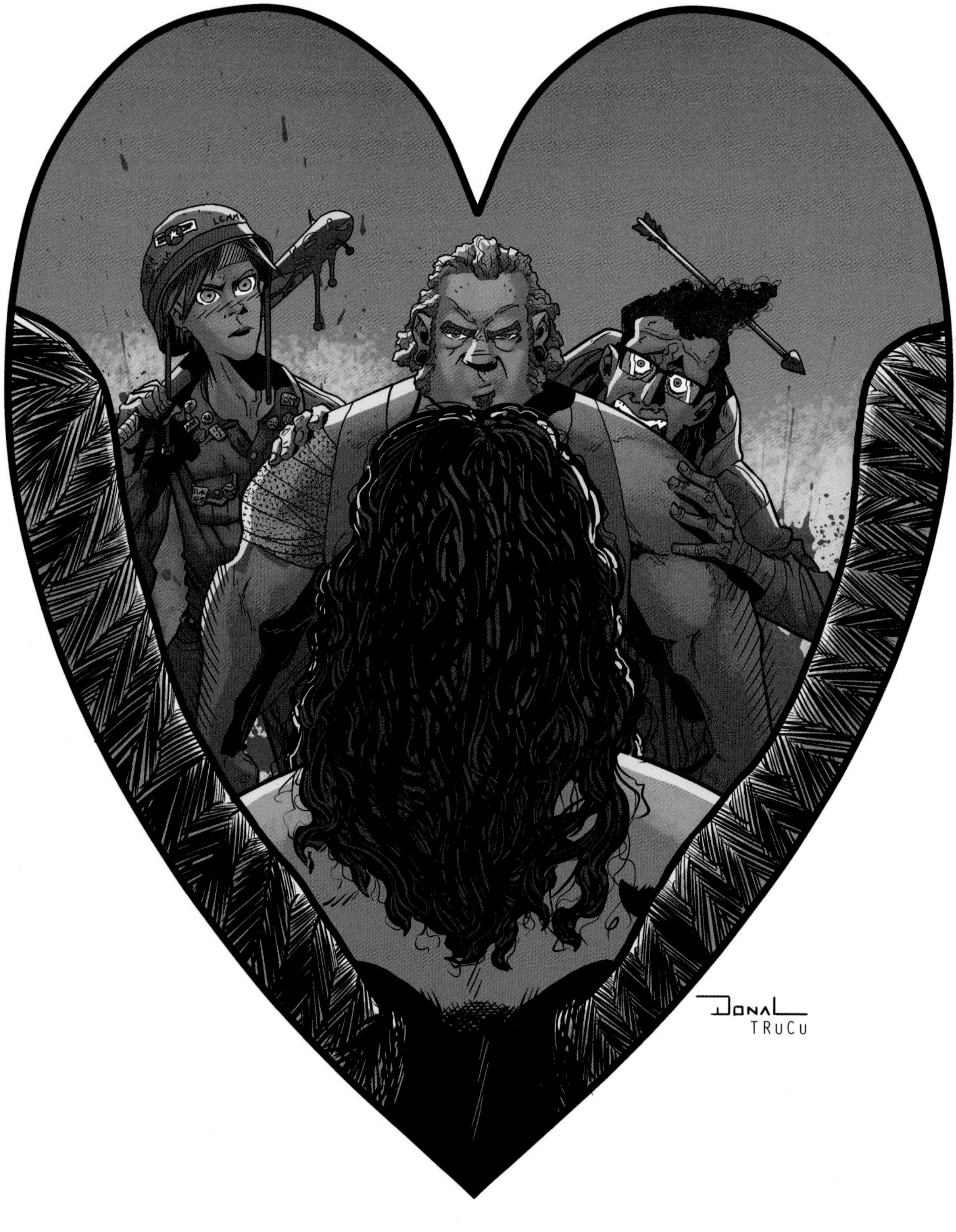
DONAL
TRUCU

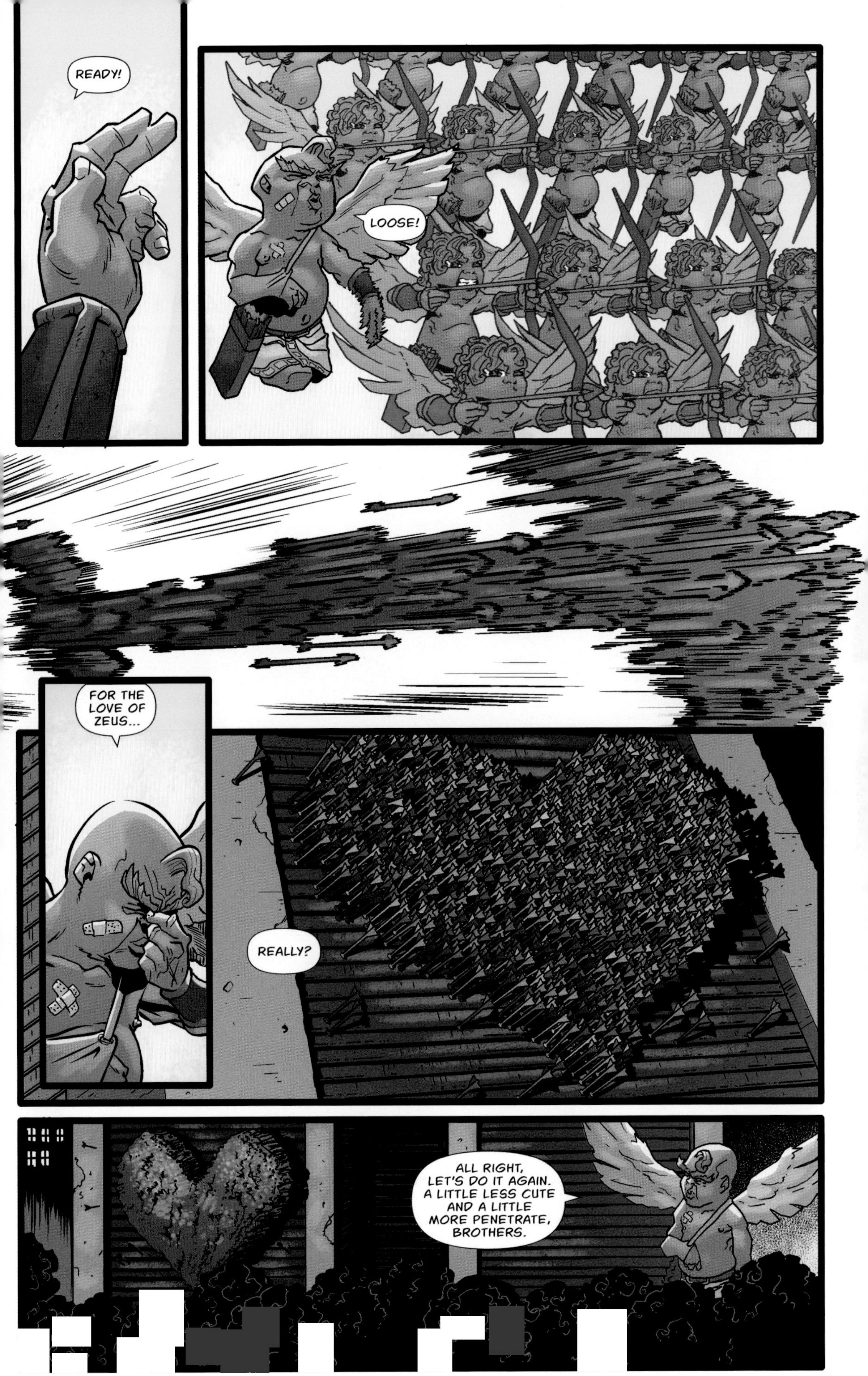
READY!
LOOSE!
FOR THE LOVE OF ZEUS...
REALLY?
ALL RIGHT, LET'S DO IT AGAIN. A LITTLE LESS CUTE AND A LITTLE MORE PENETRATE, BROTHERS.

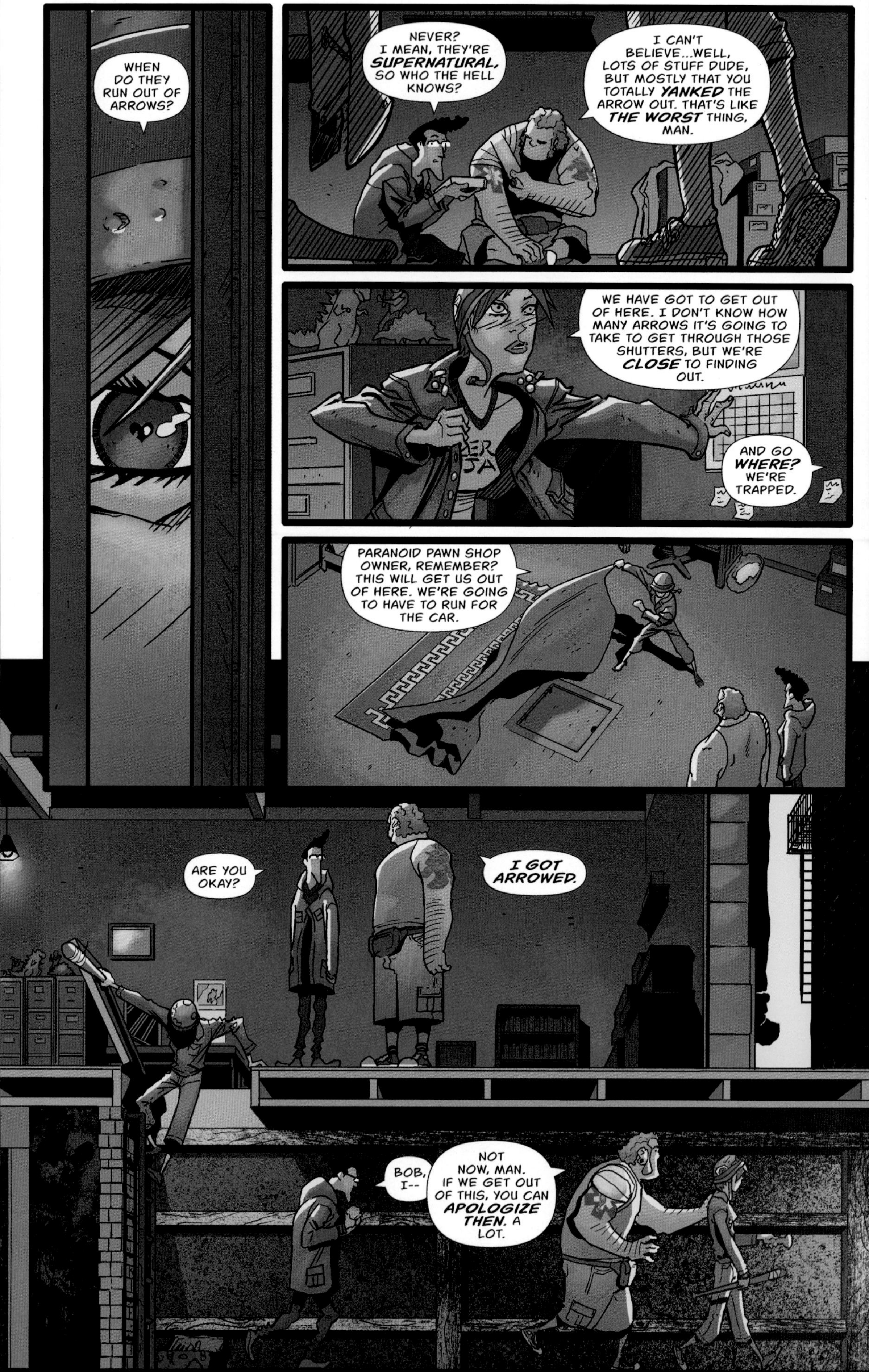

WHEN DO THEY RUN OUT OF ARROWS?
NEVER? I MEAN, THEY'RE SUPERNATURAL, SO WHO THE HELL KNOWS?
I CAN'T BELIEVE...WELL, LOTS OF STUFF DUDE, BUT MOSTLY THAT YOU TOTALLY YANKED THE ARROW OUT. THAT'S LIKE THE WORST THING, MAN.
WE HAVE GOT TO GET OUT OF HERE. I DON'T KNOW HOW MANY ARROWS IT'S GOING TO TAKE TO GET THROUGH THOSE SHUTTERS, BUT WE'RE CLOSE TO FINDING OUT.
AND GO WHERE? WE'RE TRAPPED.
PARANOID PAWN SHOP OWNER, REMEMBER? THIS WILL GET US OUT OF HERE. WE'RE GOING TO HAVE TO RUN FOR THE CAR.
ARE YOU OKAY?
I GOT ARROWED.
BOB, I--
NOT NOW, MAN. IF WE GET OUT OF THIS, YOU CAN APOLOGIZE THEN. A LOT.

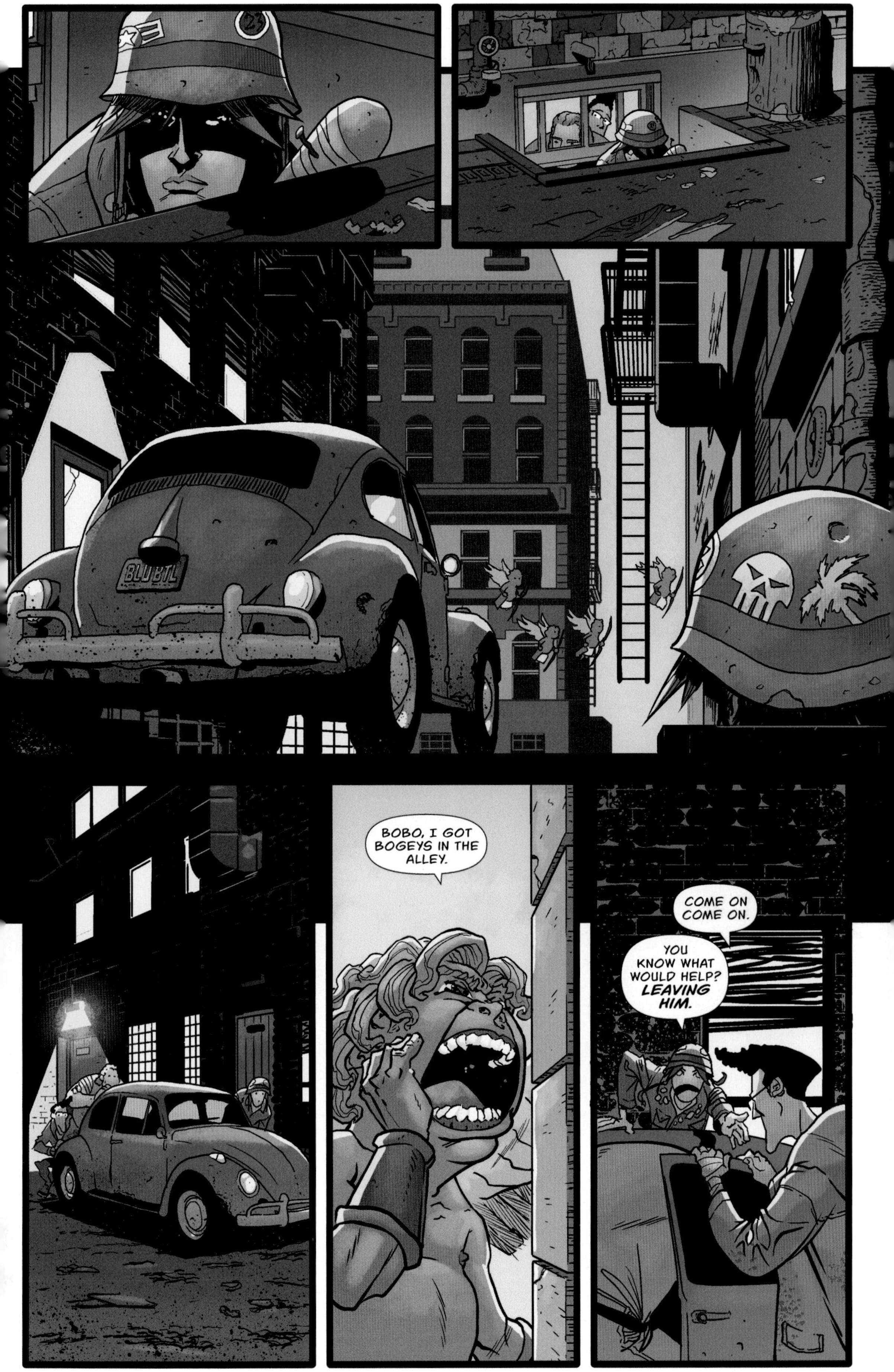
BLU BTL
BOBO, I GOT BOGEYS IN THE ALLEY.
COME ON COME ON.
YOU KNOW WHAT WOULD HELP? **LEAVING HIM.**

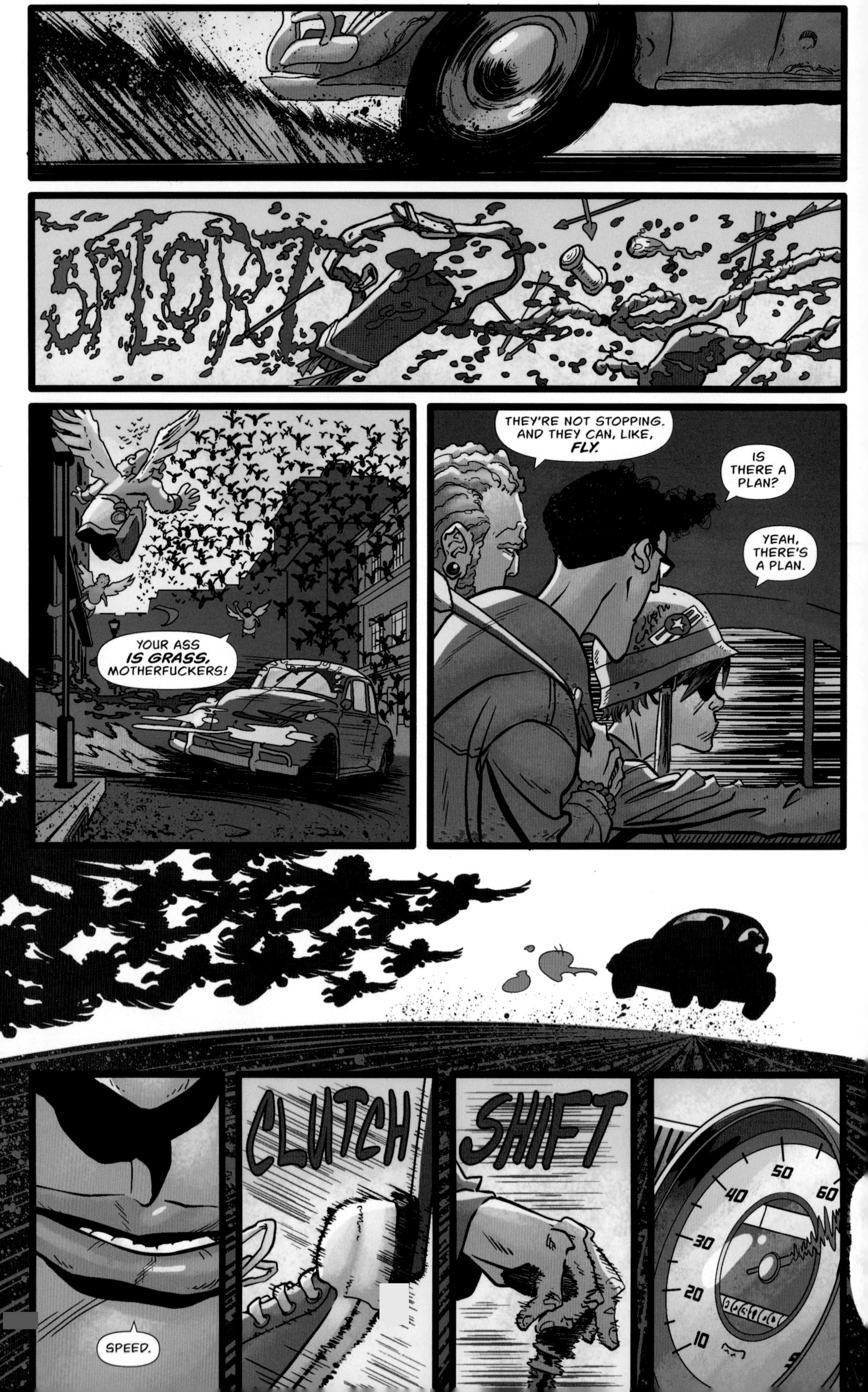
SPLORT
YOUR ASS IS GRASS, MOTHERFUCKERS!
THEY'RE NOT STOPPING. AND THEY CAN, LIKE, FLY.
IS THERE A PLAN?
YEAH, THERE'S A PLAN.
SPEED.
CLUTCH
SHIFT
10 20 30 40 50 60

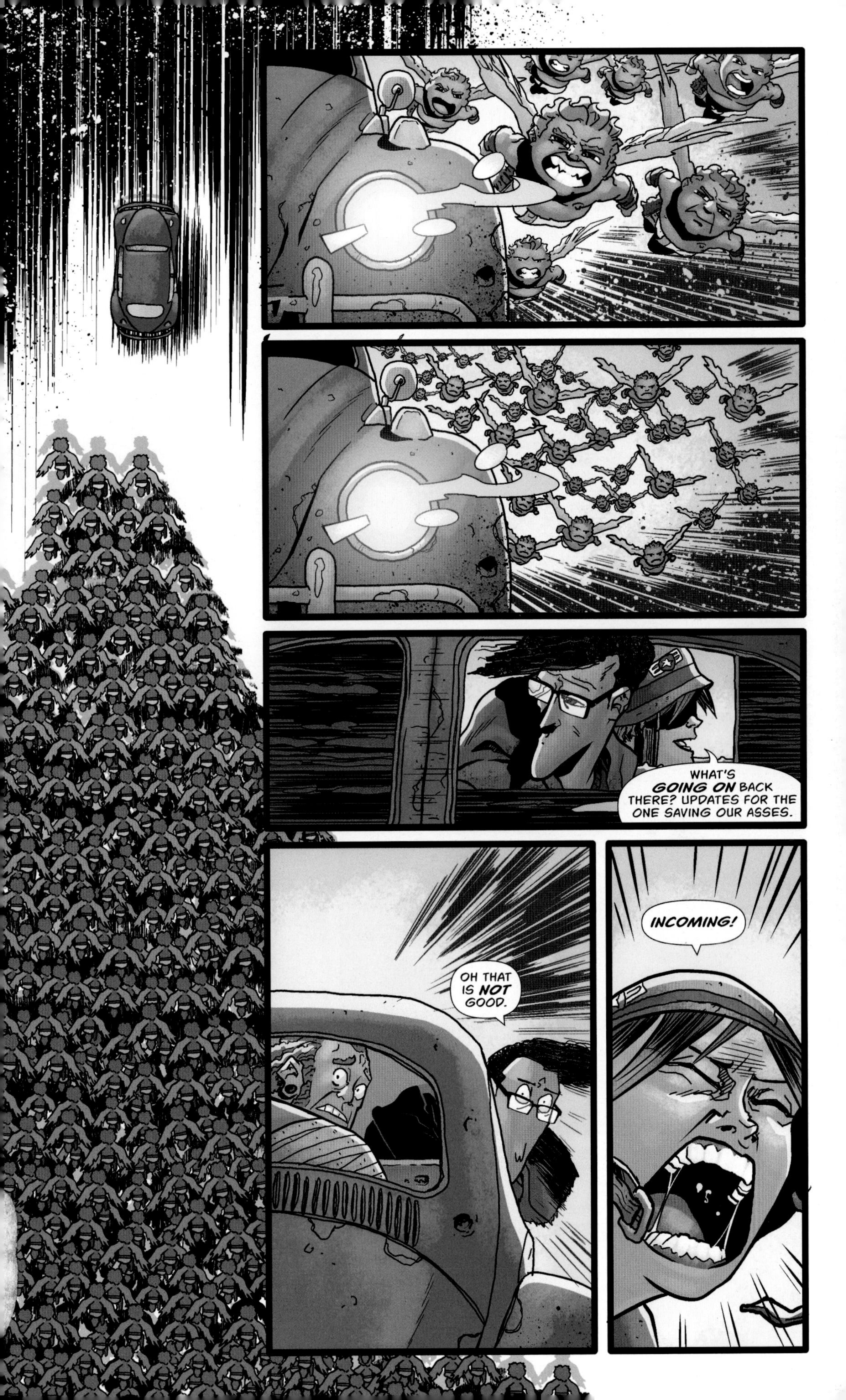
WHAT'S **GOING ON** BACK THERE? UPDATES FOR THE ONE SAVING OUR ASSES.
OH THAT IS **NOT** GOOD.
INCOMING!

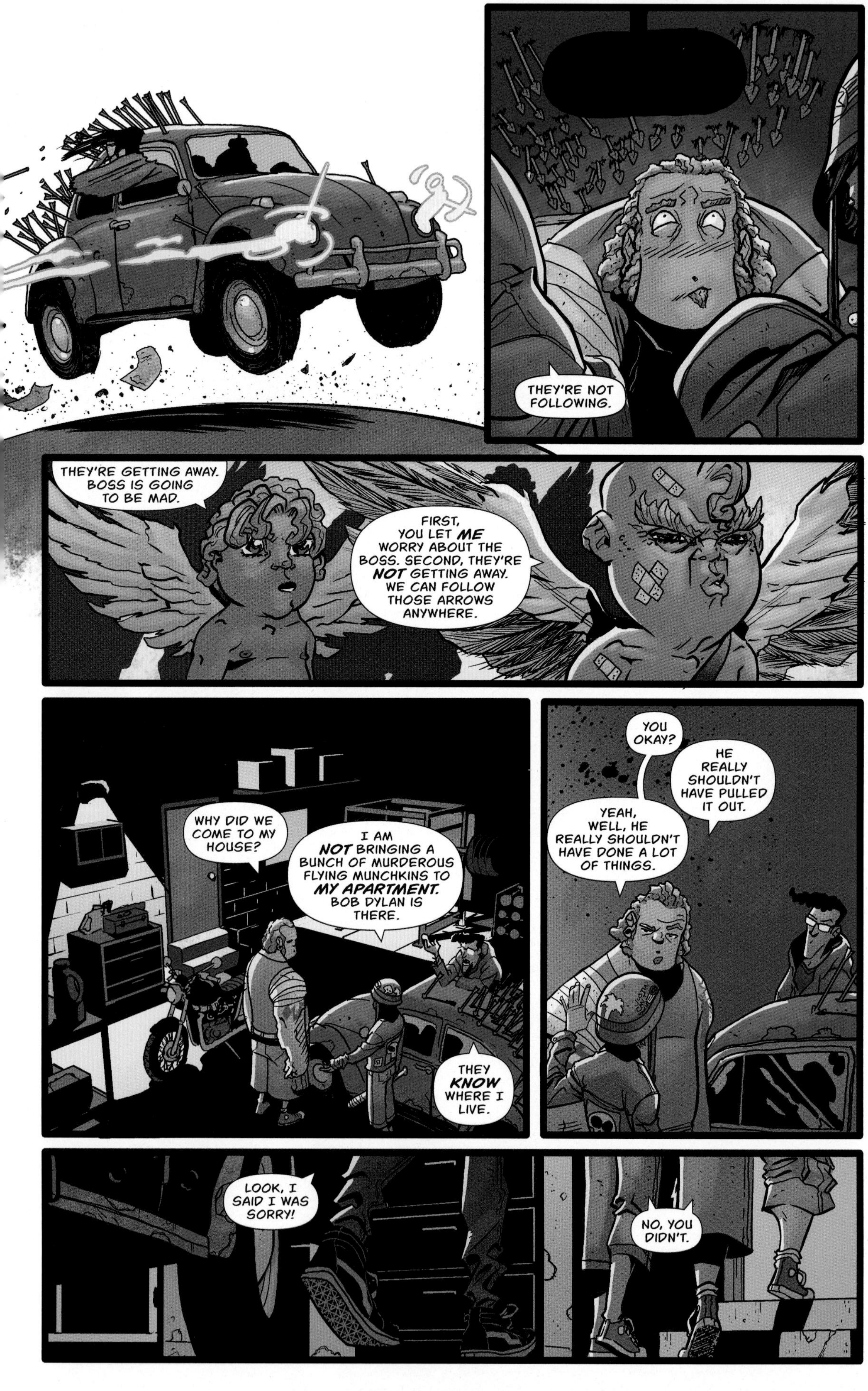
THEY'RE NOT FOLLOWING.
THEY'RE GETTING AWAY. BOSS IS GOING TO BE MAD.
FIRST, YOU LET **ME** WORRY ABOUT THE BOSS. SECOND, THEY'RE **NOT** GETTING AWAY. WE CAN FOLLOW THOSE ARROWS ANYWHERE.
WHY DID WE COME TO MY HOUSE?
I AM **NOT** BRINGING A BUNCH OF MURDEROUS FLYING MUNCHKINS TO **MY APARTMENT.** BOB DYLAN IS THERE.
THEY **KNOW** WHERE I LIVE.
YOU OKAY?
HE REALLY SHOULDN'T HAVE PULLED IT OUT.
YEAH, WELL, HE REALLY SHOULDN'T HAVE DONE A LOT OF THINGS.
LOOK, I SAID I WAS SORRY!
NO, YOU DIDN'T.

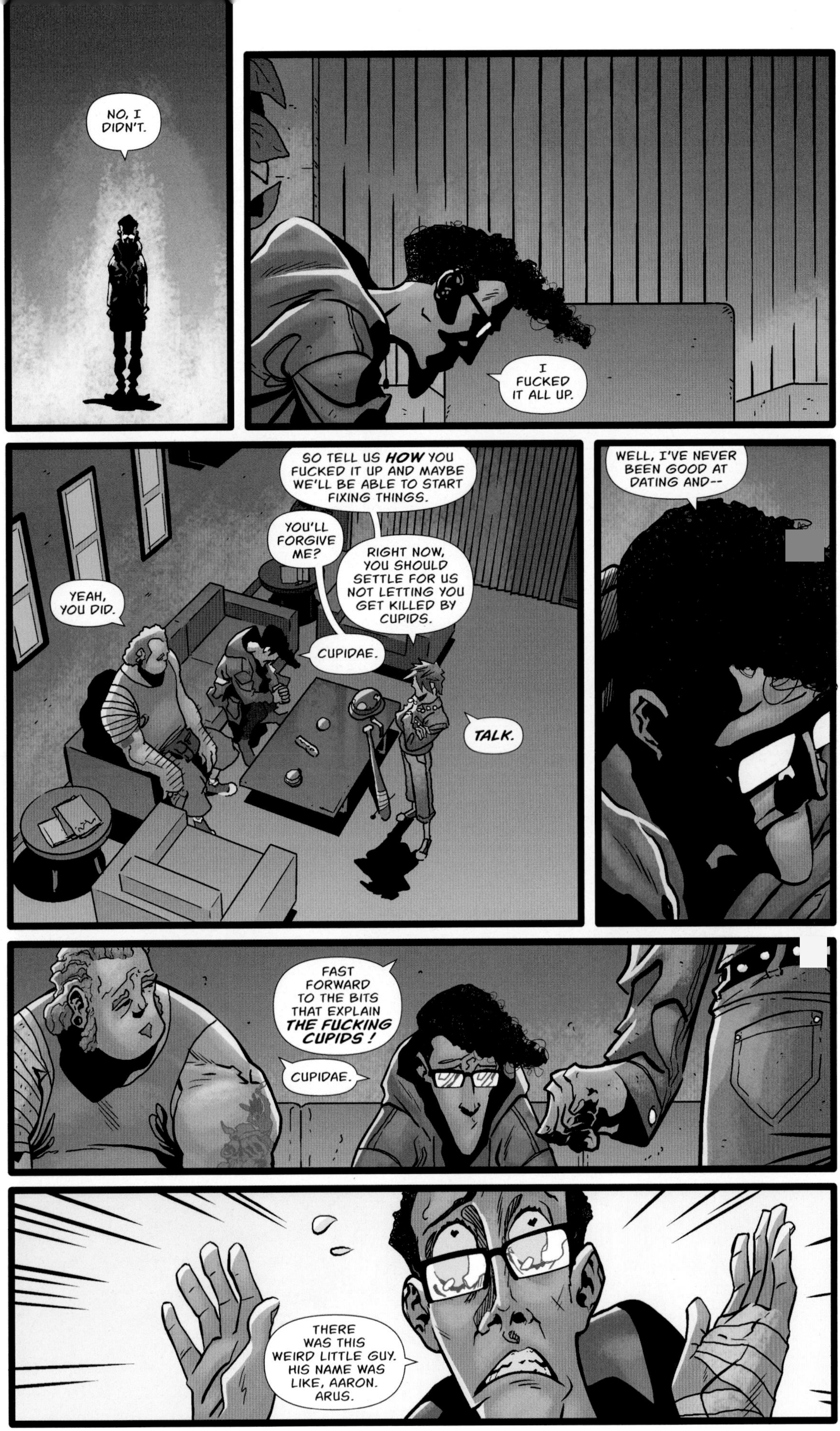
NO, I DIDN'T.
I FUCKED IT ALL UP.
YEAH, YOU DID.
SO TELL US HOW YOU FUCKED IT UP AND MAYBE WE'LL BE ABLE TO START FIXING THINGS.
YOU'LL FORGIVE ME?
RIGHT NOW, YOU SHOULD SETTLE FOR US NOT LETTING YOU GET KILLED BY CUPIDS.
CUPIDAE.
TALK.
WELL, I'VE NEVER BEEN GOOD AT DATING AND--
FAST FORWARD TO THE BITS THAT EXPLAIN THE FUCKING CUPIDS!
CUPIDAE.
THERE WAS THIS WEIRD LITTLE GUY. HIS NAME WAS LIKE, AARON. ARUS.

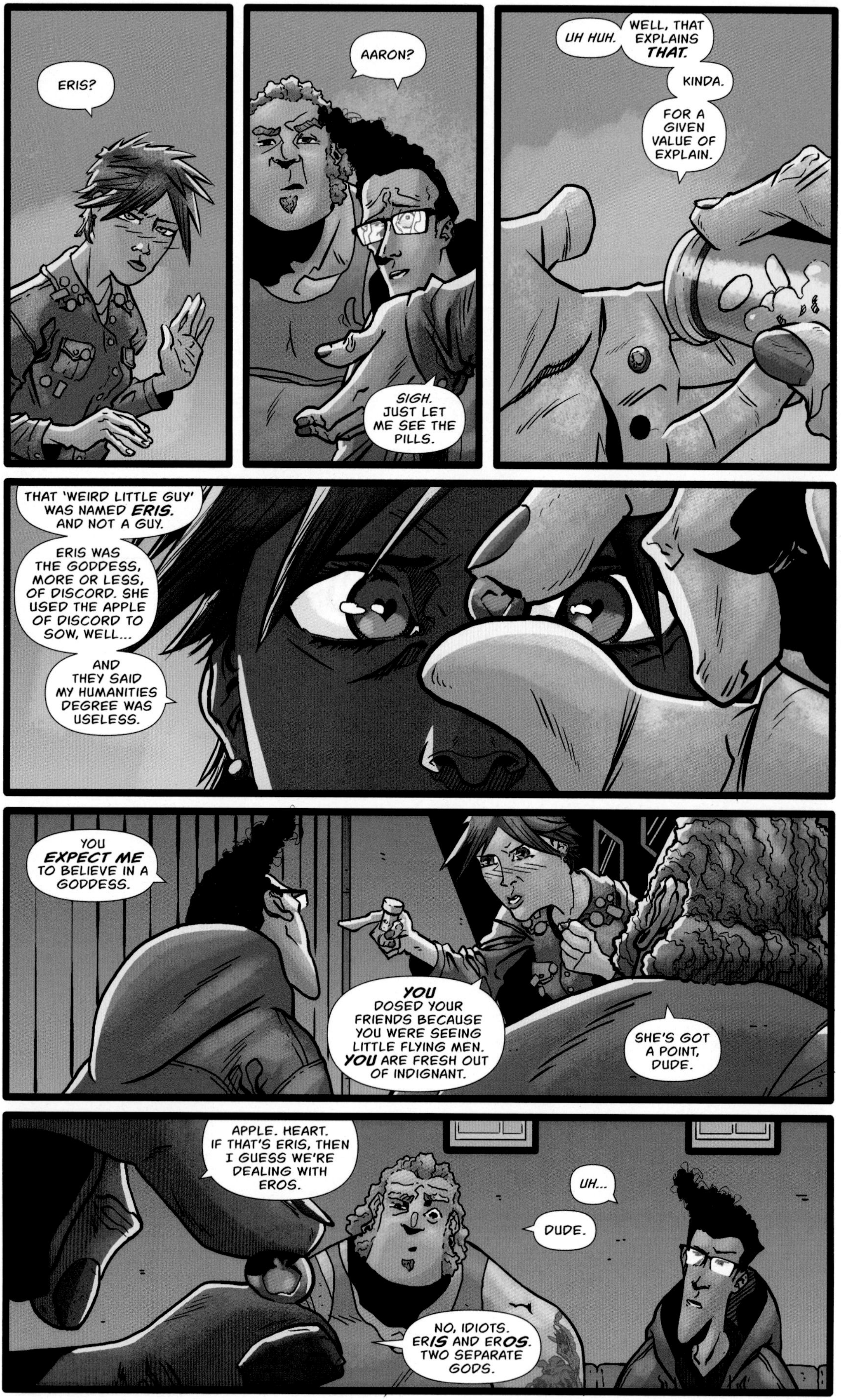
ERIS?
AARON?
SIGH. JUST LET ME SEE THE PILLS.
UH HUH.
WELL, THAT EXPLAINS THAT.
KINDA.
FOR A GIVEN VALUE OF EXPLAIN.
THAT 'WEIRD LITTLE GUY' WAS NAMED ERIS. AND NOT A GUY.
ERIS WAS THE GODDESS, MORE OR LESS, OF DISCORD. SHE USED THE APPLE OF DISCORD TO SOW, WELL...
AND THEY SAID MY HUMANITIES DEGREE WAS USELESS.
YOU EXPECT ME TO BELIEVE IN A GODDESS.
YOU DOSED YOUR FRIENDS BECAUSE YOU WERE SEEING LITTLE FLYING MEN. YOU ARE FRESH OUT OF INDIGNANT.
SHE'S GOT A POINT, DUDE.
APPLE. HEART. IF THAT'S ERIS, THEN I GUESS WE'RE DEALING WITH EROS.
UH...
DUDE.
NO, IDIOTS. ERIS AND EROS. TWO SEPARATE GODS.

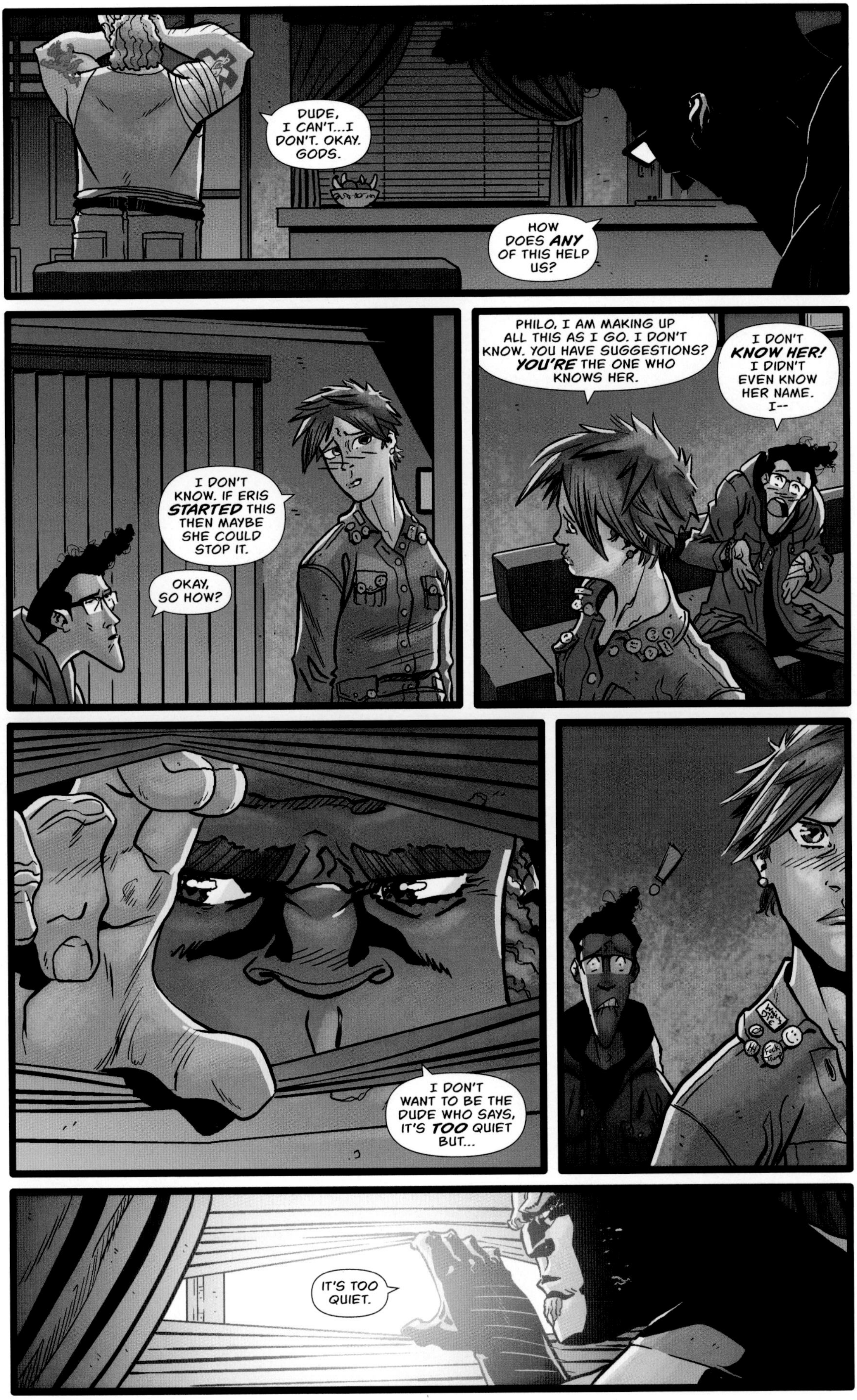
DUDE, I CAN'T...I DON'T. OKAY. GODS.
HOW DOES **ANY** OF THIS HELP US?
I DON'T KNOW. IF ERIS **STARTED** THIS THEN MAYBE SHE COULD STOP IT.
OKAY, SO HOW?
PHILO, I AM MAKING UP ALL THIS AS I GO. I DON'T KNOW. YOU HAVE SUGGESTIONS? **YOU'RE** THE ONE WHO KNOWS HER.
I DON'T **KNOW HER!** I DIDN'T EVEN KNOW HER NAME. I--
I DON'T WANT TO BE THE DUDE WHO SAYS, IT'S **TOO** QUIET BUT...
IT'S TOO QUIET.

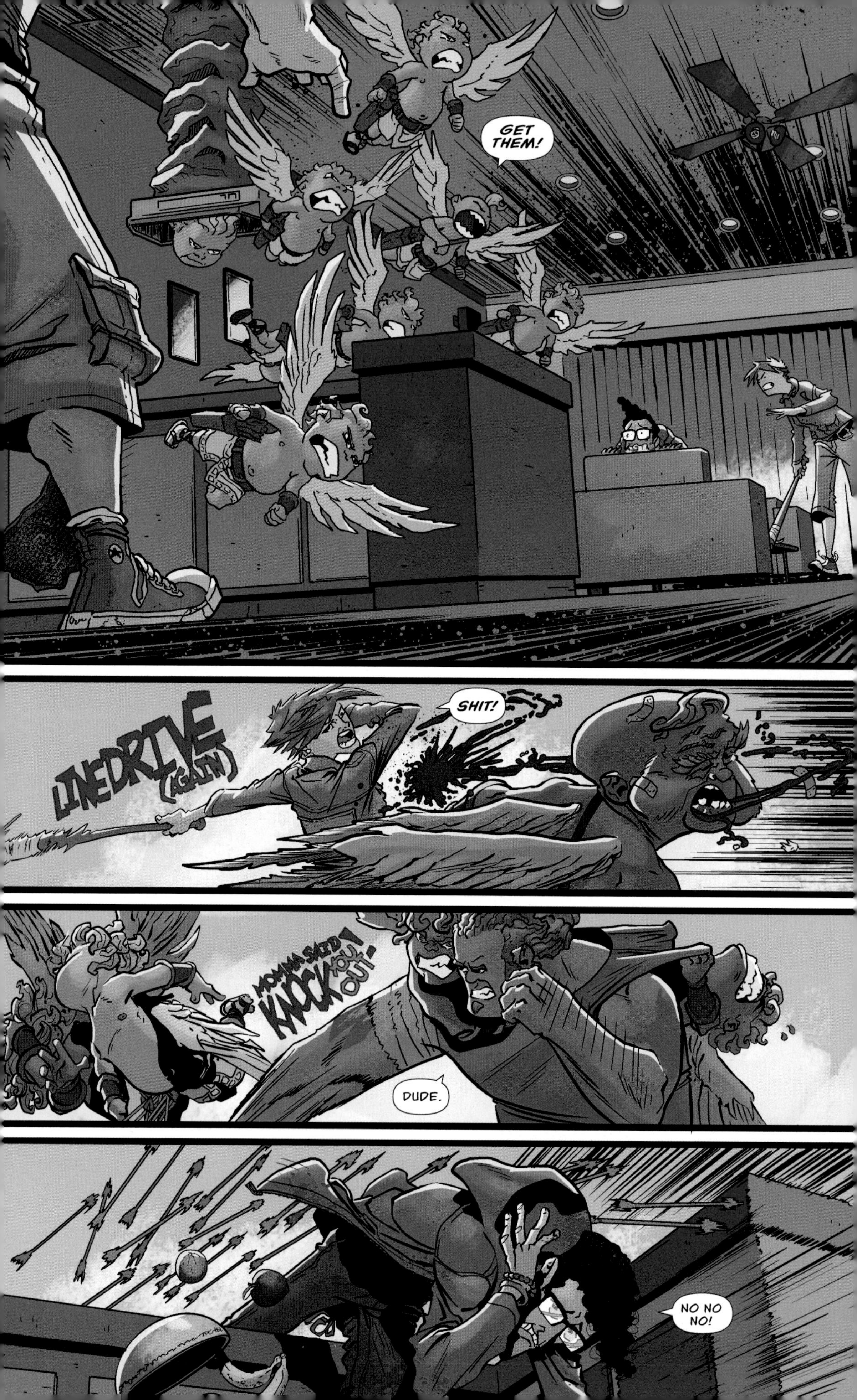
GET THEM!
LINEDRIVE (AGAIN)
SHIT!
MOMMA SAID KNOCK YOU OUT!
DUDE.
NO NO NO!

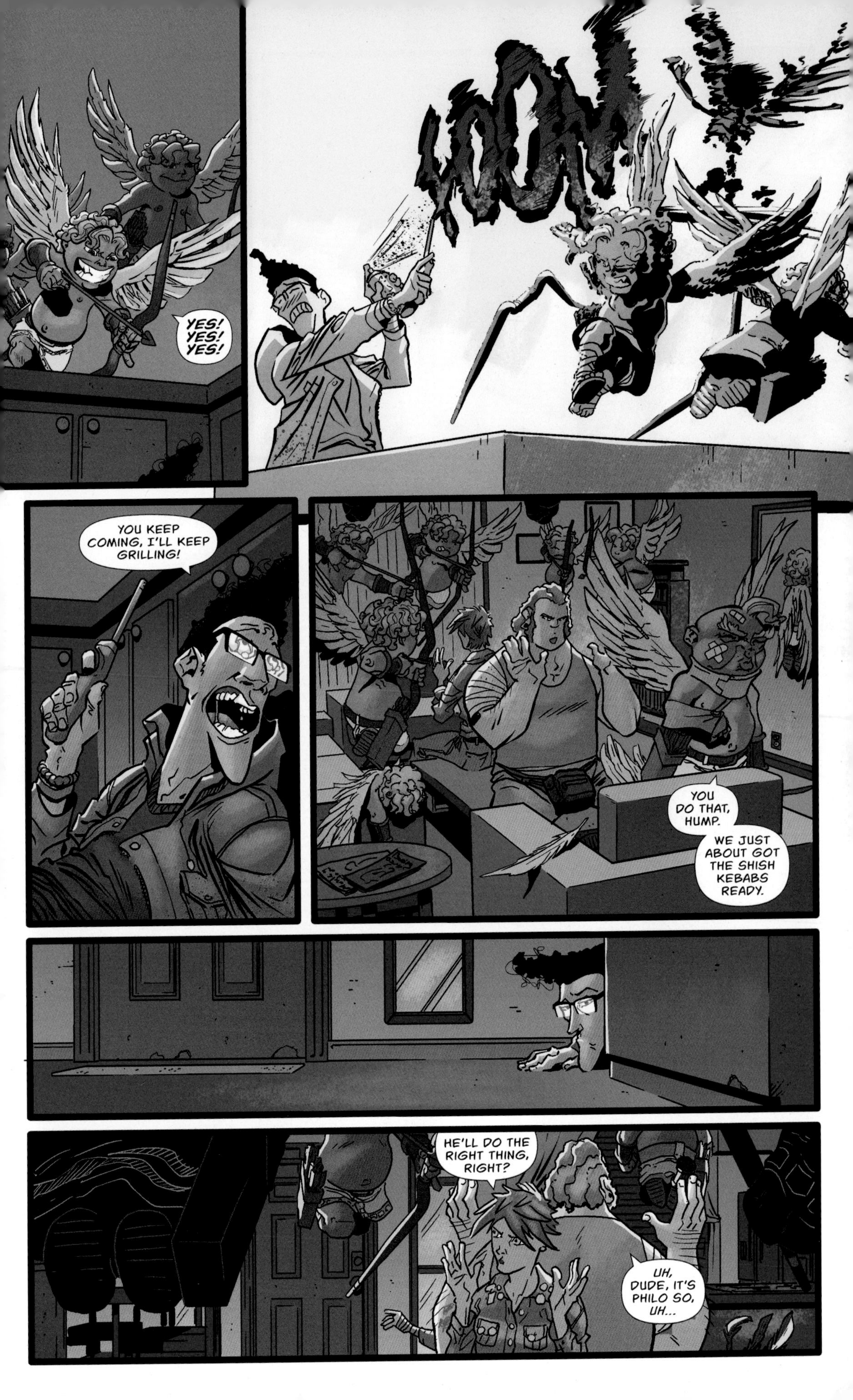
YES! YES! YES!
VOOM
YOU KEEP COMING, I'LL KEEP GRILLING!
YOU DO THAT, HUMP.
WE JUST ABOUT GOT THE SHISH KEBABS READY.
HE'LL DO THE RIGHT THING, RIGHT?
UH, DUDE, IT'S PHILO SO, UH...

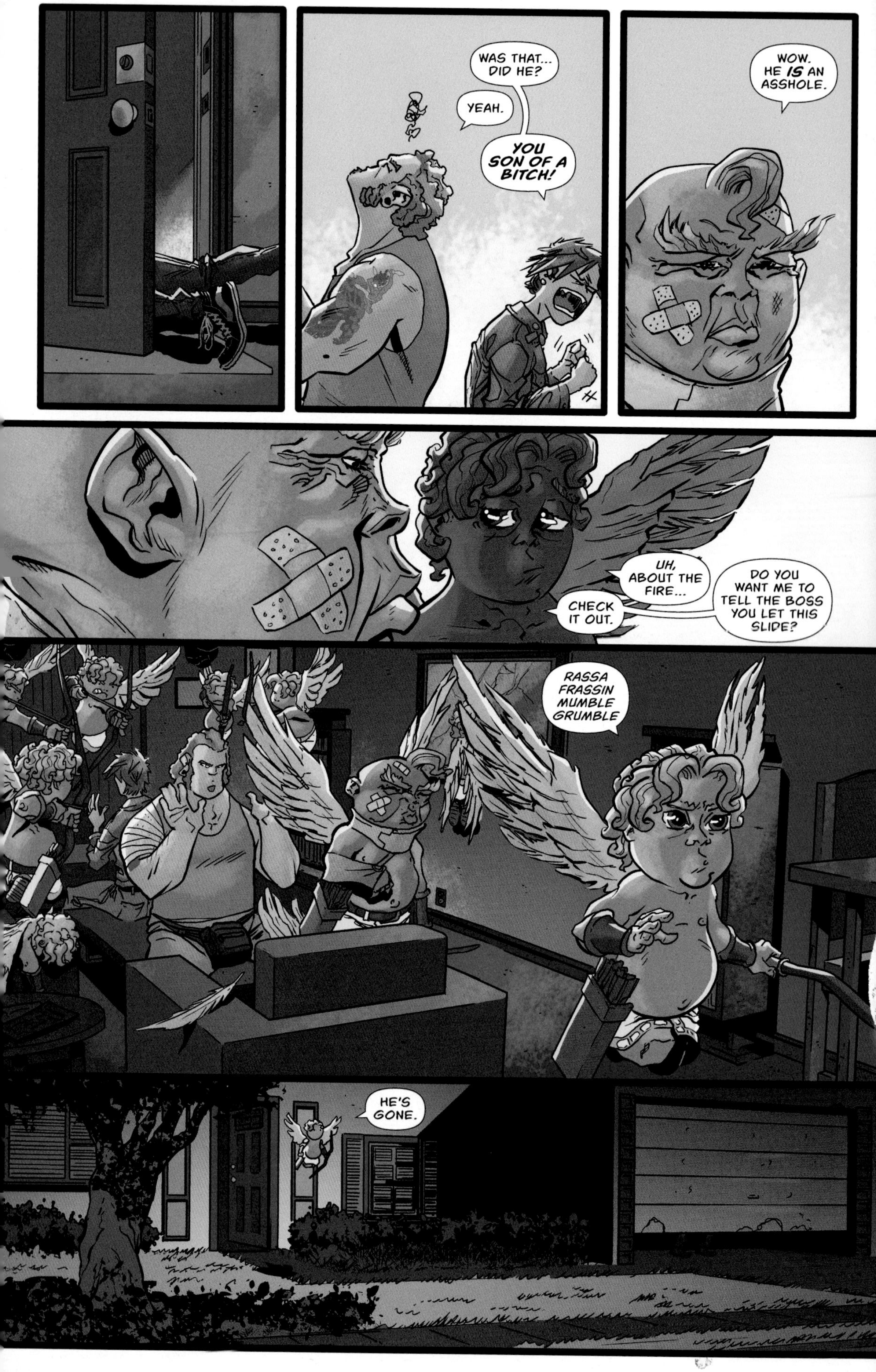
WAS THAT... DID HE?
YEAH.
YOU SON OF A BITCH!
WOW. HE IS AN ASSHOLE.
UH, ABOUT THE FIRE...
CHECK IT OUT.
DO YOU WANT ME TO TELL THE BOSS YOU LET THIS SLIDE?
RASSA FRASSIN MUMBLE GRUMBLE
HE'S GONE.

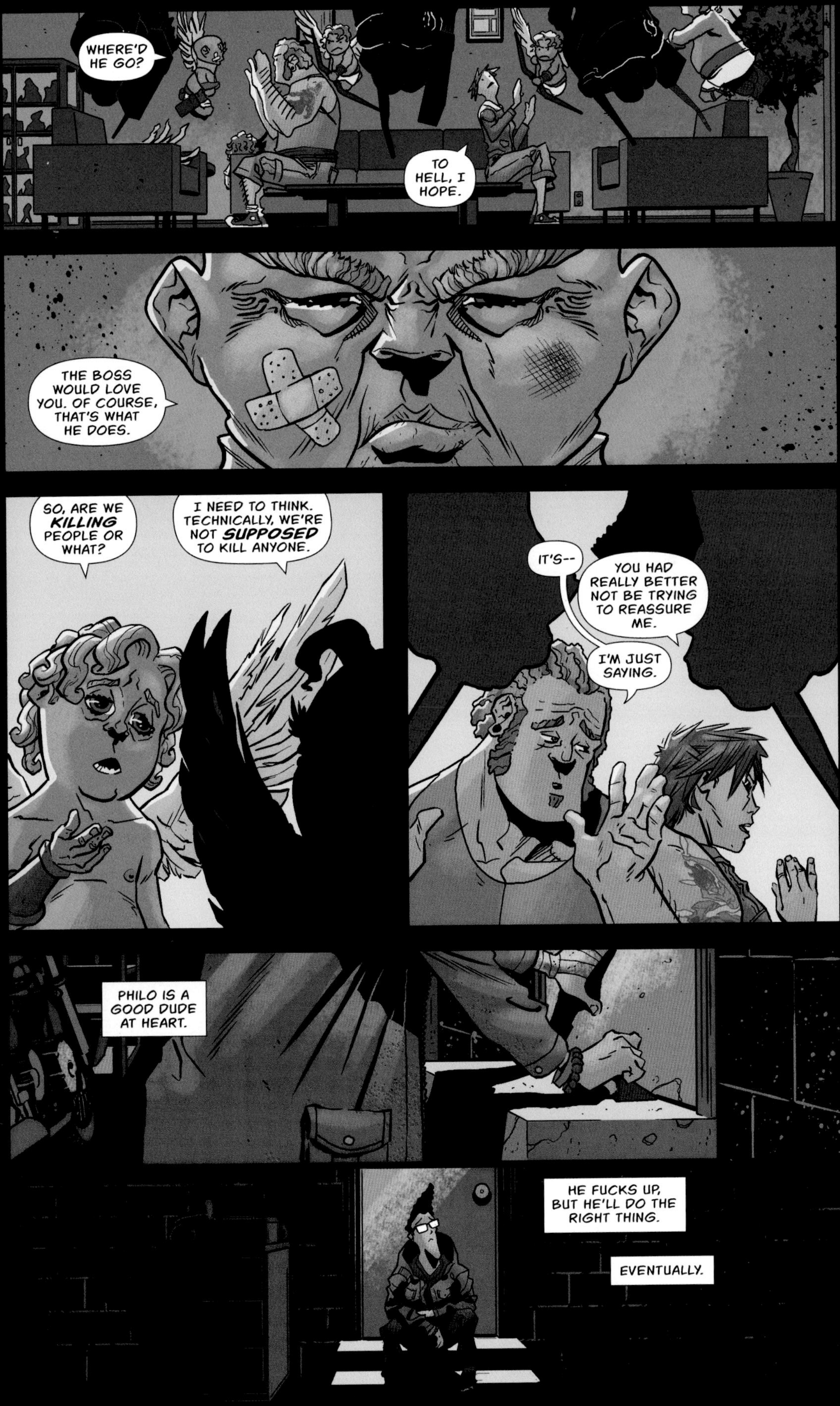
WHERE'D HE GO?
TO HELL, I HOPE.
THE BOSS WOULD LOVE YOU. OF COURSE, THAT'S WHAT HE DOES.
SO, ARE WE KILLING PEOPLE OR WHAT?
I NEED TO THINK. TECHNICALLY, WE'RE NOT SUPPOSED TO KILL ANYONE.
IT'S--
YOU HAD REALLY BETTER NOT BE TRYING TO REASSURE ME.
I'M JUST SAYING.
PHILO IS A GOOD DUDE AT HEART.
HE FUCKS UP, BUT HE'LL DO THE RIGHT THING.
EVENTUALLY.

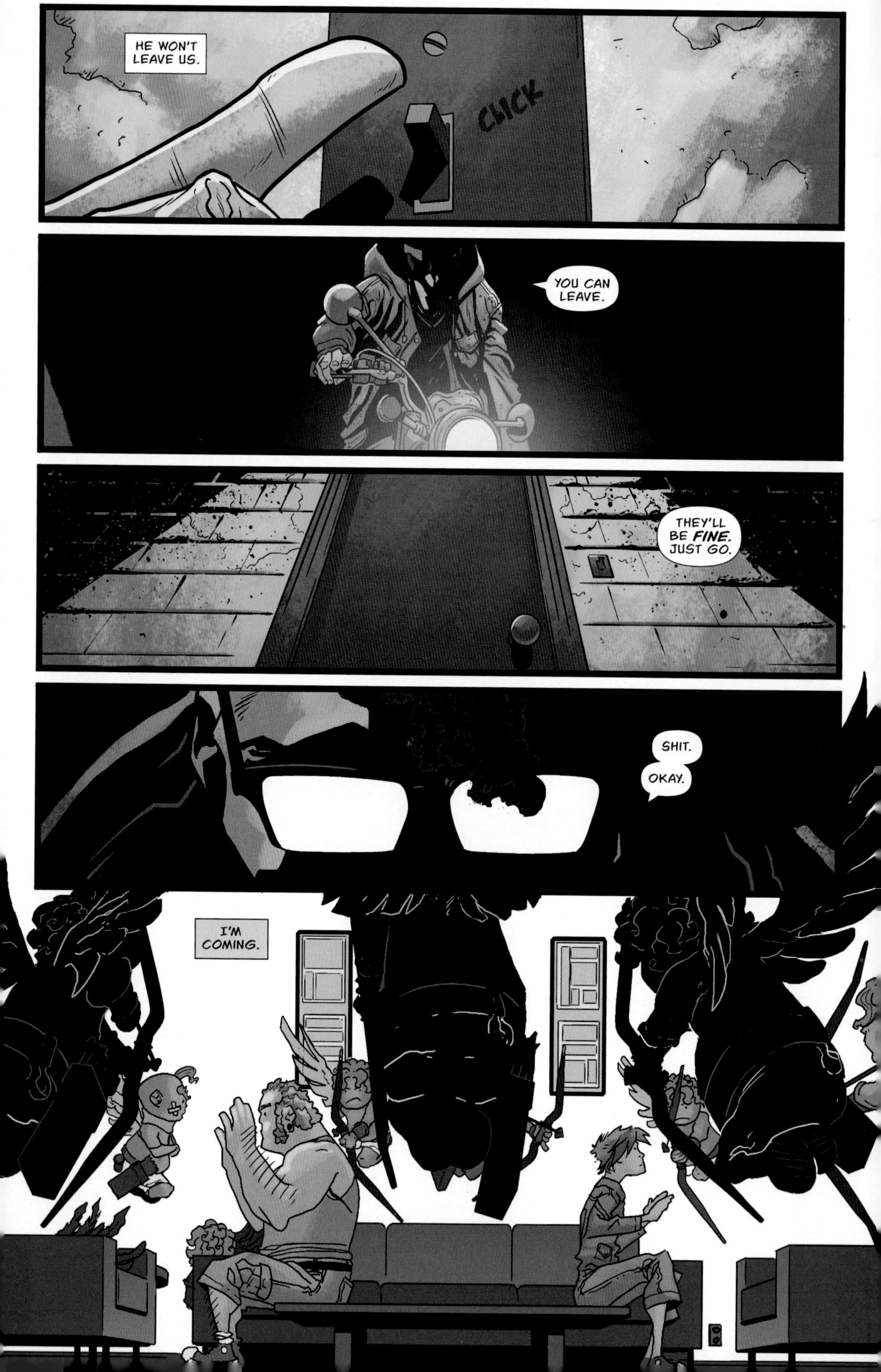
HE WON'T LEAVE US.
CLICK
YOU CAN LEAVE.
THEY'LL BE FINE. JUST GO.
SHIT.
OKAY.
I'M COMING.

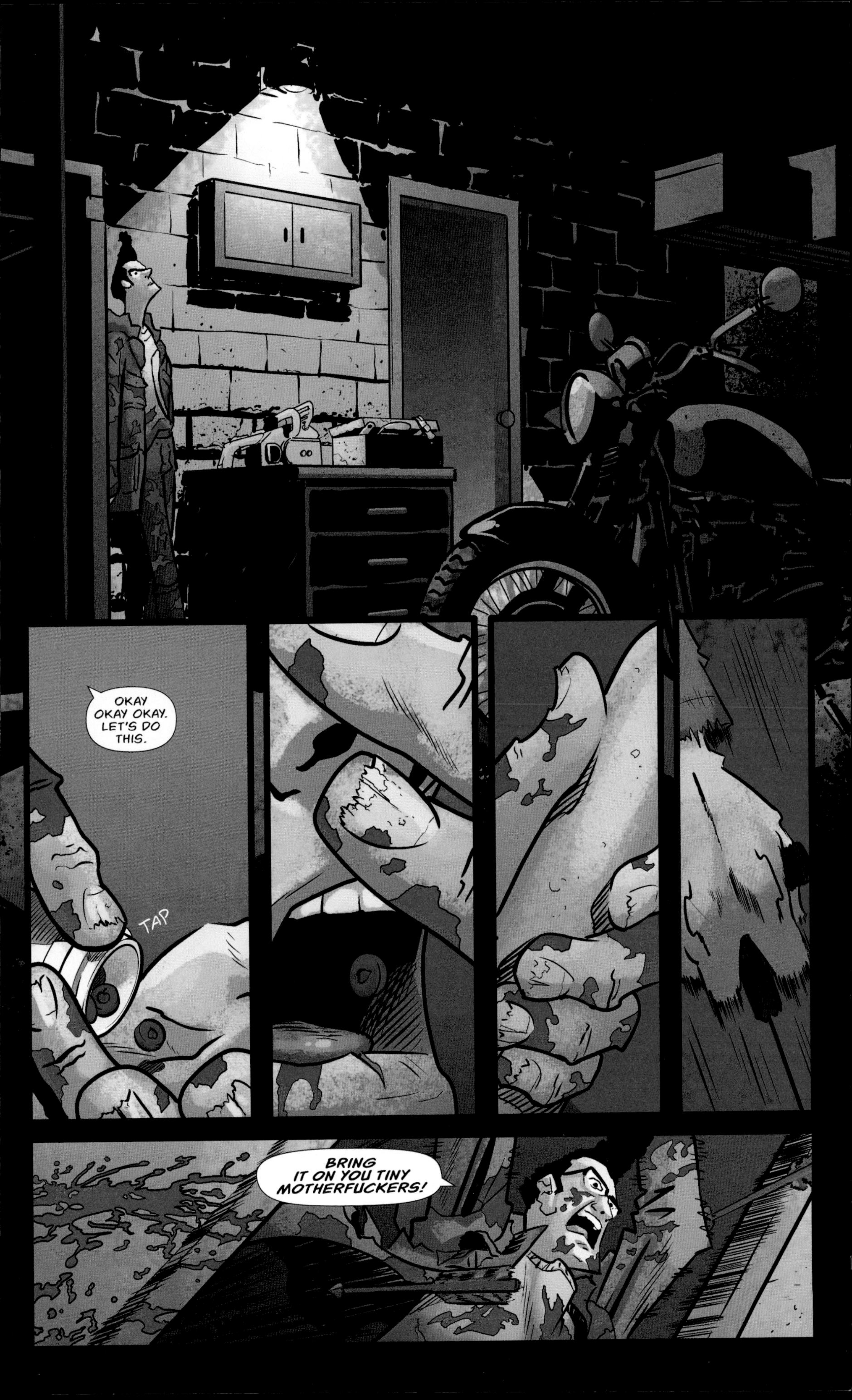
OKAY OKAY OKAY. LET'S DO THIS.
TAP
BRING IT ON YOU TINY MOTHERFUCKERS!

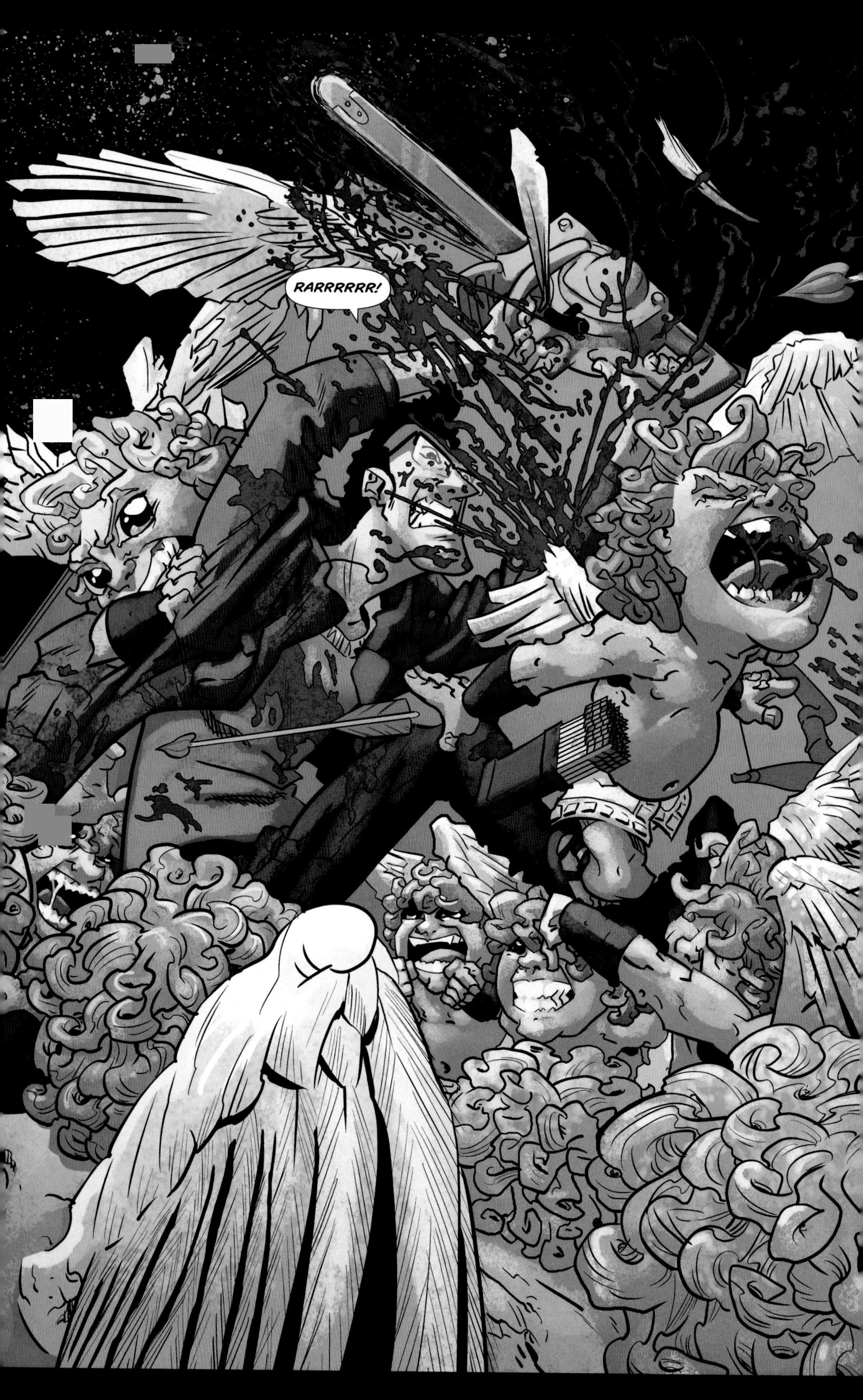
RARRRRRR!

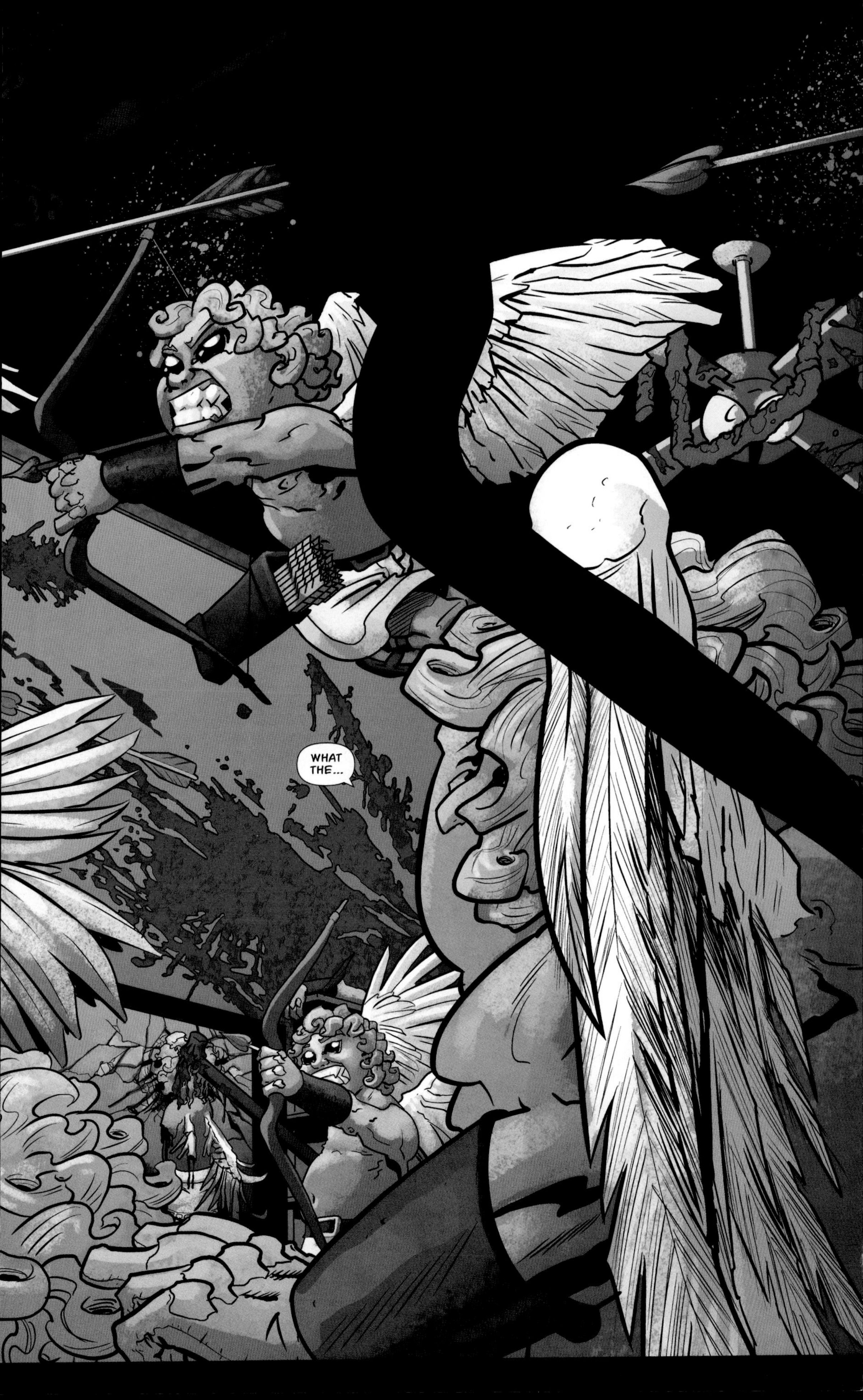
WHAT THE...

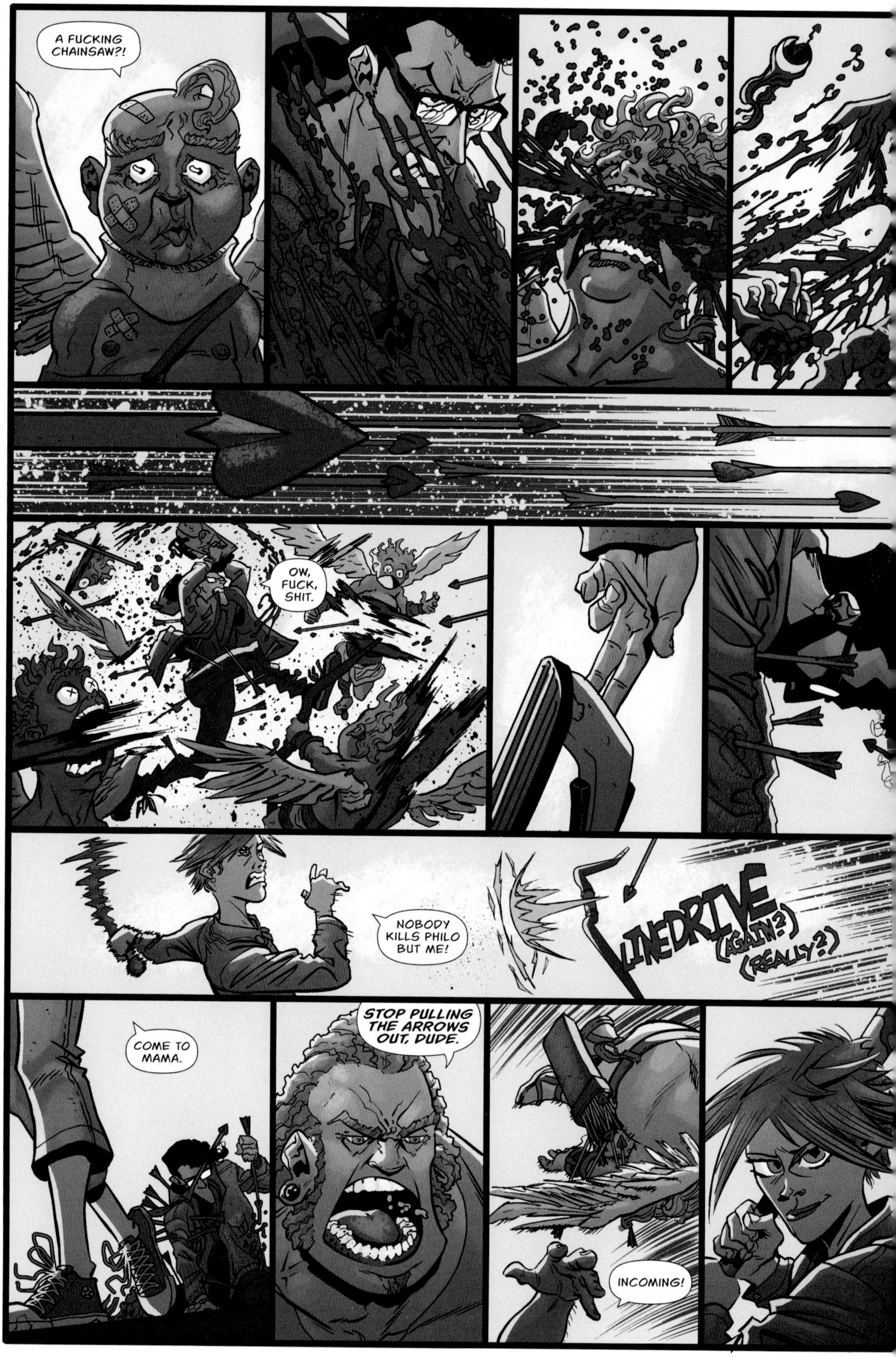
A FUCKING CHAINSAW?!
OW, FUCK, SHIT.
NOBODY KILLS PHILO BUT ME!
LINEDRIVE
(AGAIN?)
(REALLY?)
COME TO MAMA.
STOP PULLING THE ARROWS OUT, DUDE.
INCOMING!

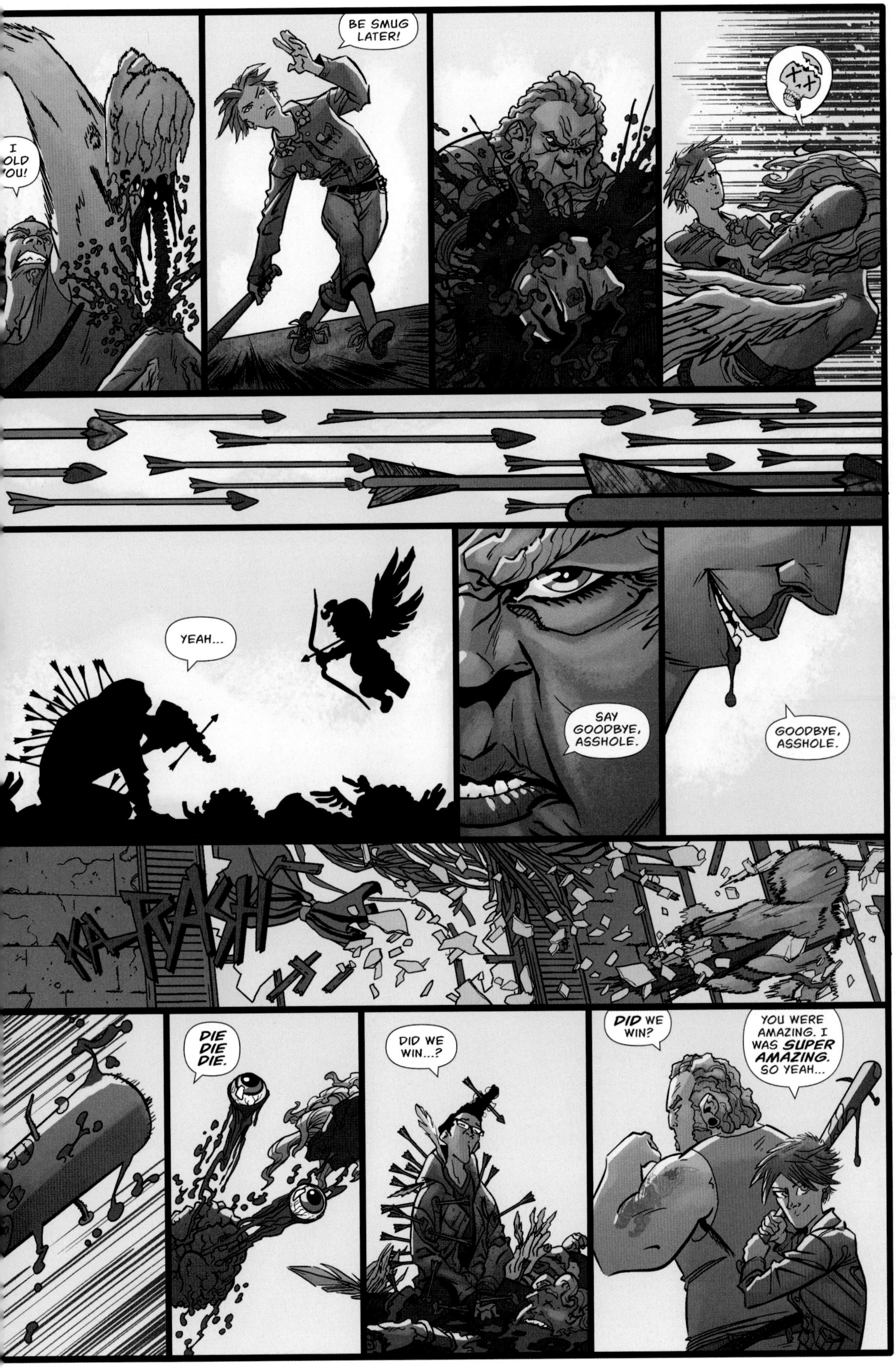

I OLD OU!
BE SMUG LATER!
YEAH...
SAY GOODBYE, ASSHOLE.
GOODBYE, ASSHOLE.
KA-RASH
DIE DIE DIE.
DID WE WIN...?
DID WE WIN?
YOU WERE AMAZING. I WAS SUPER AMAZING. SO YEAH...

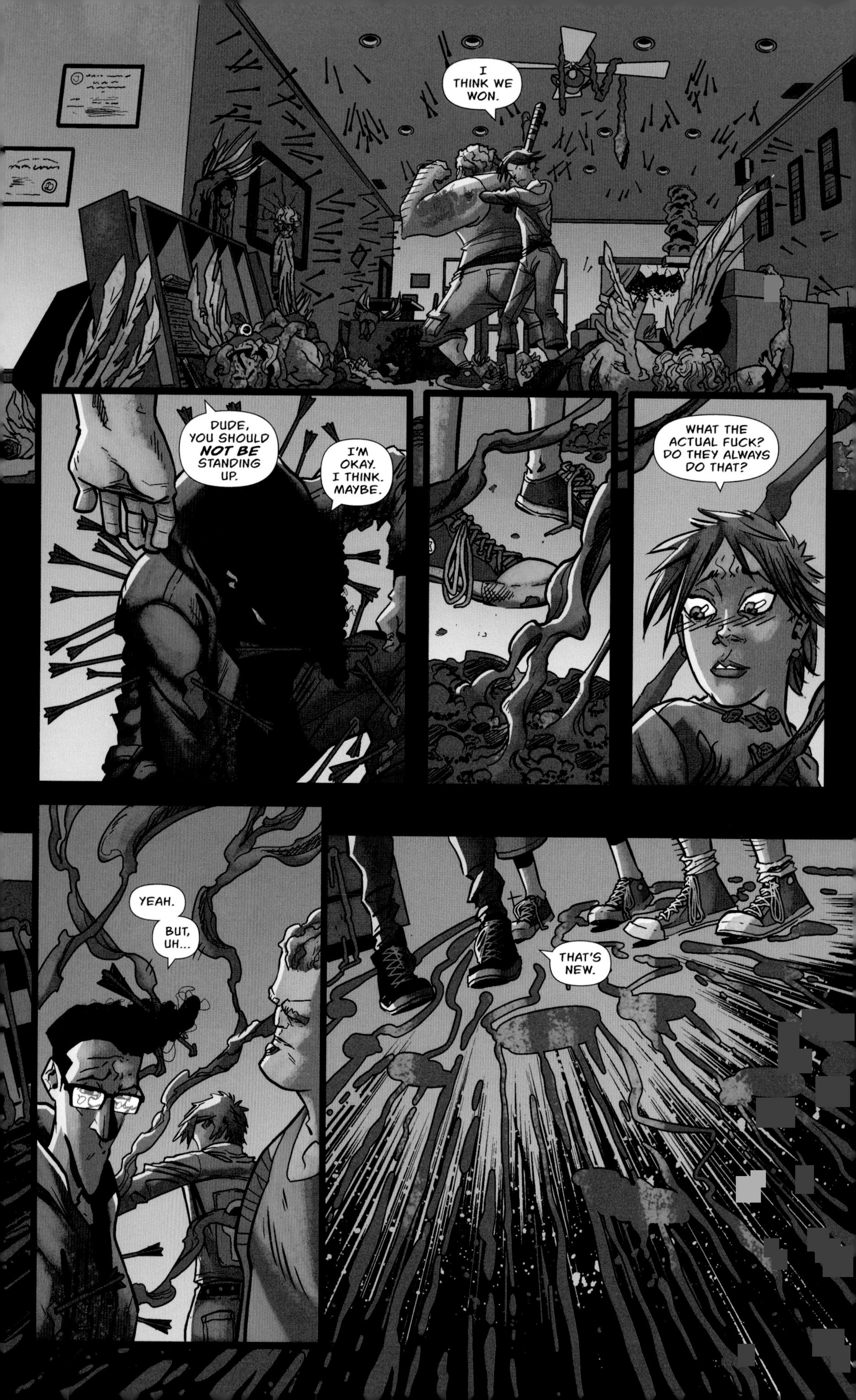
I THINK WE WON.
DUDE, YOU SHOULD NOT BE STANDING UP.
I'M OKAY. I THINK. MAYBE.
WHAT THE ACTUAL FUCK? DO THEY ALWAYS DO THAT?
YEAH.
BUT, UH...
THAT'S NEW.

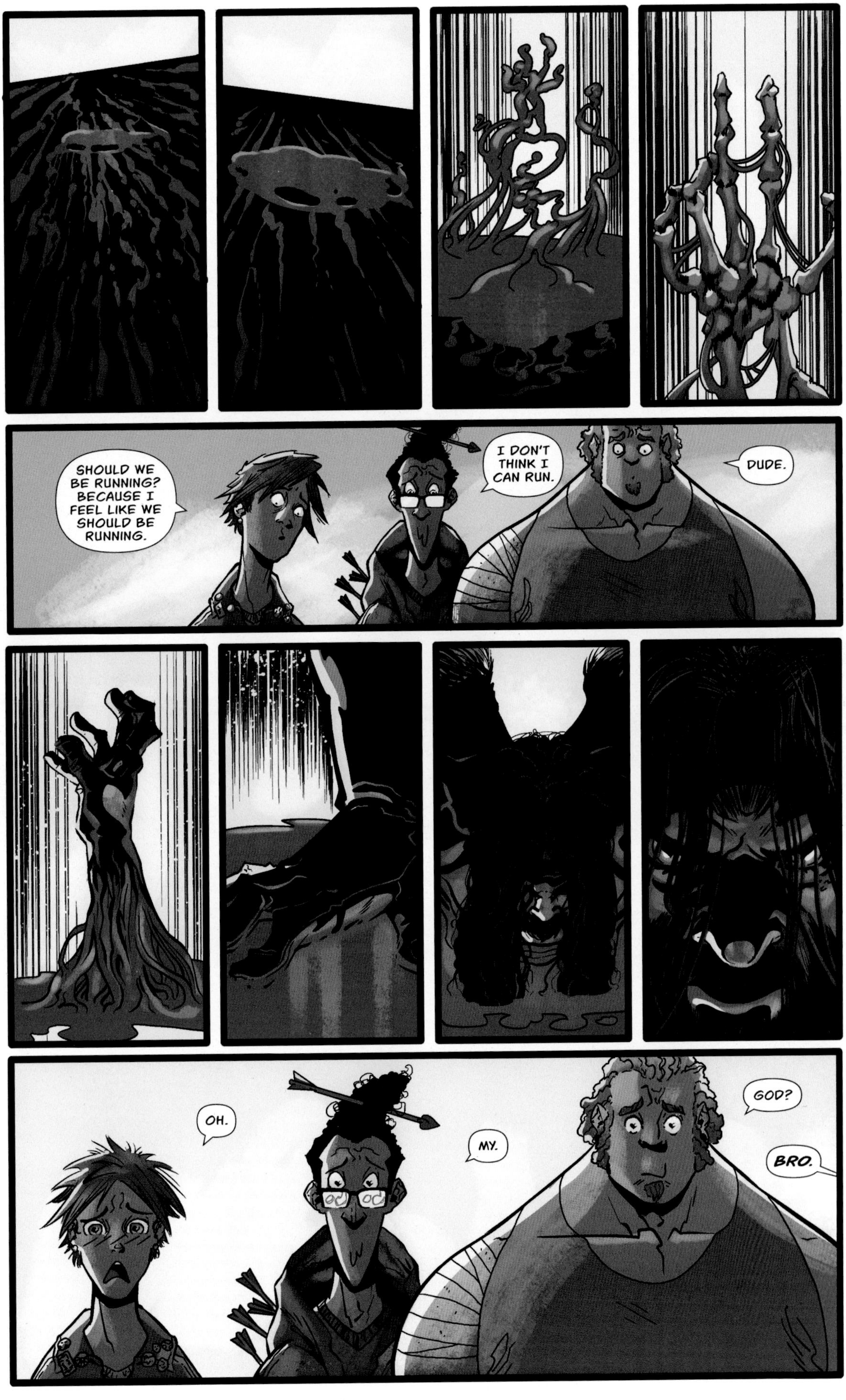
SHOULD WE BE RUNNING? BECAUSE I FEEL LIKE WE SHOULD BE RUNNING.
I DON'T THINK I CAN RUN.
DUDE.
OH.
MY.
GOD?
BRO.

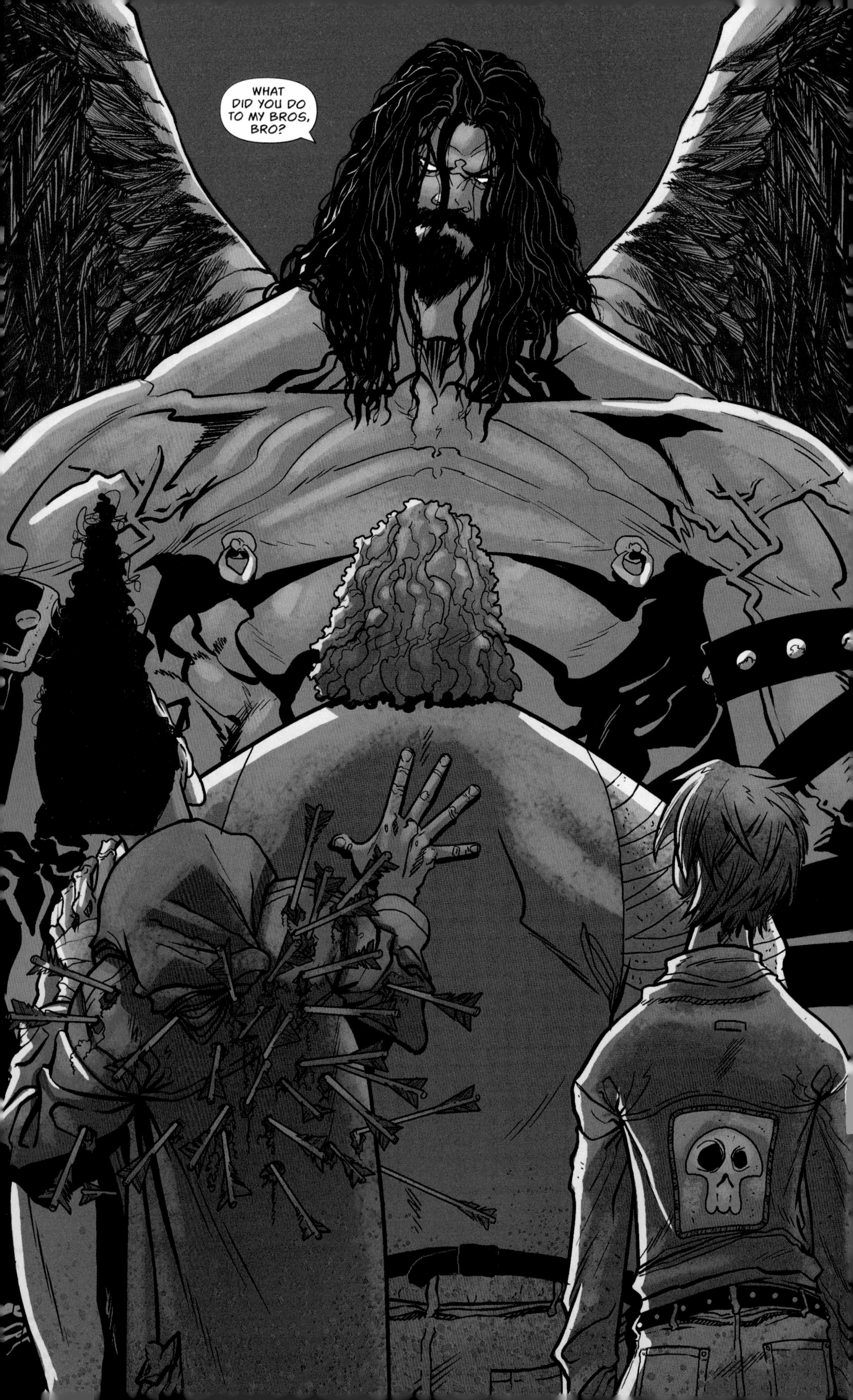
WHAT DID YOU DO TO MY BROS, BRO?

Five

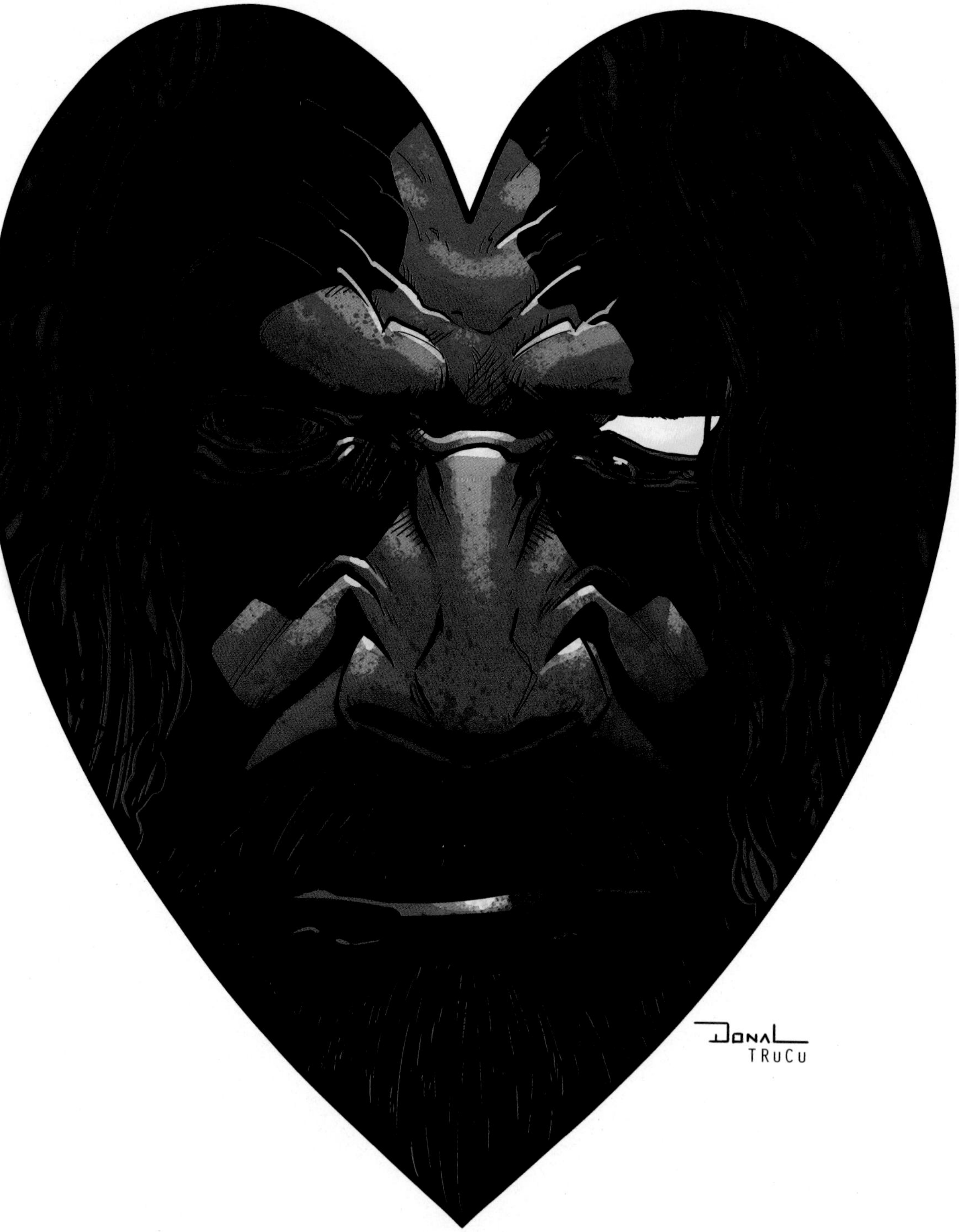
DONAL
TRUCU

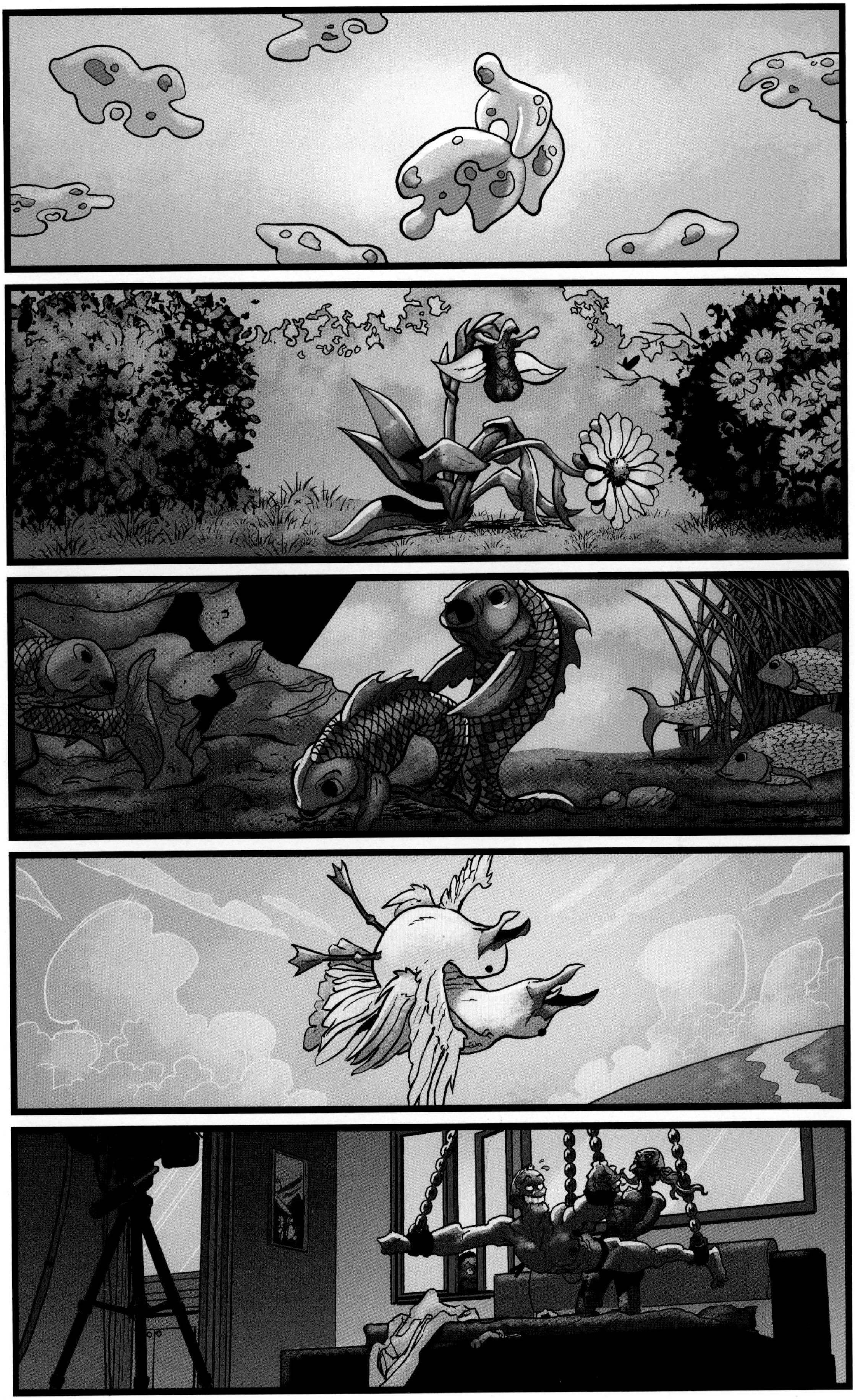

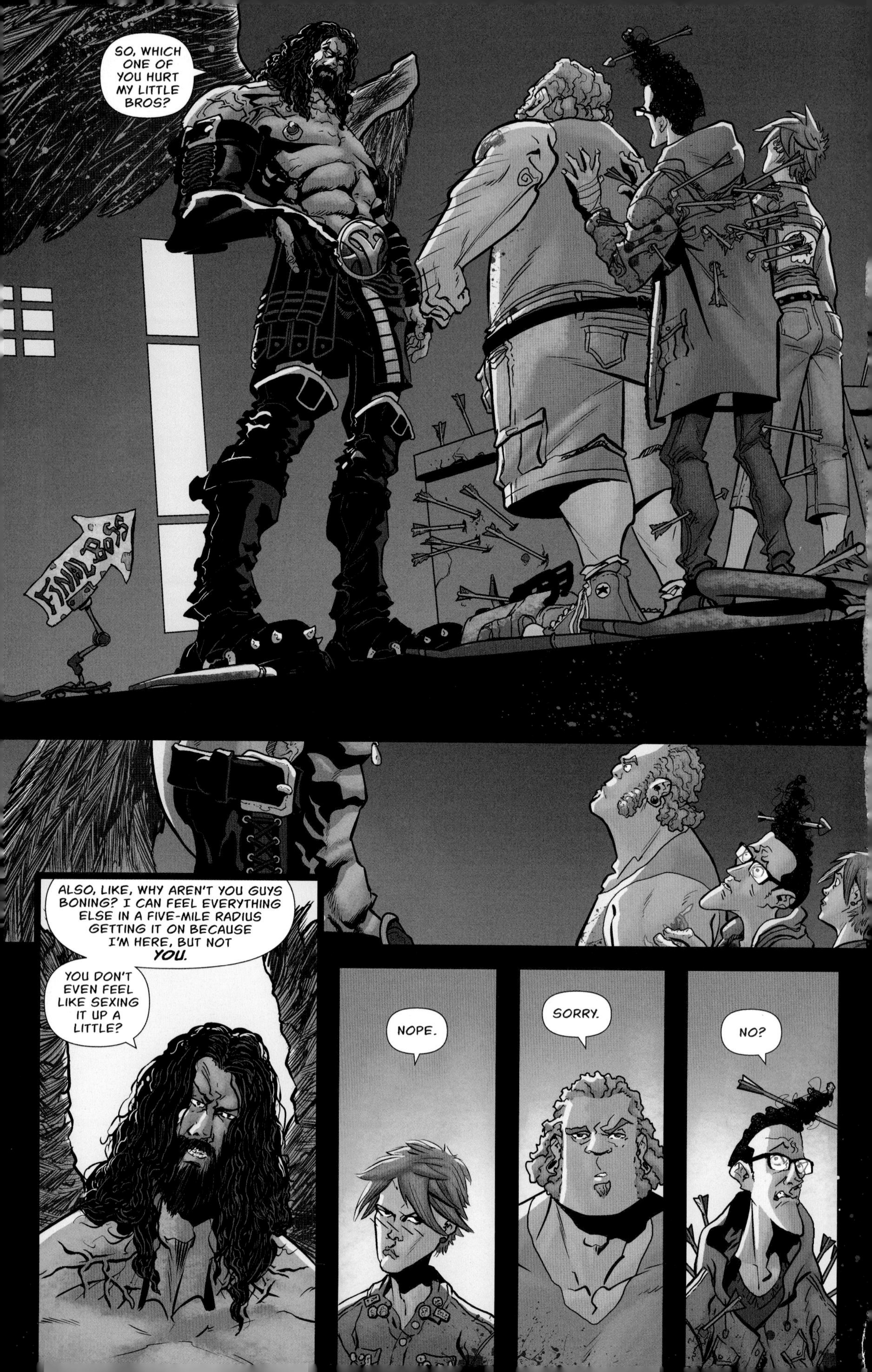
SO, WHICH ONE OF YOU HURT MY LITTLE BROS?
FINAL BOSS
ALSO, LIKE, WHY AREN'T YOU GUYS BONING? I CAN FEEL EVERYTHING ELSE IN A FIVE-MILE RADIUS GETTING IT ON BECAUSE I'M HERE, BUT NOT *YOU.*
YOU DON'T EVEN FEEL LIKE SEXING IT UP A LITTLE?
NOPE.
SORRY.
NO?

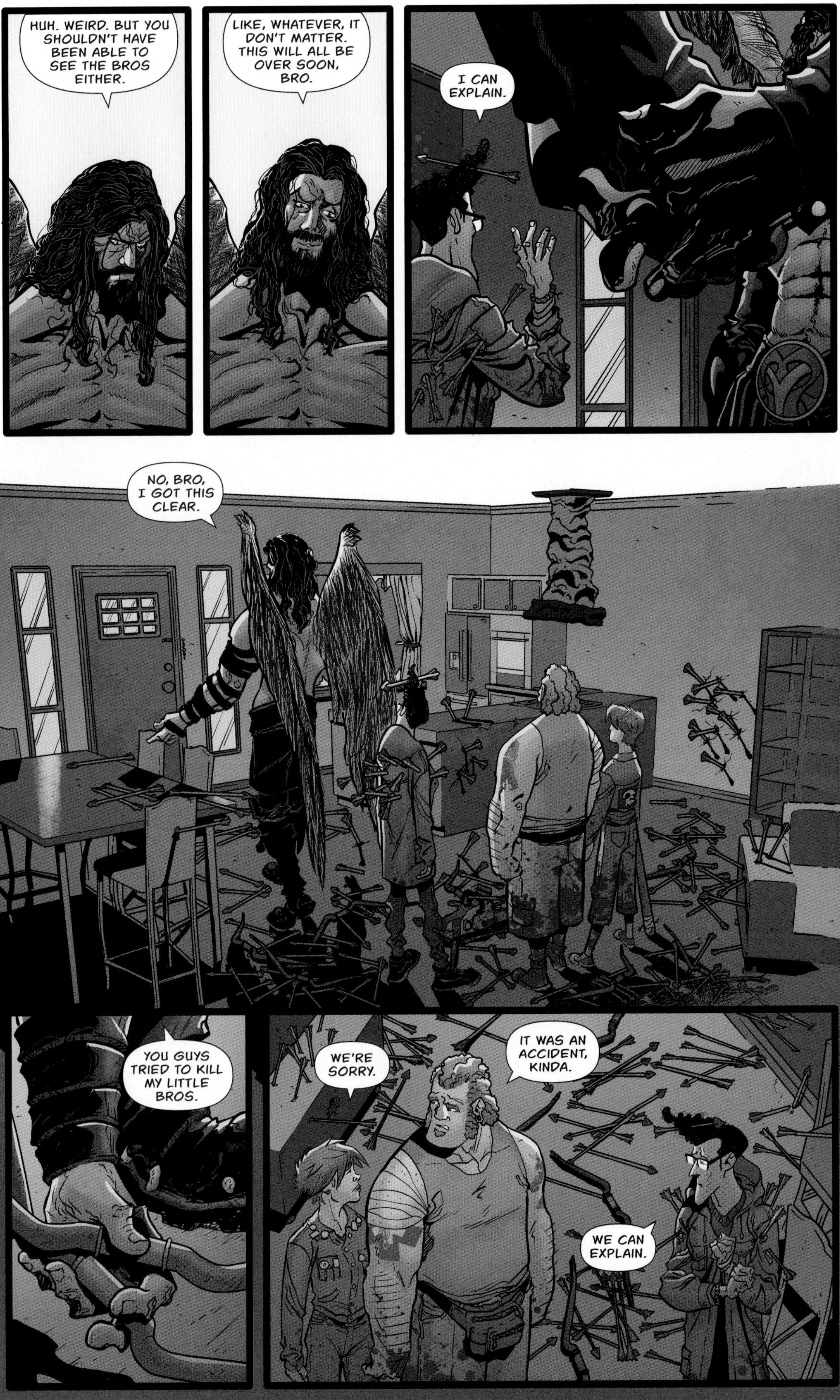
HUH. WEIRD. BUT YOU SHOULDN'T HAVE BEEN ABLE TO SEE THE BROS EITHER.
LIKE, WHATEVER, IT DON'T MATTER. THIS WILL ALL BE OVER SOON, BRO.
I CAN EXPLAIN.
NO, BRO, I GOT THIS CLEAR.
YOU GUYS TRIED TO KILL MY LITTLE BROS.
WE'RE SORRY.
IT WAS AN ACCIDENT, KINDA.
WE CAN EXPLAIN.

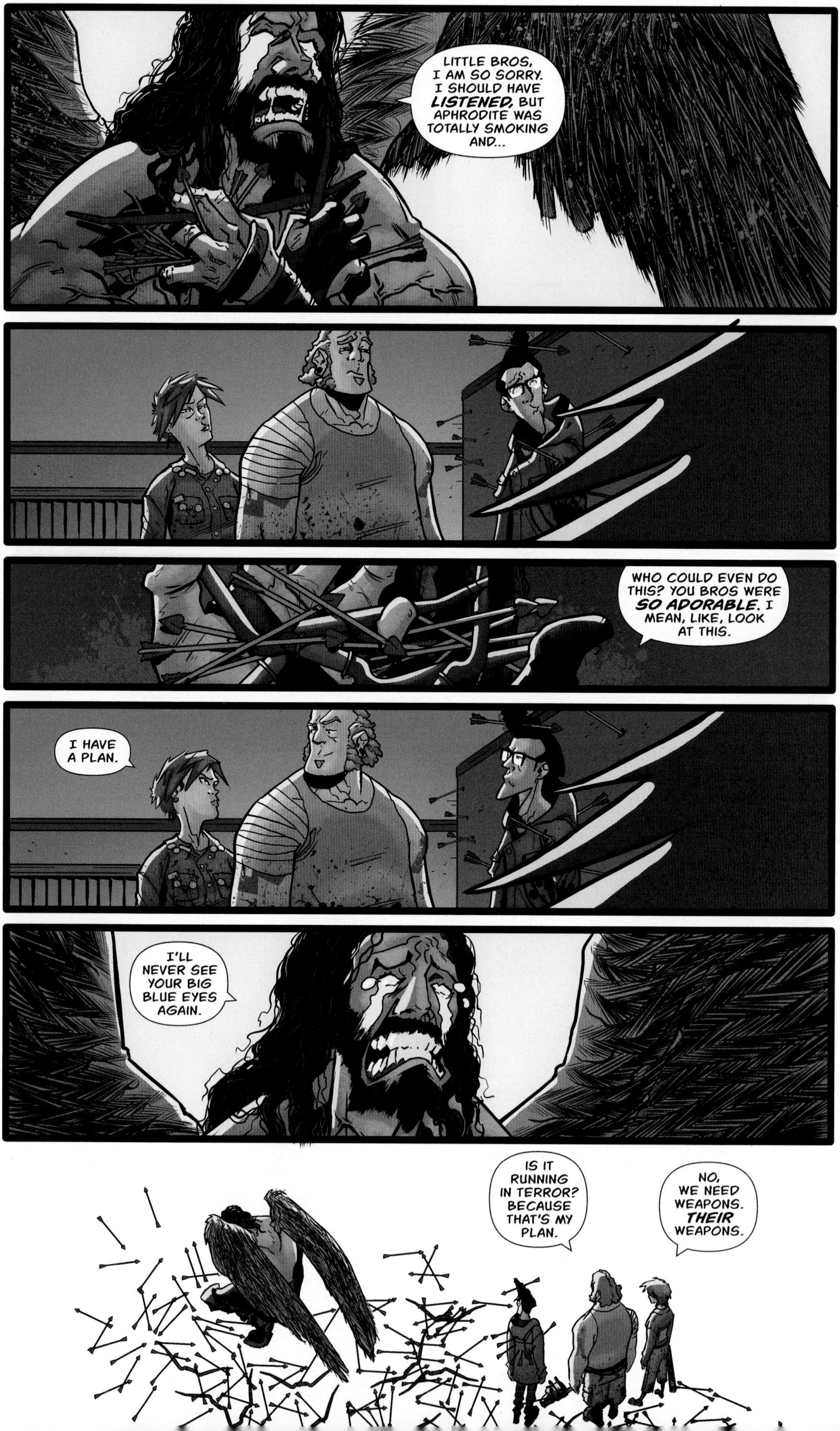
LITTLE BROS, I AM SO SORRY. I SHOULD HAVE LISTENED, BUT APHRODITE WAS TOTALLY SMOKING AND...
WHO COULD EVEN DO THIS? YOU BROS WERE SO ADORABLE. I MEAN, LIKE, LOOK AT THIS.
I HAVE A PLAN.
I'LL NEVER SEE YOUR BIG BLUE EYES AGAIN.
IS IT RUNNING IN TERROR? BECAUSE THAT'S MY PLAN.
NO, WE NEED WEAPONS. THEIR WEAPONS.

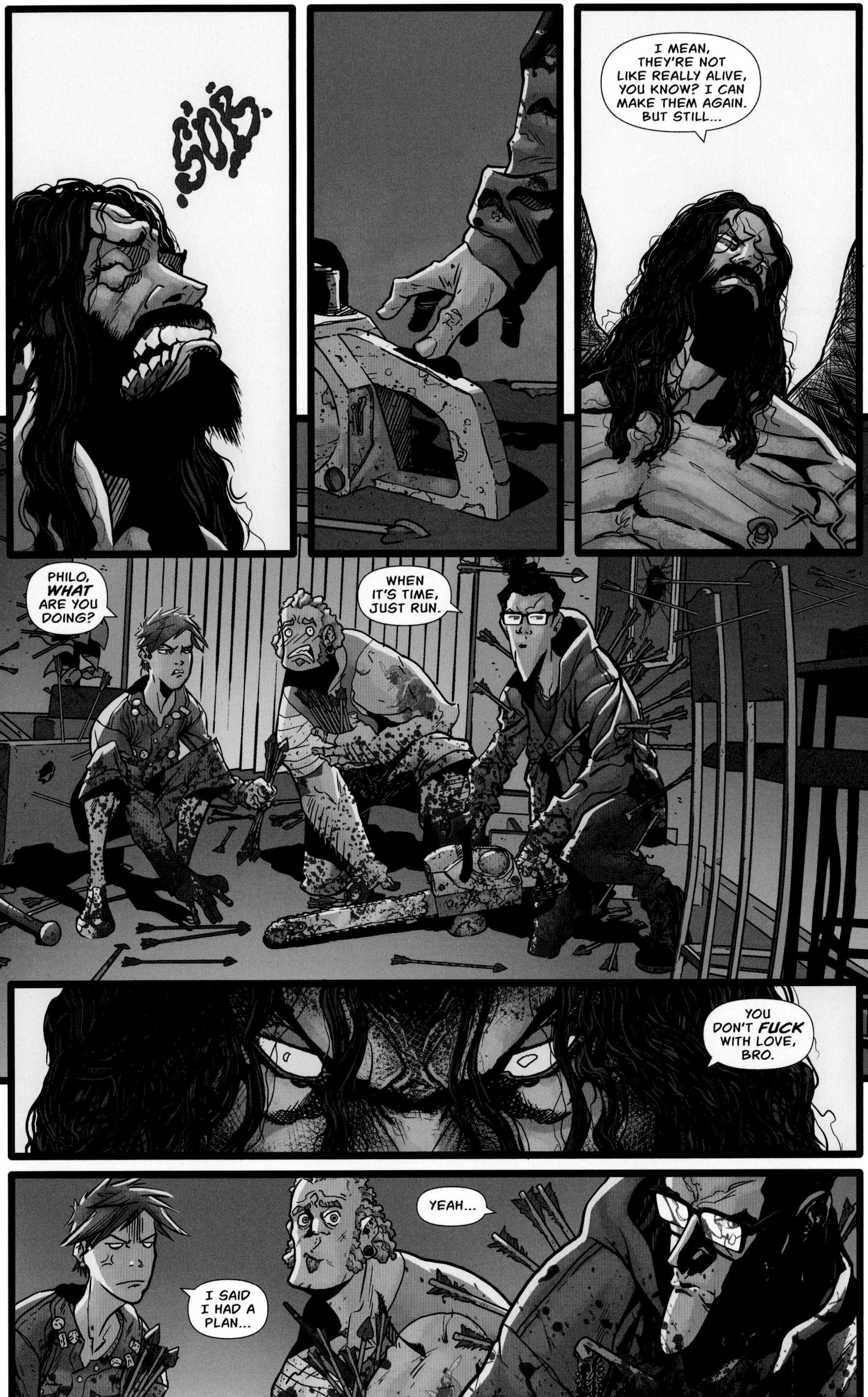
SOB
I MEAN, THEY'RE NOT LIKE REALLY ALIVE, YOU KNOW? I CAN MAKE THEM AGAIN. BUT STILL...
PHILO, WHAT ARE YOU DOING?
WHEN IT'S TIME, JUST RUN.
YOU DON'T FUCK WITH LOVE, BRO.
YEAH...
I SAID I HAD A PLAN...

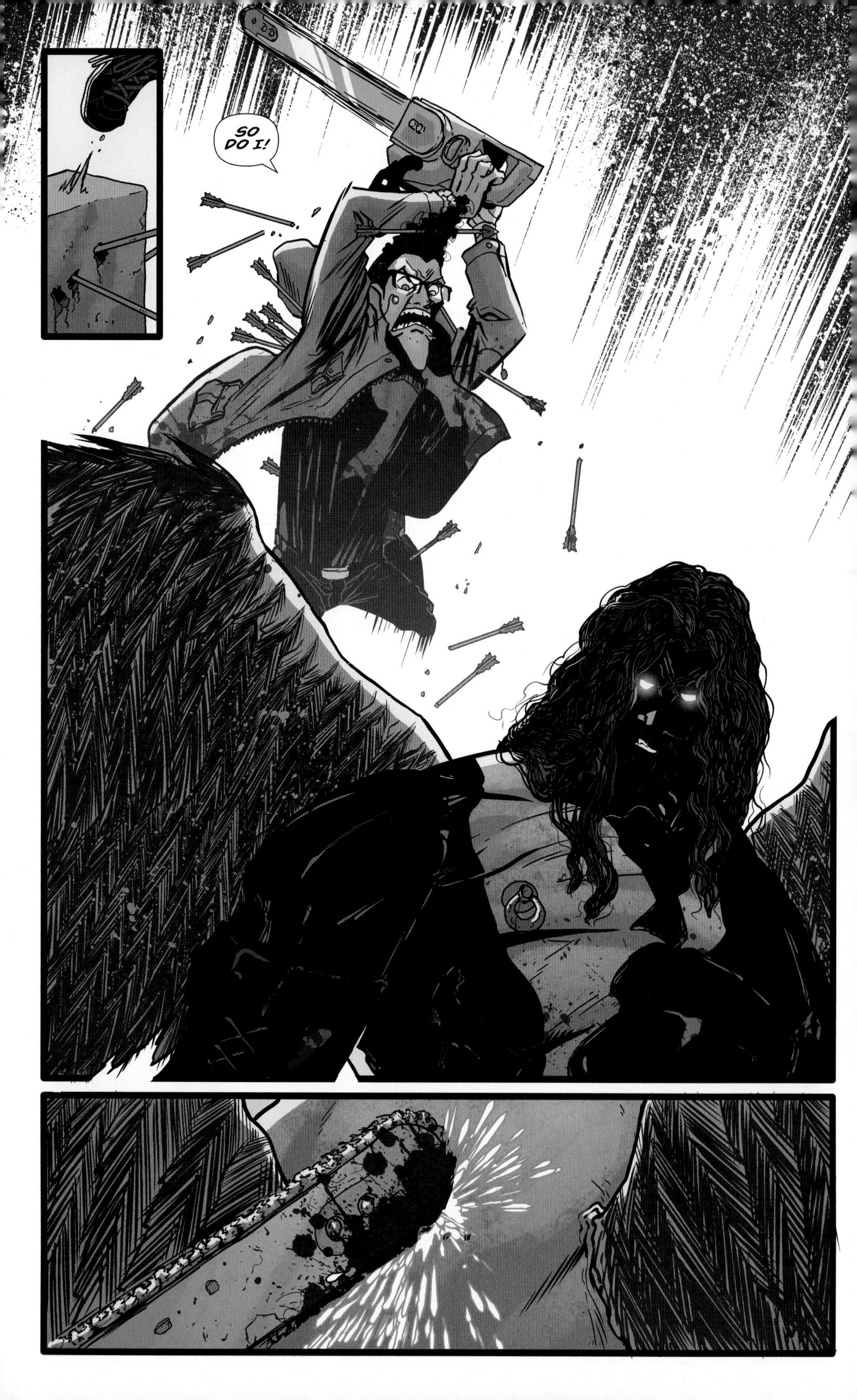
SO DO I!

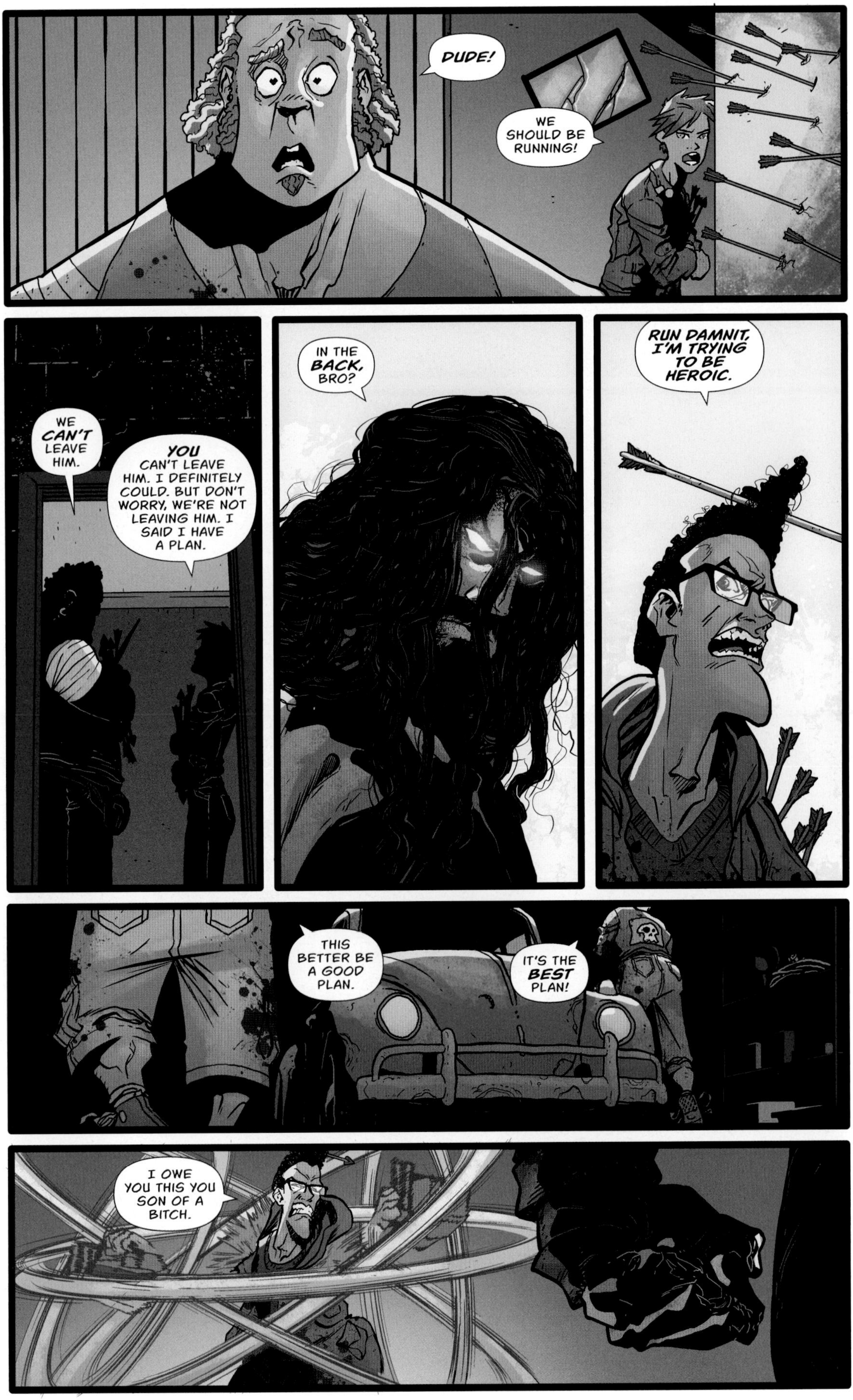
DUDE!
WE SHOULD BE RUNNING!
WE CAN'T LEAVE HIM.
YOU CAN'T LEAVE HIM. I DEFINITELY COULD. BUT DON'T WORRY, WE'RE NOT LEAVING HIM. I SAID I HAVE A PLAN.
IN THE BACK, BRO?
RUN DAMNIT, I'M TRYING TO BE HEROIC.
THIS BETTER BE A GOOD PLAN.
IT'S THE BEST PLAN!
I OWE YOU THIS YOU SON OF A BITCH.

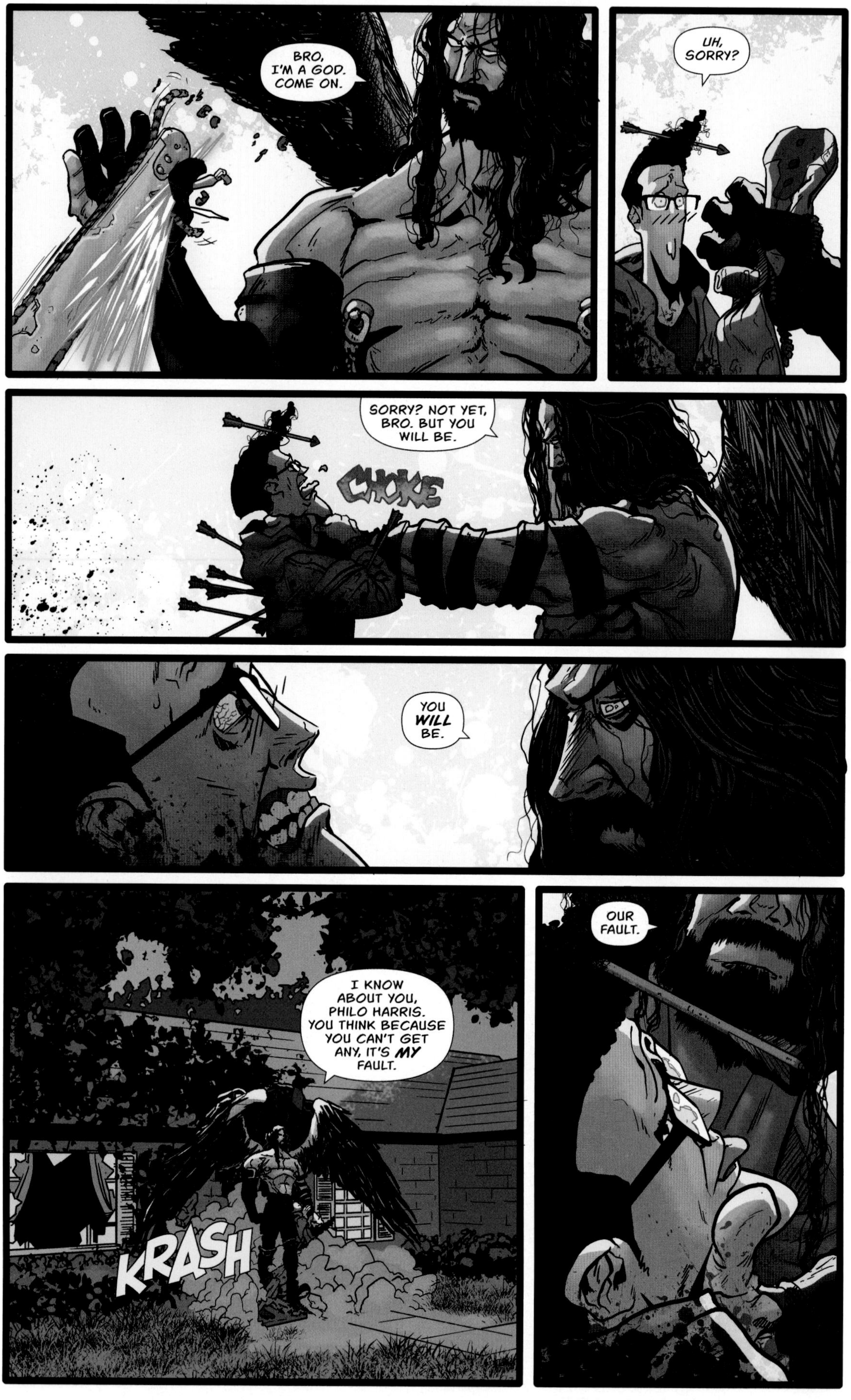
BRO, I'M A GOD. COME ON.
UH, SORRY?
SORRY? NOT YET, BRO. BUT YOU WILL BE.
CHOKE
YOU *WILL* BE.
I KNOW ABOUT YOU, PHILO HARRIS. YOU THINK BECAUSE YOU CAN'T GET ANY, IT'S *MY* FAULT.
KRASH
OUR FAULT.

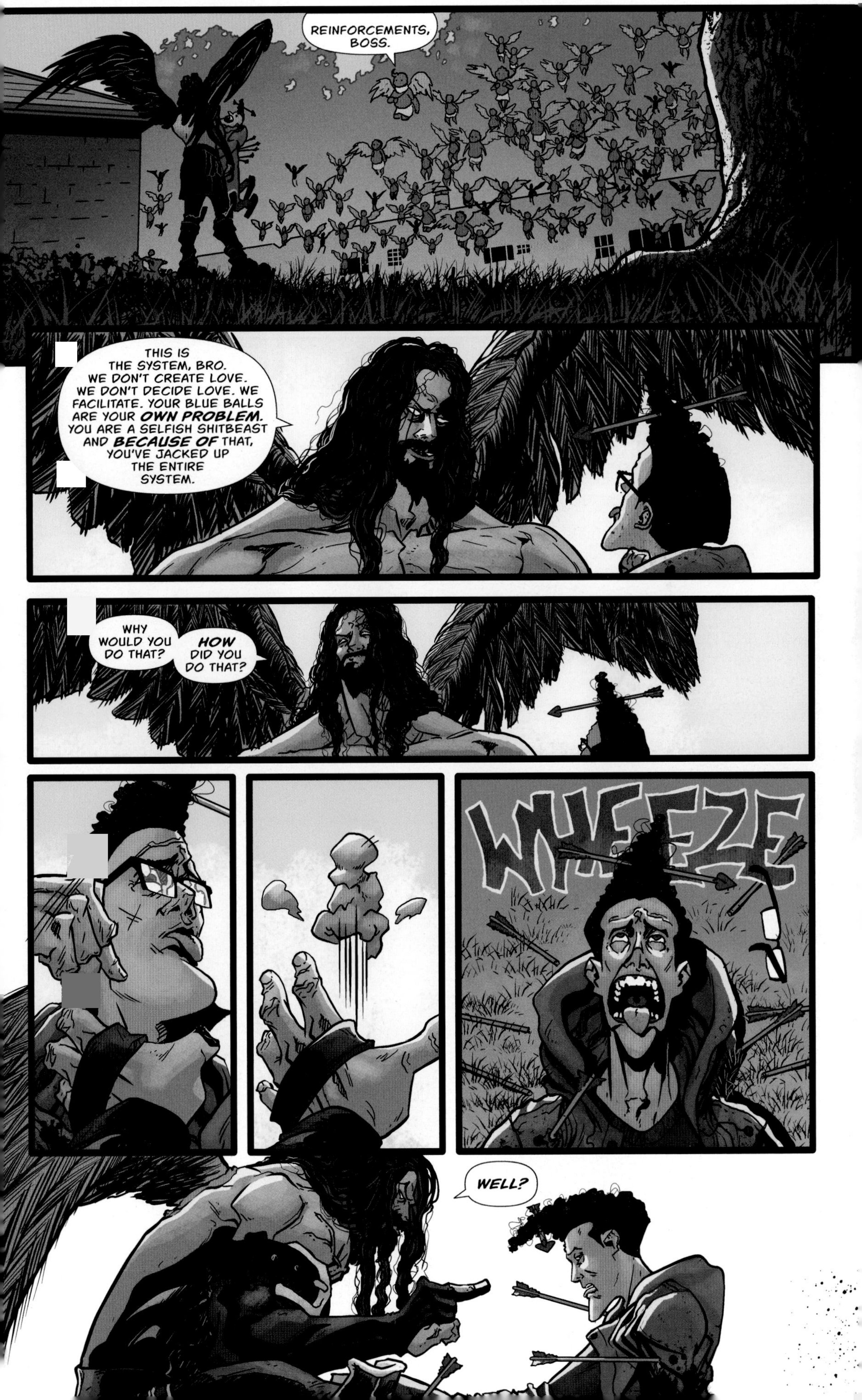
REINFORCEMENTS, BOSS.
THIS IS THE SYSTEM, BRO. WE DON'T CREATE LOVE. WE DON'T DECIDE LOVE. WE FACILITATE. YOUR BLUE BALLS ARE YOUR ***OWN PROBLEM.*** YOU ARE A SELFISH SHITBEAST AND ***BECAUSE OF*** THAT, YOU'VE JACKED UP THE ENTIRE SYSTEM.
WHY WOULD YOU DO THAT?
HOW DID YOU DO THAT?
WHEEZE
WELL?

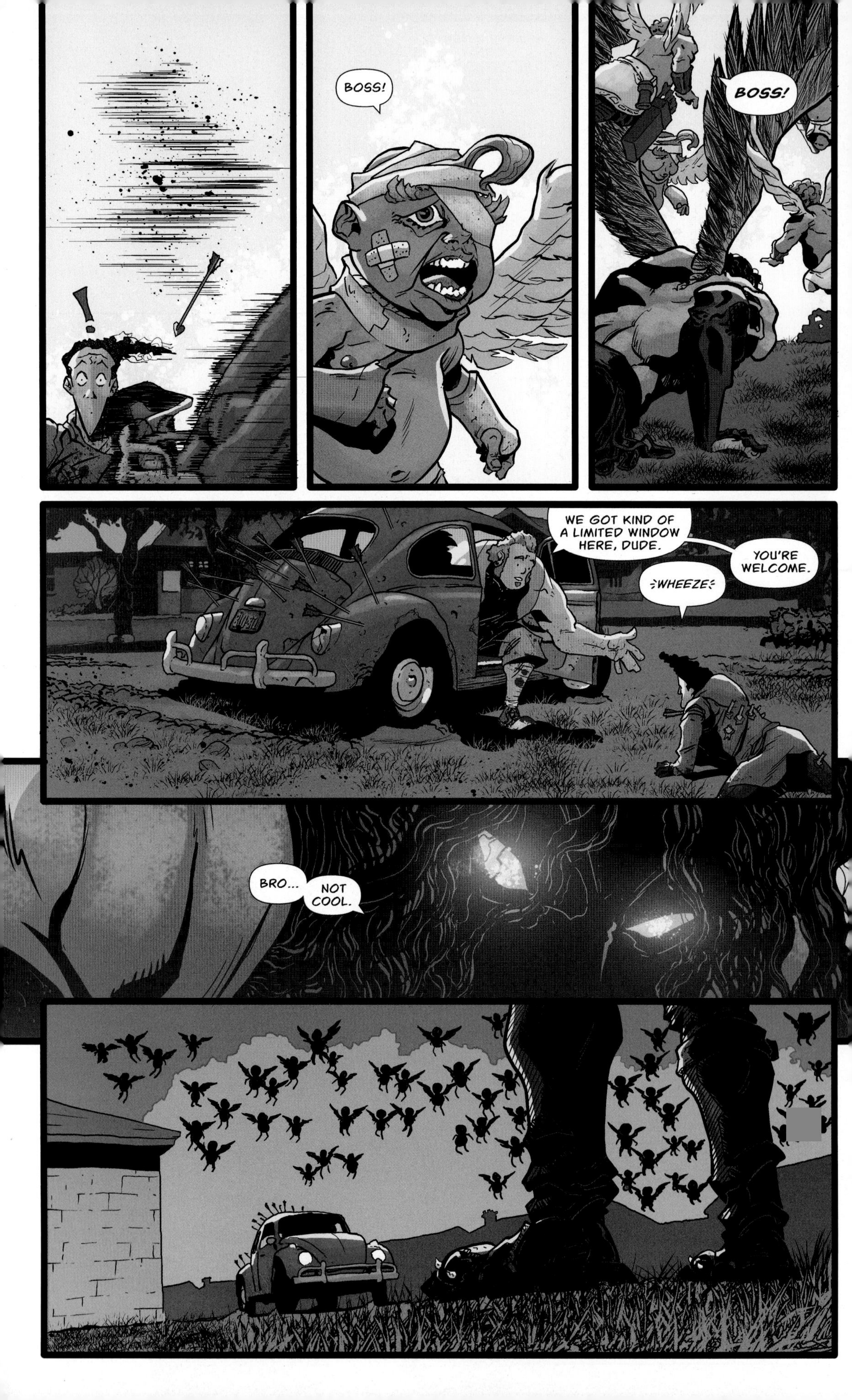
!
BOSS!
BOSS!
WE GOT KIND OF A LIMITED WINDOW HERE, DUDE.
YOU'RE WELCOME.
WHEEZE
BRO...
NOT COOL.

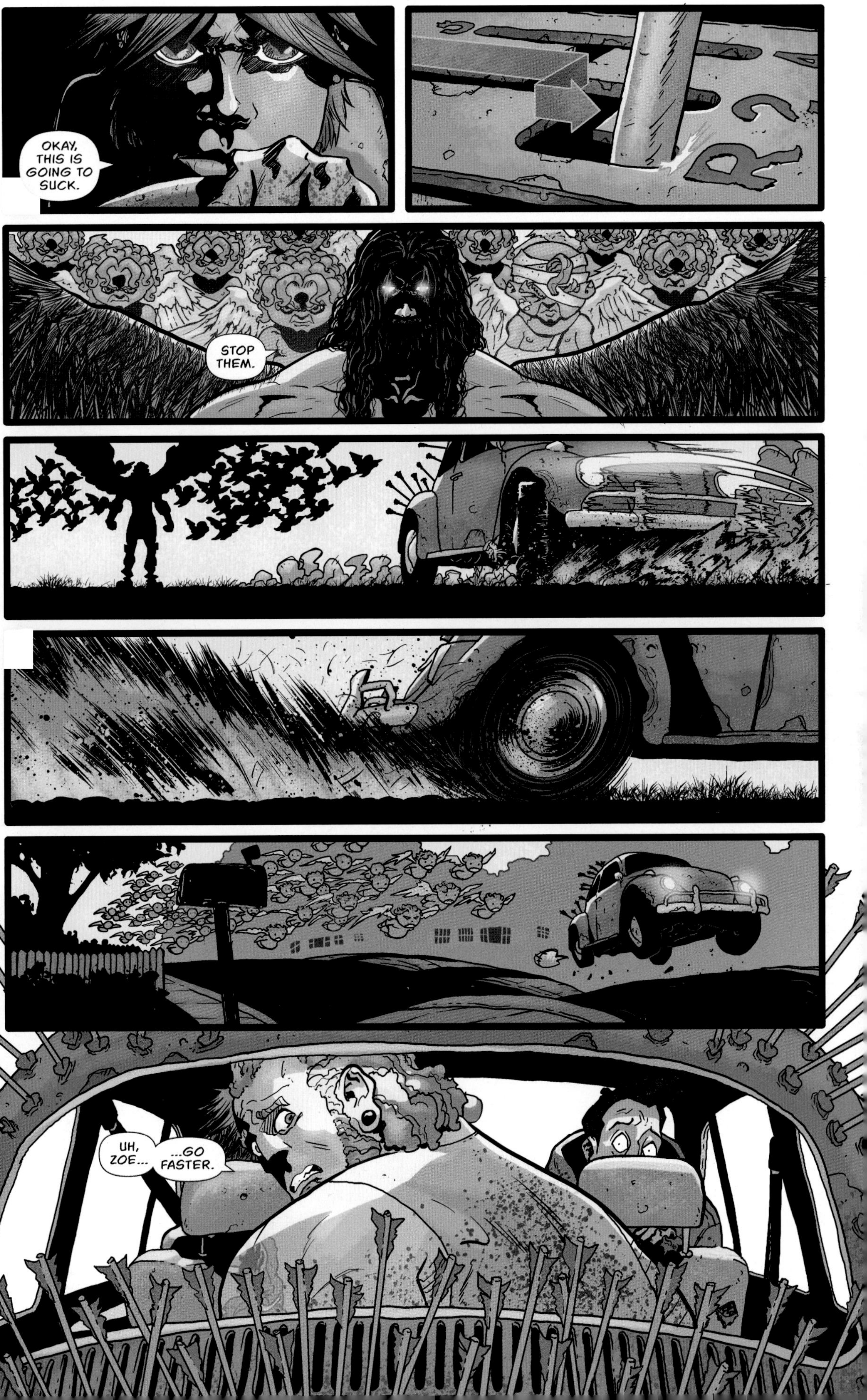
OKAY, THIS IS GOING TO SUCK.
STOP THEM.
UH, ZOE...
...GO FASTER.

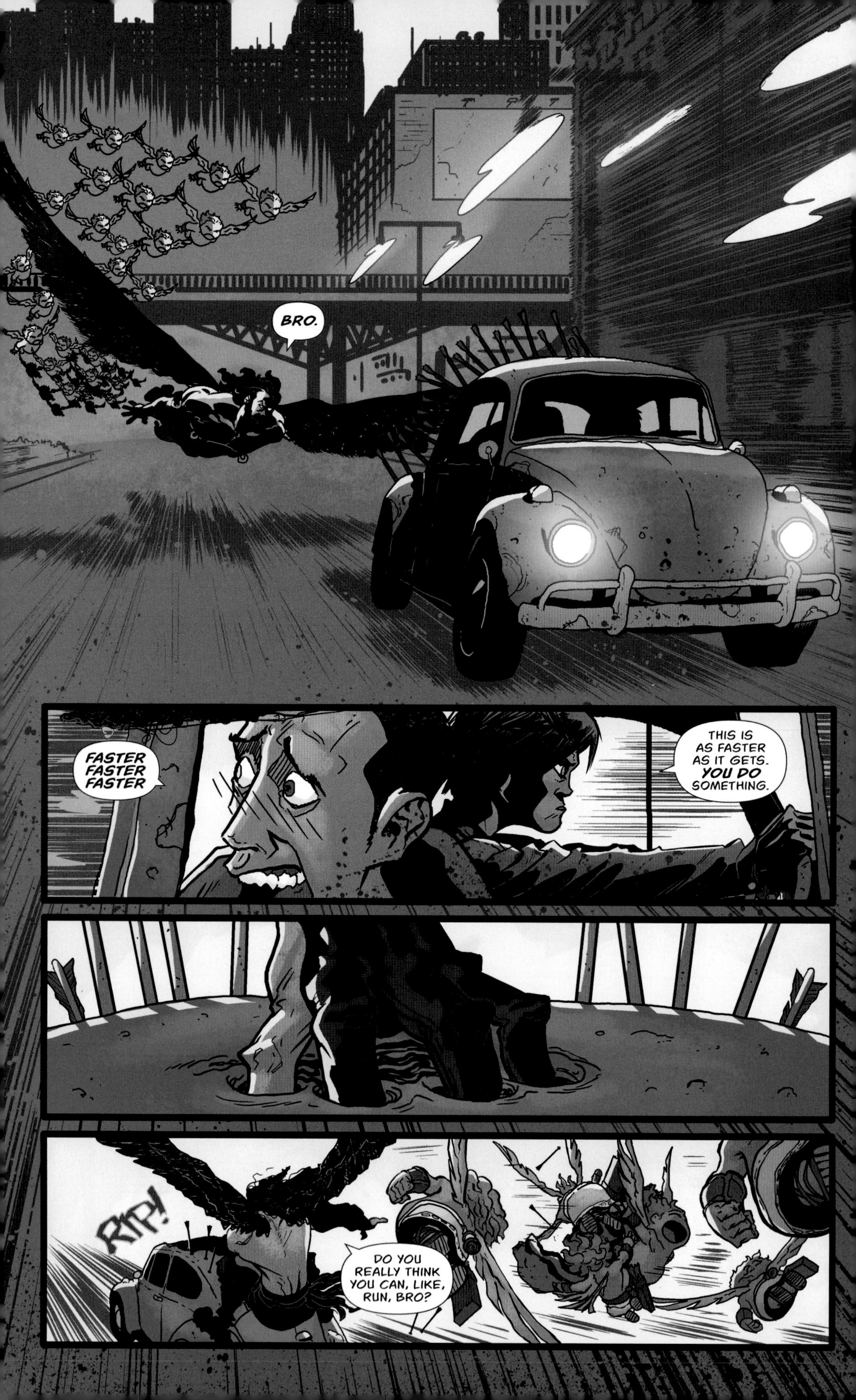
BRO.
FASTER FASTER FASTER
THIS IS AS FASTER AS IT GETS. YOU DO SOMETHING.
RIP!
DO YOU REALLY THINK YOU CAN, LIKE, RUN, BRO?

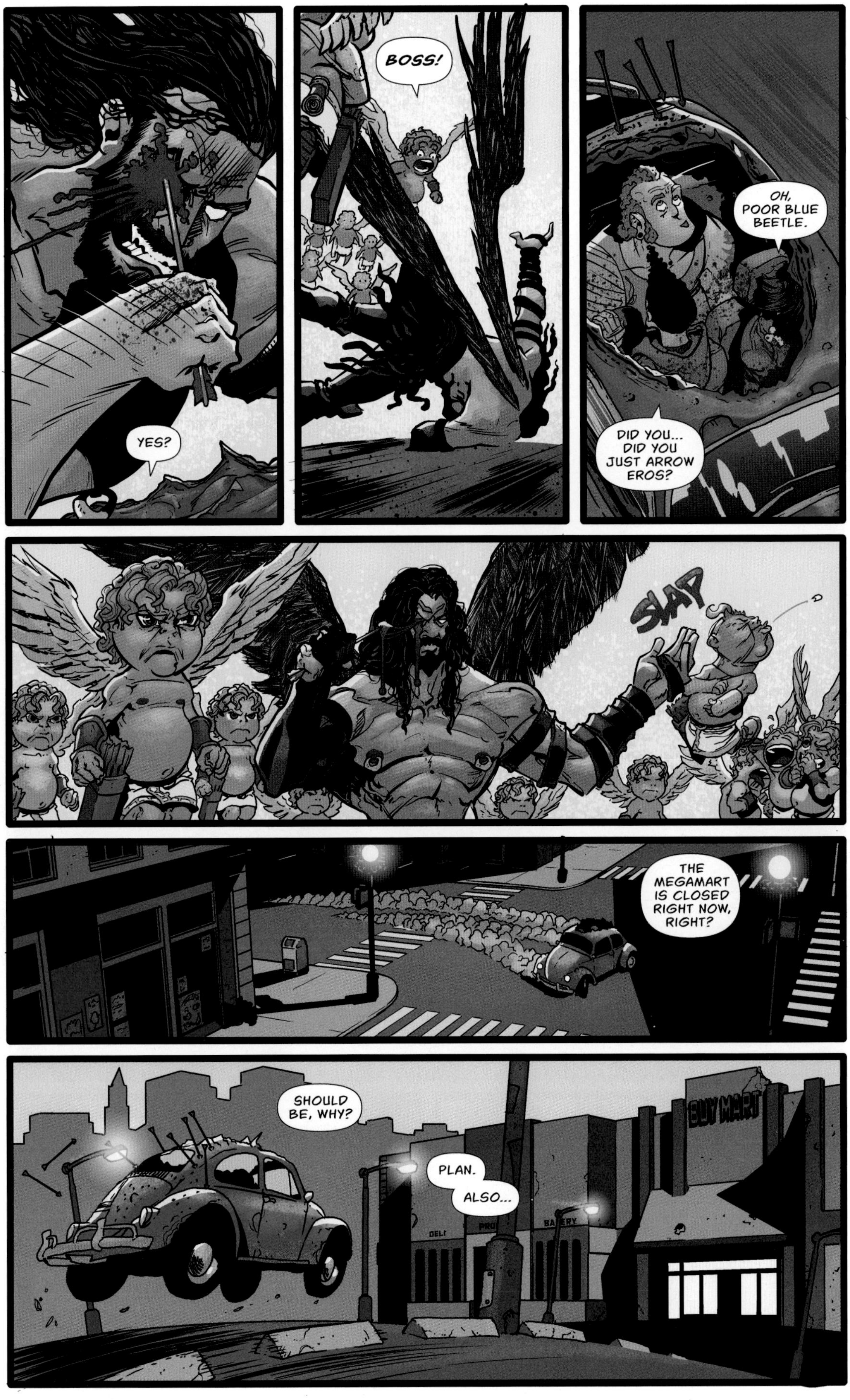
YES?
BOSS!
OH, POOR BLUE BEETLE.
DID YOU... DID YOU JUST ARROW EROS?
SLAP
THE MEGAMART IS CLOSED RIGHT NOW, RIGHT?
SHOULD BE, WHY?
PLAN.
ALSO...
BUY MART
DELI
BAKERY

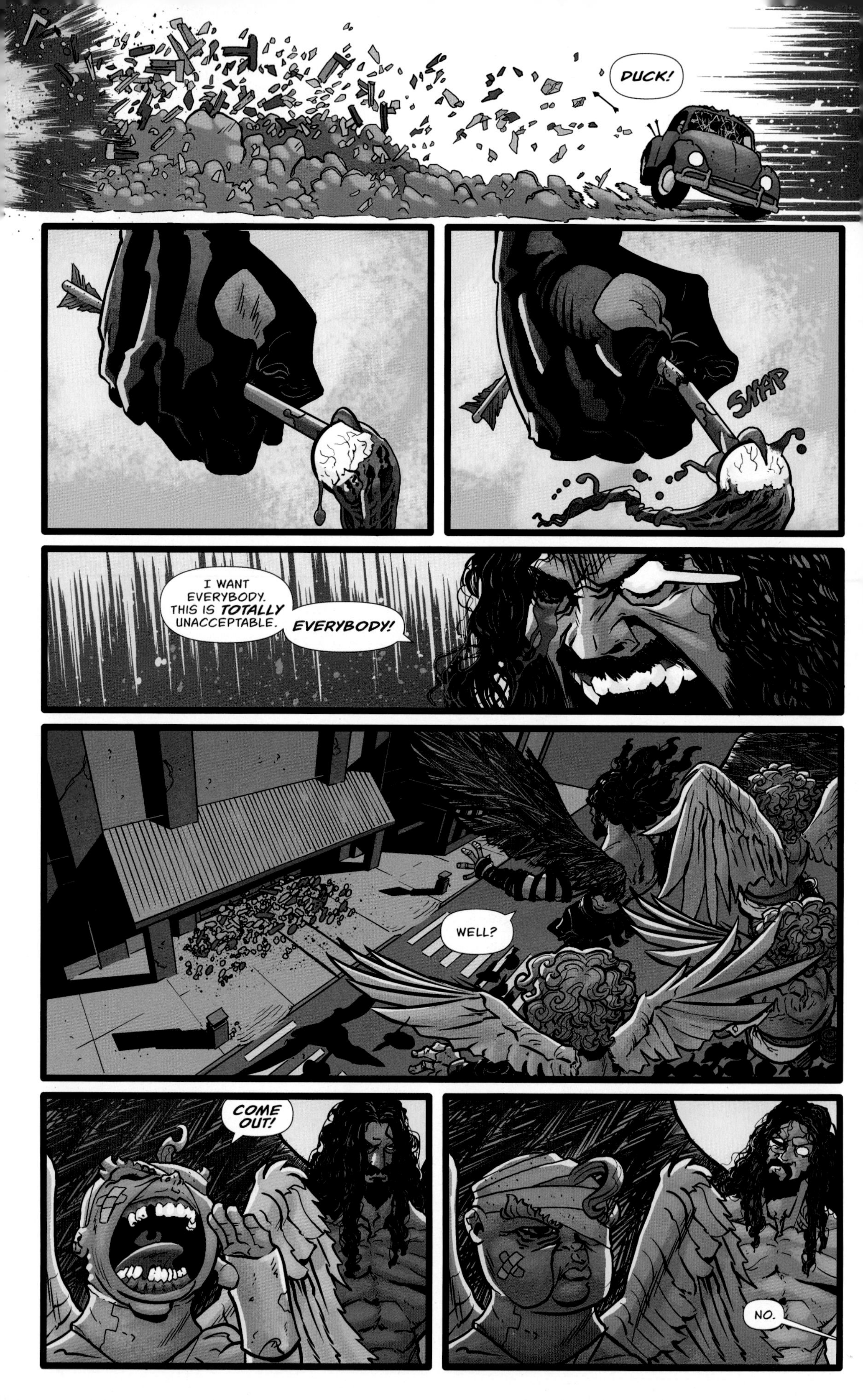
DUCK!
SNAP
I WANT EVERYBODY. THIS IS TOTALLY UNACCEPTABLE.
EVERYBODY!
WELL?
COME OUT!
NO.

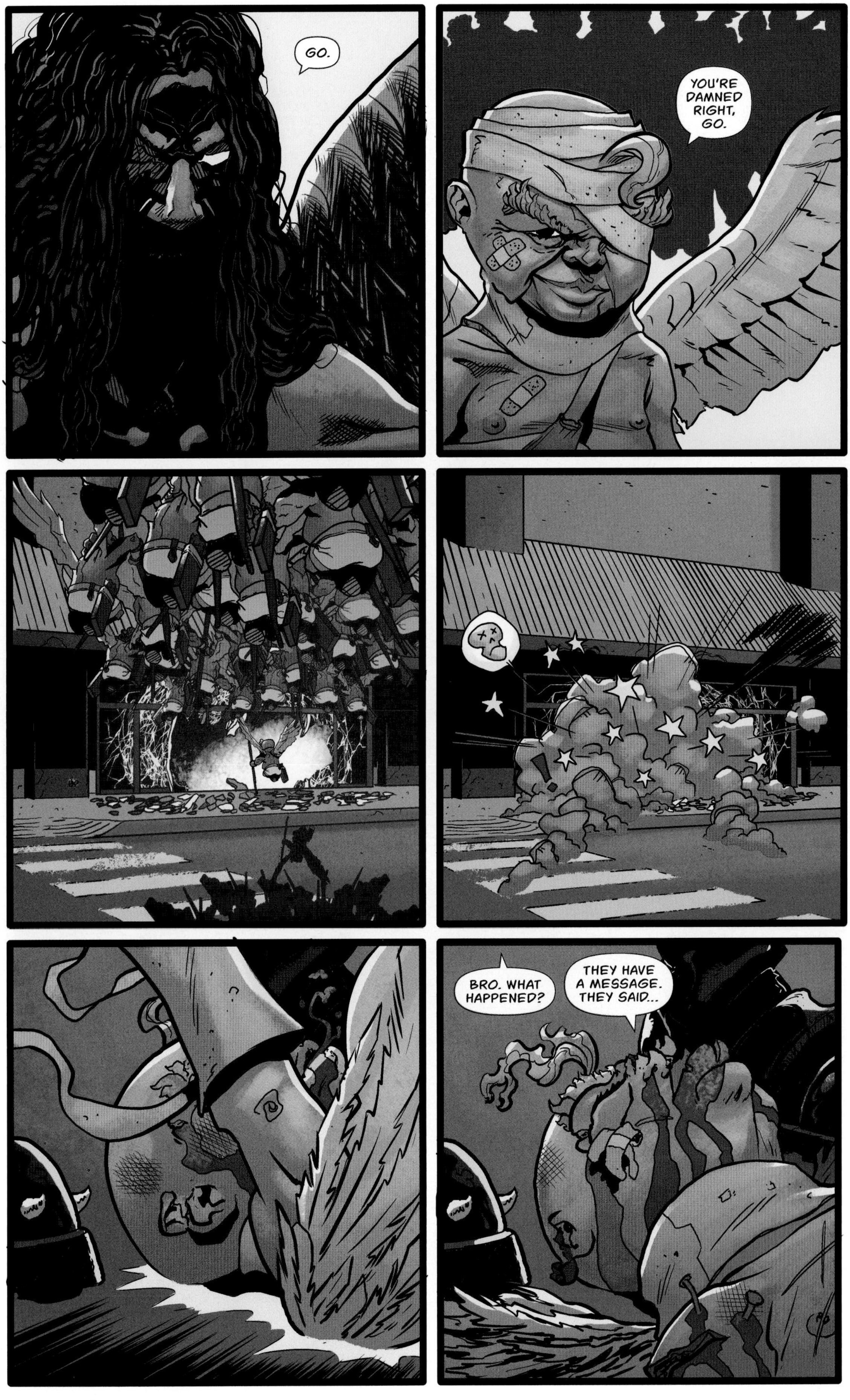
GO.
YOU'RE DAMNED RIGHT, GO.
BRO. WHAT HAPPENED?
THEY HAVE A MESSAGE. THEY SAID...

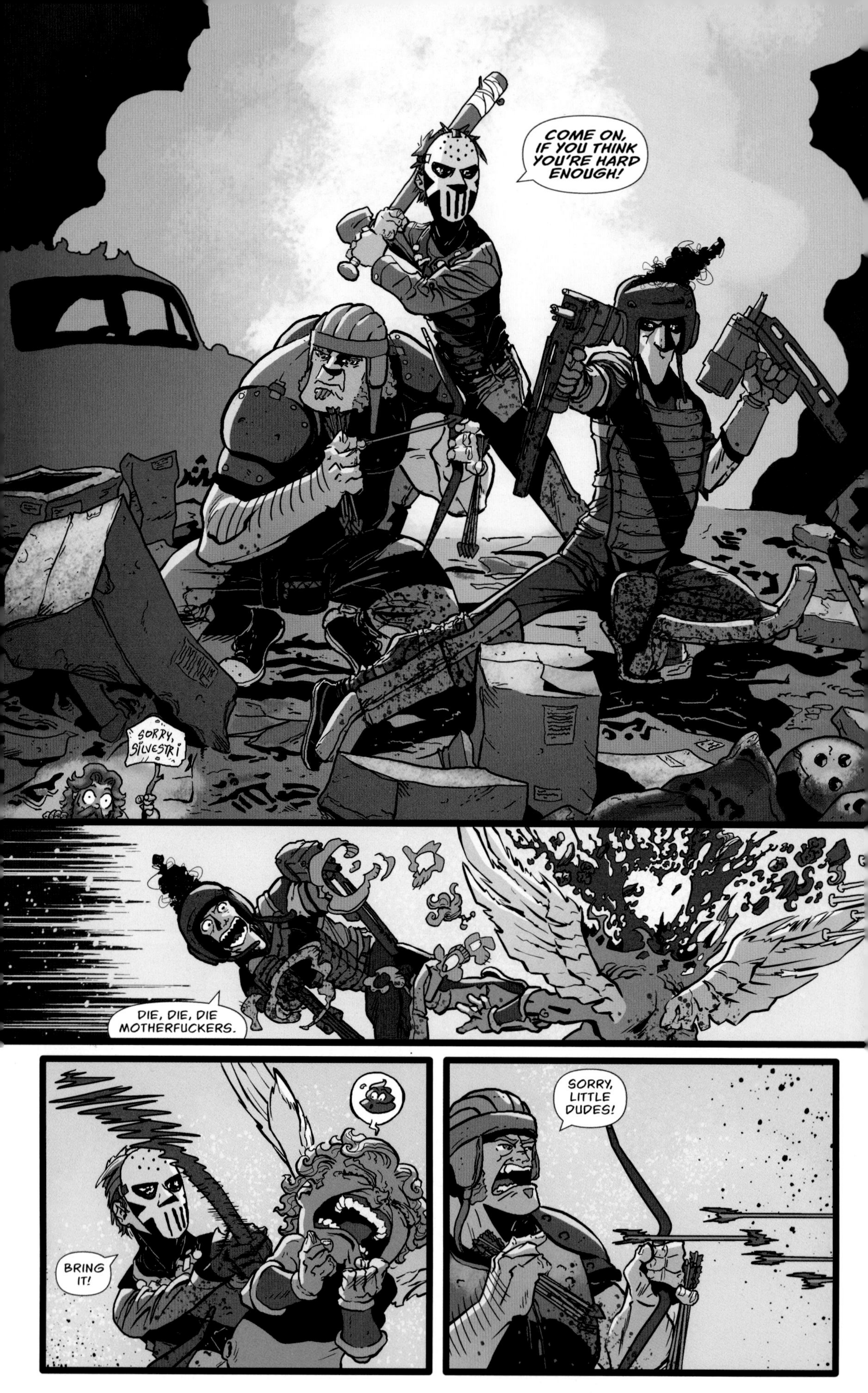
COME ON, IF YOU THINK YOU'RE HARD ENOUGH!
SORRY, SILVESTRI
DIE, DIE, DIE MOTHERFUCKERS.
BRING IT!
SORRY, LITTLE DUDES!

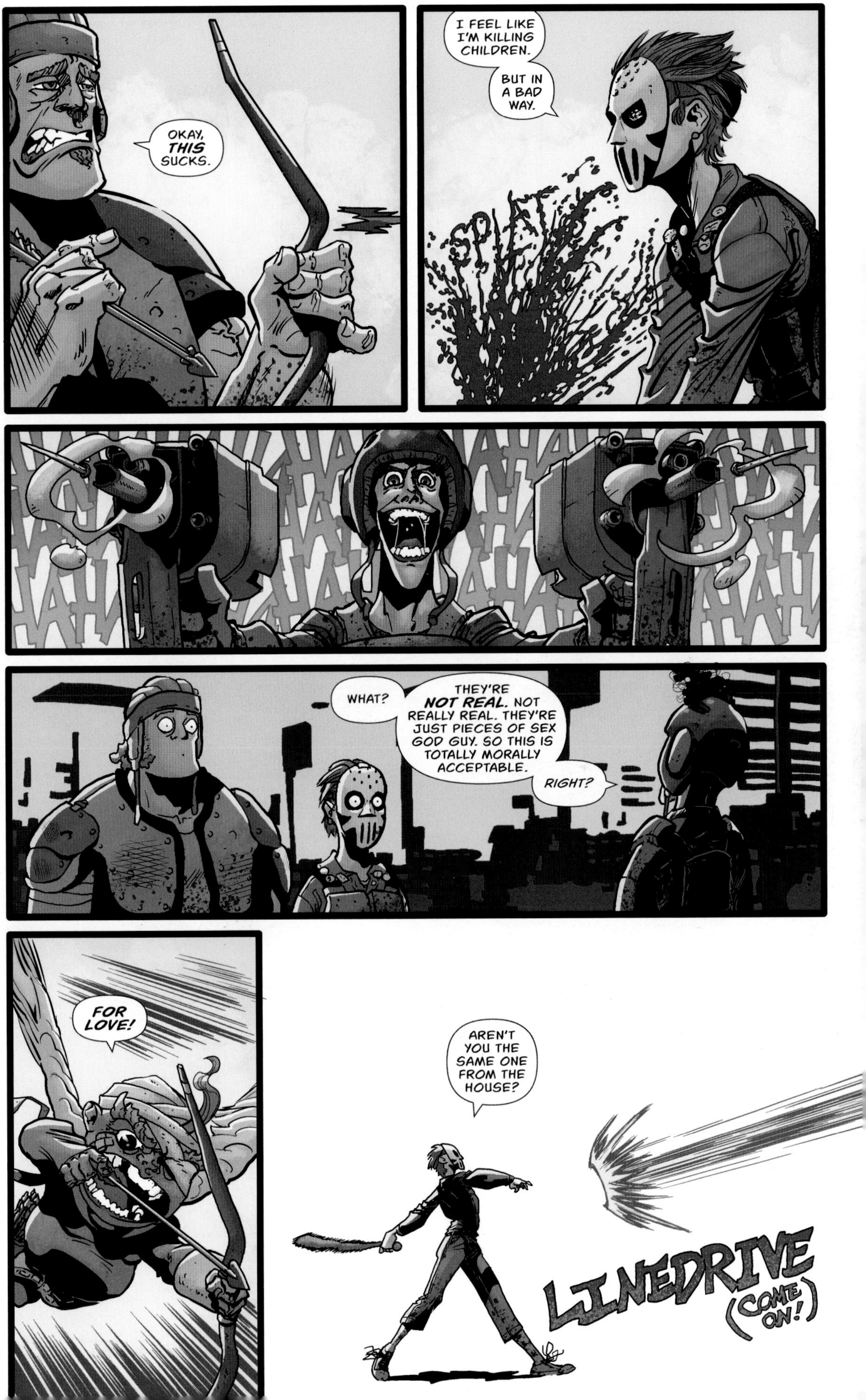
OKAY, THIS SUCKS.
I FEEL LIKE I'M KILLING CHILDREN.
BUT IN A BAD WAY.
SPLAT
WHAT?
THEY'RE NOT REAL. NOT REALLY REAL. THEY'RE JUST PIECES OF SEX GOD GUY. SO THIS IS TOTALLY MORALLY ACCEPTABLE.
RIGHT?
FOR LOVE!
AREN'T YOU THE SAME ONE FROM THE HOUSE?
LINEDRIVE
(COME ON!)

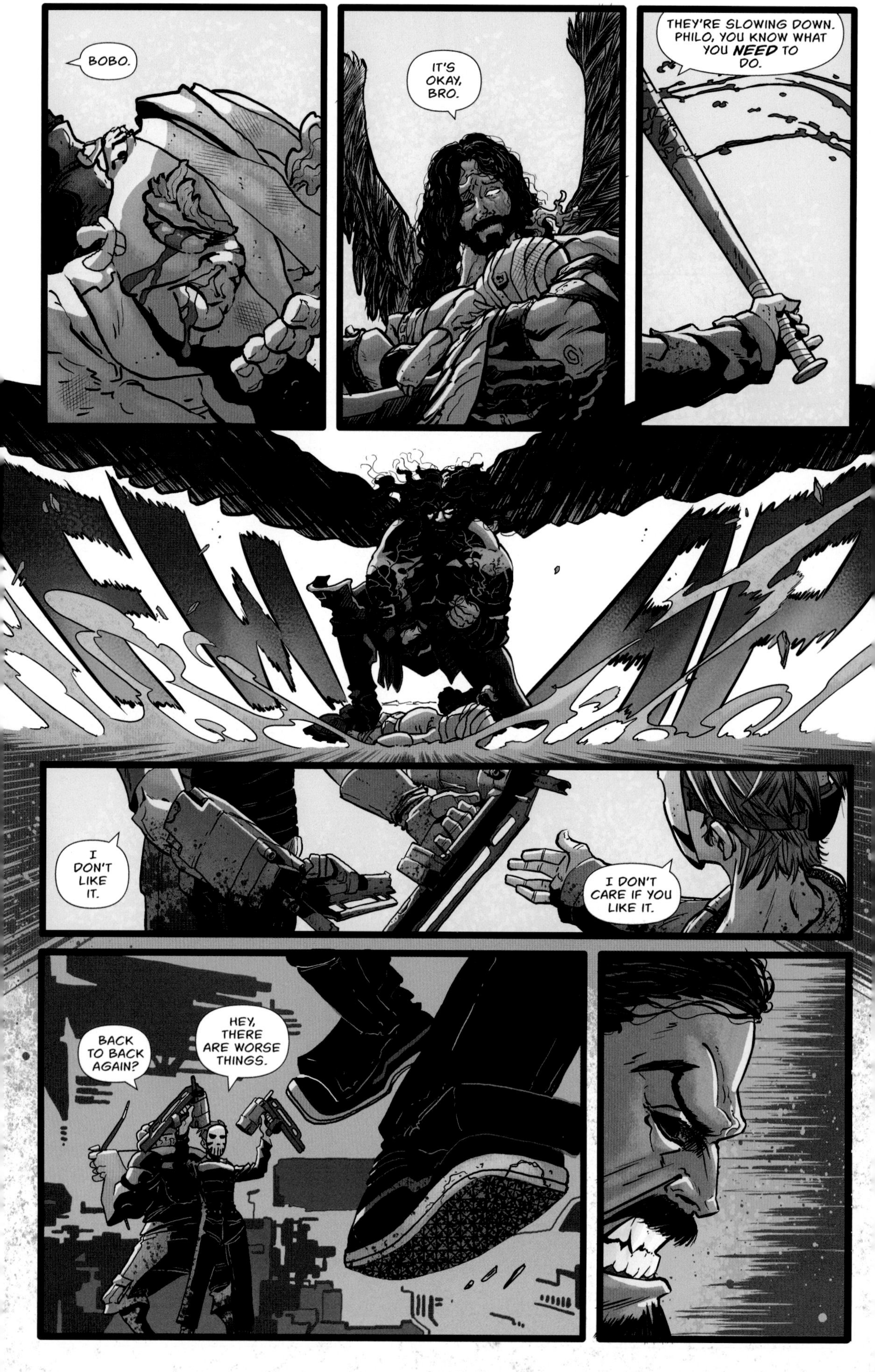
BOBO.
IT'S OKAY, BRO.
THEY'RE SLOWING DOWN. PHILO, YOU KNOW WHAT YOU NEED TO DO.
I DON'T LIKE IT.
I DON'T CARE IF YOU LIKE IT.
BACK TO BACK AGAIN?
HEY, THERE ARE WORSE THINGS.

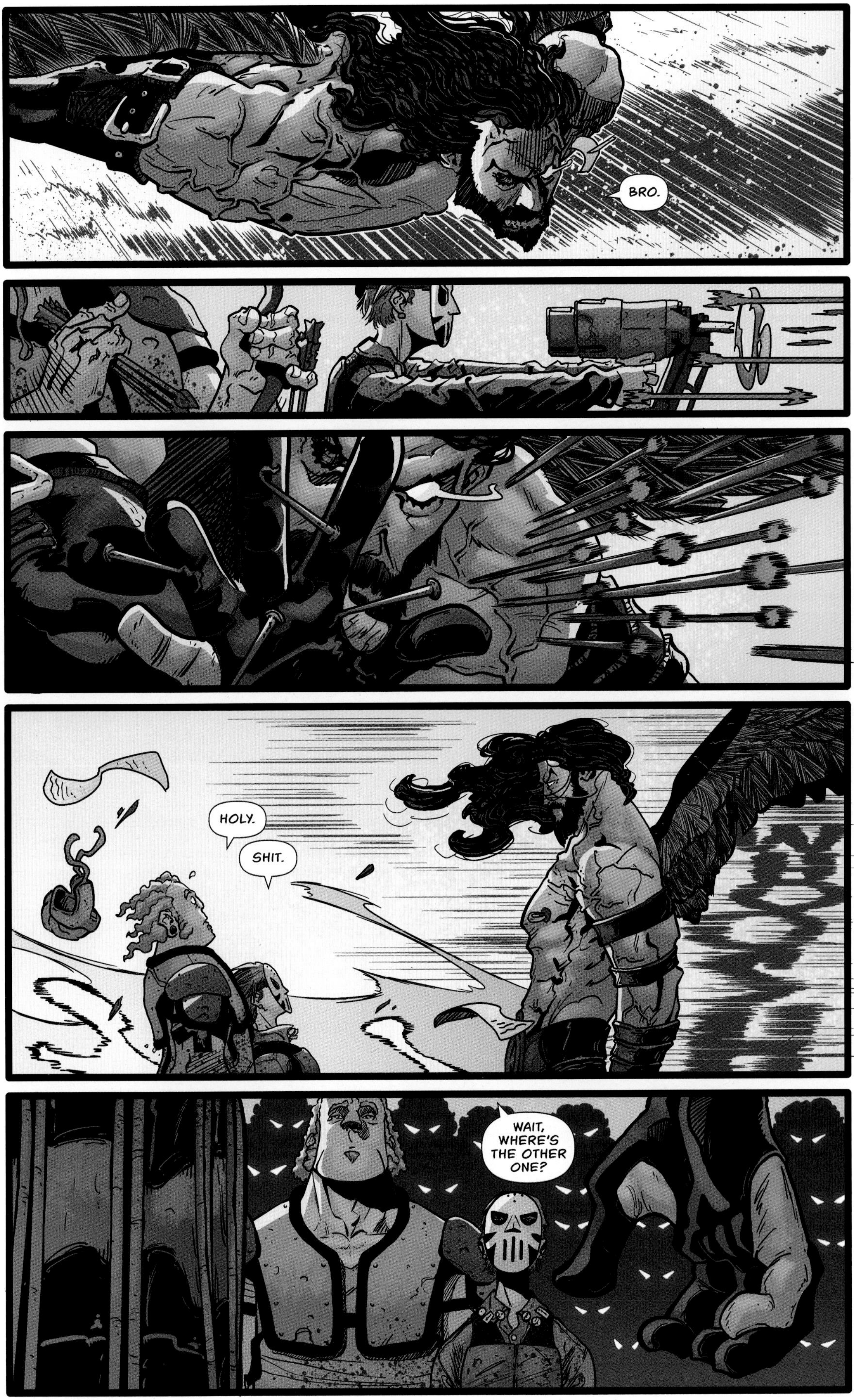
BRO.
HOLY.
SHIT.
WAIT, WHERE'S THE OTHER ONE?

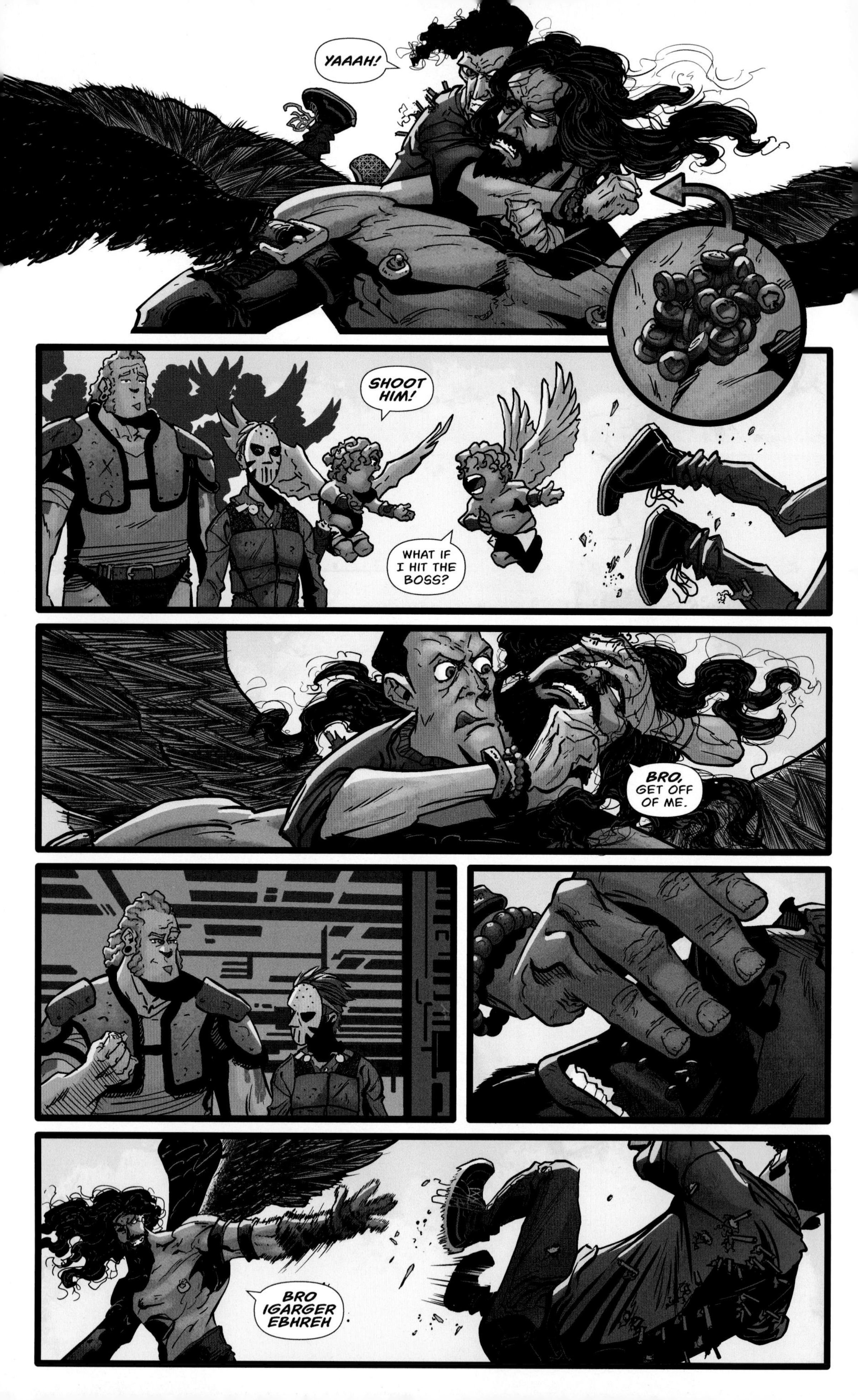
YAAAH!
SHOOT HIM!
WHAT IF I HIT THE BOSS?
BRO, GET OFF OF ME.
BRO IGARGER EBHREH

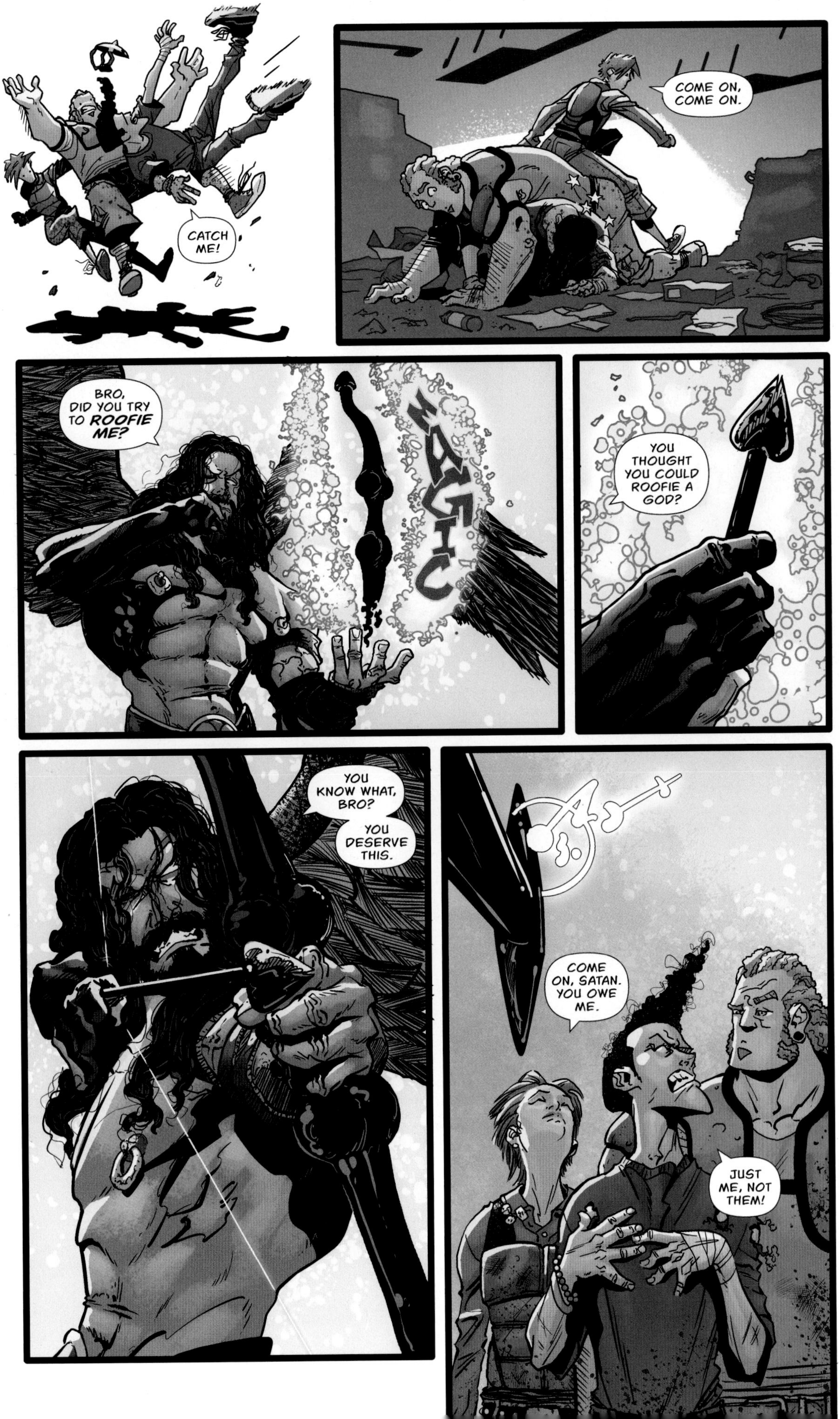
CATCH ME!
COME ON, COME ON.
BRO, DID YOU TRY TO ***ROOFIE ME?***
YOU THOUGHT YOU COULD ROOFIE A GOD?
YOU KNOW WHAT, BRO?
YOU DESERVE THIS.
COME ON, SATAN. YOU OWE ME.
JUST ME, NOT THEM!

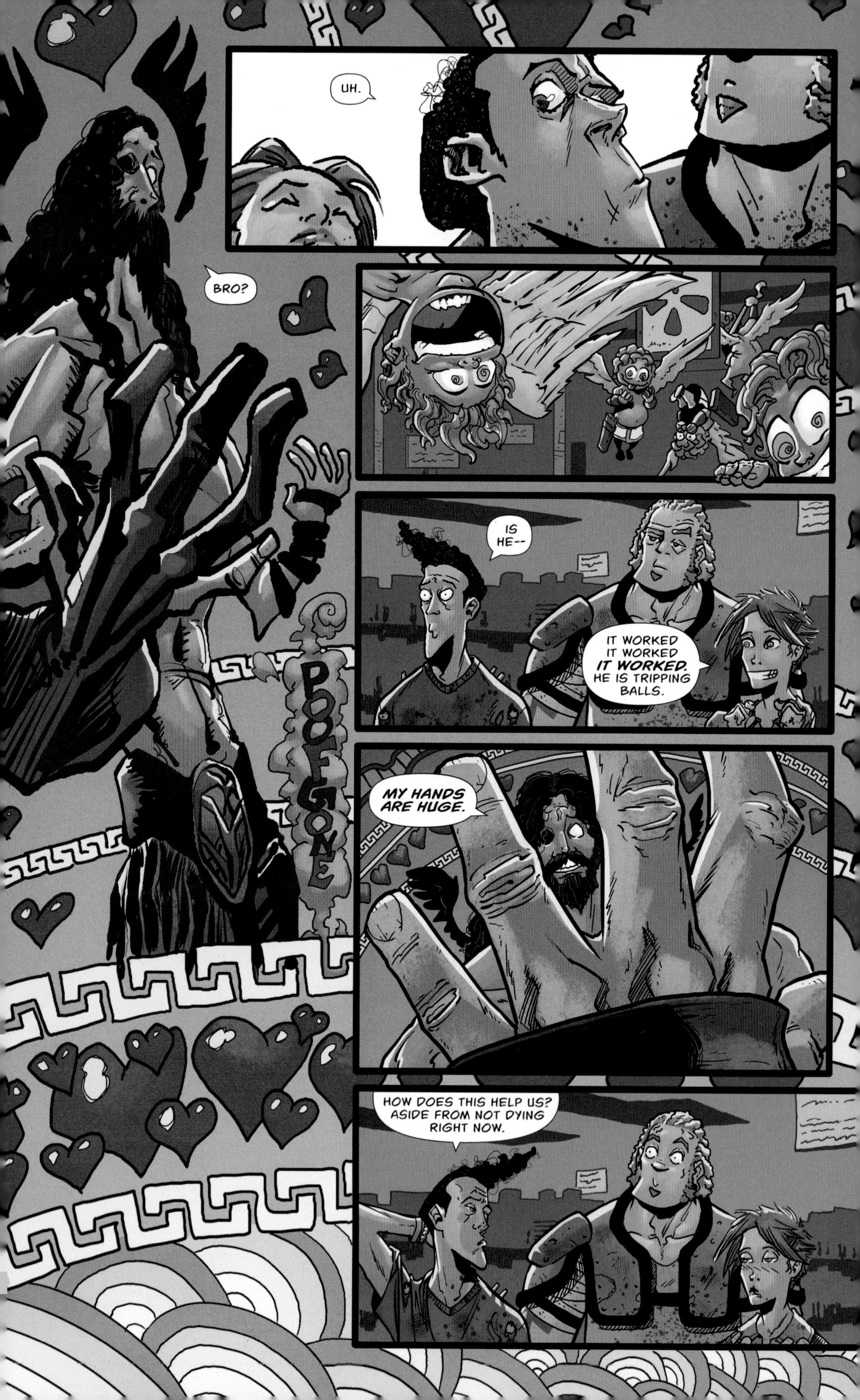
UH.
BRO?
IS HE--
IT WORKED IT WORKED IT WORKED. HE IS TRIPPING BALLS.
MY HANDS ARE HUGE.
HOW DOES THIS HELP US? ASIDE FROM NOT DYING RIGHT NOW.
POOF GONE

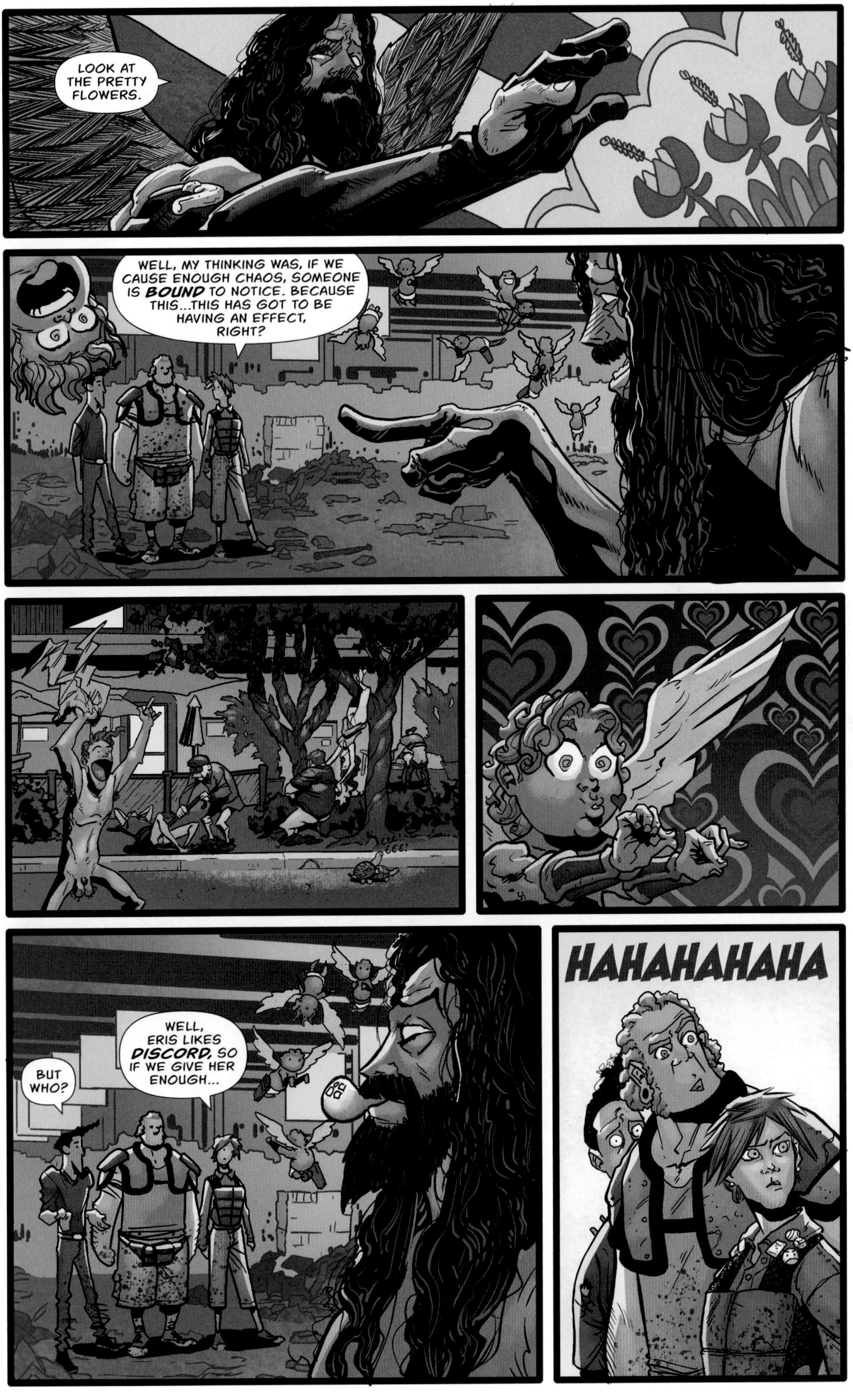
LOOK AT THE PRETTY FLOWERS.
WELL, MY THINKING WAS, IF WE CAUSE ENOUGH CHAOS, SOMEONE IS **BOUND** TO NOTICE. BECAUSE THIS...THIS HAS GOT TO BE HAVING AN EFFECT, RIGHT?
EEE! EEE!
BUT WHO?
WELL, ERIS LIKES **DISCORD**, SO IF WE GIVE HER ENOUGH...
HAHAHAHAHA

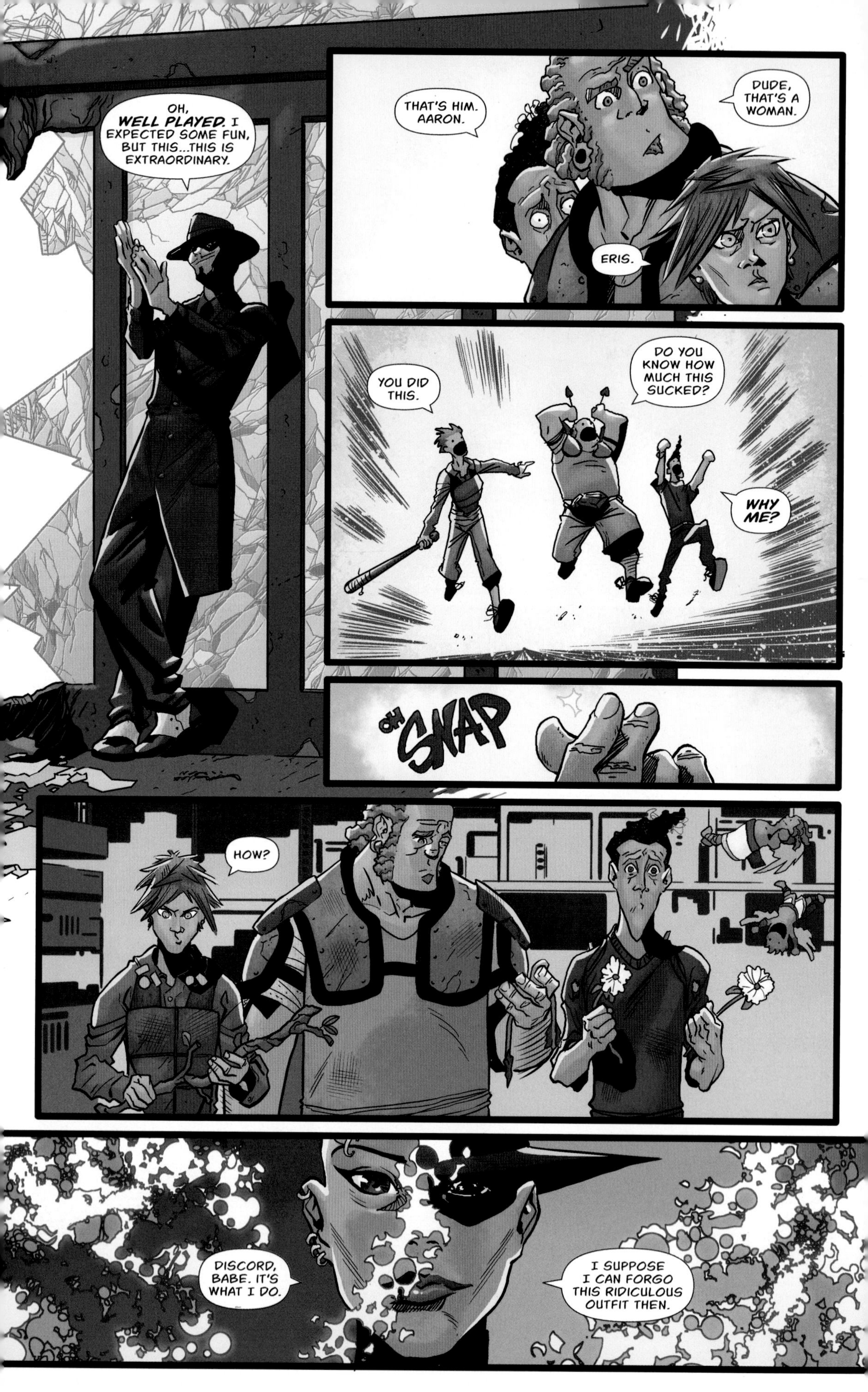
OH, WELL PLAYED. I EXPECTED SOME FUN, BUT THIS...THIS IS EXTRAORDINARY.
THAT'S HIM. AARON.
DUDE, THAT'S A WOMAN.
ERIS.
YOU DID THIS.
DO YOU KNOW HOW MUCH THIS SUCKED?
WHY ME?
SNAP
HOW?
DISCORD, BABE. IT'S WHAT I DO.
I SUPPOSE I CAN FORGO THIS RIDICULOUS OUTFIT THEN.

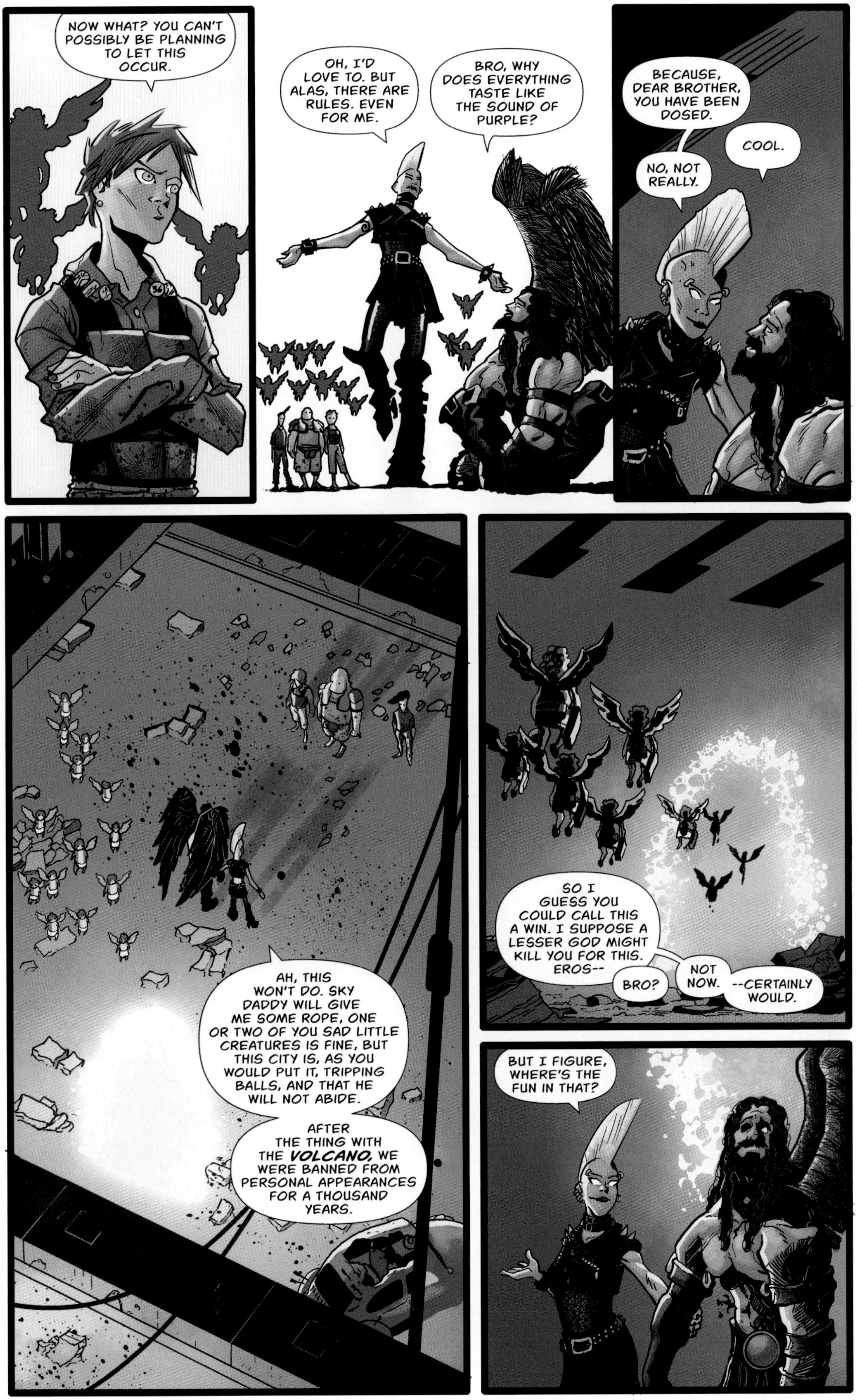
NOW WHAT? YOU CAN'T POSSIBLY BE PLANNING TO LET THIS OCCUR.
OH, I'D LOVE TO. BUT ALAS, THERE ARE RULES. EVEN FOR ME.
BRO, WHY DOES EVERYTHING TASTE LIKE THE SOUND OF PURPLE?
BECAUSE, DEAR BROTHER, YOU HAVE BEEN DOSED.
COOL.
NO, NOT REALLY.
AH, THIS WON'T DO. SKY DADDY WILL GIVE ME SOME ROPE, ONE OR TWO OF YOU SAD LITTLE CREATURES IS FINE, BUT THIS CITY IS, AS YOU WOULD PUT IT, TRIPPING BALLS, AND THAT HE WILL NOT ABIDE.
AFTER THE THING WITH THE ***VOLCANO,*** WE WERE BANNED FROM PERSONAL APPEARANCES FOR A THOUSAND YEARS.
SO I GUESS YOU COULD CALL THIS A WIN. I SUPPOSE A LESSER GOD MIGHT KILL YOU FOR THIS. EROS--
BRO?
NOT NOW.
--CERTAINLY WOULD.
BUT I FIGURE, WHERE'S THE FUN IN THAT?

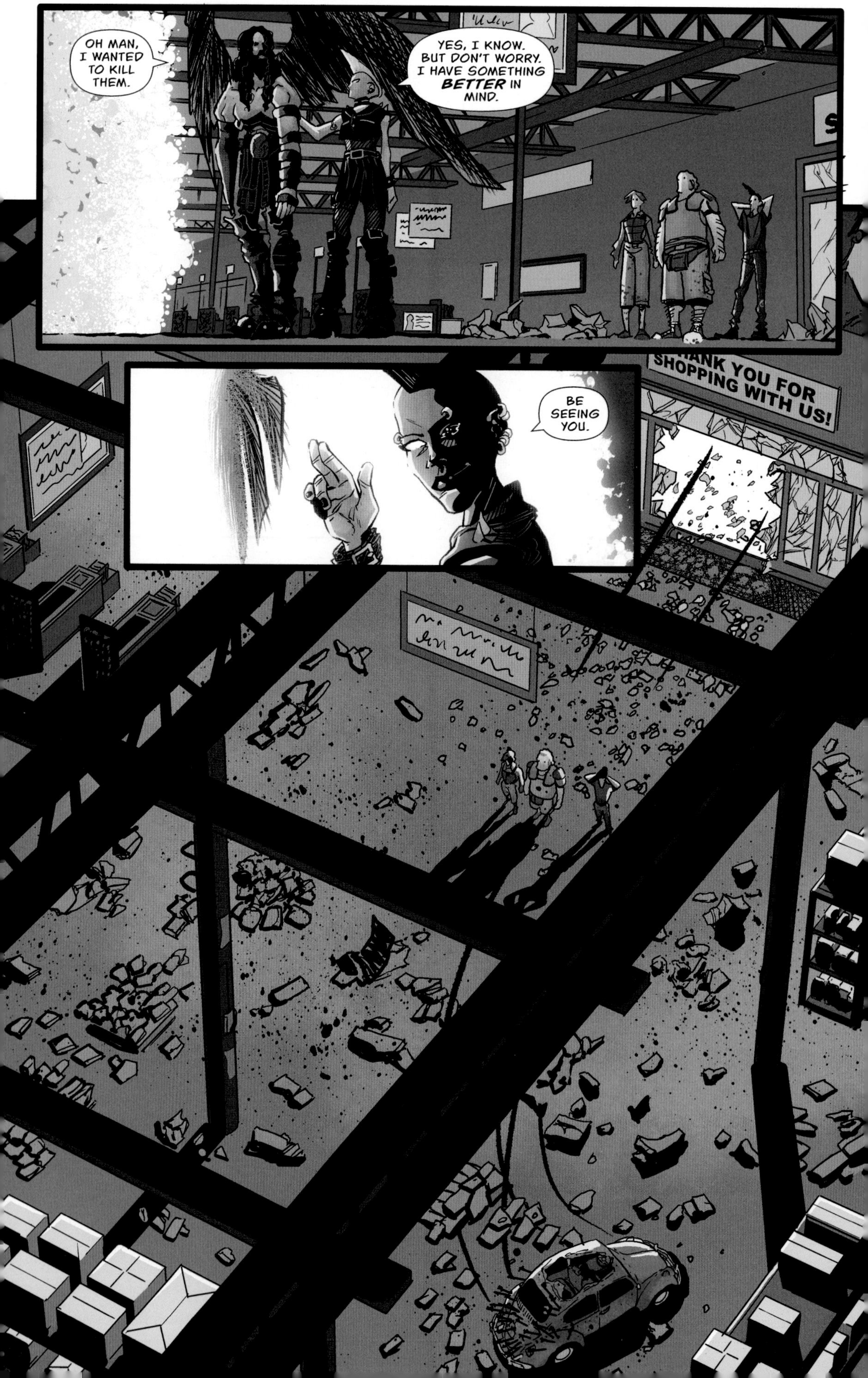
OH MAN, I WANTED TO KILL THEM.
YES, I KNOW. BUT DON'T WORRY. I HAVE SOMETHING BETTER IN MIND.
BE SEEING YOU.
THANK YOU FOR SHOPPING WITH US!

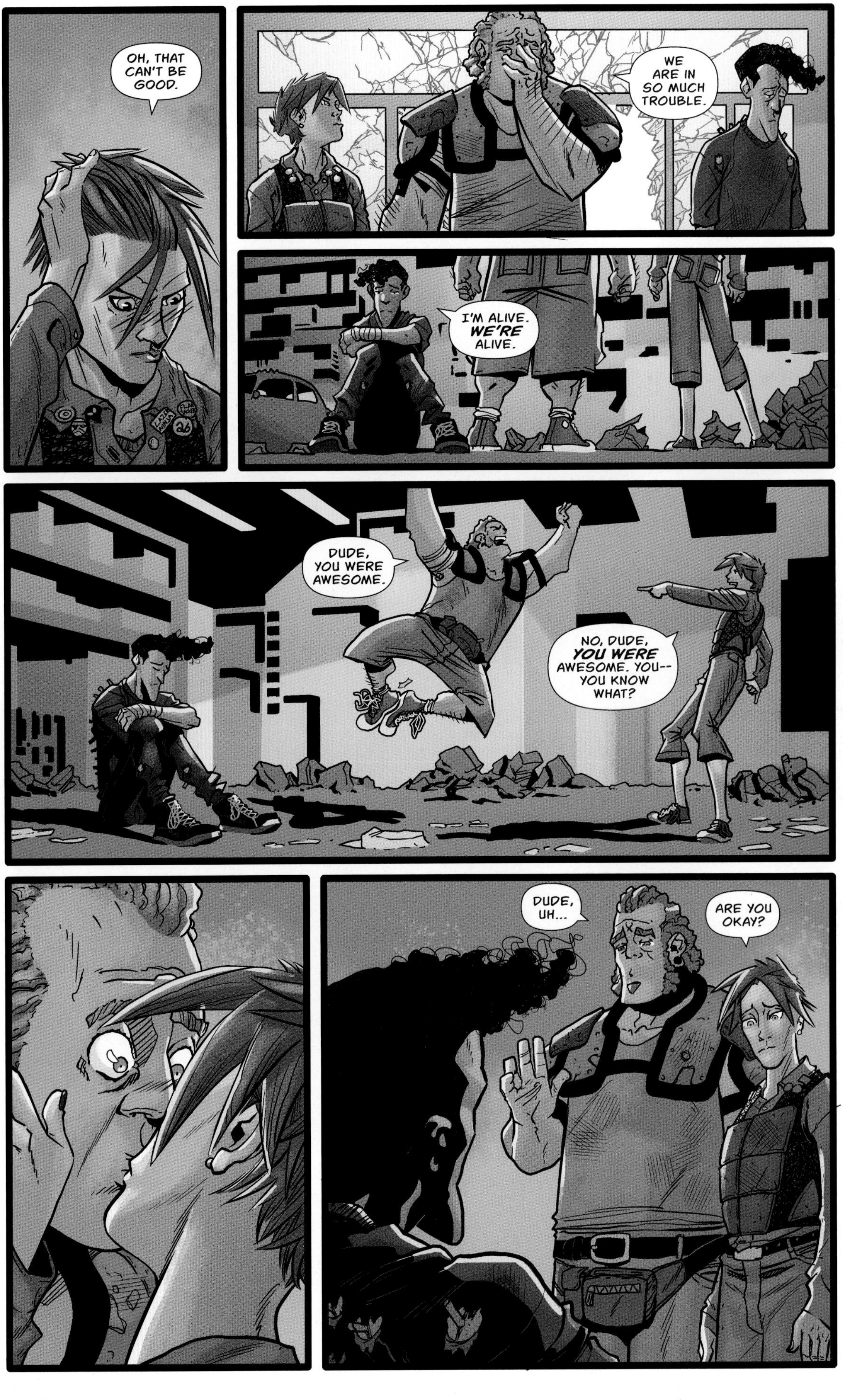
OH, THAT CAN'T BE GOOD.
WE ARE IN SO MUCH TROUBLE.
I'M ALIVE. *WE'RE* ALIVE.
DUDE, YOU WERE AWESOME.
NO, DUDE, *YOU WERE* AWESOME. YOU-- YOU KNOW WHAT?
DUDE, UH...
ARE YOU OKAY?

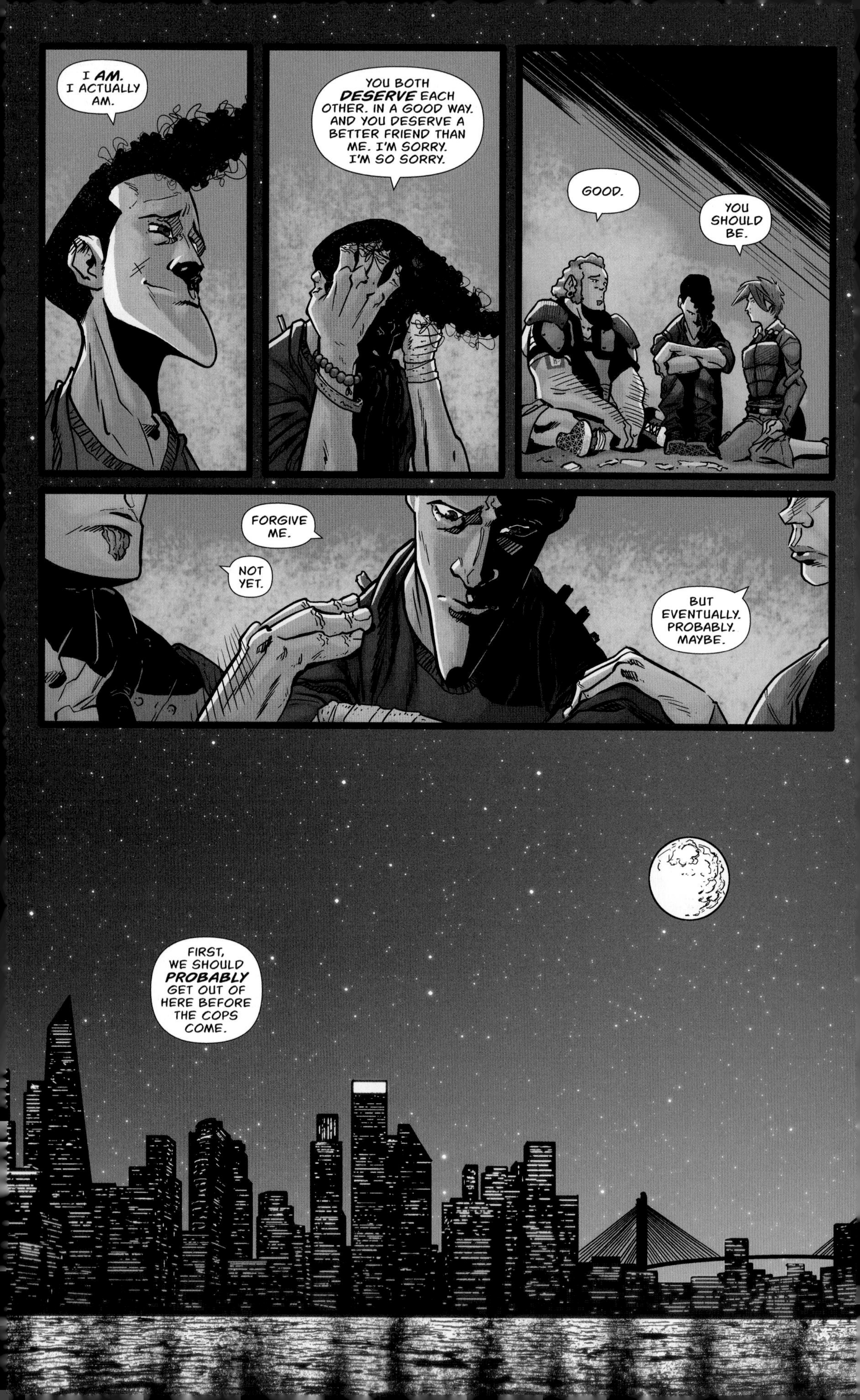
I AM. I ACTUALLY AM.
YOU BOTH DESERVE EACH OTHER. IN A GOOD WAY. AND YOU DESERVE A BETTER FRIEND THAN ME. I'M SORRY. I'M SO SORRY.
GOOD.
YOU SHOULD BE.
FORGIVE ME.
NOT YET.
BUT EVENTUALLY. PROBABLY. MAYBE.
FIRST, WE SHOULD PROBABLY GET OUT OF HERE BEFORE THE COPS COME.

Extras

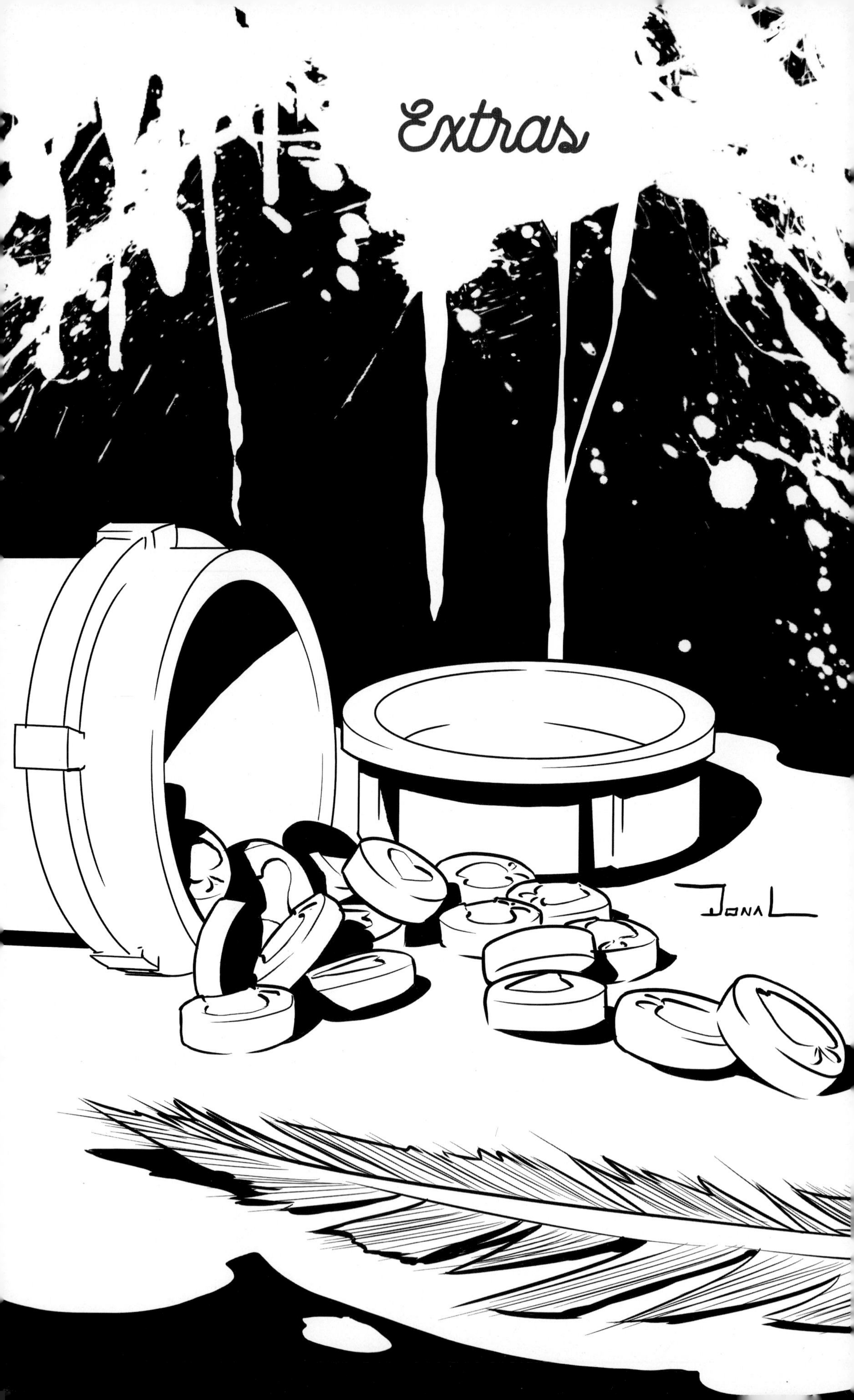
JonaL

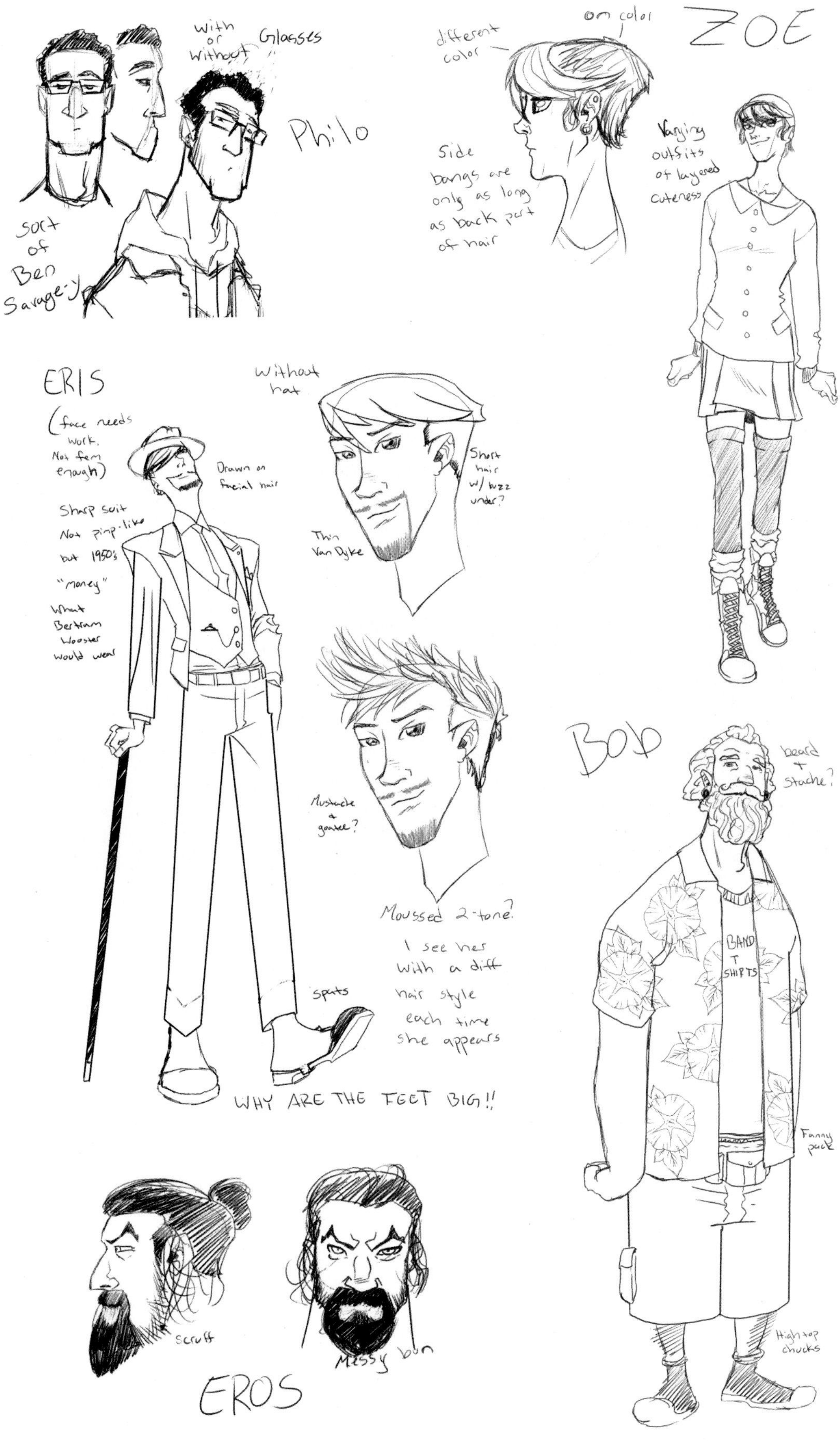

With or Without Glasses
Philo
sort of Ben Savage-y
ZOE
on color
different color
Side bangs are only as long as back part of hair
Varying outfits of layered cuteness
ERIS
(face needs work. Not fem enough)
Drawn on facial hair
Sharp suit
Not pimp-like but 1950's "money"
What Bertram Wooster would wear
Without hat
Short hair w/ buzz under?
Thin Van Dyke
Mustache + goatee?
Moussed 2-tone?
I see her with a diff hair style each time she appears
spats
WHY ARE THE FEET BIG!!
BOB
beard + stache?
BAND T SHIRTS
Fanny pack
High top chucks
scruff
Messy bun
EROS

early character designs by Donal DeLay

Paging Doctor NerdLove

with Harris O'Malley aka Doctor NerdLove

Love hurts.

I mean, that's the cliche, isn't it? Poke Spotify or iTunes in just the right spot and it'll vomit out more than five dozen variations on love. All you need is love, love is all around, love is in the air and that's great and all but love bites, love stinks and oh hey, it's going to blow your freakin' mind but it's also going to be awful. You're going to fall in love with someone you randomly see on the subway, the person you love is going to love someone else and you're going to have to just live with only ever being the supportive best friend in *their* love story while you wonder how you're going to live without them. If they just don't up and leave you and destroy your car in the process, anyway.

And that's if you're lucky.

And while love may be a many-splendored thing, it's also a humongous pain in the ass because while we're all growing up being taught about happy endings and True Love™, we tend to get sweet-fuck-all about how to *find* that love…or even the nearest facsimile thereof. We get marched over to the threshold and a hearty clap on the shoulder. "Hey, there's what you're supposed to be living for over yonder. Figure out how to get there, watch out for badgers, good luck" and a swift boot to the tail out the door.

If you're one of the lucky ones — someone who has that intuitive, instinctive grasp of social dynamics, who may or may or not also have teeth like chiclets and abs like woah — then you're more or less set. These are the bastards who seem to trip over their shoelaces and find themselves with someone incredible. Meanwhile, there's the rest of us who're trying to figure out increasingly arcane and baroque mating rules and rituals — ones that seem to change every couple of minutes, with no rhyme, nor reason.

And to make matters worse, we're *all* playing by different rules. Straight men get one playbook — you get the girl by being Billy Bad-Ass, the high-status man with the plan, the skills, the job or the looks. Be the guy who's large and in charge because alpha fucks, beta bucks yo.

Straight women get told to be sexy but not *too* sexy, available but not *too* available unless you're a modern woman who wants it all so in that case go out and make sure you have the career *and* the pilates-sculpted booty *and* chase your man but not *too* aggressively lest he feel emasculated and by the way, have you seen what *Cosmo* says you should do with a donut?.

Gay men get told that you they need to be like the straights but also not like the straights because really isn't marriage and monogamy a heteronormative trap? Meanwhile gay women get jokes about cats and bringing U-hauls to the second date and bi people get told that they don't exist, that they're selfish, indecisive or all of the above.

Except wait, all of pop culture tells us differently. That's where the alphas are the assholes to be overcome and the nerds and Nice Guys win the girl like the prize for beating Bowser and the douche from the Cobra Kai. Lewis Skolnick wins through trickery and deceit and Andrew Lincoln took time off from killing zombies to tell Keira Knightly he's going to go bang some models but he loves her anyway, just FYI. Han Solo made sure his busted-ass shaggin' wagon with the fuzzy dice was going to strand him in the middle of nowhere with the Princess, while Mr. Darcy was kind of a dick to everyone. Meanwhile, Saint Ducky, patron of The Friend Zone gets rewarded with a girlfriend after striking out with Andi and maybe the key is just to try to be her best friend for as long as it takes until she realizes that you're Mr. Perfect.

All the while Alex Forrest is the nightmare crazy ex-girlfriend and every woman with a career needs to wake up to realize what she *really* needs is to quit being so *ambitious* and *driven* and *make time for love and family, yo.*

Small wonder we're all confused and frustrated and scared. We try to follow the rules and we're positioned to work against each other like a round of *Clash of Clans* designed by coked-up divorce lawyers.

And reaching out for advice isn't any help. Women get *The Rules* and *Think Like A Man, Act Like a Lady*—be as unavailable and mysterious as the stars. Make him *work* for it because men don't like what they get too easily. Men get *The Game* and The Red Pill—women are targets bro, make those hamsters run in their wheels and keep the chicks off balance. Trigger those Demonstrations of Higher Value and flip the attraction switches that they evolved with. Treat love like a flowchart or the last match of *DOTA* at the International—push the lanes, drop negs to lower their bitch shields, deploy C's vs. U's to build attraction, call your wing to carry, now *isolate* go go go.

And never, *ever* let them think that you might *like* them. No no my dudes and my dudettes, that way lies madness because he or she who cares *least* has the power. And really isn't having the power what love is all about?

Small wonder so many of us lie awake at night, terrified that we're going to be Forever Alone. We're going to be the guy left at the end of the movie without even the consolation prize partner, the "sorry you weren't good enough to be the main character but we don't want the audiences to feel guilty they were rooting for your breakup" award. Only the lucky few get to be the OTP and everyone else gets to pair the spares and you're the guy left hoping somebody likes you enough to throw you in their fanfic later.

In the words of the sages, thank God for Mom and Dad for sticking through together because we sure as hell don't know how.

And yet, we *still* go through with it all. We suffer the slings and arrows of outrageous fortune and bear up under the seemingly arbitrary designs of Cupid and Eros and Himeros and Pothos because in each of our love stories, we have that moment.

We have that moment when get fed up and we're about to give up and then we say "You know what? Screw it."

We take a breath and decide to just...drop the bullshit. We decide to not give a damn about how many times we are or aren't supposed to call. We quit trying to find the perfect clever line to send to our Tinder matches. We stop trying to think of what avatar we need to project that will represent everything we think we're *supposed* to be and we say "You know what? Fuck it, here I am.

"Here's all the weird shit that makes me, me. Here's all the anxieties I keep trying to pretend I don't have, here's all the stuff that I dig that I think nobody else could possibly understand and ok, *fine* here's all the crap that I just need to finally take responsibility for.

"Here I am and *I have no idea what I'm doing*. I'm alone and I'm a little scared. Does anyone else feel this way?"

And that's when it happens.

That moment when we let go of all the rules and the standards, the arbitrary bullshit about how we're "*supposed*" to find love—that is the moment we feel the doors open. We let down our guard and our facades and just *reach out* to someone. Simple human contact, free of artifice for once. We bare our hearts and our souls as we stand naked, trembling and vulnerable before one another, we feel that *click*, when two sparks ignite.

And in that moment, we touch *the infinite*.

And in that moment, we *know*.

And in that moment, we face the truth: that not every love story is going to be an epic poem. Some love stories are meant to be novellas. Some are just a dirty limerick.

But every moment, every line and stanza makes it *worth* it.

Love bites, love stinks and love may well just be blood screaming to work its will...

But it brings us together and makes us whole. It makes us want to be able to live up to what we see reflected in someone else's eyes.

Love leaves scars. Love may be ugly and cruel sometimes.

But it's *worth* it.

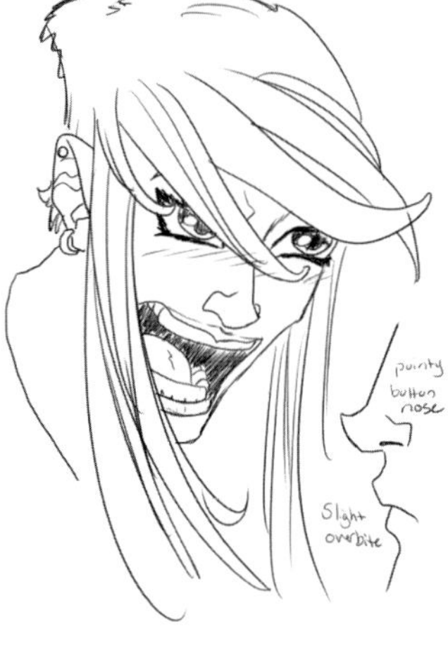
pointy button nose,
Slight overbite

It's 2018 and we have literal sex ATMs on our phones. Love or a reasonable approximation is available to us with the click of a button, the swipe of a finger and $29.99 a month if you want to have access to the premium features including hotter singles, the "OHSWEETJESUSIDIDN'TMEANTHAT-UNDOUNDOUNDO" function and also the "don't let them see me creeping" option.

And yet, despite our futurephones doing everything short of doing the pushing for us, we still feel the pressure to perform in person. We cling to the belief that even as we live in a corporate run cyberpunk dystopia, we're still supposed to get our freak on with someone we pulled in meatspace. Tinder feels too simple, OKCupid is a frustrating wasteland of women tired of unicorn hunters, dodging dick pics that beg to be sent like viruses conveniently labeled "virus do not open" in big, tempting, red letters and Plenty o' Fish reminds us that "Standards are for closers!"

But there's a comfort conveyed by the distance from face to phone to face. We live more and more of our lives behind screens, moving bits and bytes and so we get so very skilled with talking with our thumbs, like God intended.

Even so, there's that perception that dating apps don't "count," that they're another modern convenience that distances us from our rugged individualist ancestors who had to test their might in order to win a mate. Grandpa Alpha Male would never have resorted to something as convenient as Spring Street Personals to meet Grandma, not when he could go uphill in the snow both ways just to be worthy of getting someone's number.

But moving from behind the screen to the world around us is intimidating. We can grind our social meters in peace from our keyboards and carefully cultivate our social proof on social media. Meatspace is sloppy. It's messy. It's less easy to control, to curate and conceal.

And yet we still believe that meeting women on apps is lesser. It's to live a life of the fake alpha, knowing in your hearts that you just don't measure up to the asshole "bad boys" who can roll up on the woman *you* like in a cloud of testosterone and brow-to-chin

ratios and take her home with a smile and a nudge.

The binary of the world never makes itself more known than the 1s of those who are good with women and the 0s who aren't. Even the Molière of iMessage, the Oscar Wilde of WhatsApp and the Kierkegaard of Kik can find themselves bereft of wit and charm when we find ourselves in front of our preferred hotties in the too, too solid flesh.

And woe betide he who *admits* that he doesn't know what he is doing when it comes to women for he has committed the cardinal sin of masculinity: admitting weakness where others can see.

Baser still are those who want to *do* something about it. The man who tries to better his place and develop game has forgotten the face of his father. He who can be found surreptitiously buying the Writ of Mystery is to be mocked for the shame he brings upon his house.

And yet, despite the prohibitions, we can't forget how we watched another crush fall to the charms of That Friend, the one who attracts women like cheese attracts mice. And while we hear them in the next room as we sit there crying and using our tears as lube, we think to ourselves "no more. No more."

So we have our Batman moment: the sudden arrival of an omen (found by Googling "how to get good with girls"). The crash of The Game through our windows as a sign — YES FATHER, I SHALL BECOME A PICKUP ARTIST.

After all, it isn't fair that God didn't bless us with the gift of gab or the smooth charms that everyone else had. We were in the wrong room when the perfect abs were handed out. We missed the lecture on how to talk to women. We were cheated by the universe of our birthright, so we may as well cheat ourselves.

And that market is out there waiting for us, promising occult knowledge. The cheat codes to sex could be ours if we're just willing to prove our commitment. You want the knowledge you were denied, the handbook everyone else got, right? Never mind the queer allegories of black men telling multi-racial saviors that they're being exploited by old white men, take the Red Pill and see just how far the bitter rabbit hole goes.

Because they're not selling you magic beans, they're selling you magic bullets. They promise you that One Weird Trick that will bypass women's conscious minds and reach their primal core and leave you in charge. Get certified in the neurolinguistic programming language and be the Killgrave you always wish you could be. Find your inner gorilla mind and manhandle your way to sexual superiority. Flip these primal attraction switches and let evolution do the work for you. Master the Dark Triad and finally get the princess who's coming back to *your* castle.

And of course they all give you a wink and a smile as they make you promise that you're not going to *abuse* your newfound prowess, you're totally not going to take these secret techniques and bang out with every celebrity and crush you've ever had. No, not you, you're not going to exploit this unstoppable power that's under daily threat from angry feminists who think that it's just *too unfair*.

Nor do they want you to think too much about what it means to have to use tricks to get women into bed.

Or that what they describe as "getting past last minute resistance" sounds an awful lot like pressuring someone to give in because they're at your house and where else are they going to go?

Or that "buyers remorse" sounds a lot like "had sex they didn't want to have."

Don't think about those things. Think about how much less intimidating social interaction is when you describe it like performing an end-level raid in *Destiny*. Think of how much easier it is to meet women when attraction works like a flowchart. Sure, it's somebody else's stories coming from your mouth but isn't less scary to just if-then-else your way into bed?

Don't think about how this teaches you to treat women as opponents, not collaborators, think of all those women who'll never say no to you because now you know how to fuck like a super-villain. Sex is a competition and you've been losing for so long that it's *ok* to slot in a Game Genie so you can start winning again. You're going to win so much that you'll get *tired of winning*.

If it means lying and deceit, is that so bad? If the mutual intimacy of two people is replaced by a system of false fronts and invented personas, do you really lose *that* much?

And when your friends hit the wall because they can't keep up the manipulation, when you realize that *your every social encounter* is being weighed in terms of "who's the AMOG, who's the beta? How much value must I be showing, what's my status in this room?"

That's when you have to ask yourself: are you even *happy*? Even if it worked as advertised (SPOILER ALERT it doesn't, two out of five stars on Yelp), how long do you think you can keep it going before the fakeness gets to you? Before you realize you're still empty and alone, just stickier than before?

How long before you want just simple human intimacy, untainted by trickery and deceit?

Intimacy and vulnerability and making yourself open to strangers and lovers is scary, sure. There's power there, raw and pure and glittering in the sun. But with the fear comes the elation and the rush of a connection—whether it's casual or committed, for one night or for life.

But it doesn't come with special secret tricks or pseudoscientific gobbledygook found in ancient tomes. It doesn't come with the promise of sexual riches beyond dreams of avarice.

It comes when we embrace the suck.

It comes when we open ourselves up, reach deep within and find that core truth.

It comes, not with systems or routines but from authenticity.

It comes when we come to it honestly. When we're our true selves. Our best selves.

We may not have the hypnotic words or the evolutionary switches.

Because we don't need them.

We have *us*. And that is enough.

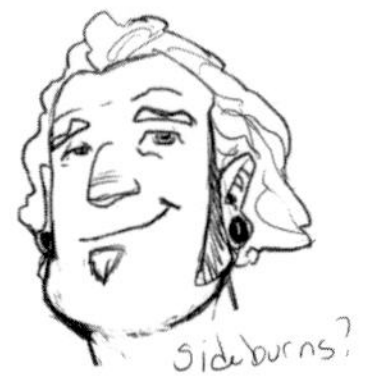
Sideburns?

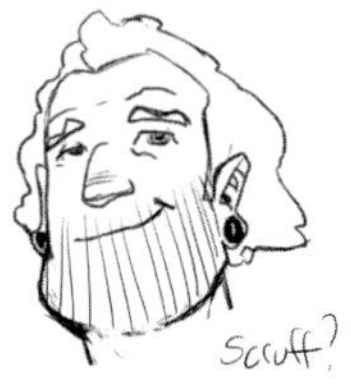
Scruff?

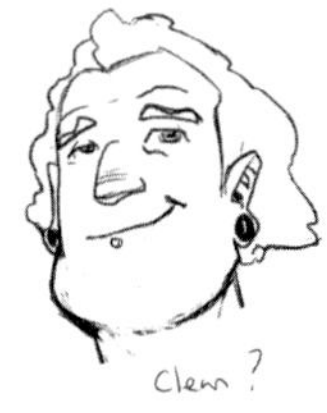
Clean?

THE NICE GUY

Why do we still hear the siren call of the Nice Guy, with a capital N, capital G?

If ever there were a trope so beaten into the ground, so nigh-universally reviled, it would be The Nice Guy. To be a woman who dates men is to inevitably have been the recipient of a patchy-facial-hair-bearing, that-is-not-a-fedora-it's-a-trilby-get-it-right tipping m'lady. It's to have known someone who posits themselves as a friend, a gentleman, a squire of a more genteel age who knows how to respect a lady who then will turn around and complain that she hasn't paid for his kindness with the expected handjob.

There is no poison arrow frog with brighter coloring, no clearer way (short of Tap Out and Ed Hardy shirts) that nature tells us Do Not Touch. After all, the rate of success for those who have studied The Blade with their mall-bought katanas is somewhere between jack and shit. So why, then, do so many men fall prey to the call of The Nice Guy identity?

It's easy enough to blame entitlement; after all, the lament of The Nice Guy is that he's reached the bare minimum and why hasn't he been rewarded with all the sex? Has he not collected enough Power Points on his reward card that he can hop on down to the store and turn them in for blowjobs? Haven't we all seen the complaints shared via Tumblr and Twitter and drama sub-Reddits lamenting that women who ask "where have all the nice guys gone" only have themselves to blame?

But entitlement alone isn't what leads men to become Nice Guys.

Some self-described NGs would say it's women's fault. That they heard "I wish I could find a nice guy" one time too many and, like a fool, took women at their word. They hear "I wish I could find a nice guy" and think "Well, that's me. I'm nice." And when women inevitably fall for that asshole, you know the one with the leather jacket and the look that says "I smell like Drakkar and other women's panties," it can only be because women say one thing but mean another entirely — two-faced to the end. Promising the glory with one hand but cruelly pushing the Knight in Tin Foil Armor of their dreams aside for cultivated stubble, teeth like chiclets and black leather.

But misunderstanding what women want isn't what leads men to become Nice Guys either.

It's fear. Fear of a word.

"No."

And Nice Guys know this.

They know this because they *know* that women aren't genetically attracted to someone who'll borrow money without repaying it, gaslight her when she catches them sleeping with her best friend and then repeat the cycle again with the next contender to put all of his points in The Dark Triad. Just as they know that when women say that they wish they could find a nice guy, there is the codicil of "...that I was actually attracted to," less unspoken, less dog whistle and more akin to cats ignoring any sound but the sound of a can being opened as uninteresting.

And they know — more than anything they know — one truth: that *she just doesn't like him that way.* And we know that they know this because a Nice Guy will never, *never* be up front about his interest. That way lies the potential for rejection.

(Can't get rejected if you never ask them out in the first place.)

Better to live in illusory hope than to face the reality of being definitively turned down. Better to suffer like a lover from gothic poetry than to admit defeat and move on. Better to build up the fantasy that attraction, like mushrooms, can grow on you over time.

(They never stop to think that mushrooms only grow on dead things.)

Armed with misunderstandings of chivalry, overstuffed with the romantic notion that to suffer for "love" makes you a hero, they wait. They've read the manga and heard all the songs. They've seen the movies. They've watched the TV shows. They know that Ross inevitably gets Rachel, that the princess loves the frog, she just doesn't know it yet. Saint Ducky, patron of the unlucky in love, watches over them. They just have to wait it out, so that they can be there when fate smiles and their beloved *finally* realizes that The One She's Been Waiting For was right there.

And so they plot. They plan. They need reasons to be around. They know that love — like the dodgy Santa Claus of their youth — often comes in through the back door. And so they plan to unleash The Platonic Best Friend Backdoor Gambit. He will never admit his feelings — not yet, not until the time is right, when the stars align in their syzygy — but will profess his purely nonsexual affection for her. And this, not chemistry, not shared values or sexual attraction, will be his winning stroke.

After all, how many times has the romance finally ended when the Beloved realizes that she has been in love with her best friend all this time?

To be the Platonic Best Friend puts them into the catbird seat. It means that they are front row, center for all of her drama — the better with which to catch them when she swoons dramatically at the latest break-up with yet another Asshole Who Doesn't Deserve Her. He gets to know all of her secrets because hasn't he shown that he's a good guy, a trusted guy, someone who would never abuse her trust?

(They never stop to think of the irony.)

He becomes her indispensable confidant and companion, the Shoulder To Cry On, the Ears To Listen. He is there, almost all the time, even when she doesn't expect it. He's the one who offers to take care of her when she's sick, who wants to do things to make her life easier. And if his constant attention, slavish devotion and occasionally overly lavish gifts make her uncomfortable… well, he doesn't *mean* any harm. After all, they're Just Friends.

And all the while, he waits. He plans.

(In sunken M'yladeah, dread Ducky lies dreaming.)

In his mind, it's a matter of time, a day that can never come soon enough. And while he *tells* himself that he can wait as long as it takes, the reality is another matter entirely. He *can't* wait and each day he reads the tea leaves like they will tell him who really killed Kurt Cobain. He becomes a self-appointed master of body language, a Salieri of tonality. He can read novels in the upswing of her voice when she says his name. That touch lingered just a nanosecond longer than last time, as sure a sign of her thawing emotions as the sparrows returning from Capistrano.

But each dawn that sees her dating Yet Another Asshole is one more dagger in his heart, another reminder that he *knows* the answer that he refuses to ask. But the soul still burns and the dream refuses to die and while there may be others out there who might want what *he* has to offer, but he can't give up. He's too invested in the Sunk Cost Fallacy; to let go now would be to admit that all this time waiting was for nothing.

And so there always, *always* comes the moment when he can't suffer nobly in silence any longer. There *always* comes the moment of confession, the plea that she should be with *him* — almost always triggered by another man. Sometimes the prompt comes in the form of realizing that she's seeing someone new and this latest window of opportunity will be closed. Or the dawning realization that this one is *serious* and he thought he had more time.

And so he pleads his case. He remembers her birthday and the important events in her life. He was there for her when she needed somebody. And look at all of those times that he *didn't* take advantage of her vulnerability, like some *cad*.

Doesn't the fact that he's met the base expectations for friendship and social functionality mean that he deserves her body?

But with the confession comes the truth: it was never friendship. Friends don't come with agendas. Friendship doesn't come with expectations of things owed, with a bill that comes due when the would-be paramour's self-inflicted blue balls can no longer take the strain.

(It comes with the truth. Nice Guys *aren't*.)

And a friendship that never was dies. Hearts get broken because who wants to know that someone she trusted never respected her at all?

With luck, the Nice Guy learns. He grows. He understands that friendship with strings attached (to his penis) is no friendship in the first place. He begins to recognize that he never has the whole story about The Other Man and realizes that "asshole" sometimes means "guy who simply has what I want."

But to get there, first the formerly Nice Guy has to admit fault. He has to recognize that his emotional torture was his own doing. It was not just a prison of his own making but one that he attempted to drag others into.

Some never get that far. It's not their fault. Women lied to them. They're being denied what they are owed.

The ones who do? The ones who learn to turn their back on the bullshit they once espoused, who walk away from the promises of a red-pill'd Omelas?

They're the ones who step out, blinking in the newfound sunlight, to join the rest of the world. In hope. In happiness.

In love.

HOW TO ESCAPE THE FRIEND ZONE

Alright, folks, this week I'm going to give you what you've all been waiting for. I'm going to take you by the hand, lead you through the maze, give you the answer to the Riddles Three and show you, once and for all, how you get out of The Friend Zone.

Because if there's anything a nerd fears more than getting shut out from that ultra-rare Amiibo, losing a shot at a shiny Gyrados or getting a crease in the cover of their mint copy of New Mutants #87, it's getting stuck in The Friend Zone. The Friend Zone: a realm so horrible that no hope can escape. It is a singularity of suck, the place where romantic attraction goes to die. It's the Oubliette d'Amour and once you are condemned to it, there you shall remain until the end of time where you shall die, alone, unmourned and unloved.

Or so one would think.

More digital ink has been spilled about the *unfairness* of The Friend Zone than almost any relationship topic you can imagine. The concept of The Friend Zone as a Relationship Stalag 17 has driven more men to the pick-up scene than LITERALLY anything else. To enter the phrase "The Friend Zone" into YouTube's search bar is to be a pilgrim in an unholy place, the running of a gauntlet lined with carnival barkers, each and every one of them swearing up and down that *they* and they alone have the secret to open up the gates of Heaven.

Small wonder that so many will offer to teach you the secrets, from secret sex-getting texts, Boyfriend Destroyers, to hugs GUARANTEED to unlock the gates of Heaven. In its own way, promising the key to escaping Eros' Phantom Zone becomes a license to print money. Promise somebody that you can teach them to pick the lock to the Sex Jail and they will flock to your door, bringing their get-a-life savings with them.

Which is an impressive feat, considering that The Friend Zone *doesn't actually exist*. It's a fiction, a *tulpa* given shape by bad 80s romantic comedies and brought to life by the fevered belief of young, socially inexperienced men — and it *is* men who complain the most of being tricked and trapped in The Friend Zone. To be in The Friend Zone is to be caught in a prison of one's own making, a Platonic cave that we condemn ourselves to by squeezing our eyes closed tight.

Because women as a gender didn't gather into a council to judge men and build The Friend Zone Projector to punish nerds for the crime of wanting to date. There is no Friend Zone; there are just women *who don't want to fuck you*.

And despite how it may feel, nobody not-fucks at you. Somebody's lack of attraction to you isn't an act of aggression, a sexual *casus beli*, it's a null state. The fact that they didn't leap into your arms at the mere revelation of your existence isn't a nefarious auto-rejection, nor do women lure men into their doom like a spider drawing you in by the fly. It's a simple case that somebody isn't down to clown because they don't dig on what you have to offer.

Which is fair; after all, you aren't attracted to every person you see out there. But when it's *your* pants-feels on the line, it feels personal indeed.

But to be in The Friend Zone is to tacitly acknowledge that you already know what you don't want to admit. You may want answers but *you can't handle the truth*. The power to leave was within you all this time, should you ever let yourself admit it. But leaving The Friend Zone means doing the one thing you *can't* let yourself do.

Because a man who wishes to leave The Friend Zone has to make his move. He has to call the question — to himself, to his fantasy paramour, to the world at large — and commit or quit. But to do so would be The End of All Hope. Better to live in the state of quantum uncertainty, where Schrödinger's Girlfriend is both attracted to you and not, than to collapse the waveform and realize that your chances aren't dead, just that they never existed in the first place.

The temptation is there; stay and hope that you can change the way someone sees you and maybe, *maybe* you can grind them down until they give in. But The Friend Zone is a self-reinforcing prison. The longer you stay, the longer you remind someone that they're just Not That Into You, carving that indelible groove into the brain that says "my interest in this person is strictly platonic."

The only way to leave The Friend Zone is to *choose* to leave. Like the elephant in the mahout, the only thing holding you there is your own belief. No woman holds you there against your will. Even if the mythical manipulative siren *did* exist, deliberately drawing you in with her song of pleasures promised but never deliver, her power requires your active participation. You have been free to walk away this entire time, should you choose. You had to consent, each time, to believe that Lucy wouldn't pull the sexual football away from you *this* time.

And you *must* choose. If you want to leave The Friend Zone, then you must choose to open your eyes and walk, blinking into the sun and realize that you were never there in the first place. It is to cure yourself of your Oneitis and recognize that your One, as amazing as she was, is not One but one of a million — each of whom are as nice if not *better* because these have a chance of actually returning your feelings.

Even if you found the Relationship Infinity Gem and have managed to slam your fist on the Cosmic Reset Button, you first have to walk away. To change the nature of someone's feelings for you, first you have to change yourself and that can't happen while you're there. Like a rock being shaped by the wind and the rain, the changes are so gradual that they can't be seen as they occur; your newness merely becomes incorporated into the same platonic image of you. They can't wonder at the newness of you if it's never new to them. They can't miss you until you go away.

To truly escape The Friend Zone, however, is to *destroy* it. To understand that you can't get caught in The Friend Zone if you don't allow it to be built in the first place. To understand that this sexual oubliette is one of your making and you laid the first brick when you let the fear of rejection overpower your desire to have an answer.

Because at the end of the day, The Friend Zone is a portal to the Demiplane of Fear. It is letting the nightmare of What If drain your resolve and lead you to adopt the Platonic Best Friend Back Door Gambit. You get caught in The Friend Zone because *you acted like a friend, not a lover.*

If you want to be a lover, you have to *show* it. You have to use your words, to make it clear that while you admire them and care for them, respect them and enjoy their company, what you want more than anything else, is their *love*. You don't ask to "hang out some time" or to "get together," you do what Johnny Testosterone and every other Bad Boy before you did: you ask them for a date. An unquestionable, undeniable *date*. You open yourself up, make yourself vulnerable and show yourself in your naked state, ready to accept the truth.

Because The Friend Zone is built from lies. You lie when you present yourself as a friend, with no other agenda. You lie when you mask your intent rather than risk being turned down. No friend offers their friendship with strings, making their relationship contingent on the possibility of a sex upgrade path.

If you would be a lover, then *be* a lover. If you want to escape The Friend Zone, then like demons of old, you must deny The Friend Zone's hold over you.

Date. Or do not date.

You know the rest.

BDSM archery style gloves
R bottom
R top
L

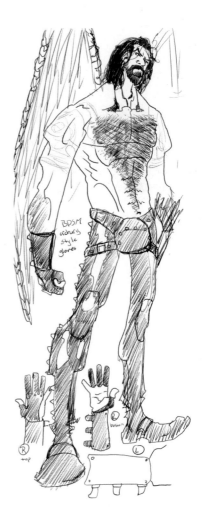

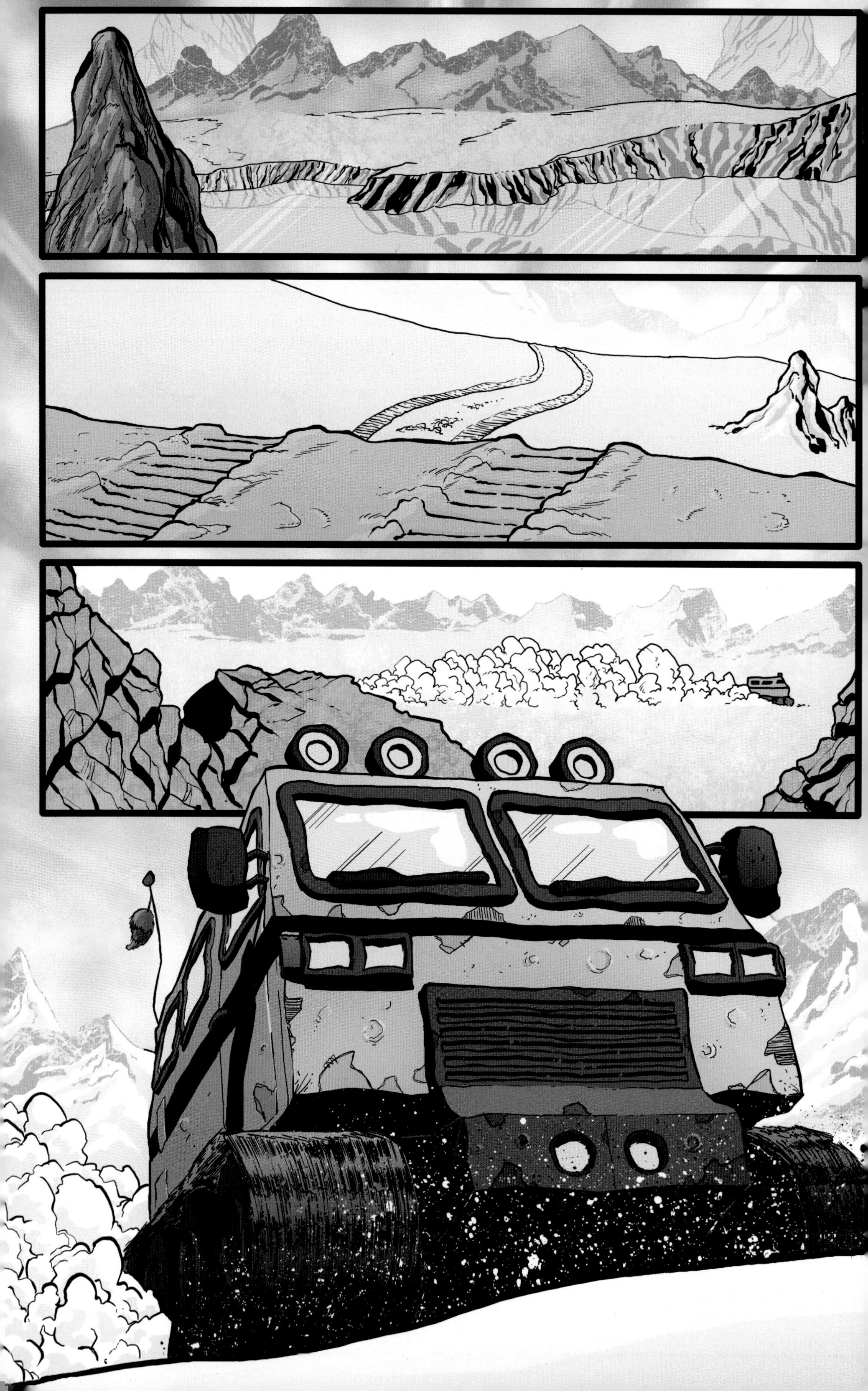

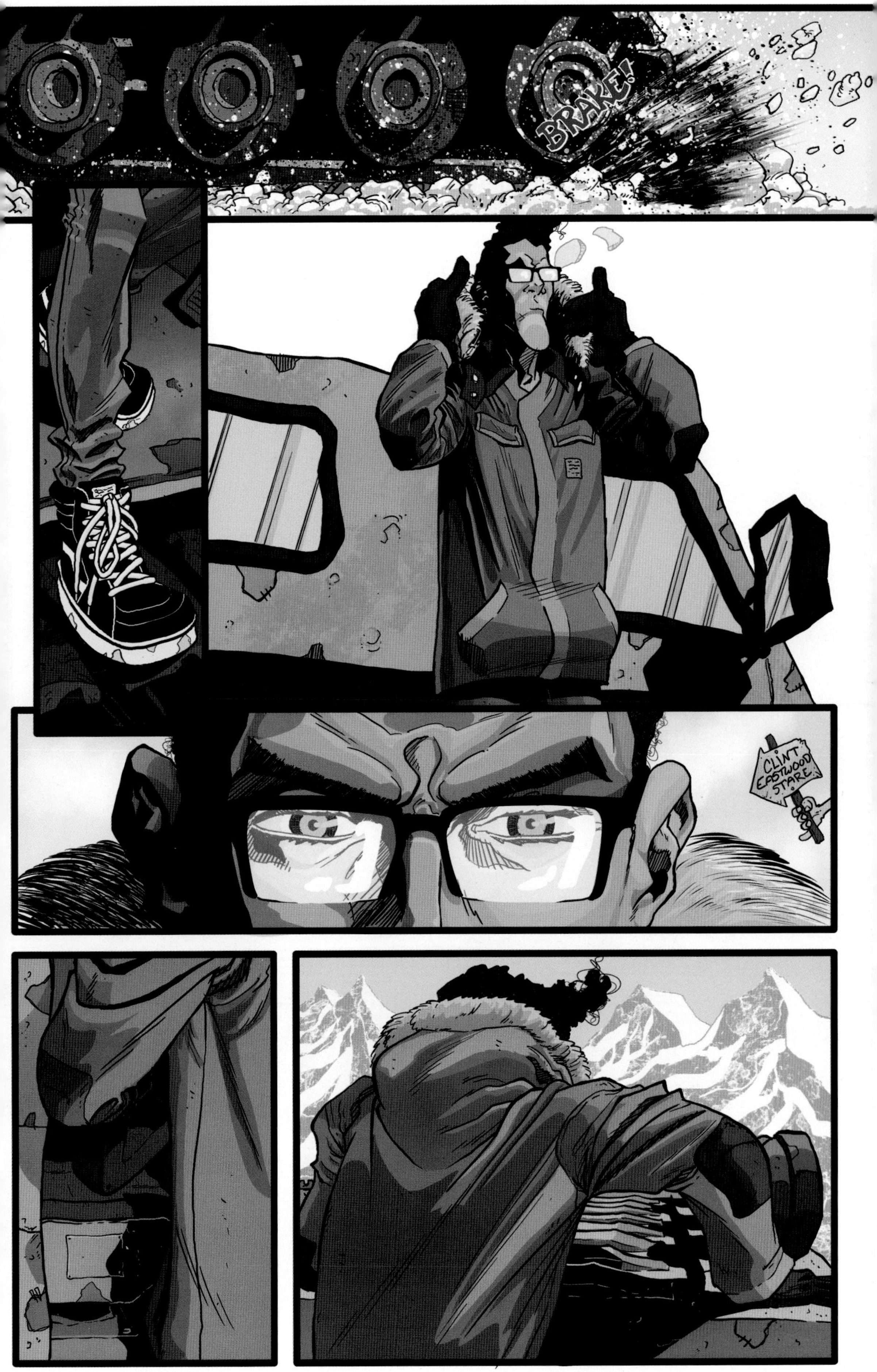
BRAKE!
CLINT EASTWOOD STARE.

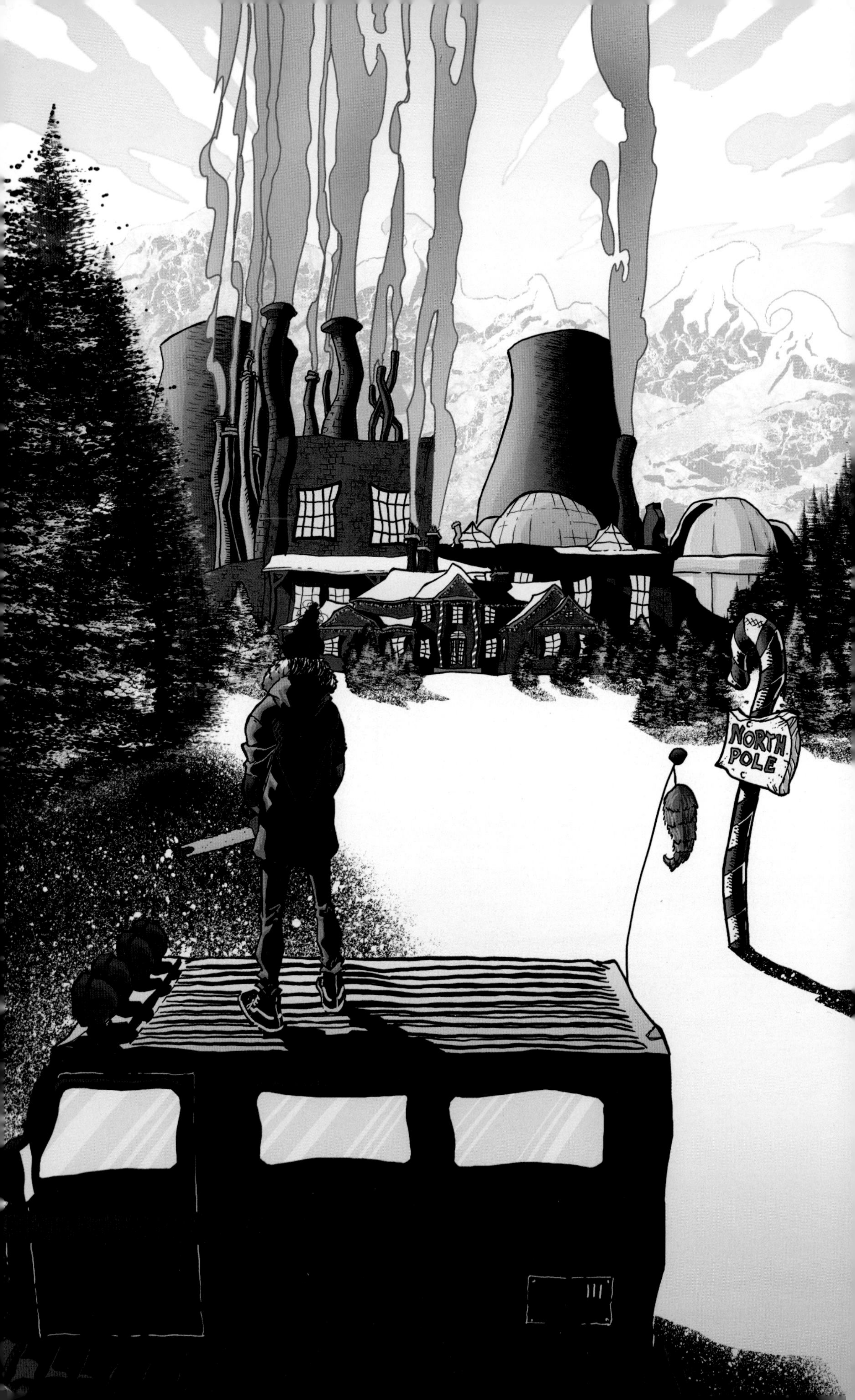
NORTH POLE

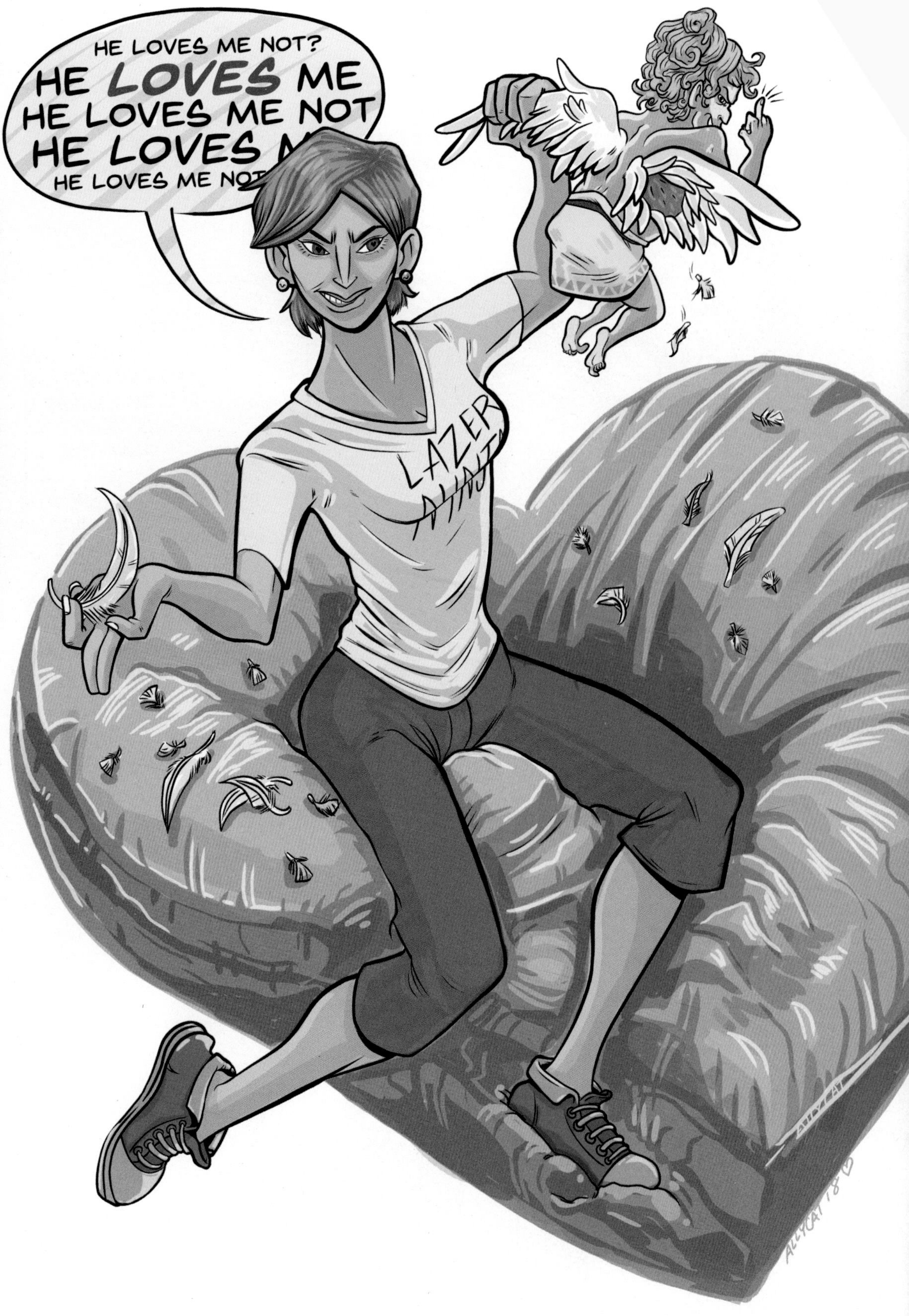
HE LOVES ME NOT?
HE LOVES ME
HE LOVES ME NOT
HE LOVES M
HE LOVES ME NO
LAZER

pinup by Ally Cat · @pompadorablecat

T
TED
IT ALL!

JUSTIN HAS A HABIT OF POSTING RANDOM IDEAS ON FACEBOOK, AND THIS ONE CAUGHT MY EYE.

Justin Jordan
February 8, 2016 ·

The Death of Love

A lonely man figures out how to see Cupids, goes on a killing spree.

Like Comment Share

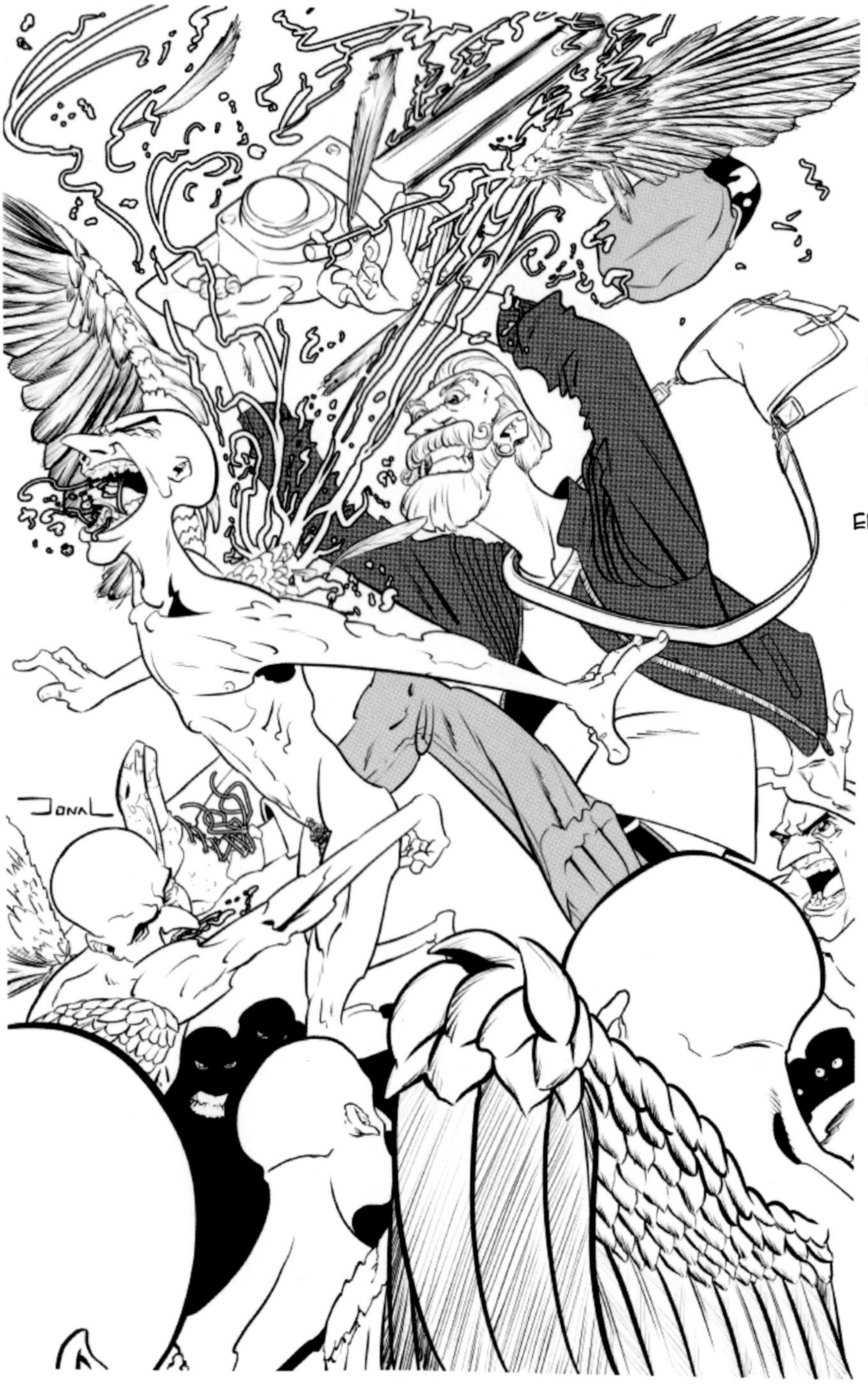

JONAL

AFTER READING IT, I HAD THIS IMAGE JUST POP IN MY HEAD, AND DECIDED TO DRAW IT AS ONE OF MY DAILY WARM-UPS.

I ENDED UP SHOWING IT TO JUSTIN AND WE DECIDED TO MAKE THE BOOK YOU NOW HOLD IN YOUR HANDS.

IT'S BEEN A FUN AND EDUCATIONAL JOURNEY!